VOLUME
NINE

IMAGE COMICS, INC.

Robert Kirkman
CHIEF OPERATING OFFICER

Erik Larsen
CHIEF FINANCIAL OFFICER

Todd McFarlane
PRESIDENT

Marc Silvestri
CHIEF EXECUTIVE OFFICER

Jim Valentino
VICE-PRESIDENT

Eric Stephenson
PUBLISHER / CHIEF CREATIVE OFFICER

Corey Hart
DIRECTOR OF SALES

Jeff Boison
DIRECTOR OF PUBLISHING PLANNING
& BOOK TRADE SALES

Chris Ross
DIRECTOR OF DIGITAL SALES

Jeff Stang
DIRECTOR OF SPECIALTY SALES

Kat Salazar
DIRECTOR OF PR & MARKETING

Drew Gill
ART DIRECTOR

Heather Doornink
PRODUCTION DIRECTOR

Nicole Lapalme
CONTROLLER

www.imagecomics.com

FIONA STAPLES
ARTIST

BRIAN K. VAUGHAN
WRITER

FONOGRAFIKS
LETTERING+DESIGN

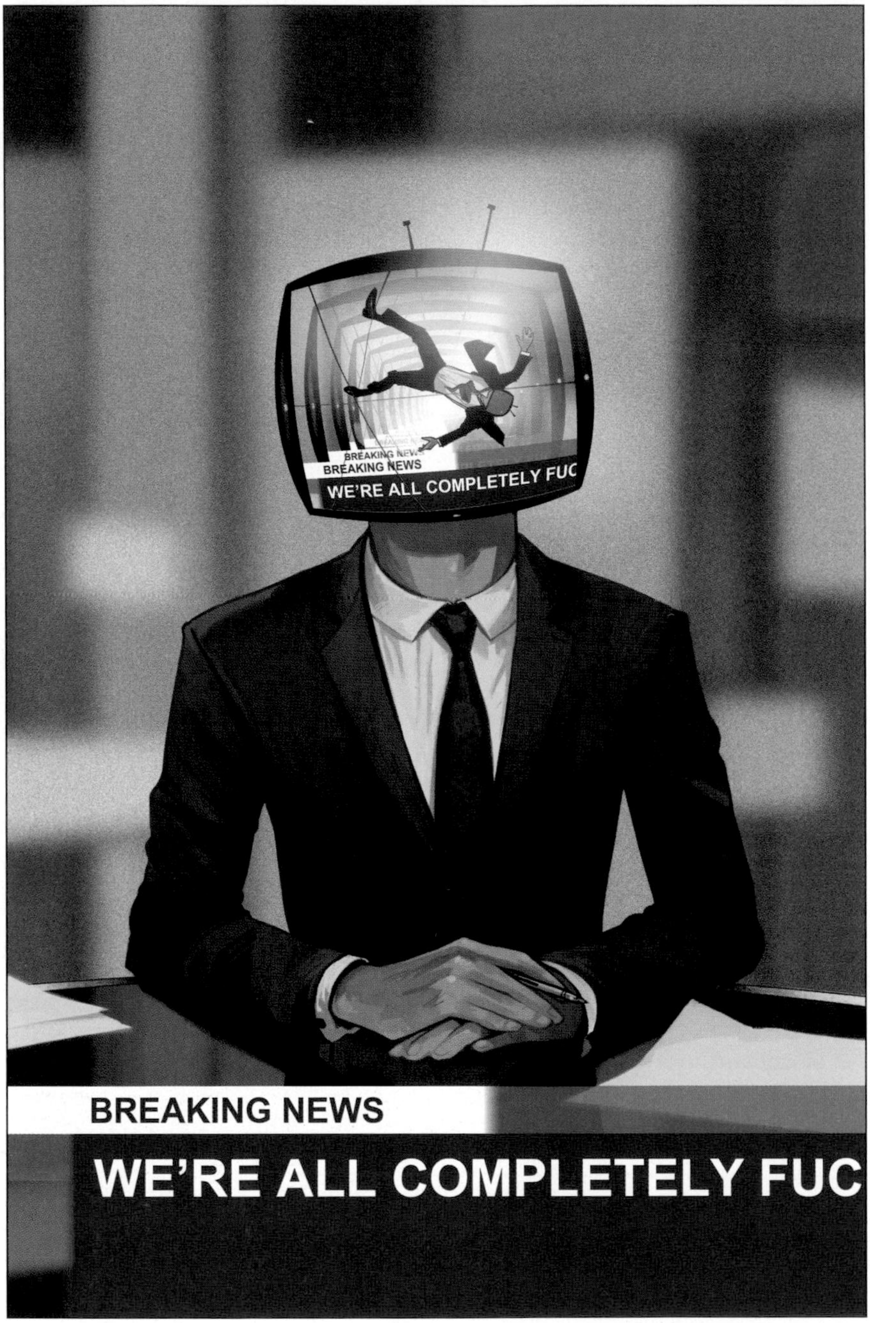
BREAKING NEWS
BREAKING NEWS
WE'RE ALL COMPLETELY FUC
BREAKING NEWS
WE'RE ALL COMPLETELY FUC

CHAPTER

FORTY-NINE

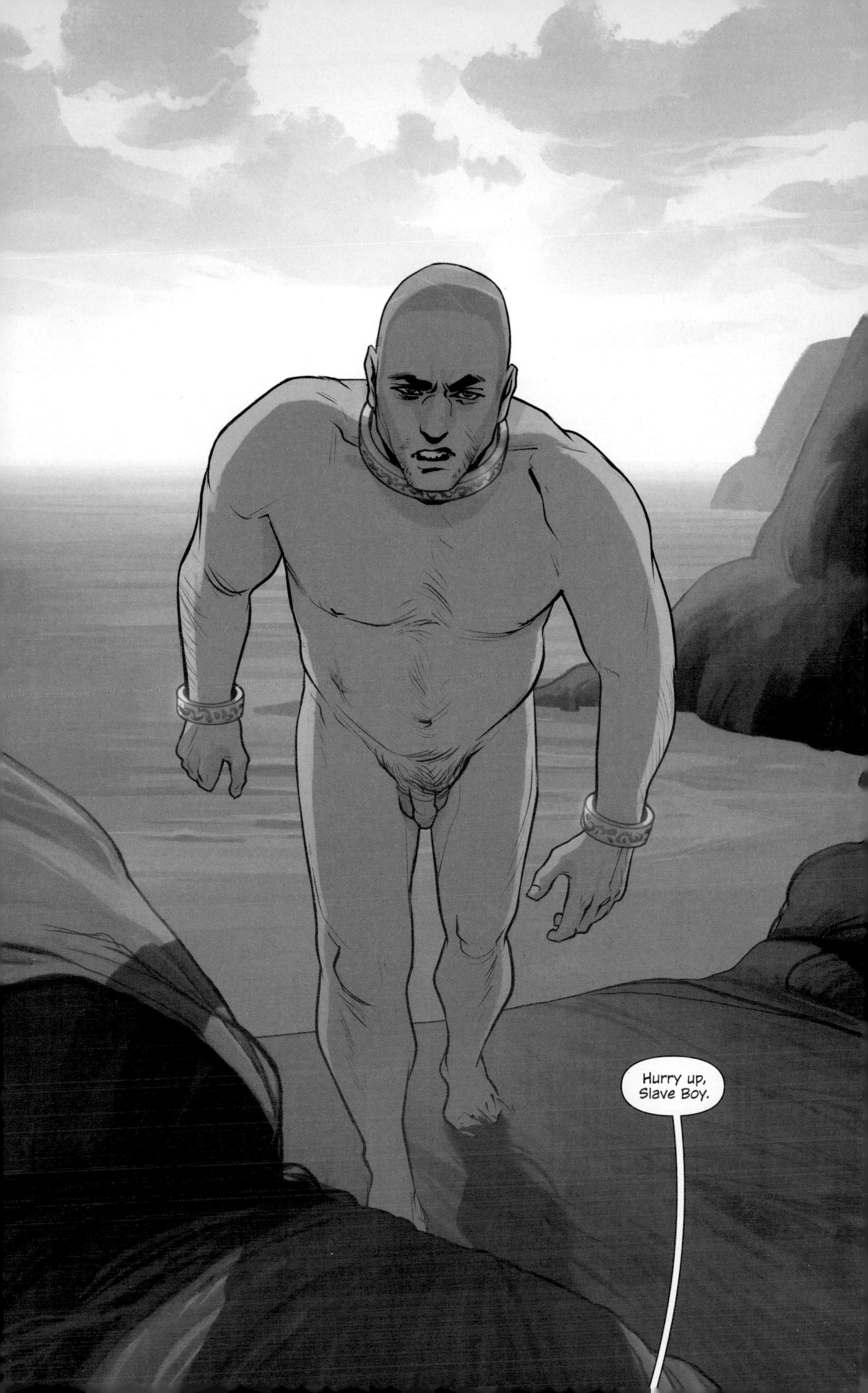
Hurry up, Slave Boy.

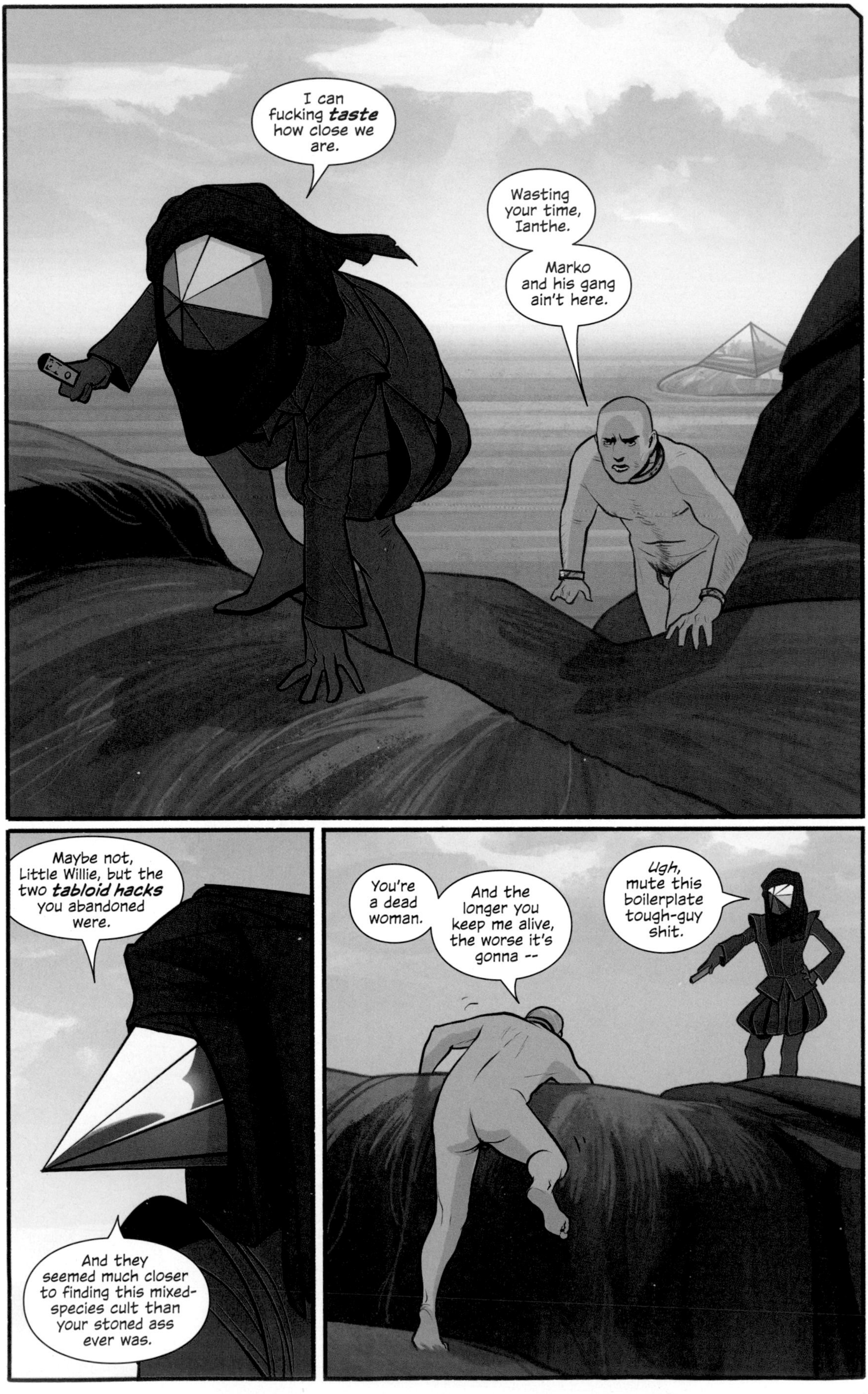

I can fucking *taste* how close we are.
Wasting your time, Ianthe.
Marko and his gang ain't here.
Maybe not, Little Willie, but the two *tabloid hacks* you abandoned were.
And they seemed much closer to finding this mixed-species cult than your stoned ass ever was.
You're a dead woman.
And the longer you keep me alive, the worse it's gonna --
Ugh, mute this boilerplate tough-guy shit.

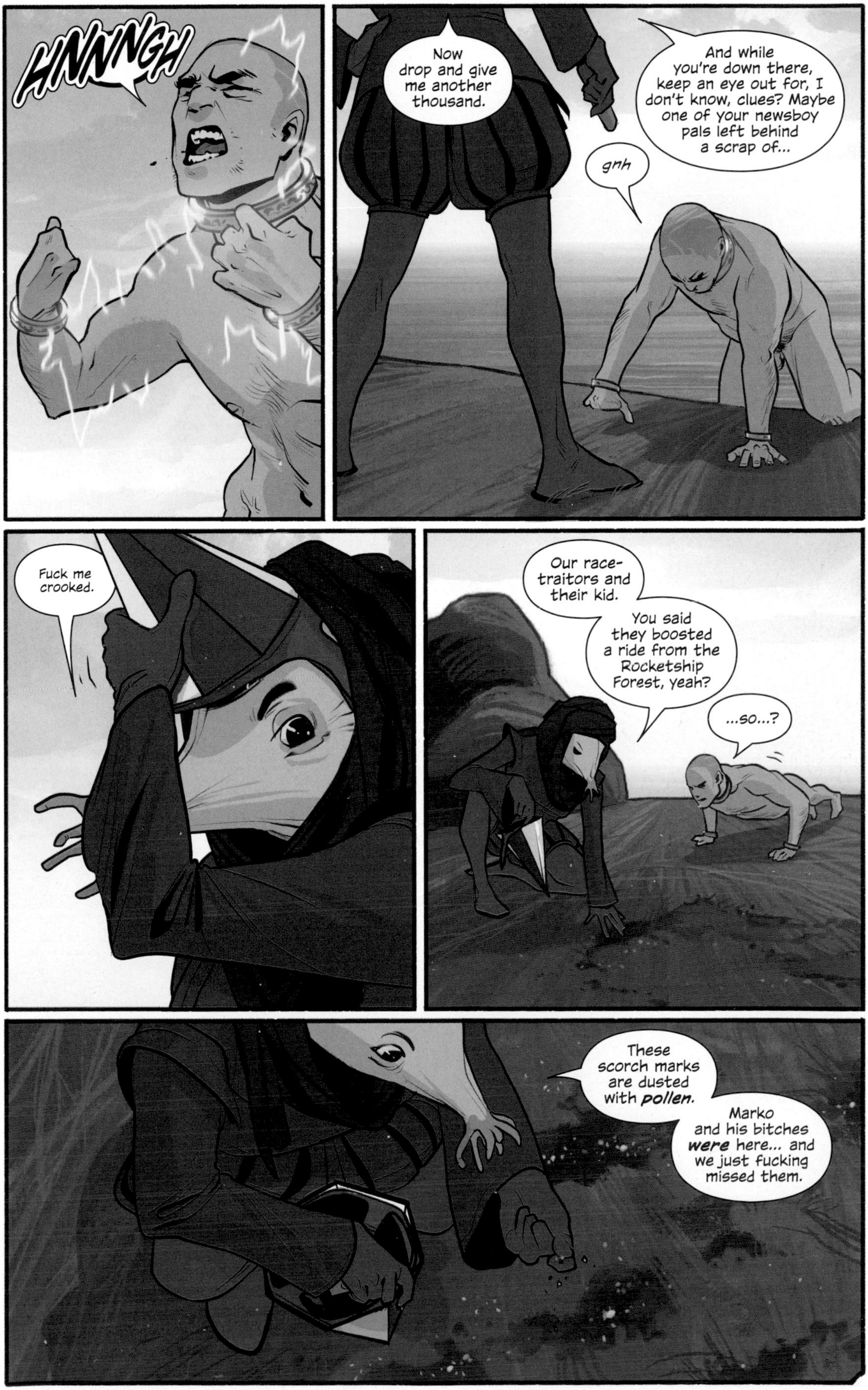
HNNNGH
Now drop and give me another thousand.
And while you're down there, keep an eye out for, I don't know, clues? Maybe one of your newsboy pals left behind a scrap of...
gnh
Fuck me crooked.
Our race-traitors and their kid.
You said they boosted a ride from the Rocketship Forest, yeah?
...so...?
These scorch marks are dusted with *pollen*.
Marko and his bitches *were* here... and we just fucking missed them.

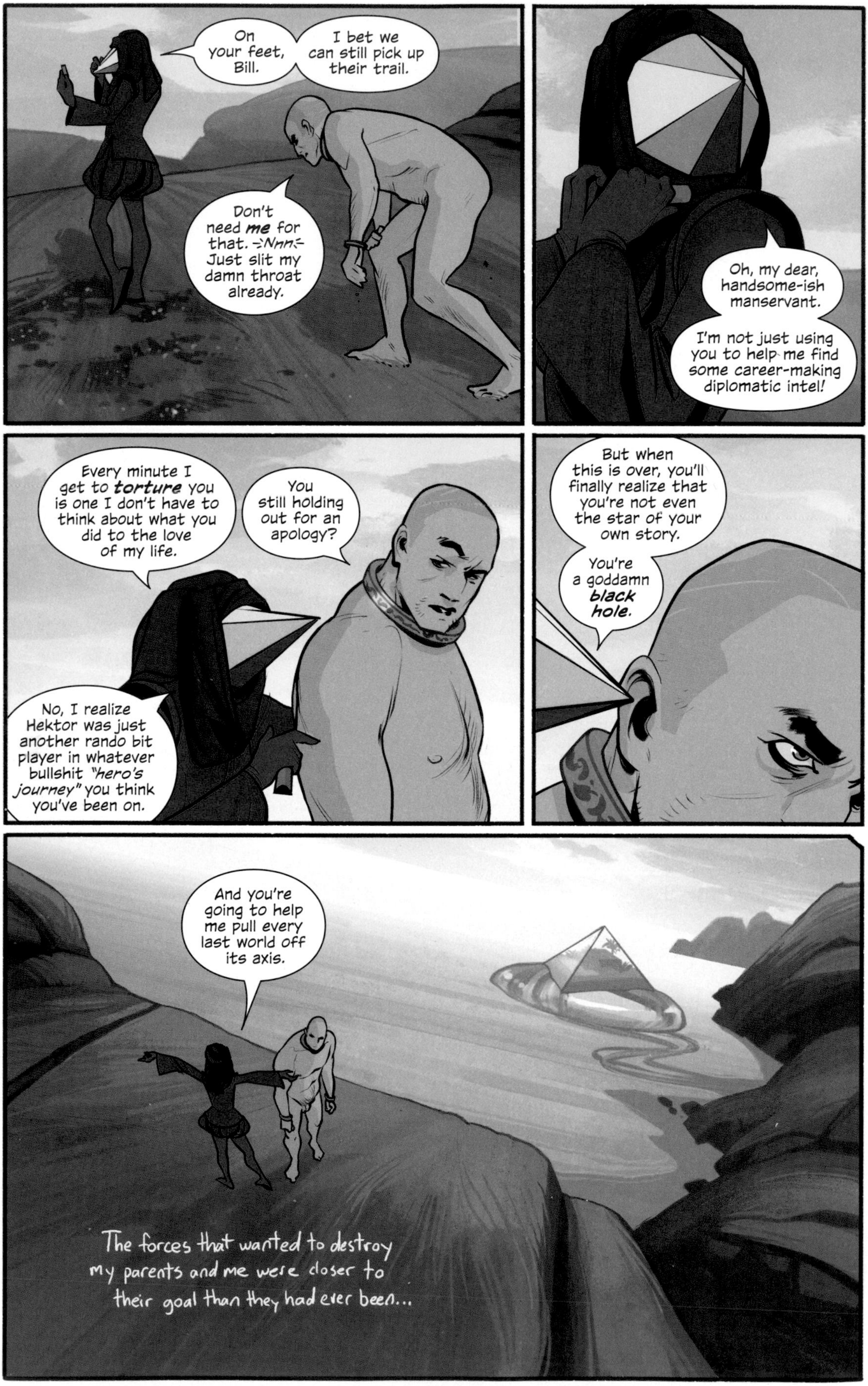
On your feet, Bill.
I bet we can still pick up their trail.
Don't need *me* for that. =Nnn= Just slit my damn throat already.
Oh, my dear, handsome-ish manservant.
I'm not just using you to help me find some career-making diplomatic intel!
Every minute I get to *torture* you is one I don't have to think about what you did to the love of my life.
You still holding out for an apology?
No, I realize Hektor was just another rando bit player in whatever bullshit *"hero's journey"* you think you've been on.
But when this is over, you'll finally realize that you're not even the star of your own story.
You're a goddamn *black hole.*
And you're going to help me pull every last world off its axis.
The forces that wanted to destroy my parents and me were closer to their goal than they had ever been...

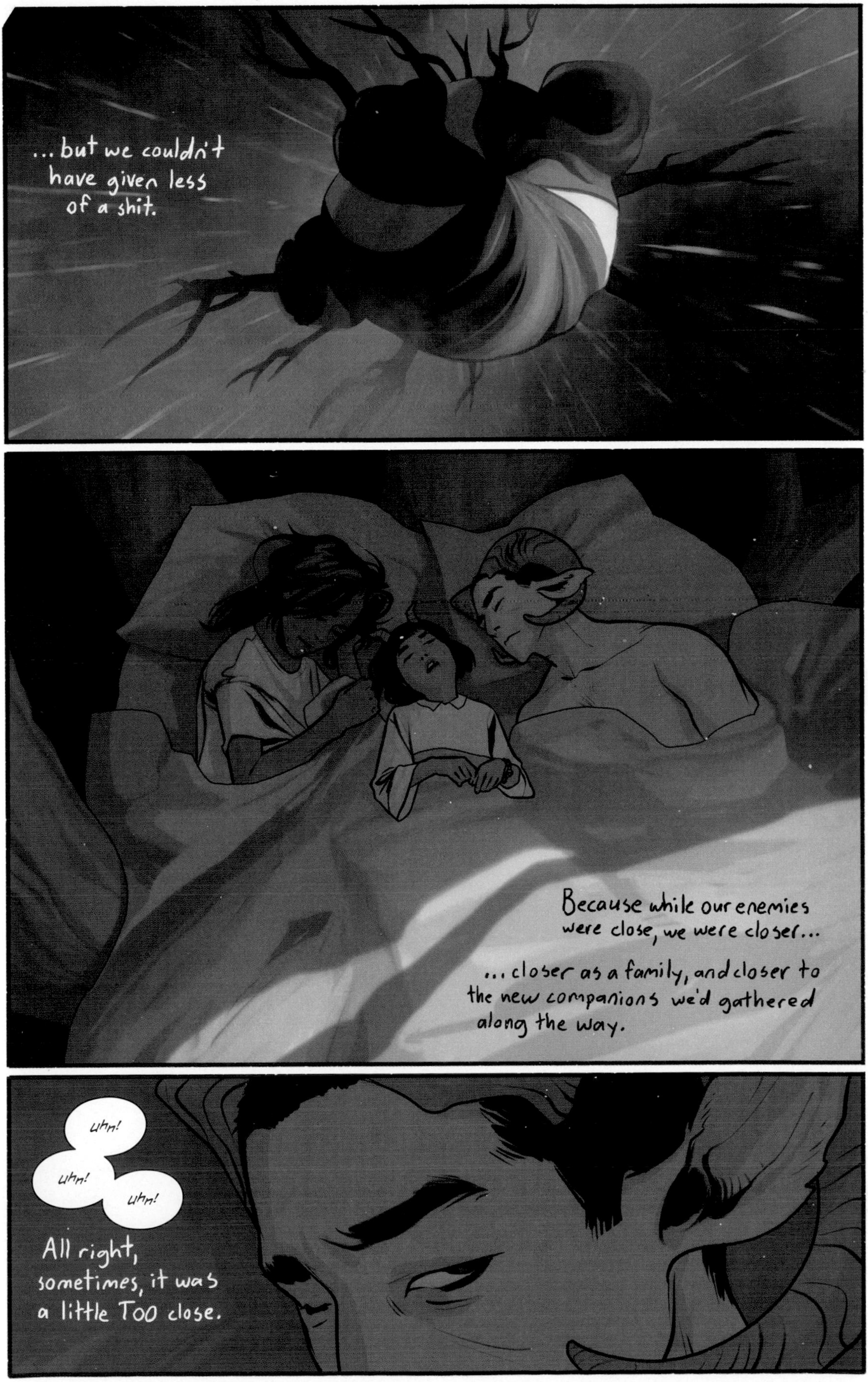
...but we couldn't have given less of a shit.
Because while our enemies were close, we were closer...
...closer as a family, and closer to the new companions we'd gathered along the way.
uhn!
uhn!
uhn!
All right, sometimes, it was a little TOO close.

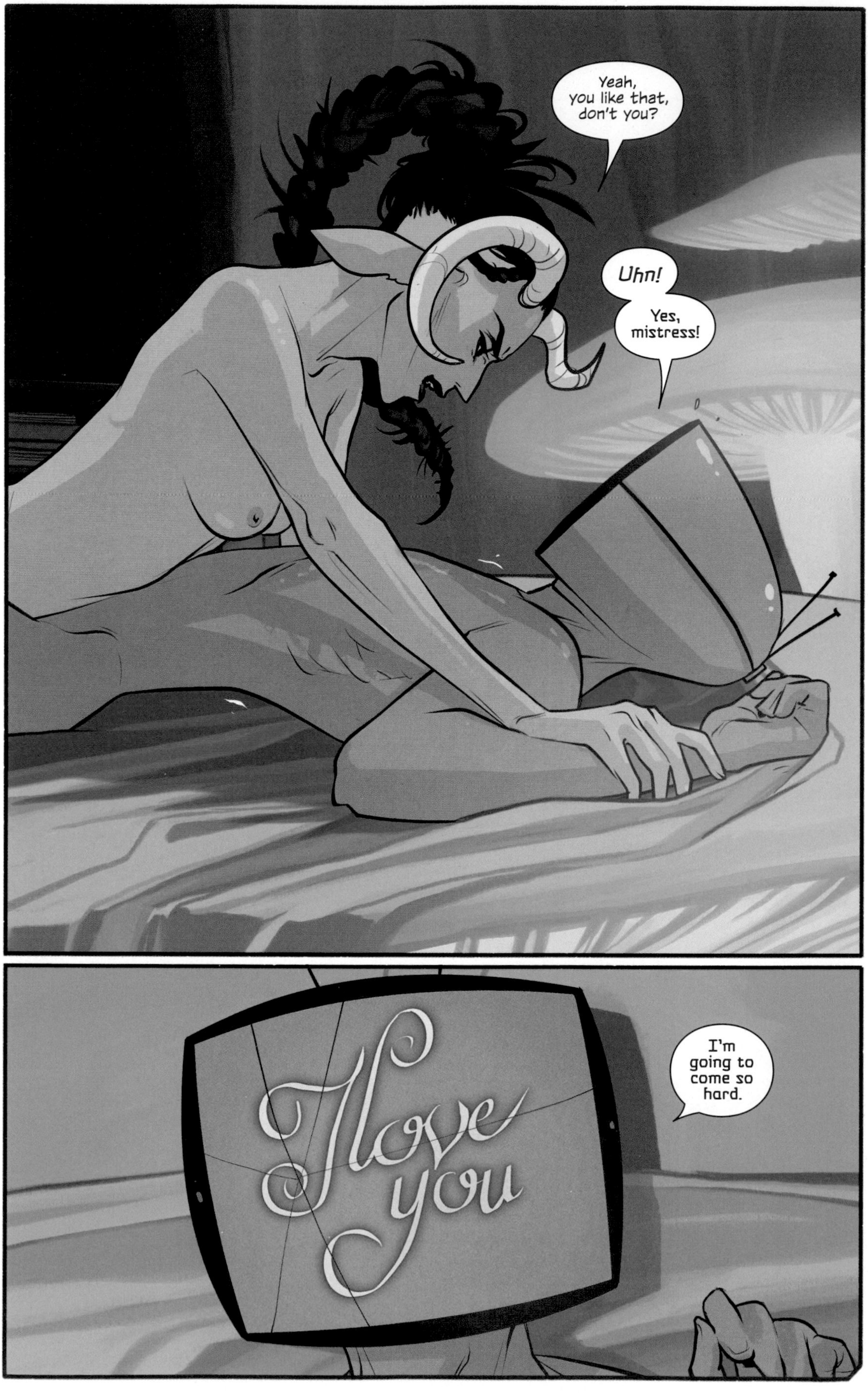

Yeah, you like that, don't you?
Uhn!
Yes, mistress!
I love you
I'm going to come so hard.

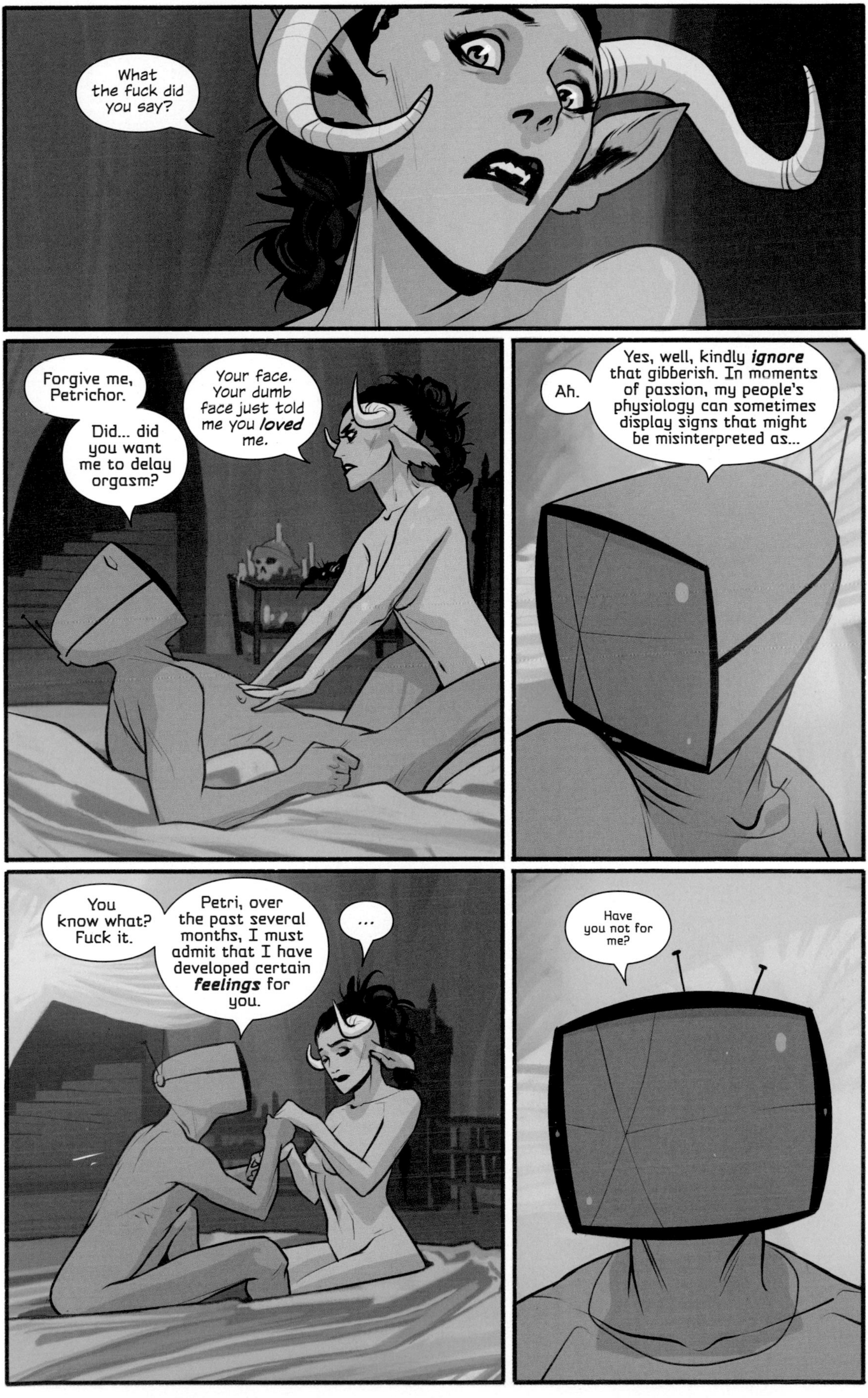
What the fuck did you say?
Forgive me, Petrichor.
Did... did you want me to delay orgasm?
Your face. Your dumb face just told me you *loved* me.
Ah.
Yes, well, kindly ***ignore*** that gibberish. In moments of passion, my people's physiology can sometimes display signs that might be misinterpreted as...
You know what? Fuck it.
Petri, over the past several months, I must admit that I have developed certain ***feelings*** for you.
...
Have you not for me?

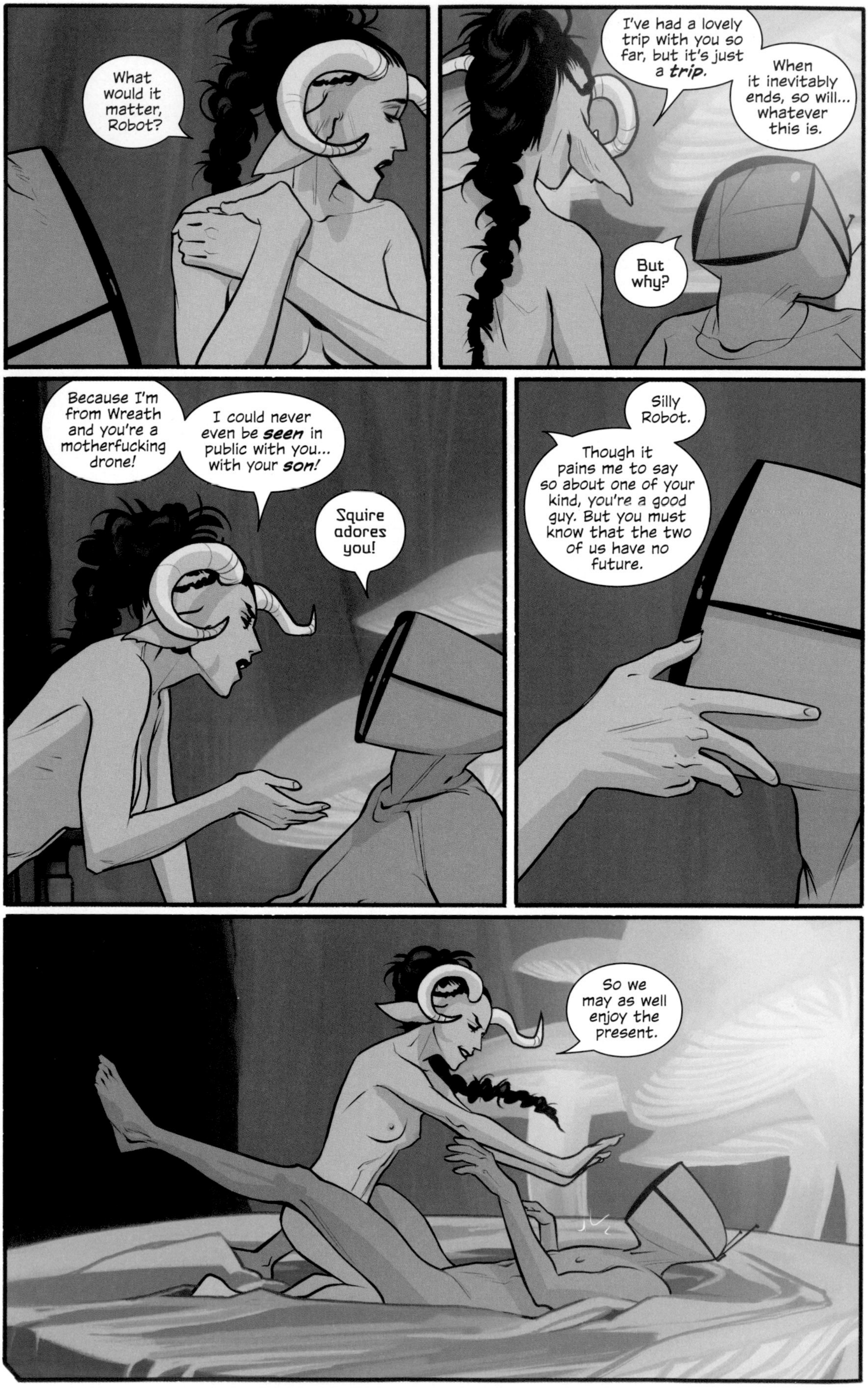
What would it matter, Robot?
I've had a lovely trip with you so far, but it's just a *trip.*
When it inevitably ends, so will... whatever this is.
But why?
Because I'm from Wreath and you're a motherfucking drone!
I could never even be *seen* in public with you... with your *son!*
Squire adores you!
Silly Robot.
Though it pains me to say so about one of your kind, you're a good guy. But you must know that the two of us have no future.
So we may as well enjoy the present.

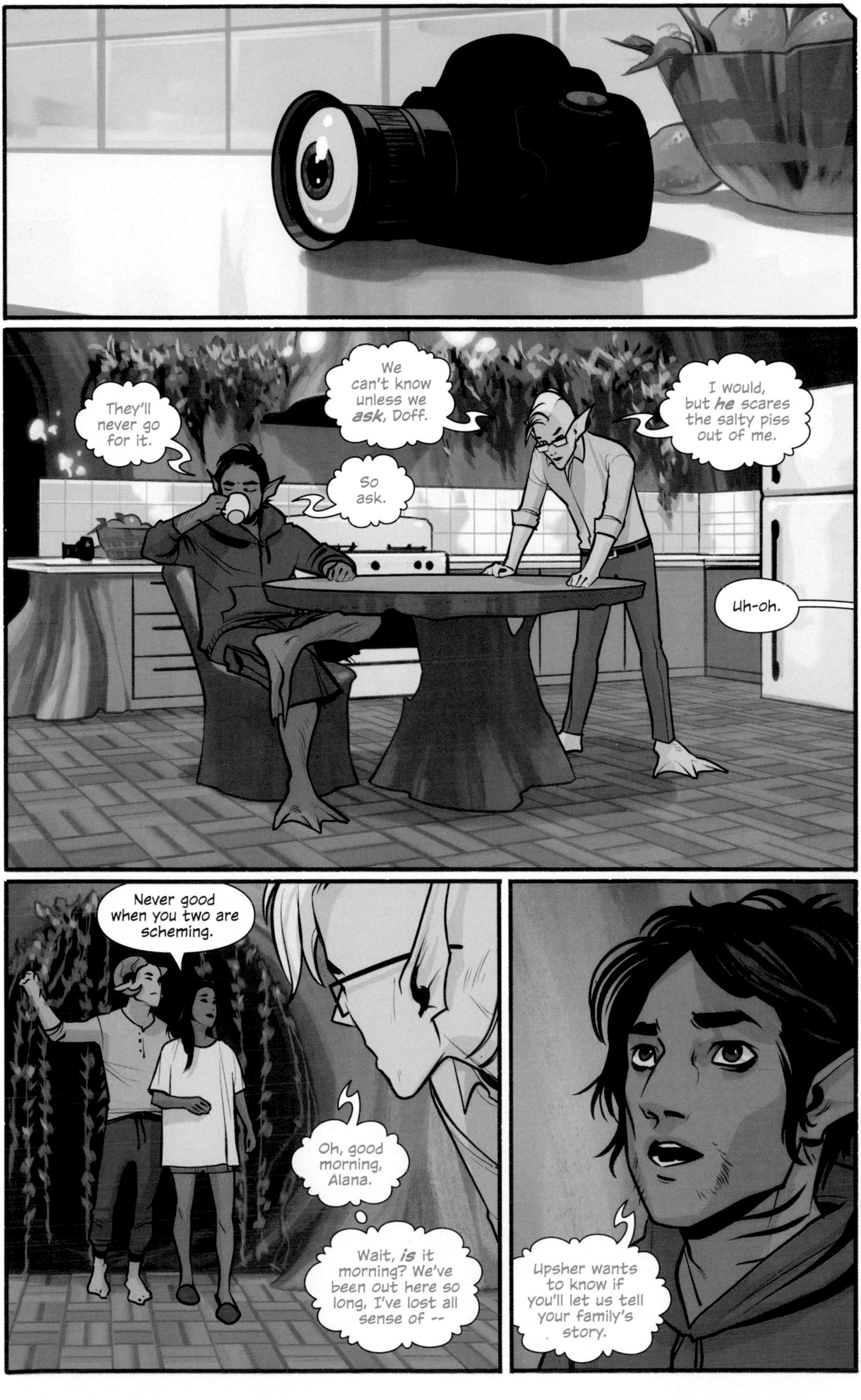
They'll never go for it.
We can't know unless we *ask*, Doff.
I would, but *he* scares the salty piss out of me.
So ask.
Uh-oh.
Never good when you two are scheming.
Oh, good morning, Alana.
Wait, *is* it morning? We've been out here so long, I've lost all sense of --
Upsher wants to know if you'll let us tell your family's story.

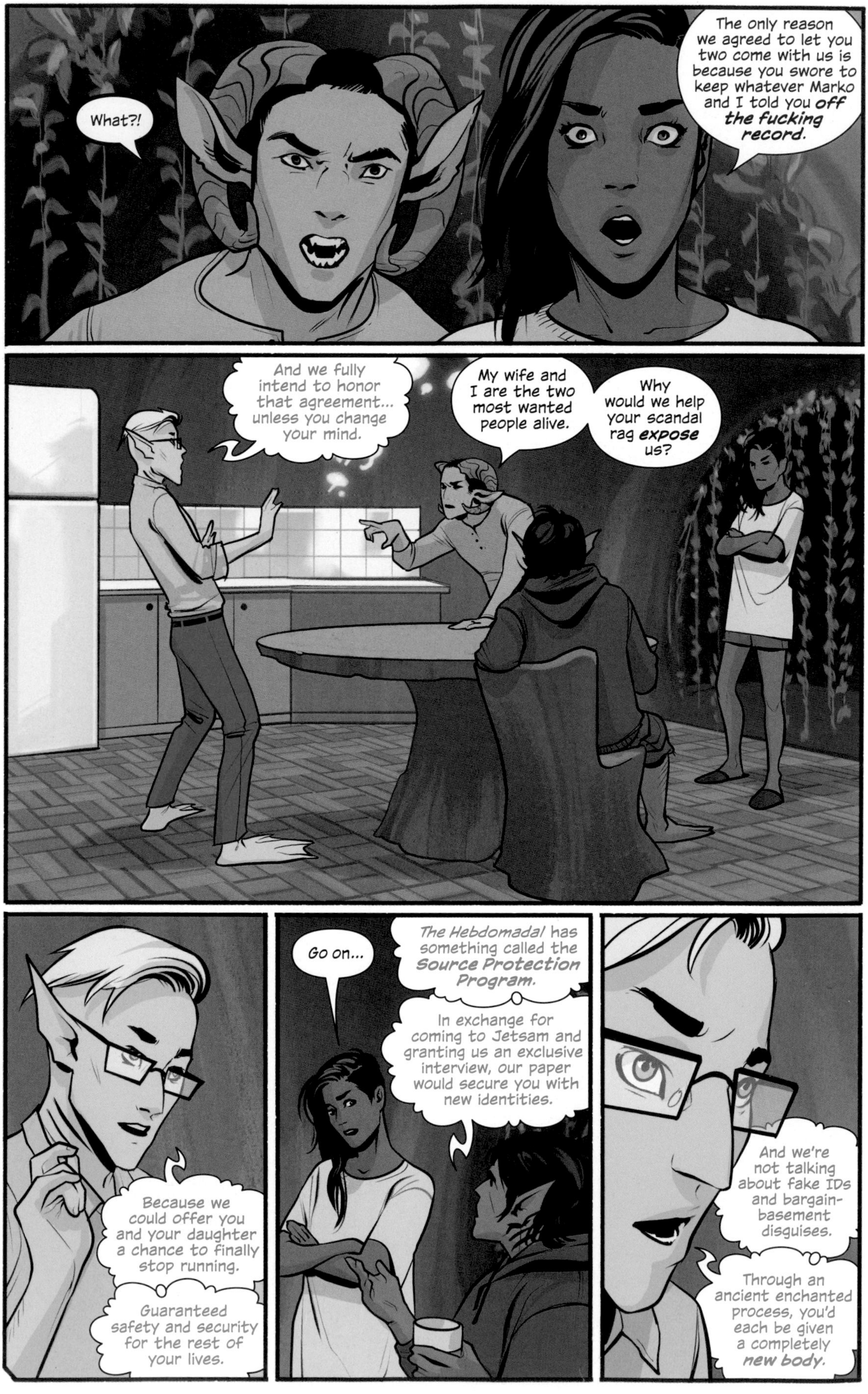

What?!
The only reason we agreed to let you two come with us is because you swore to keep whatever Marko and I told you off the fucking record.
And we fully intend to honor that agreement... unless you change your mind.
My wife and I are the two most wanted people alive.
Why would we help your scandal rag expose us?
Because we could offer you and your daughter a chance to finally stop running.
Guaranteed safety and security for the rest of your lives.
Go on...
The Hebdomadal has something called the Source Protection Program.
In exchange for coming to Jetsam and granting us an exclusive interview, our paper would secure you with new identities.
And we're not talking about fake IDs and bargain-basement disguises.
Through an ancient enchanted process, you'd each be given a completely new body.

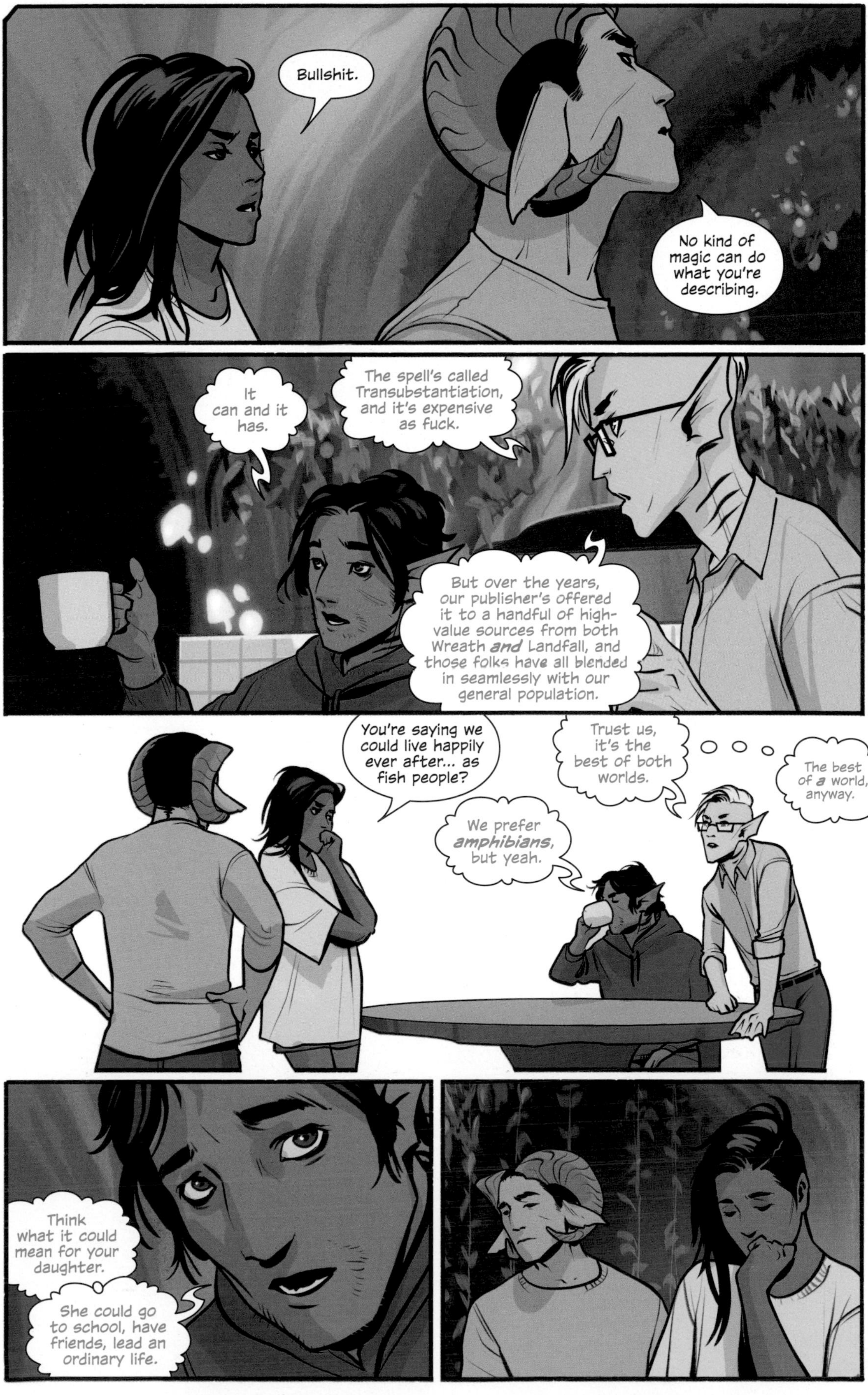
Bullshit.
No kind of magic can do what you're describing.
It can and it has.
The spell's called Transubstantiation, and it's expensive as fuck.
But over the years, our publisher's offered it to a handful of high-value sources from both Wreath *and* Landfall, and those folks have all blended in seamlessly with our general population.
You're saying we could live happily ever after... as fish people?
Trust us, it's the best of both worlds.
The best of *a* world, anyway.
We prefer *amphibians*, but yeah.
Think what it could mean for your daughter.
She could go to school, have friends, lead an ordinary life.

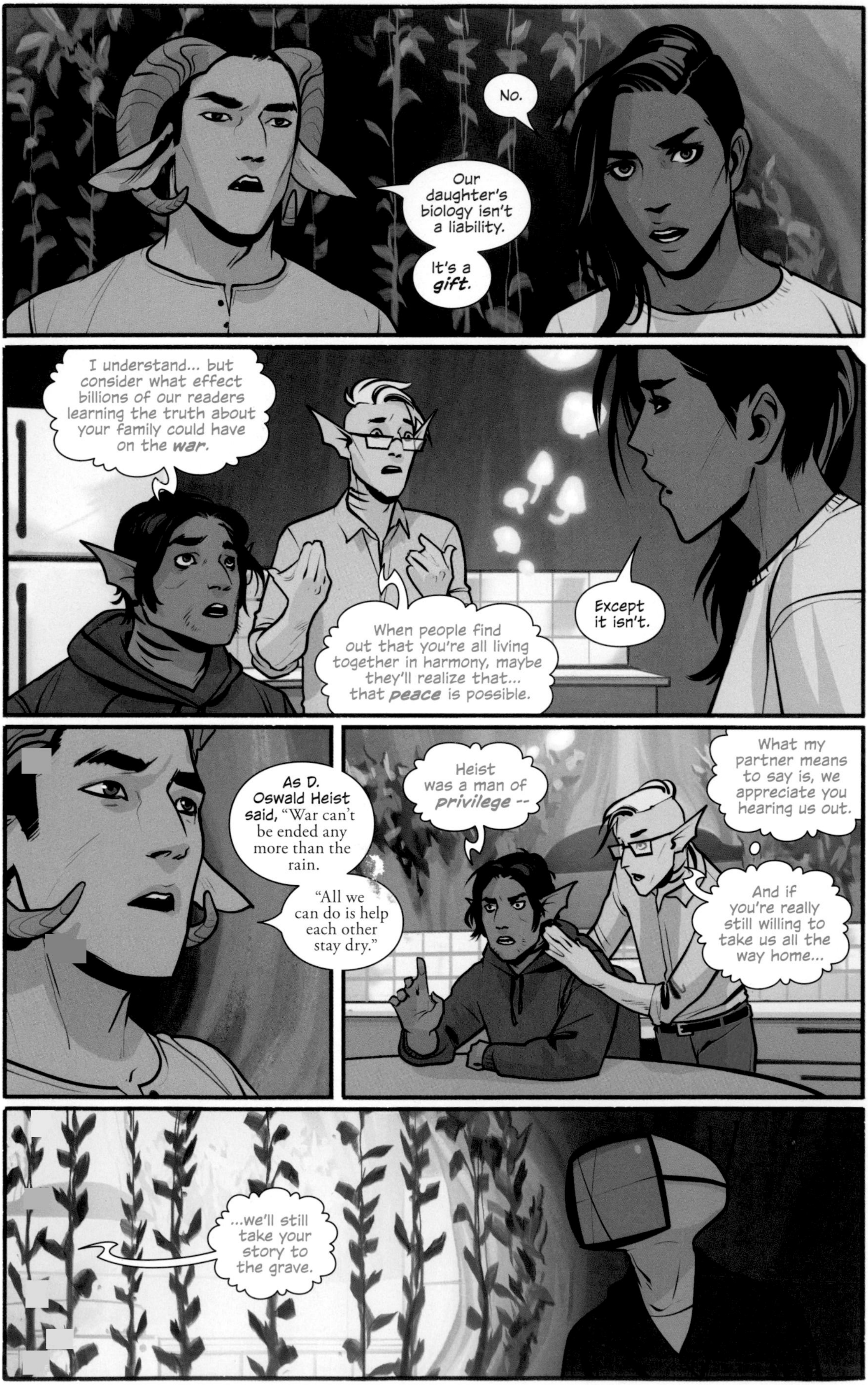

No.
Our daughter's biology isn't a liability.
It's a *gift*.
I understand... but consider what effect billions of our readers learning the truth about your family could have on the *war*.
When people find out that you're all living together in harmony, maybe they'll realize that... that *peace* is possible.
Except it isn't.
As D. Oswald Heist said, "War can't be ended any more than the rain.
"All we can do is help each other stay dry."
Heist was a man of *privilege* --
What my partner means to say is, we appreciate you hearing us out.
And if you're really still willing to take us all the way home...
...we'll still take your story to the grave.

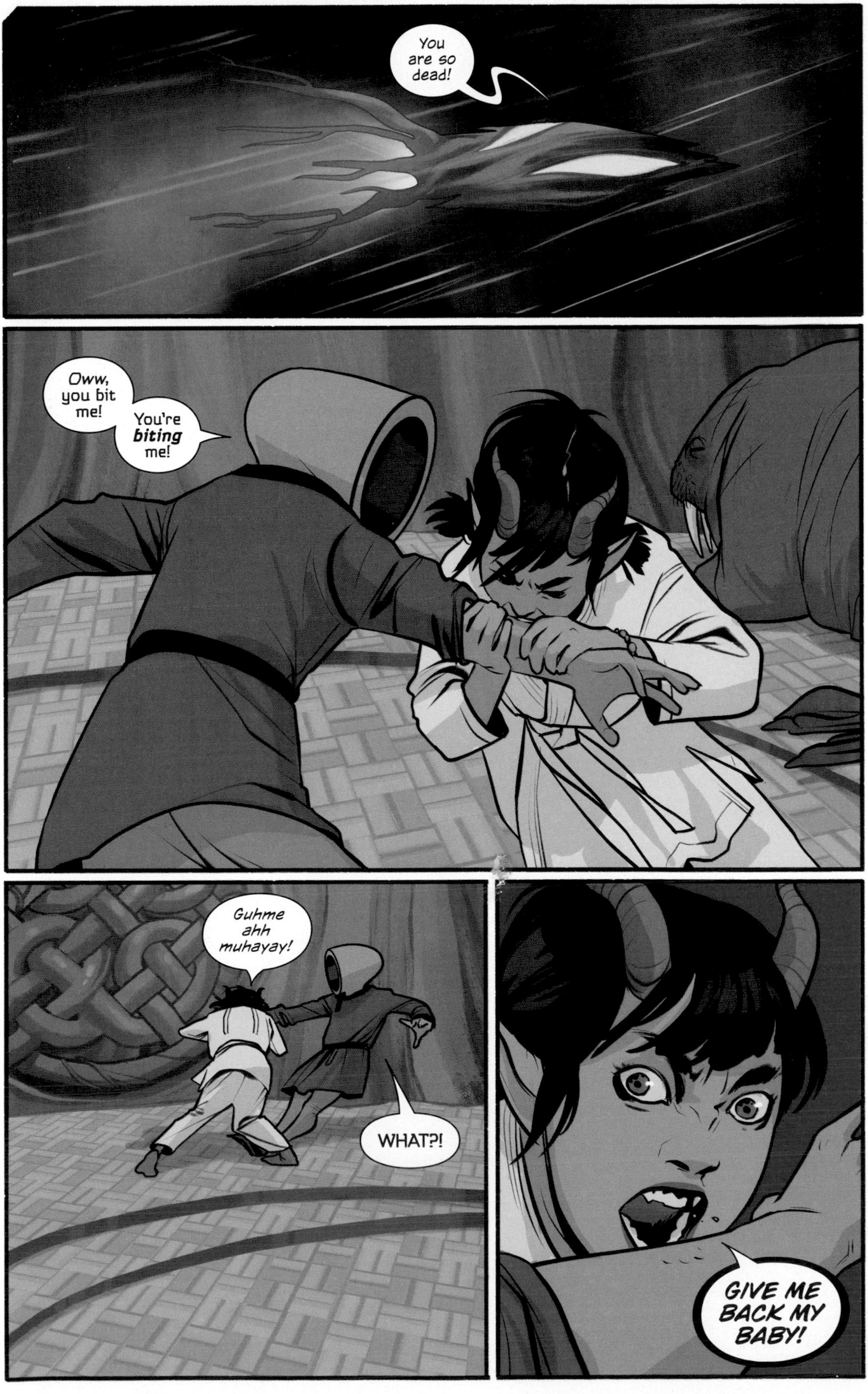
You are so dead!
Oww, you bit me!
You're *biting* me!
Guhme ahh muhayay!
WHAT?!
GIVE ME BACK MY BABY!

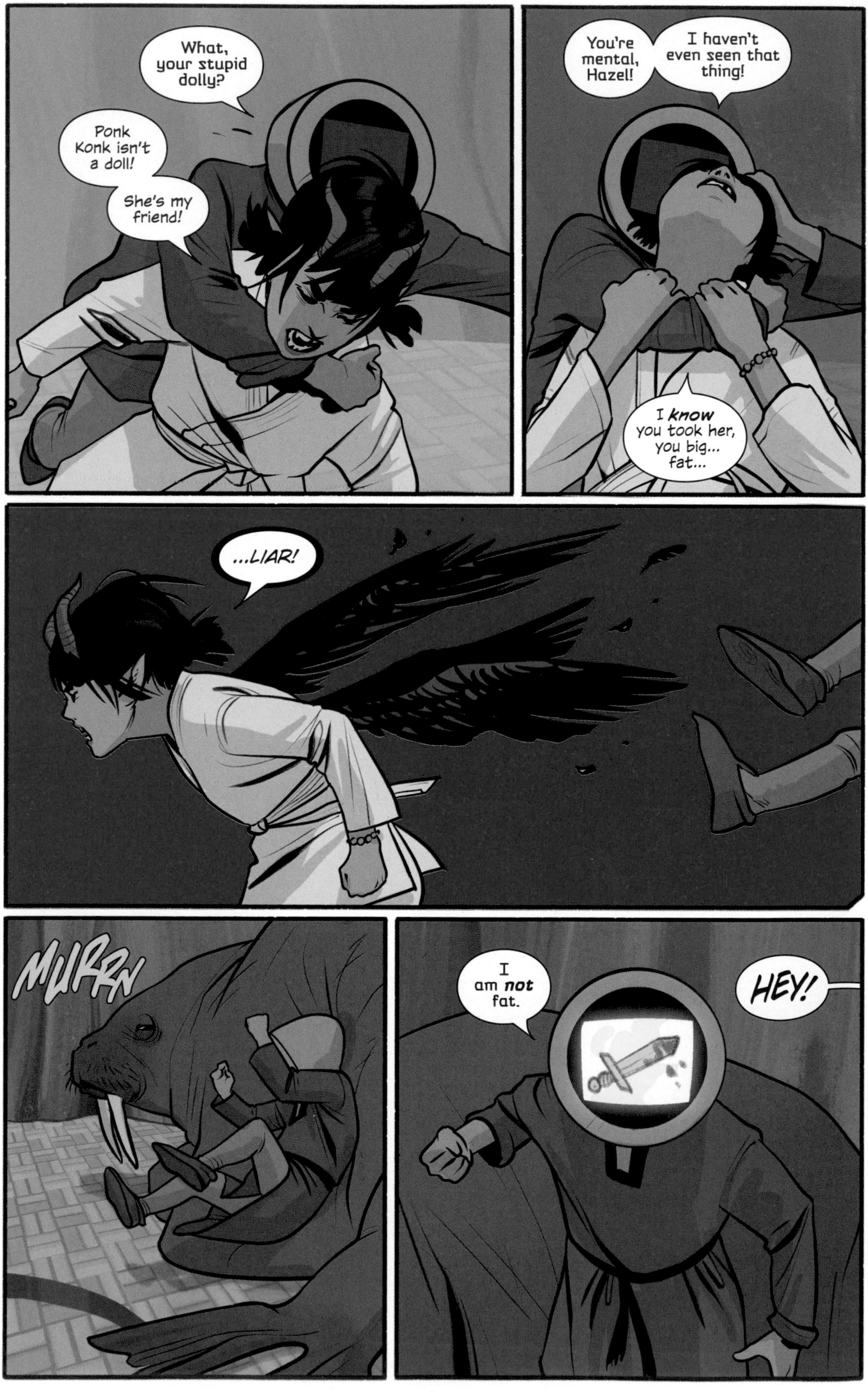

What, your stupid dolly?
Ponk Konk isn't a doll!
She's my friend!
You're mental, Hazel!
I haven't even seen that thing!
I *know* you took her, you big... fat...
...LIAR!
MURRN
I am *not* fat.
HEY!

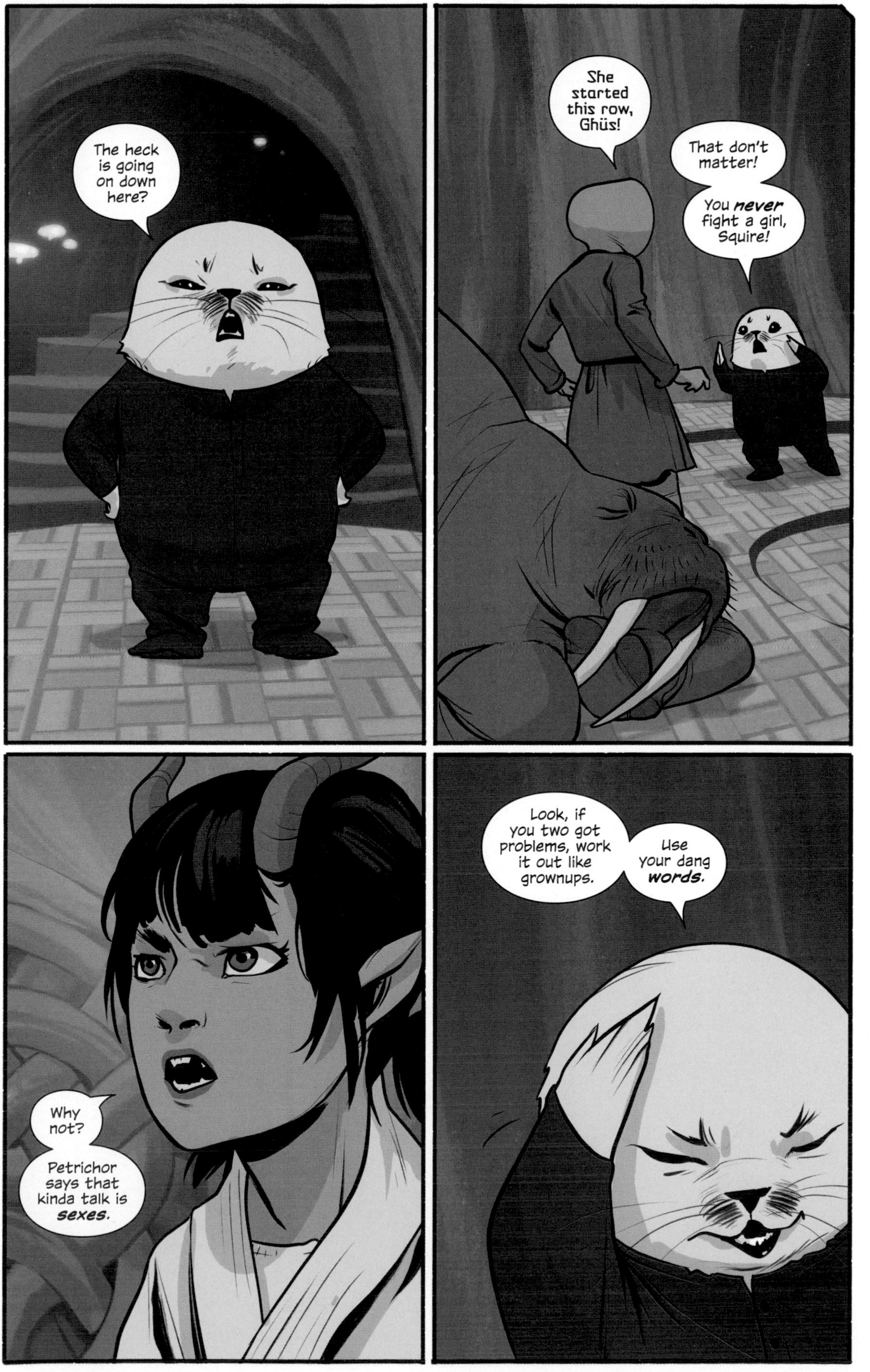
The heck is going on down here?
She started this row, Ghüs!
That don't matter!
You **never** fight a girl, Squire!
Why not?
Petrichor says that kinda talk is **sexes.**
Look, if you two got problems, work it out like grownups.
Use your dang **words.**

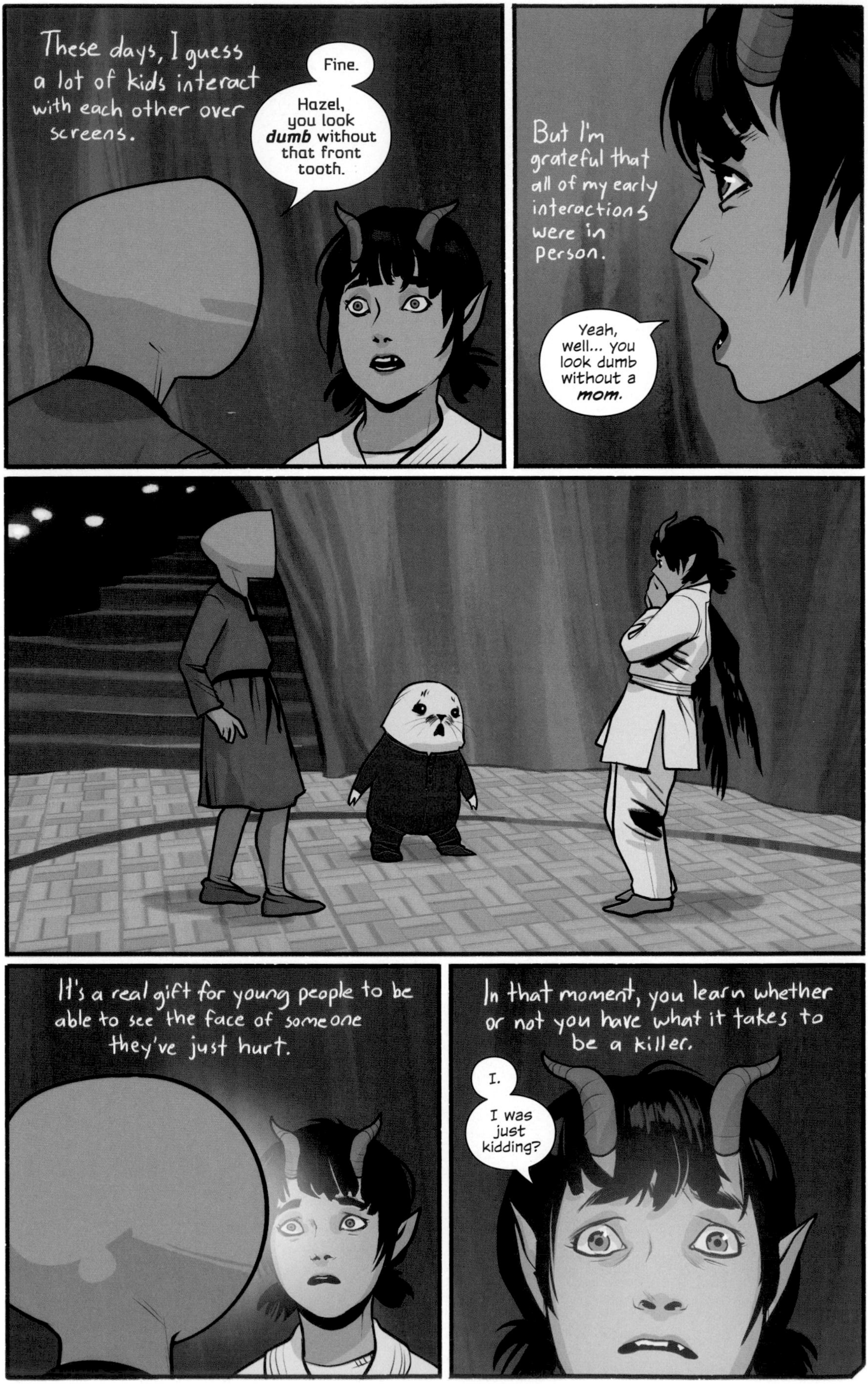
These days, I guess a lot of kids interact with each other over screens.
Fine.
Hazel, you look **dumb** without that front tooth.
But I'm grateful that all of my early interactions were in person.
Yeah, well... you look dumb without a ***mom***.
It's a real gift for young people to be able to see the face of someone they've just hurt.
In that moment, you learn whether or not you have what it takes to be a killer.
I.
I was just kidding?

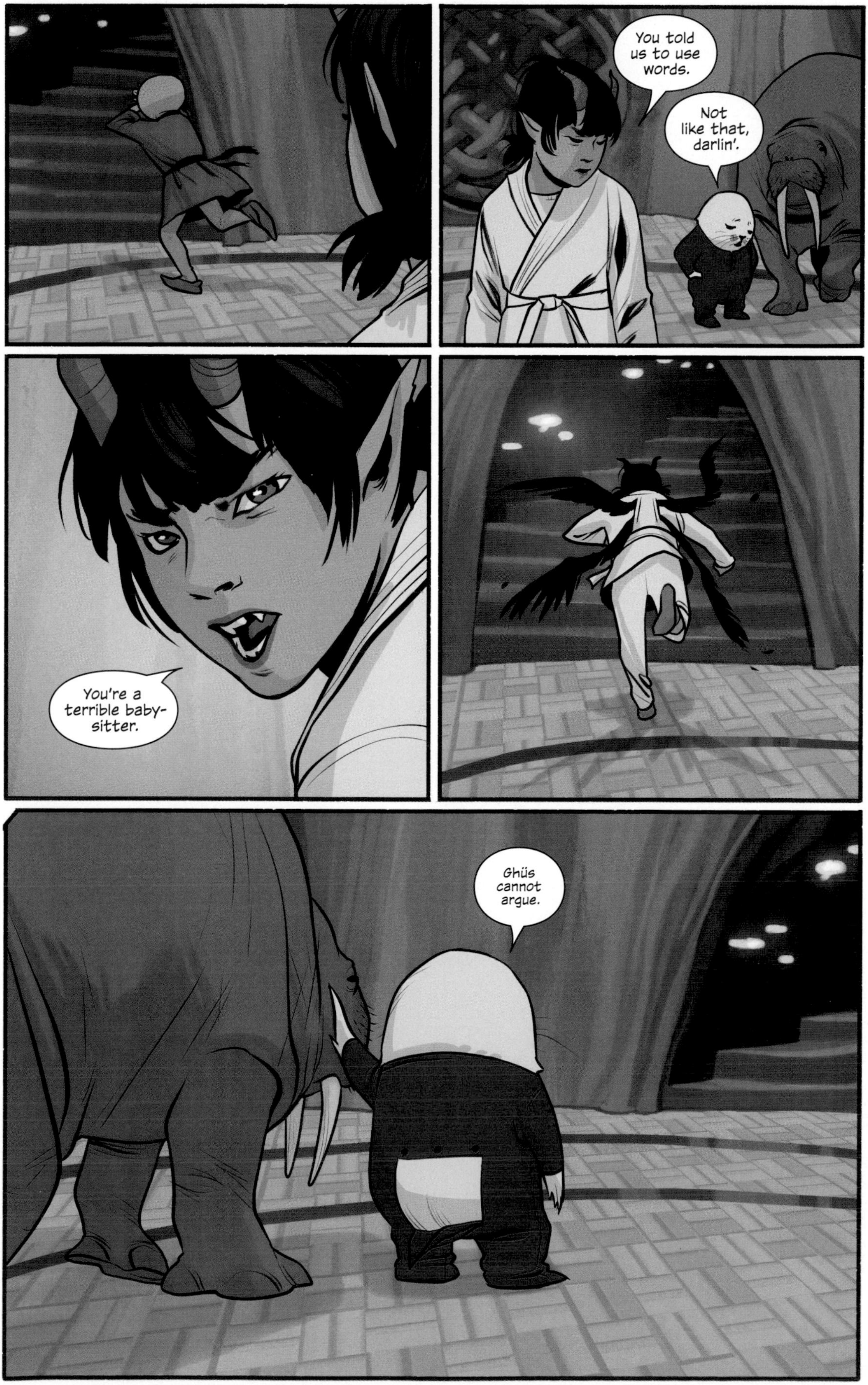
You told us to use words.
Not like that, darlin'.
You're a terrible baby-sitter.
Ghüs cannot argue.

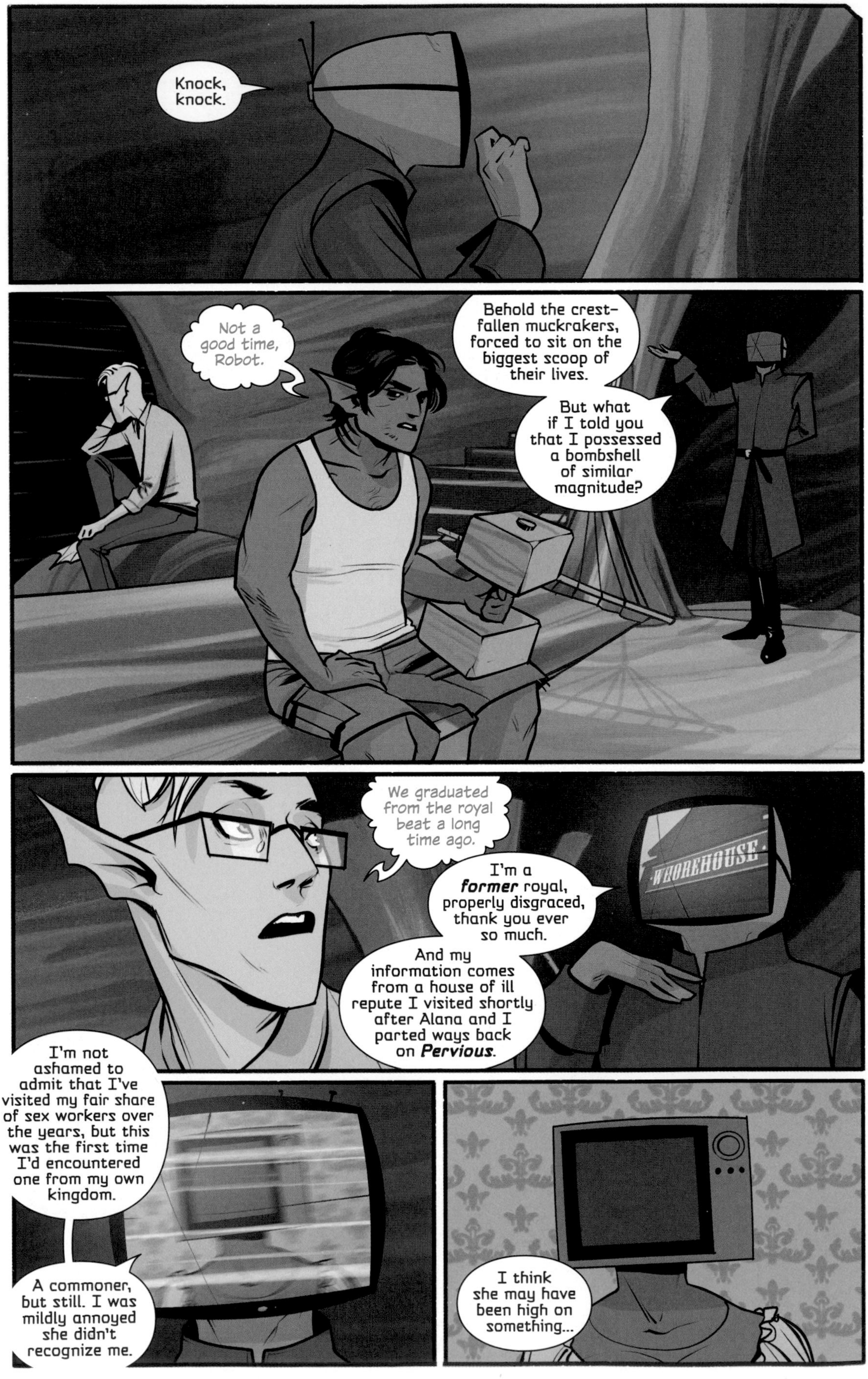
Knock, knock.
Not a good time, Robot.
Behold the crest-fallen muckrakers, forced to sit on the biggest scoop of their lives.
But what if I told you that I possessed a bombshell of similar magnitude?
We graduated from the royal beat a long time ago.
WHOREHOUSE
I'm a **former** royal, properly disgraced, thank you ever so much.
And my information comes from a house of ill repute I visited shortly after Alana and I parted ways back on **Pervious**.
I'm not ashamed to admit that I've visited my fair share of sex workers over the years, but this was the first time I'd encountered one from my own kingdom.
A commoner, but still. I was mildly annoyed she didn't recognize me.
I think she may have been high on something...

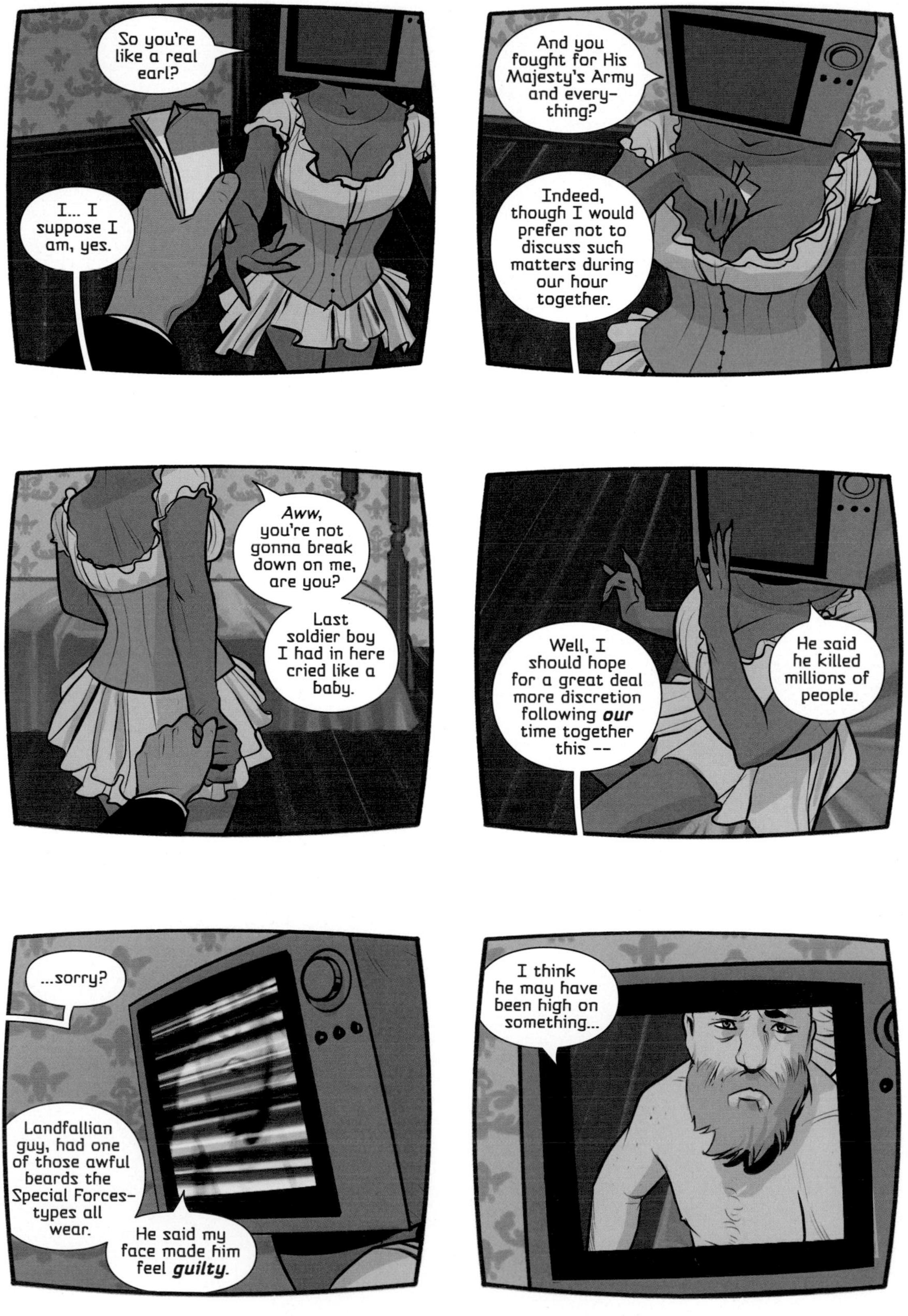
So you're like a real earl?
I... I suppose I am, yes.
And you fought for His Majesty's Army and every-thing?
Indeed, though I would prefer not to discuss such matters during our hour together.
Aww, you're not gonna break down on me, are you?
Last soldier boy I had in here cried like a baby.
Well, I should hope for a great deal more discretion following our time together this --
He said he killed millions of people.
...sorry?
Landfallian guy, had one of those awful beards the Special Forces-types all wear.
He said my face made him feel guilty.
I think he may have been high on something...

When I look at you, it reminds me, like... you people have souls, too.

That's mighty sweet of you, honey.

I mean, I don't care about whatever filthy animals we helped exterminate, but I'm sorry some of *your* folks had to get caught in the crossfire.

Say again?

You've heard of *Phang*, right?

The comet?

It wasn't some natural disaster that ended those poor fucks.

It was *us*.

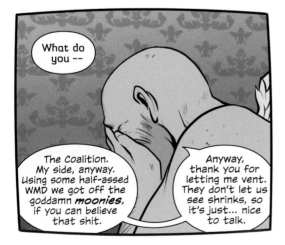

What do you --

The Coalition. My side, anyway. Using some half-assed WMD we got off the goddamn *moonies*, if you can believe that shit.

Anyway, thank you for letting me vent. They don't let us see shrinks, so it's just... nice to talk.

How much extra if I don't want to use a rubber?

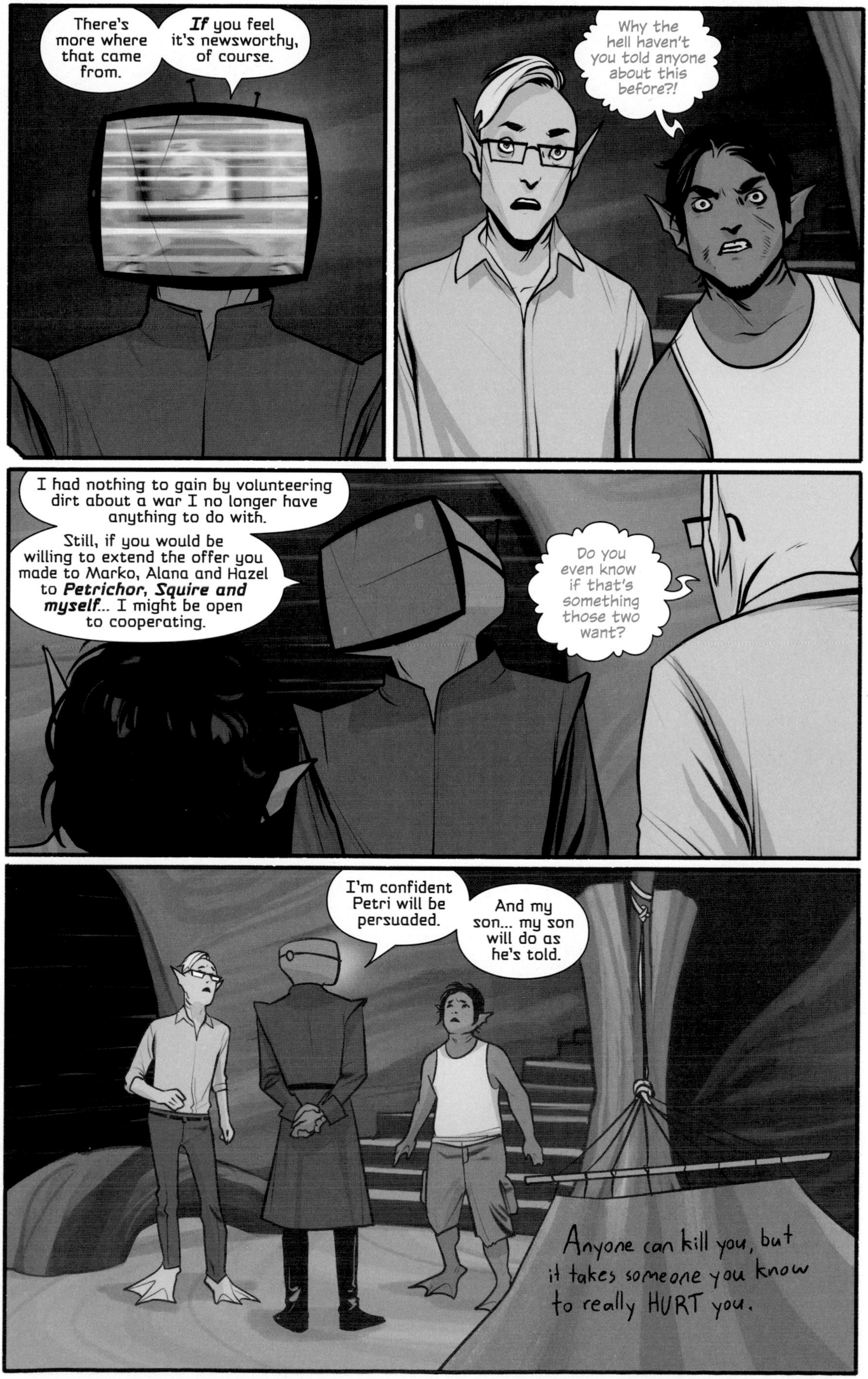
There's more where that came from.
If you feel it's newsworthy, of course.
Why the hell haven't you told anyone about this before?!
I had nothing to gain by volunteering dirt about a war I no longer have anything to do with.
Still, if you would be willing to extend the offer you made to Marko, Alana and Hazel to ***Petrichor, Squire and myself***... I might be open to cooperating.
Do you even know if that's something those two want?
I'm confident Petri will be persuaded.
And my son... my son will do as he's told.
Anyone can kill you, but it takes someone you know to really HURT you.

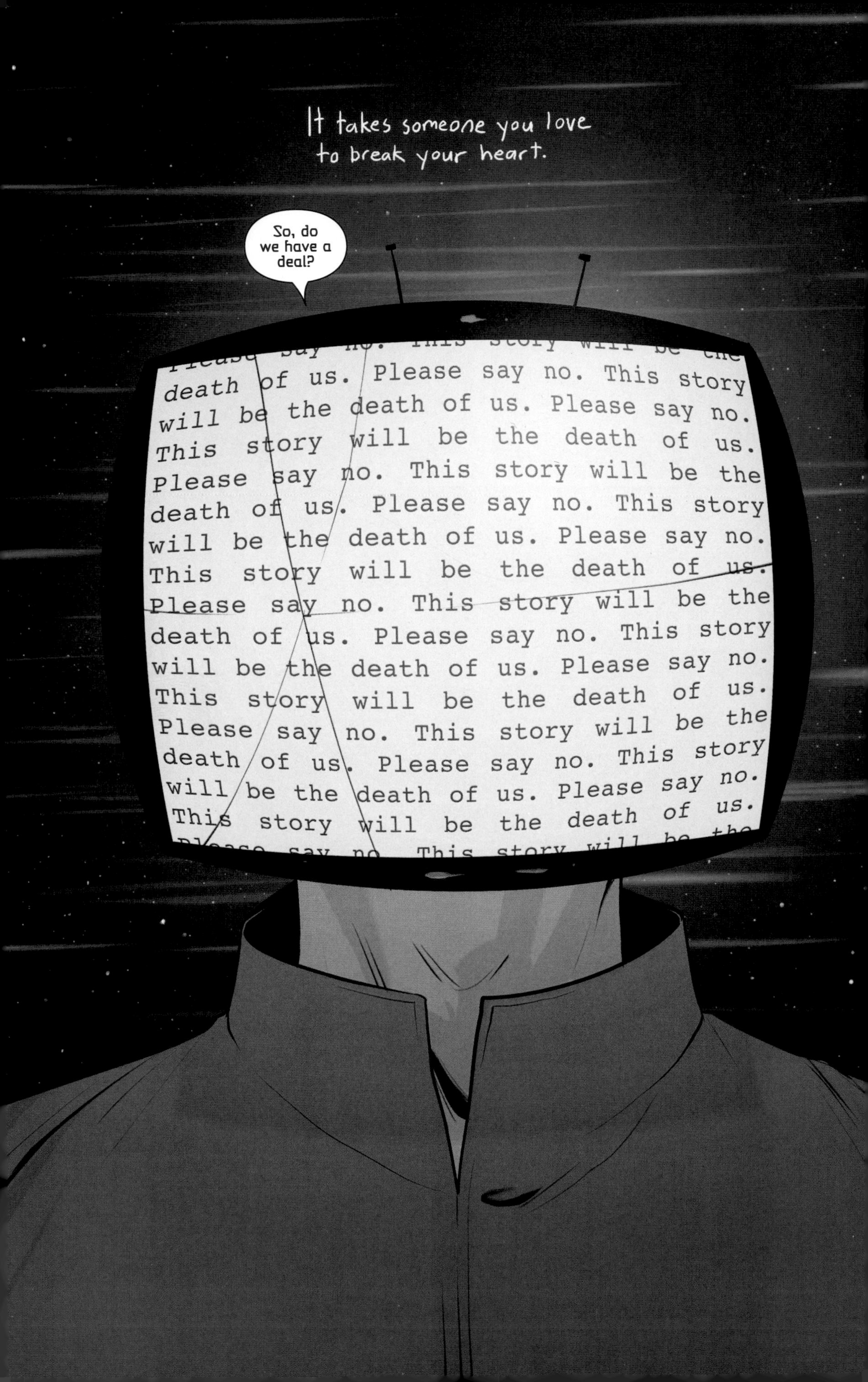

It takes someone you love
to break your heart.

So, do we have a deal?

death of us. Please say no. This story will be the death of us. Please say no. This story will be the death of us. Please say no. This story will be the death of us. Please say no. This story will be the death of us. Please say no. This story will be the death of us. Please say no. This story will be the death of us. Please say no. This story will be the death of us. Please say no. This story will be the death of us. Please say no. This story will be the death of us. Please say no. This story will be the death of us. Please say no. This story will be the death of us. Please say no. This story will be the end chapter forty-nine

CHAPTER
FIFTY

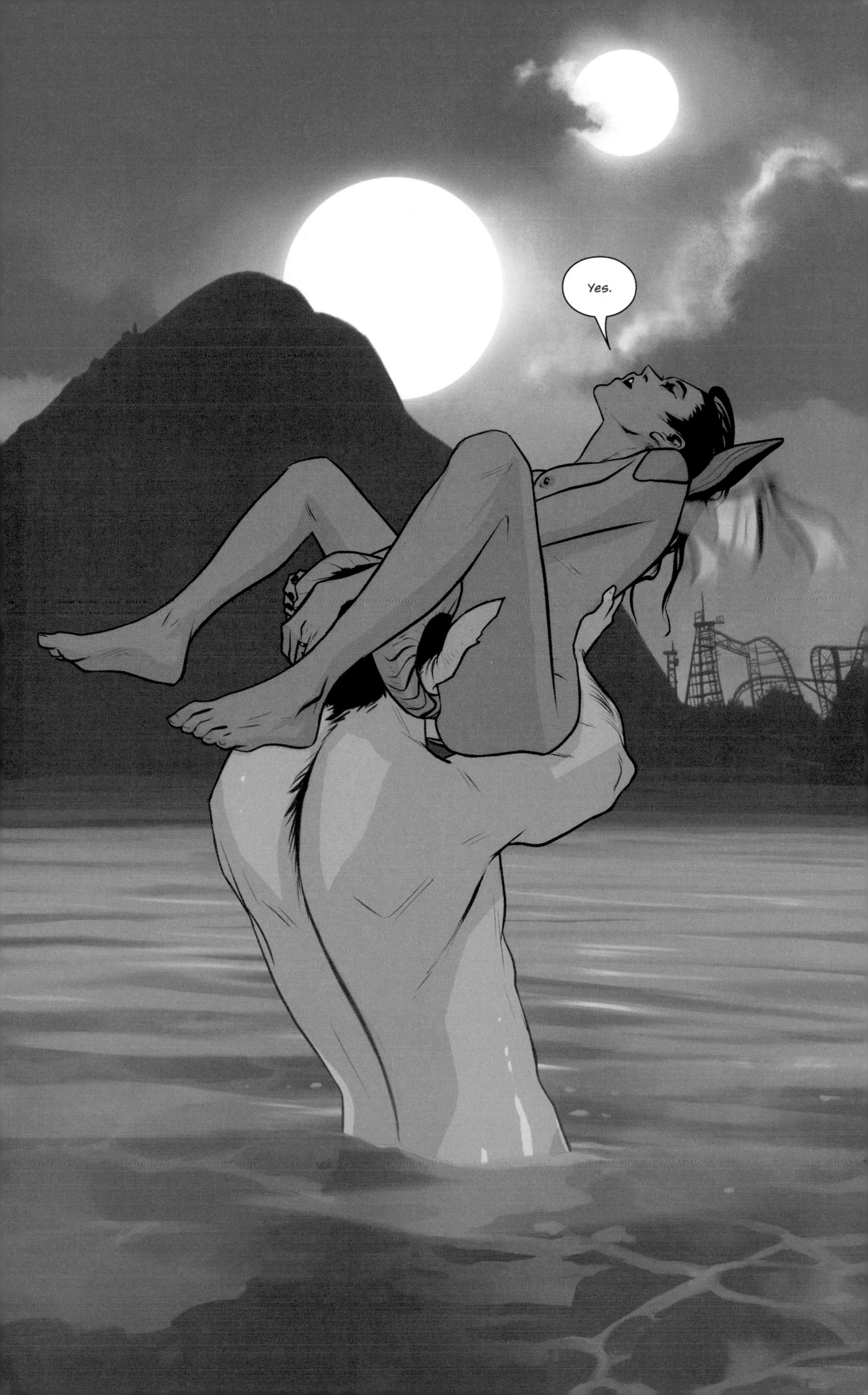
Yes.

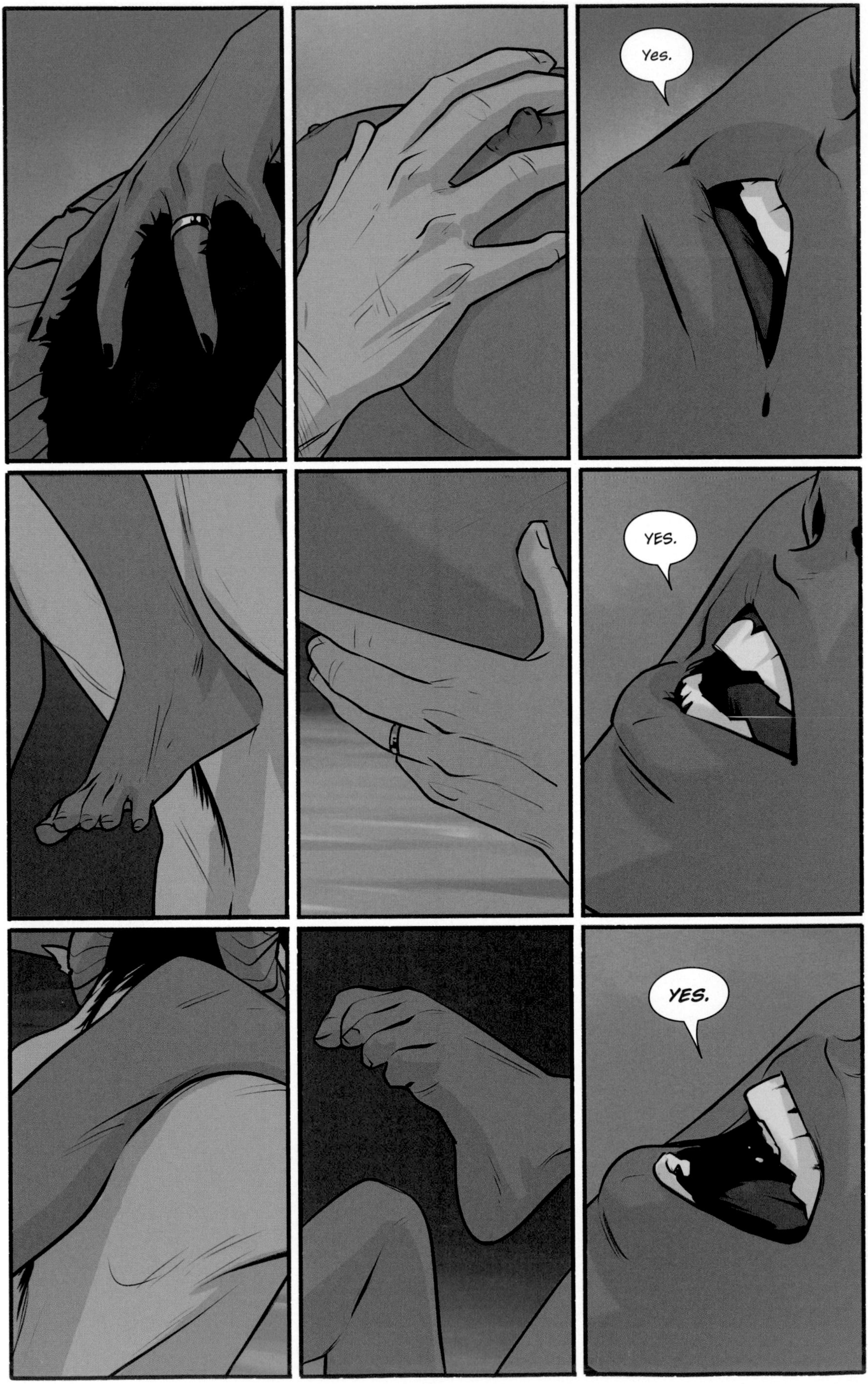
Yes.
YES.
YES.

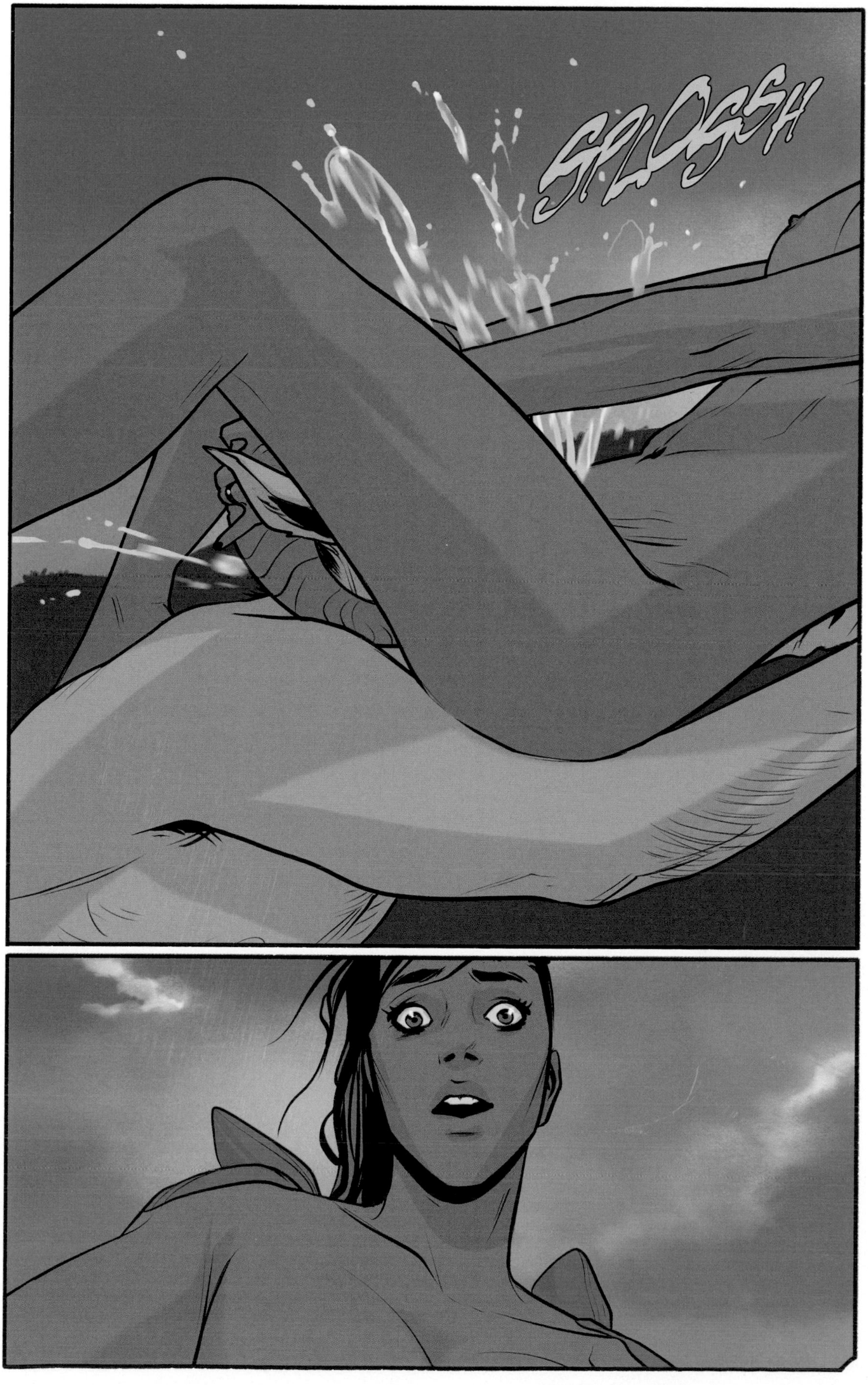
SPLOSSH

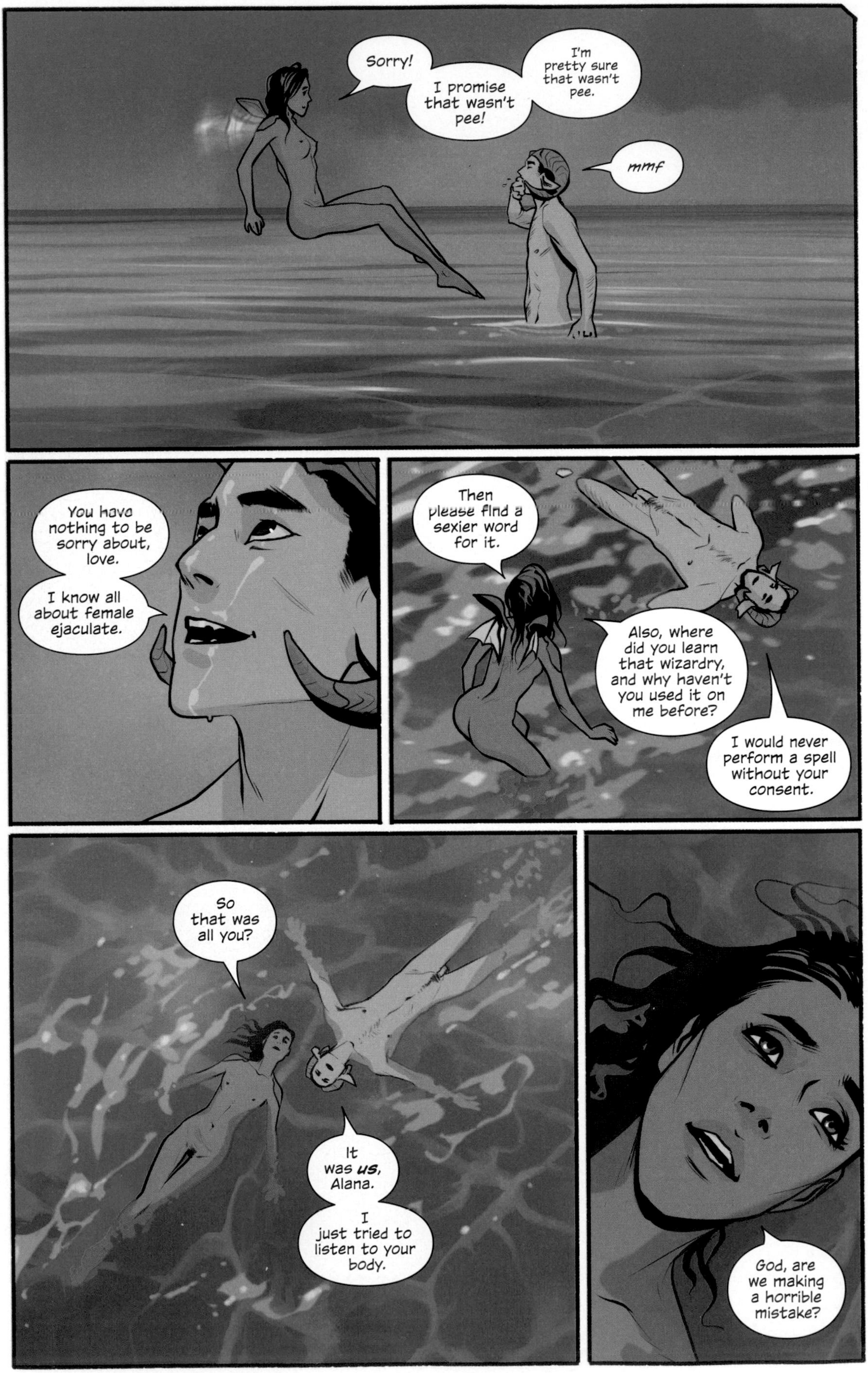
Sorry!
I promise that wasn't pee!
I'm pretty sure that wasn't pee.
mmf
You have nothing to be sorry about, love.
I know all about female ejaculate.
Then please find a sexier word for it.
Also, where did you learn that wizardry, and why haven't you used it on me before?
I would never perform a spell without your consent.
So that was all you?
It was *us*, Alana.
I just tried to listen to your body.
God, are we making a horrible mistake?

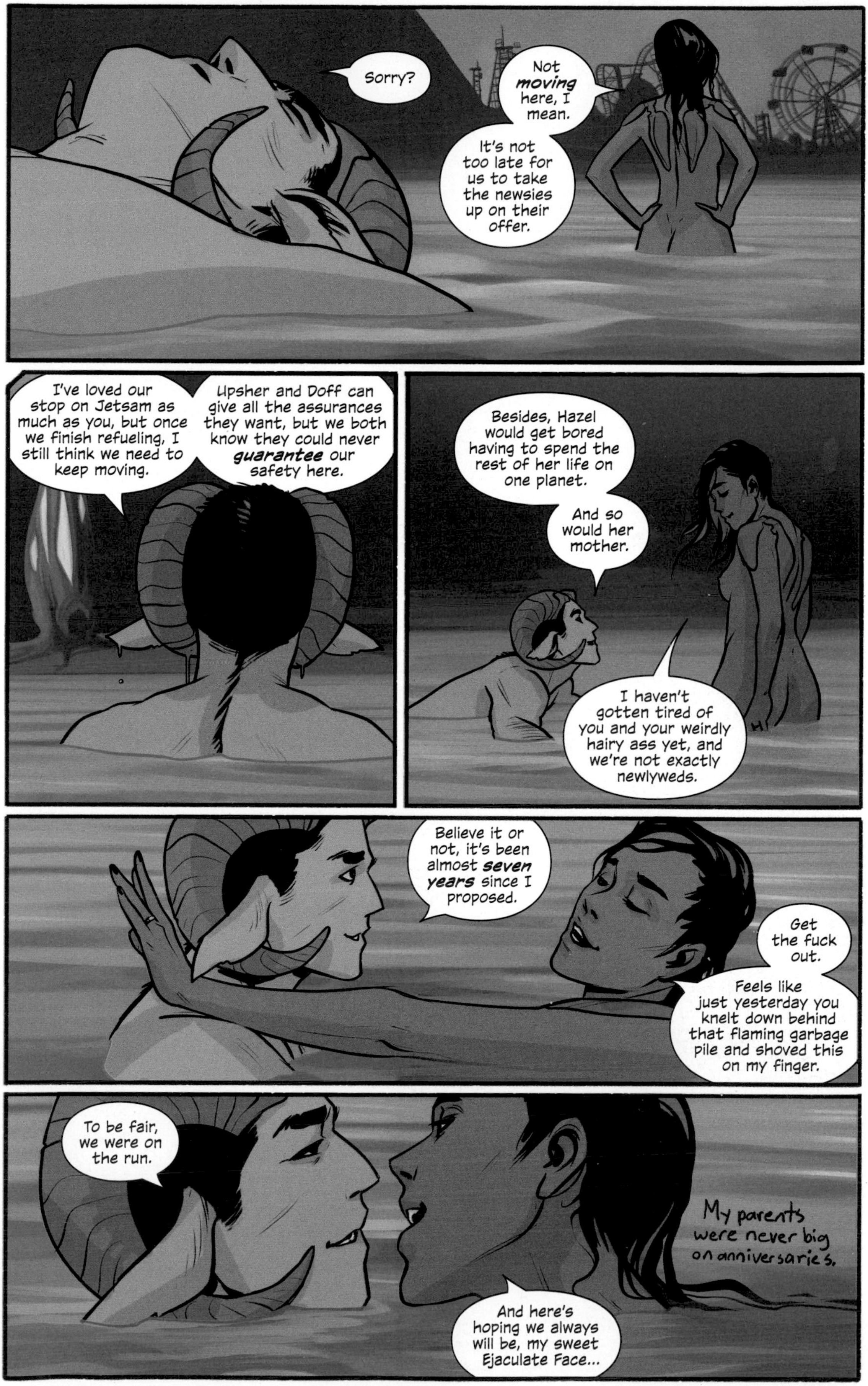
Sorry?
Not *moving* here, I mean.
It's not too late for us to take the newsies up on their offer.
I've loved our stop on Jetsam as much as you, but once we finish refueling, I still think we need to keep moving.
Upsher and Doff can give all the assurances they want, but we both know they could never *guarantee* our safety here.
Besides, Hazel would get bored having to spend the rest of her life on one planet.
And so would her mother.
I haven't gotten tired of you and your weirdly hairy ass yet, and we're not exactly newlyweds.
Believe it or not, it's been almost *seven years* since I proposed.
Get the fuck out.
Feels like just yesterday you knelt down behind that flaming garbage pile and shoved this on my finger.
To be fair, we were on the run.
My parents were never big on anniversaries.
And here's hoping we always will be, my sweet Ejaculate Face...

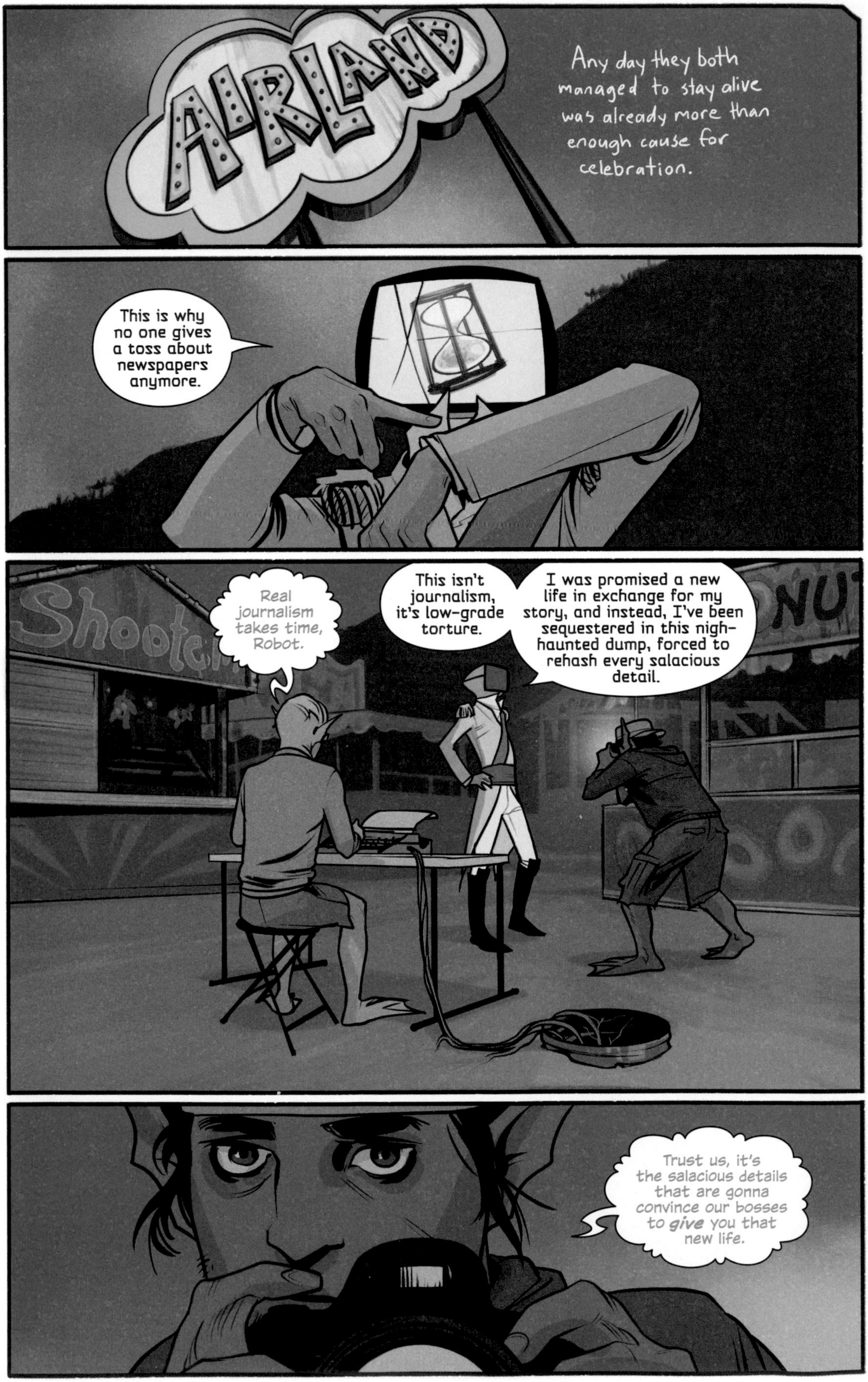

AIRLAND
Any day they both managed to stay alive was already more than enough cause for celebration.
This is why no one gives a toss about newspapers anymore.
Real journalism takes time, Robot.
This isn't journalism, it's low-grade torture.
I was promised a new life in exchange for my story, and instead, I've been sequestered in this nigh-haunted dump, forced to rehash every salacious detail.
Shootem
ONUT
Trust us, it's the salacious details that are gonna convince our bosses to *give* you that new life.

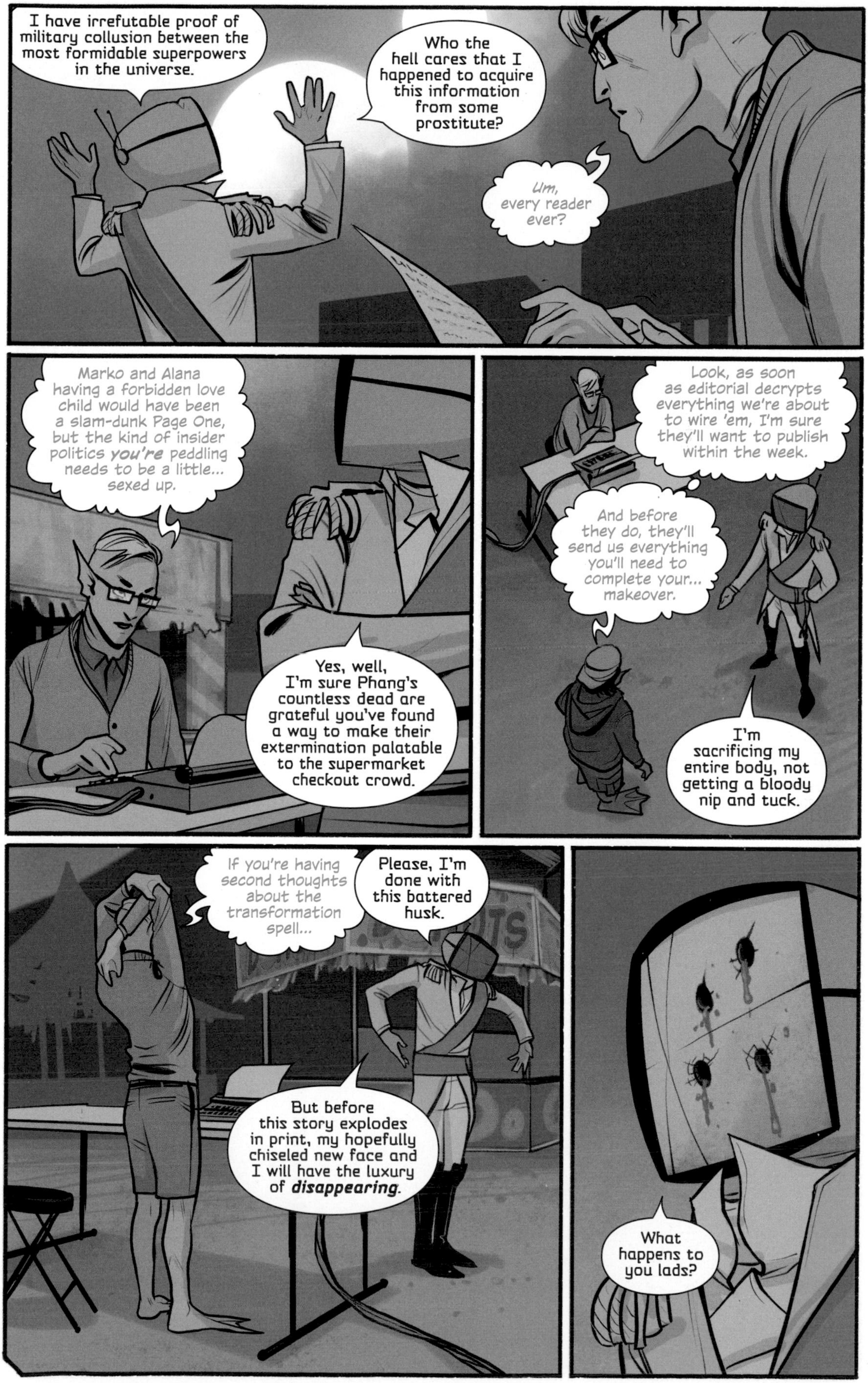
I have irrefutable proof of military collusion between the most formidable superpowers in the universe.
Who the hell cares that I happened to acquire this information from some prostitute?
Um, every reader ever?
Marko and Alana having a forbidden love child would have been a slam-dunk Page One, but the kind of insider politics *you're* peddling needs to be a little... sexed up.
Yes, well, I'm sure Phang's countless dead are grateful you've found a way to make their extermination palatable to the supermarket checkout crowd.
Look, as soon as editorial decrypts everything we're about to wire 'em, I'm sure they'll want to publish within the week.
And before they do, they'll send us everything you'll need to complete your... makeover.
I'm sacrificing my entire body, not getting a bloody nip and tuck.
If you're having second thoughts about the transformation spell...
Please, I'm done with this battered husk.
But before this story explodes in print, my hopefully chiseled new face and I will have the luxury of ***disappearing***.
What happens to you lads?

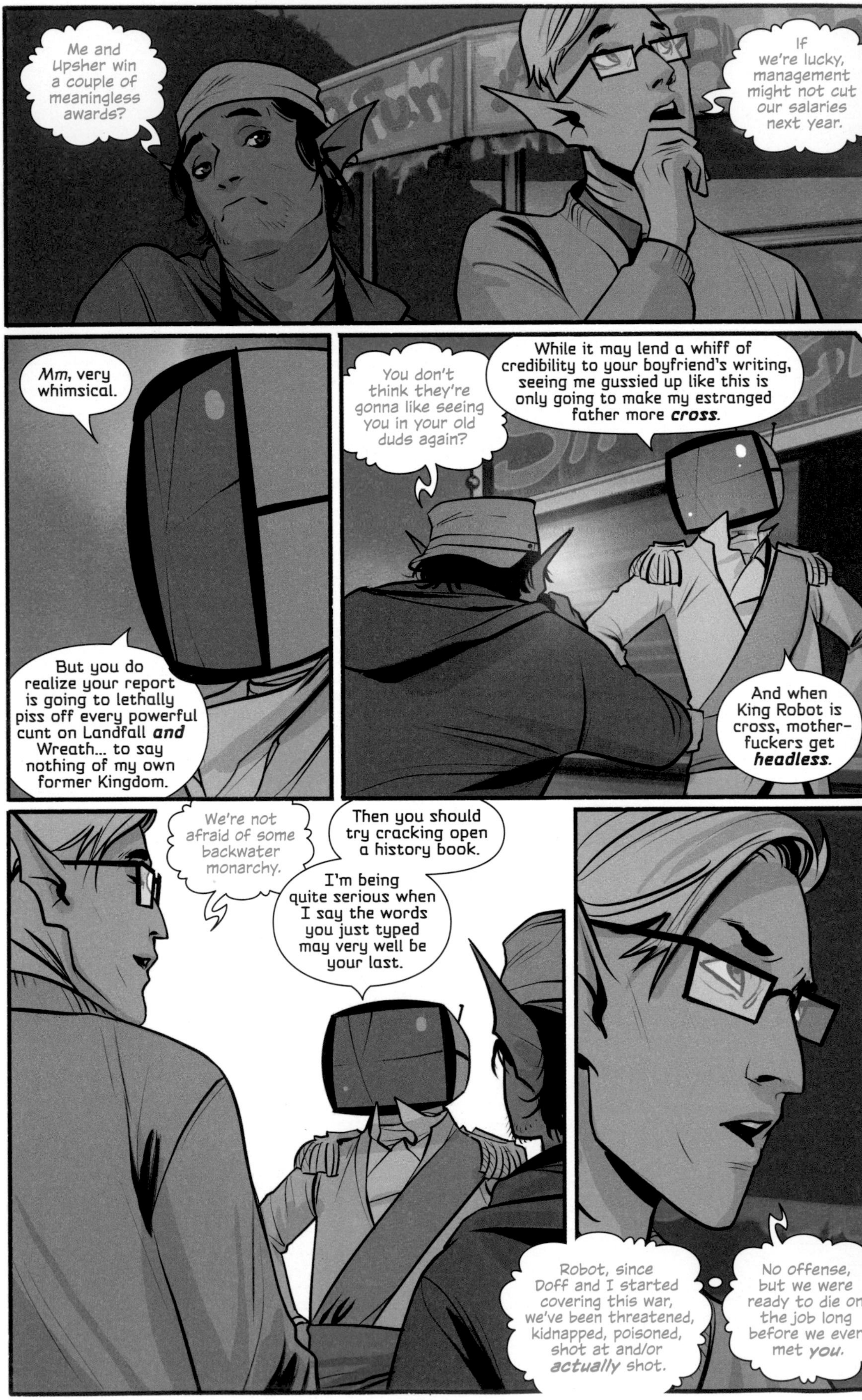
Me and Upsher win a couple of meaningless awards?
If we're lucky, management might not cut our salaries next year.
Mm, very whimsical.
But you do realize your report is going to lethally piss off every powerful cunt on Landfall ***and*** Wreath... to say nothing of my own former Kingdom.
You don't think they're gonna like seeing you in your old duds again?
While it may lend a whiff of credibility to your boyfriend's writing, seeing me gussied up like this is only going to make my estranged father more ***cross***.
And when King Robot is cross, mother-fuckers get ***headless***.
We're not afraid of some backwater monarchy.
Then you should try cracking open a history book.
I'm being quite serious when I say the words you just typed may very well be your last.
Robot, since Doff and I started covering this war, we've been threatened, kidnapped, poisoned, shot at and/or ***actually*** shot.
No offense, but we were ready to die on the job long before we ever met ***you***.

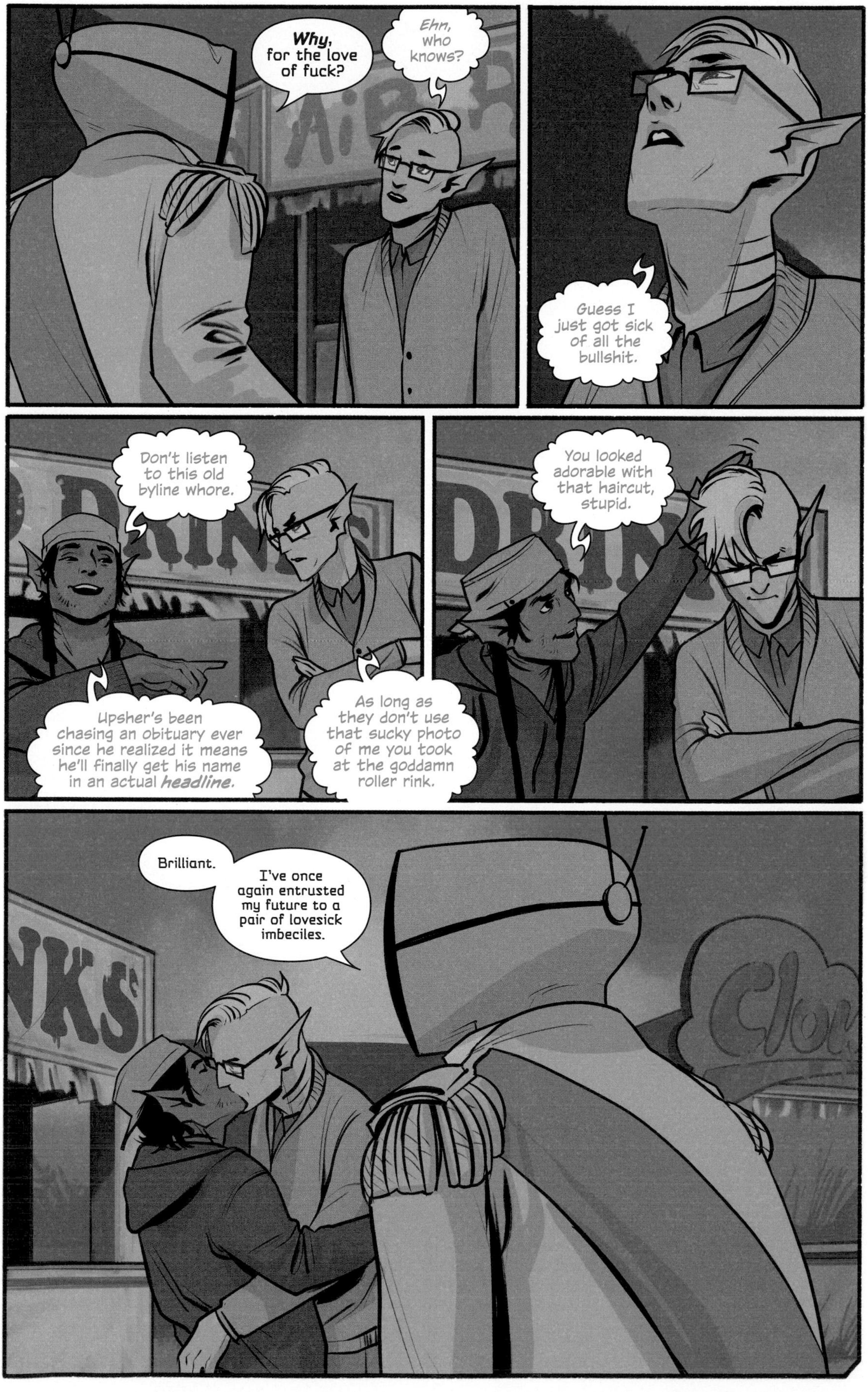

Why, for the love of fuck?
Ehn, who knows?
Guess I just got sick of all the bullshit.
Don't listen to this old byline whore.
Upsher's been chasing an obituary ever since he realized it means he'll finally get his name in an actual headline.
As long as they don't use that sucky photo of me you took at the goddamn roller rink.
You looked adorable with that haircut, stupid.
Brilliant.
I've once again entrusted my future to a pair of lovesick imbeciles.

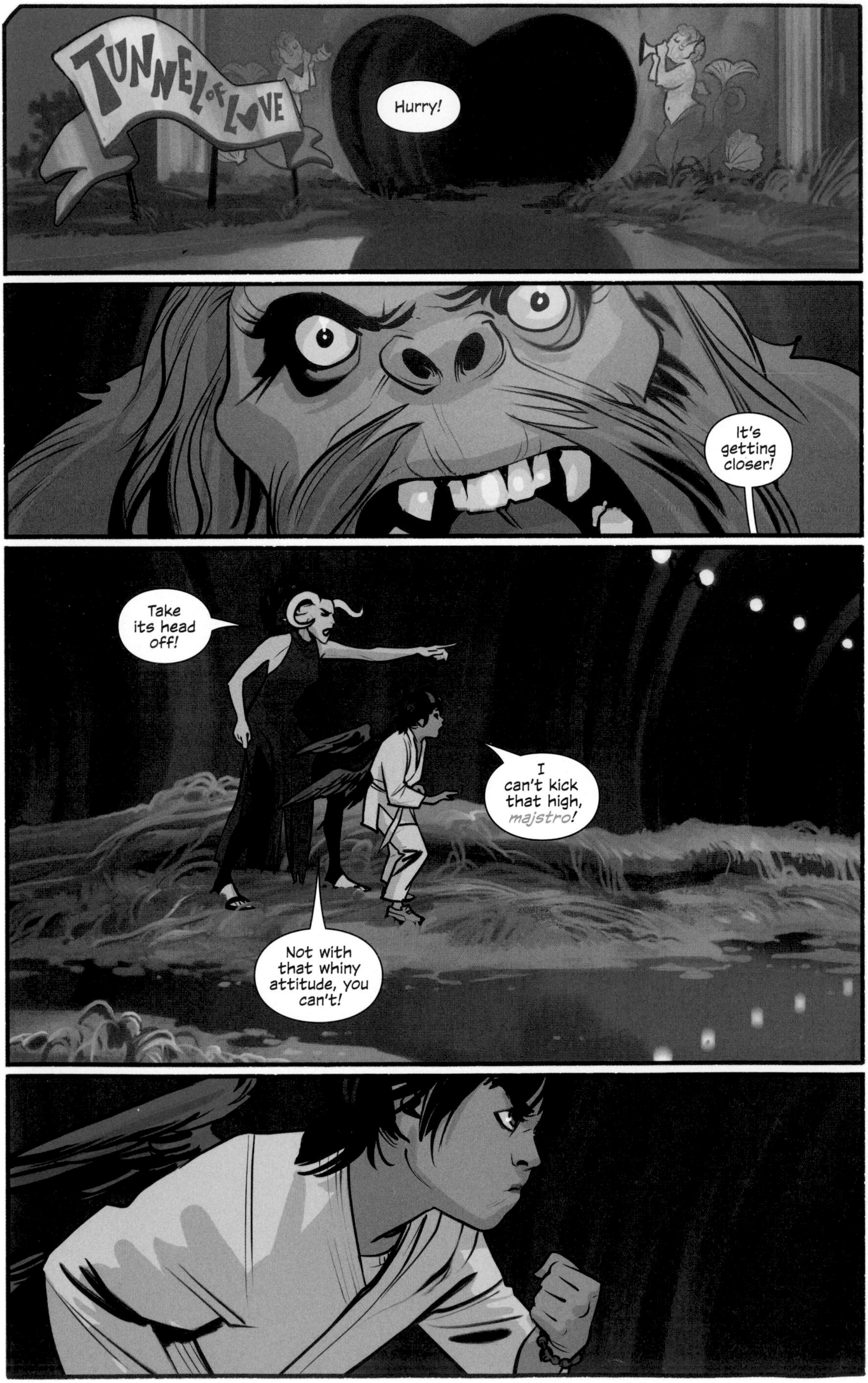
TUNNEL OF LOVE
Hurry!
It's getting closer!
Take its head off!
I can't kick that high, *majstro*!
Not with that whiny attitude, you can't!

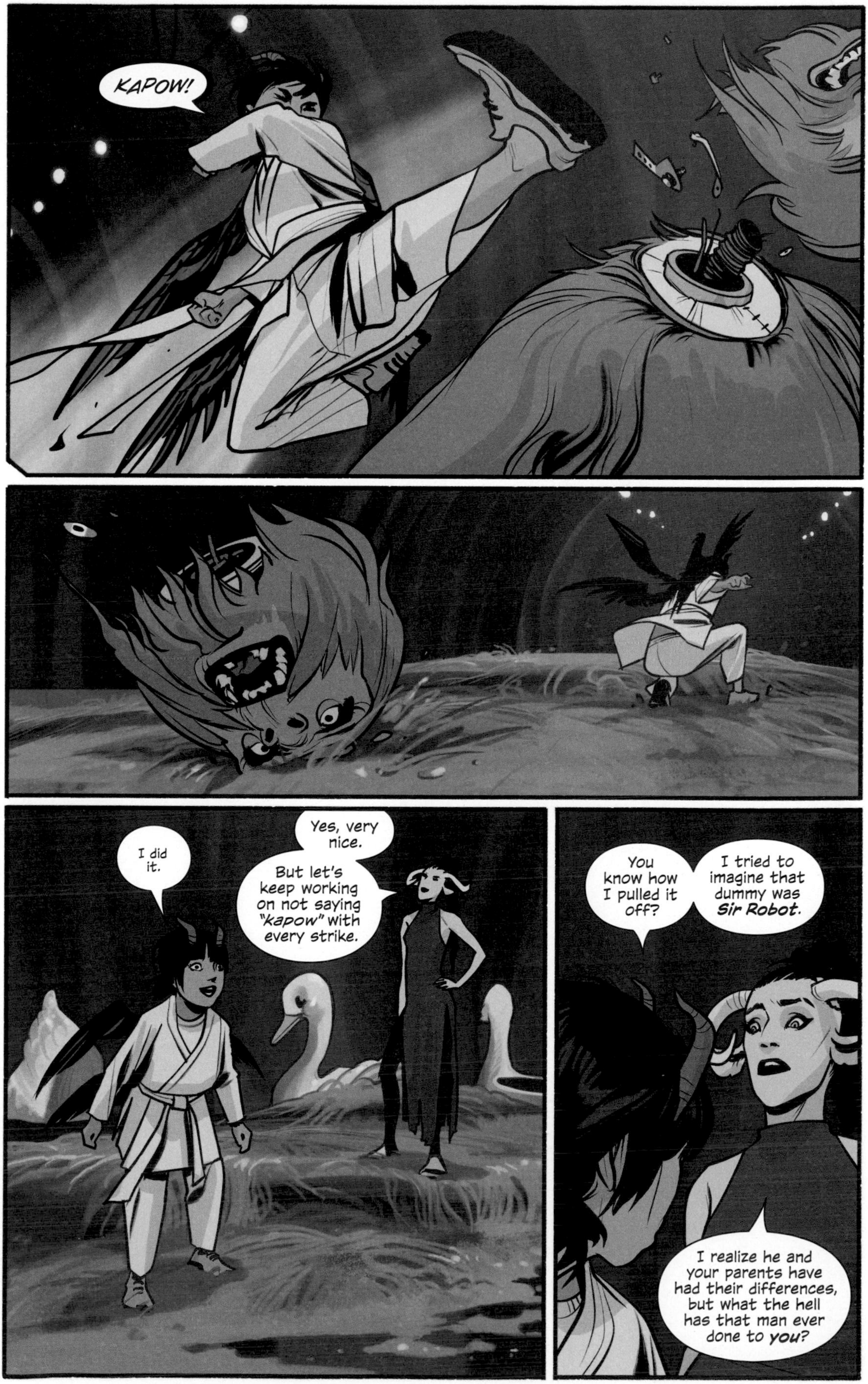
KAPOW!
I did it.
Yes, very nice.
But let's keep working on not saying "kapow" with every strike.
You know how I pulled it off?
I tried to imagine that dummy was Sir Robot.
I realize he and your parents have had their differences, but what the hell has that man ever done to you?

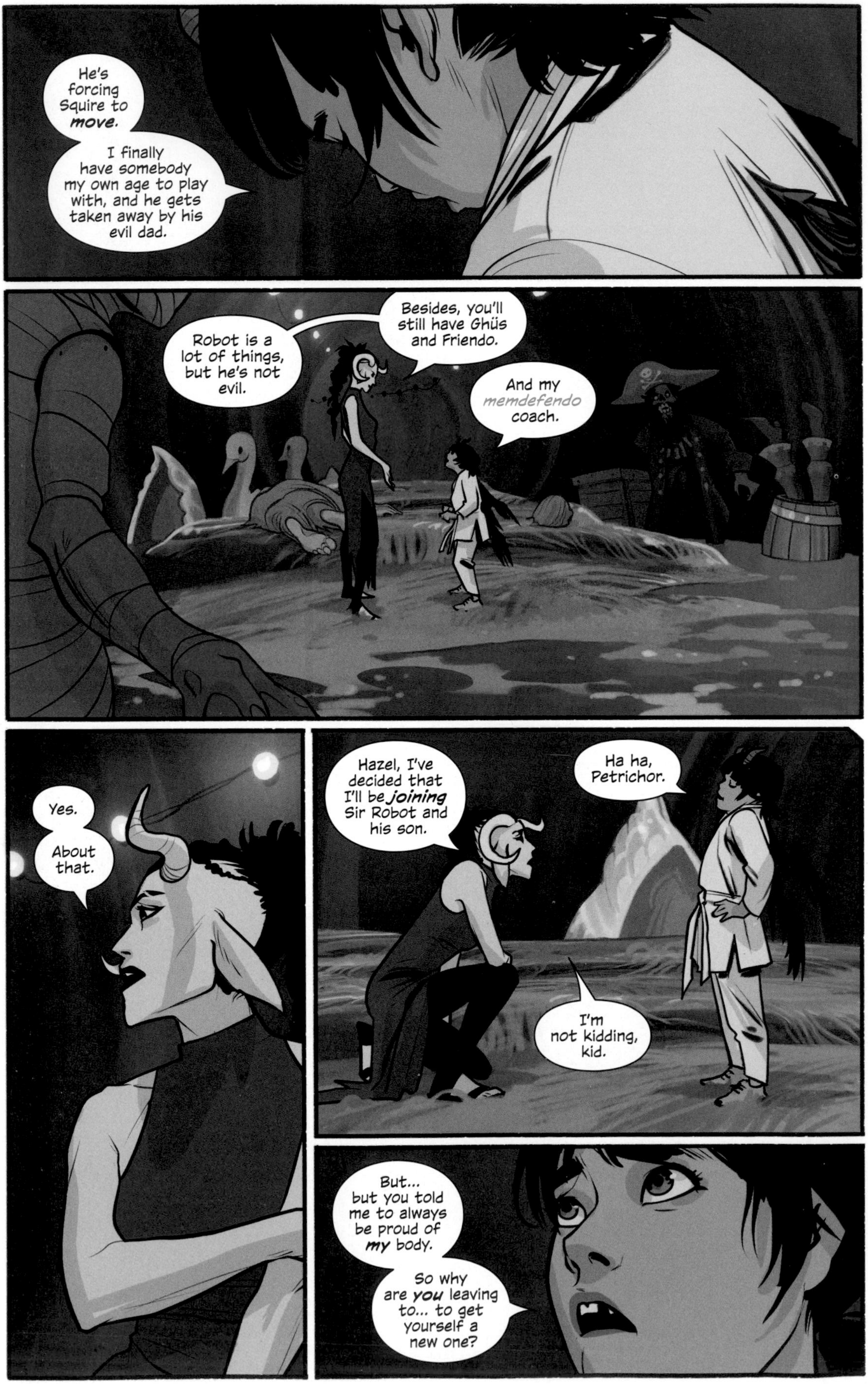
He's forcing Squire to *move*.
I finally have somebody my own age to play with, and he gets taken away by his evil dad.
Robot is a lot of things, but he's not evil.
Besides, you'll still have Ghüs and Friendo.
And my *memdefendo* coach.
Yes.
About that.
Hazel, I've decided that I'll be ***joining*** Sir Robot and his son.
Ha ha, Petrichor.
I'm not kidding, kid.
But... but you told me to always be proud of ***my*** body.
So why are ***you*** leaving to... to get yourself a new one?

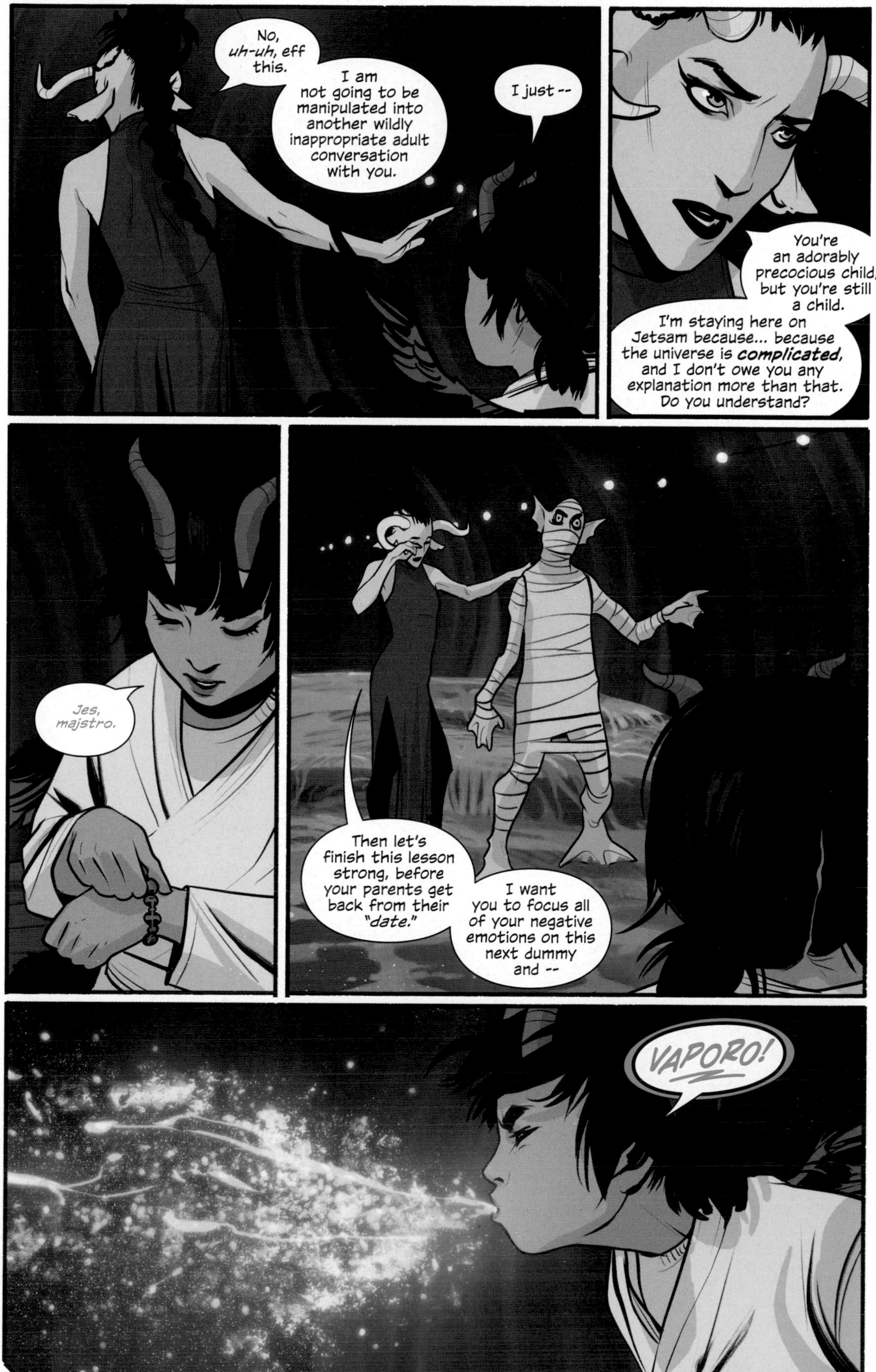
No, *uh-uh*, eff this.
I am not going to be manipulated into another wildly inappropriate adult conversation with you.
I just --
You're an adorably precocious child, but you're still a child.
I'm staying here on Jetsam because... because the universe is ***complicated***, and I don't owe you any explanation more than that. Do you understand?
Jes, majstro.
Then let's finish this lesson strong, before your parents get back from their "*date*."
I want you to focus all of your negative emotions on this next dummy and --
VAPORO!

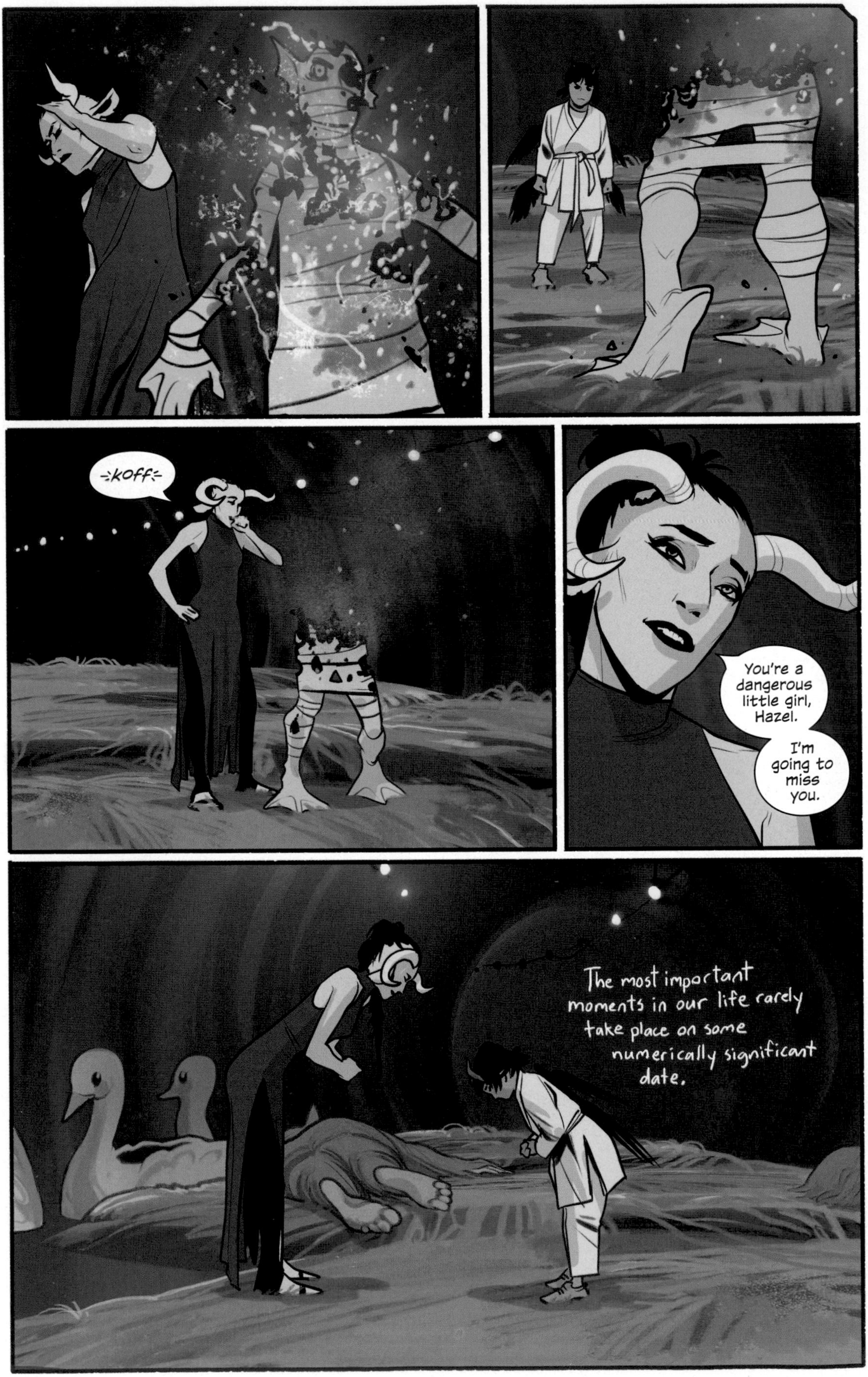
-KOFF-
You're a dangerous little girl, Hazel.
I'm going to miss you.
The most important moments in our life rarely take place on some numerically significant date.

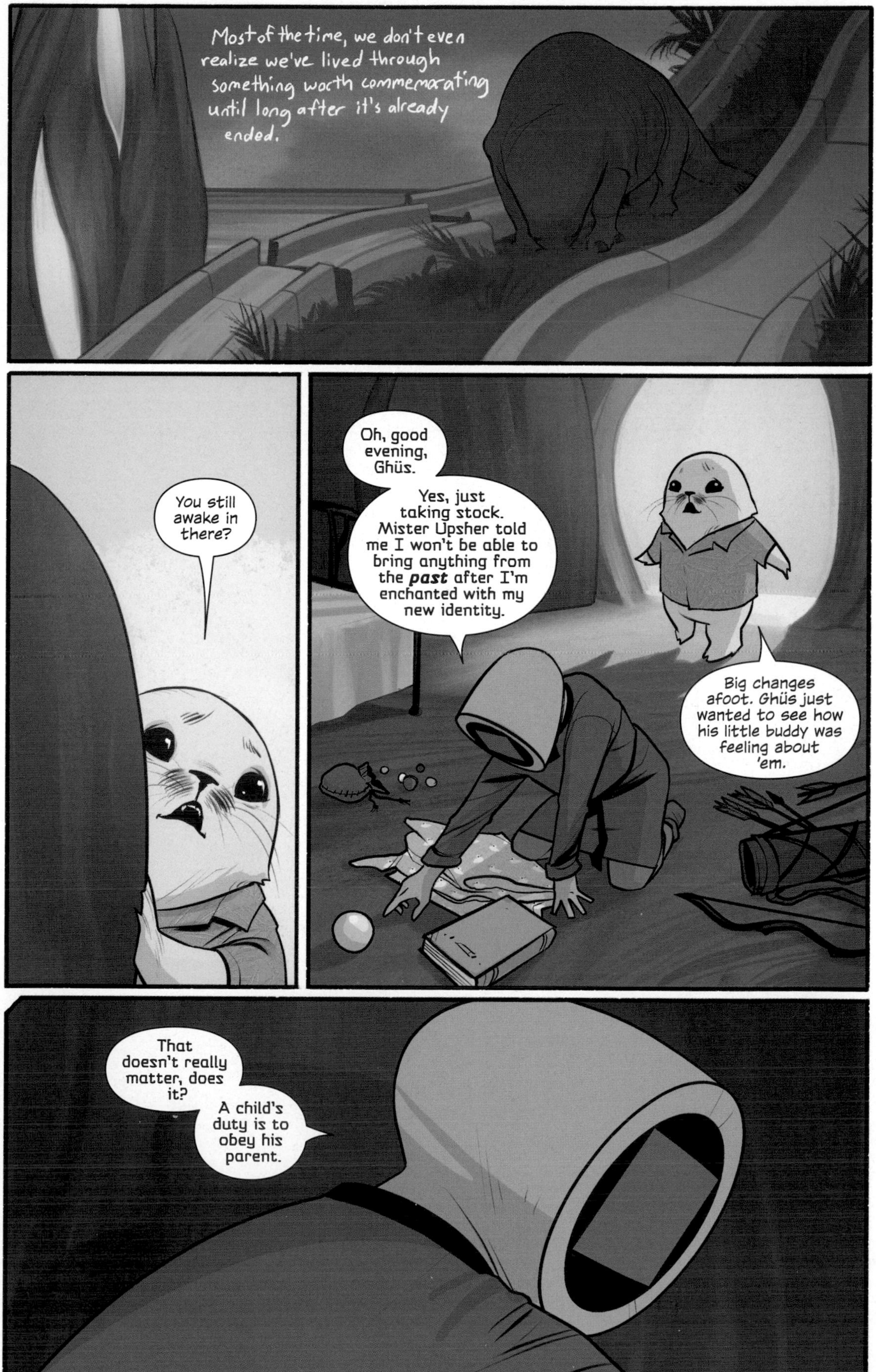

Most of the time, we don't even realize we've lived through something worth commemorating until long after it's already ended.
You still awake in there?
Oh, good evening, Ghüs.
Yes, just taking stock. Mister Upsher told me I won't be able to bring anything from the *past* after I'm enchanted with my new identity.
Big changes afoot. Ghüs just wanted to see how his little buddy was feeling about 'em.
That doesn't really matter, does it?
A child's duty is to obey his parent.

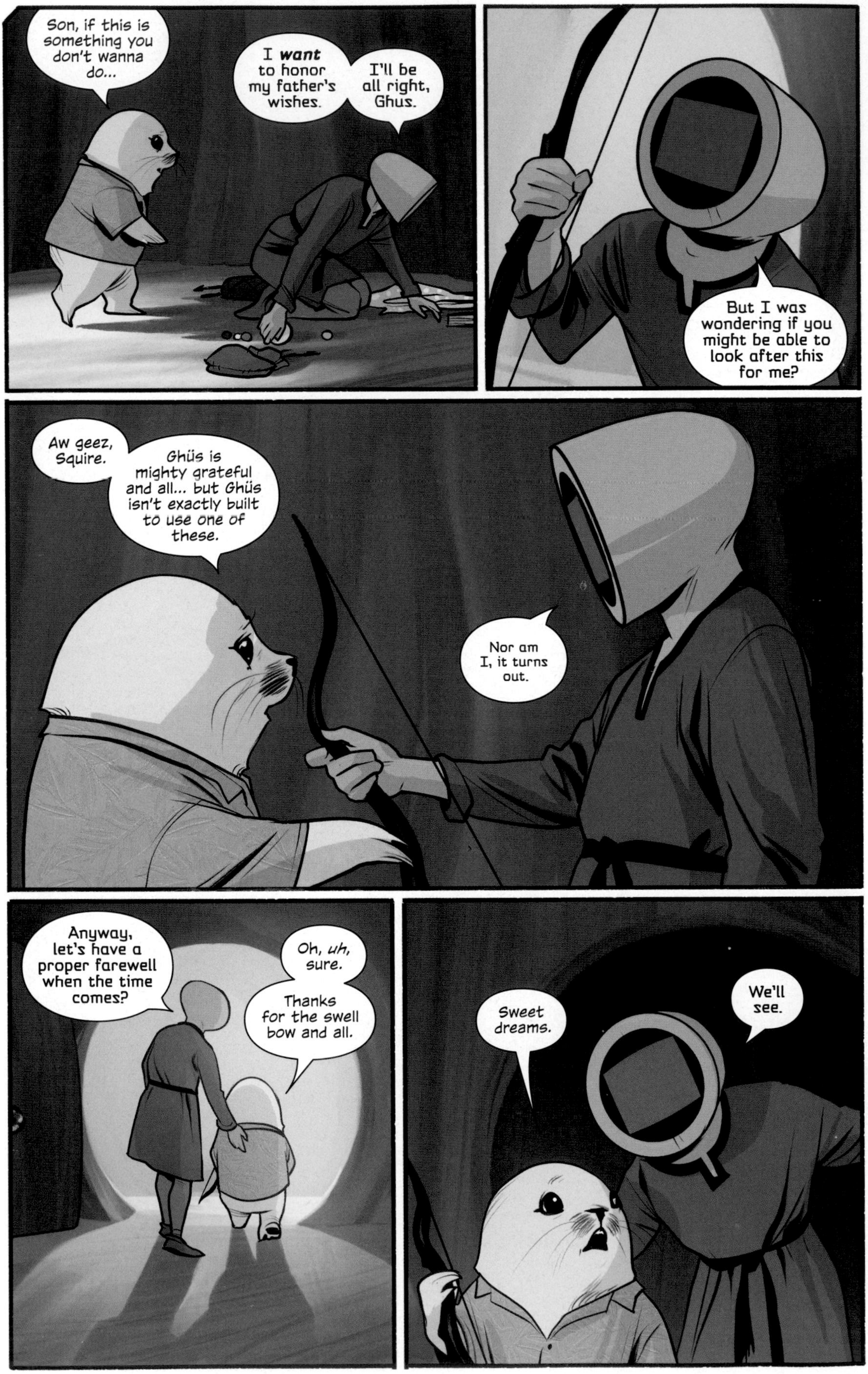
Son, if this is something you don't wanna do...
I *want* to honor my father's wishes.
I'll be all right, Ghus.
But I was wondering if you might be able to look after this for me?
Aw geez, Squire.
Ghüs is mighty grateful and all... but Ghüs isn't exactly built to use one of these.
Nor am I, it turns out.
Anyway, let's have a proper farewell when the time comes?
Oh, *uh*, sure.
Thanks for the swell bow and all.
Sweet dreams.
We'll see.

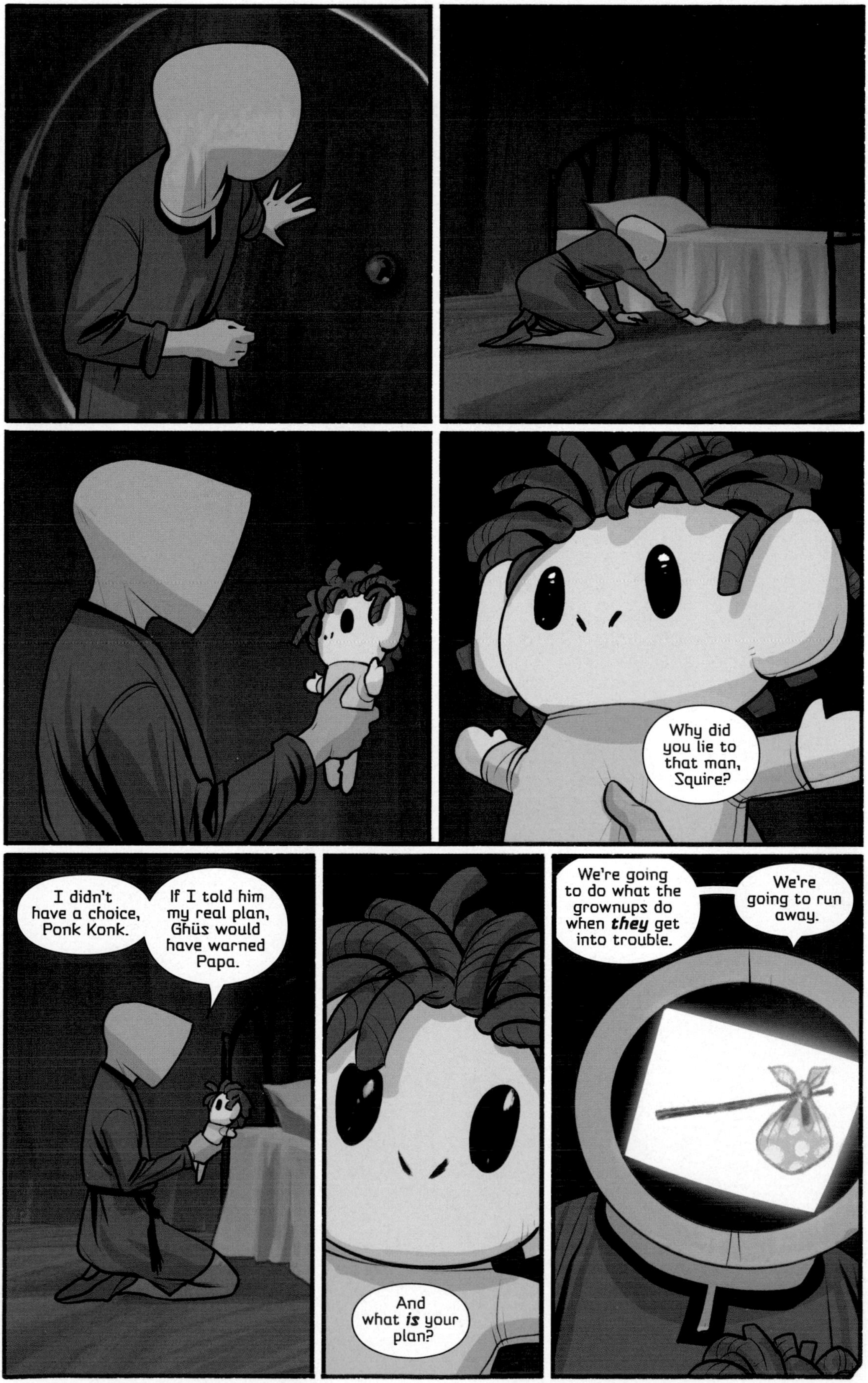
Why did you lie to that man, Squire?
I didn't have a choice, Ponk Konk.
If I told him my real plan, Ghüs would have warned Papa.
And what *is* your plan?
We're going to do what the grownups do when *they* get into trouble.
We're going to run away.

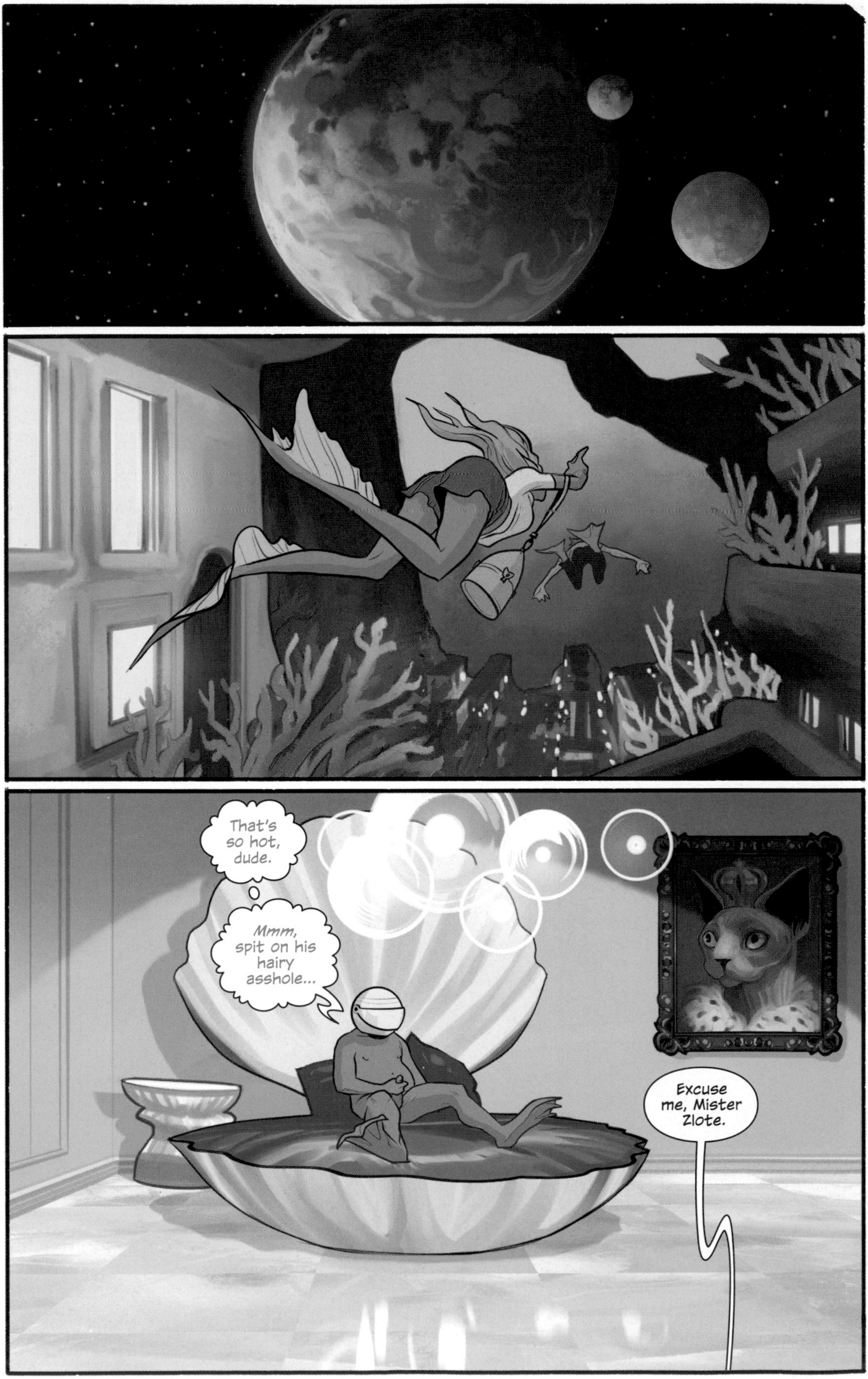
That's so hot, dude.
Mmm, spit on his hairy asshole...
Excuse me, Mister Zlote.

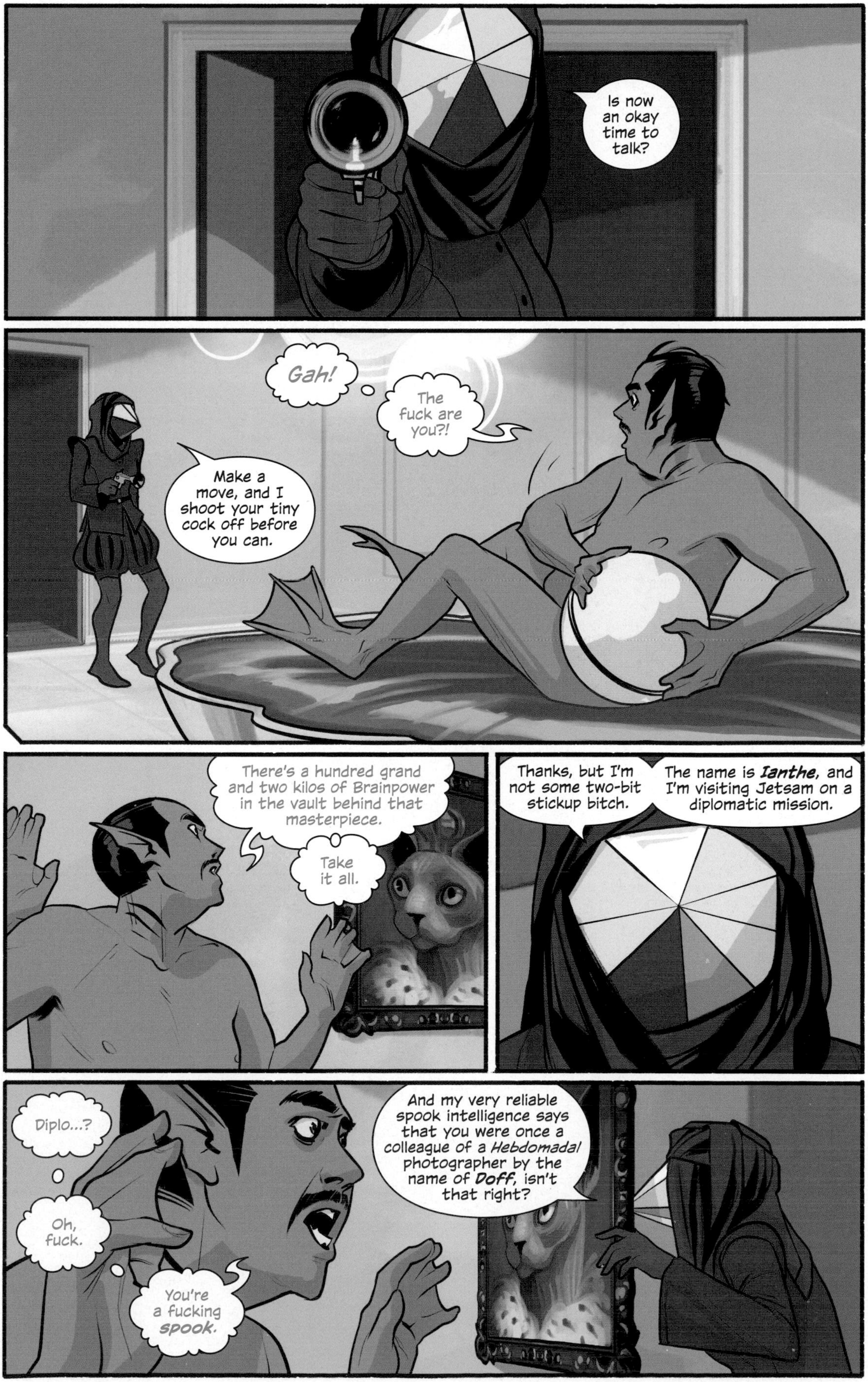
Is now an okay time to talk?
Gah!
The fuck are you?!
Make a move, and I shoot your tiny cock off before you can.
There's a hundred grand and two kilos of Brainpower in the vault behind that masterpiece.
Take it all.
Thanks, but I'm not some two-bit stickup bitch.
The name is *Ianthe*, and I'm visiting Jetsam on a diplomatic mission.
Diplo...?
Oh, fuck.
You're a fucking *spook*.
And my very reliable spook intelligence says that you were once a colleague of a *Hebdomadal* photographer by the name of *Doff*, isn't that right?

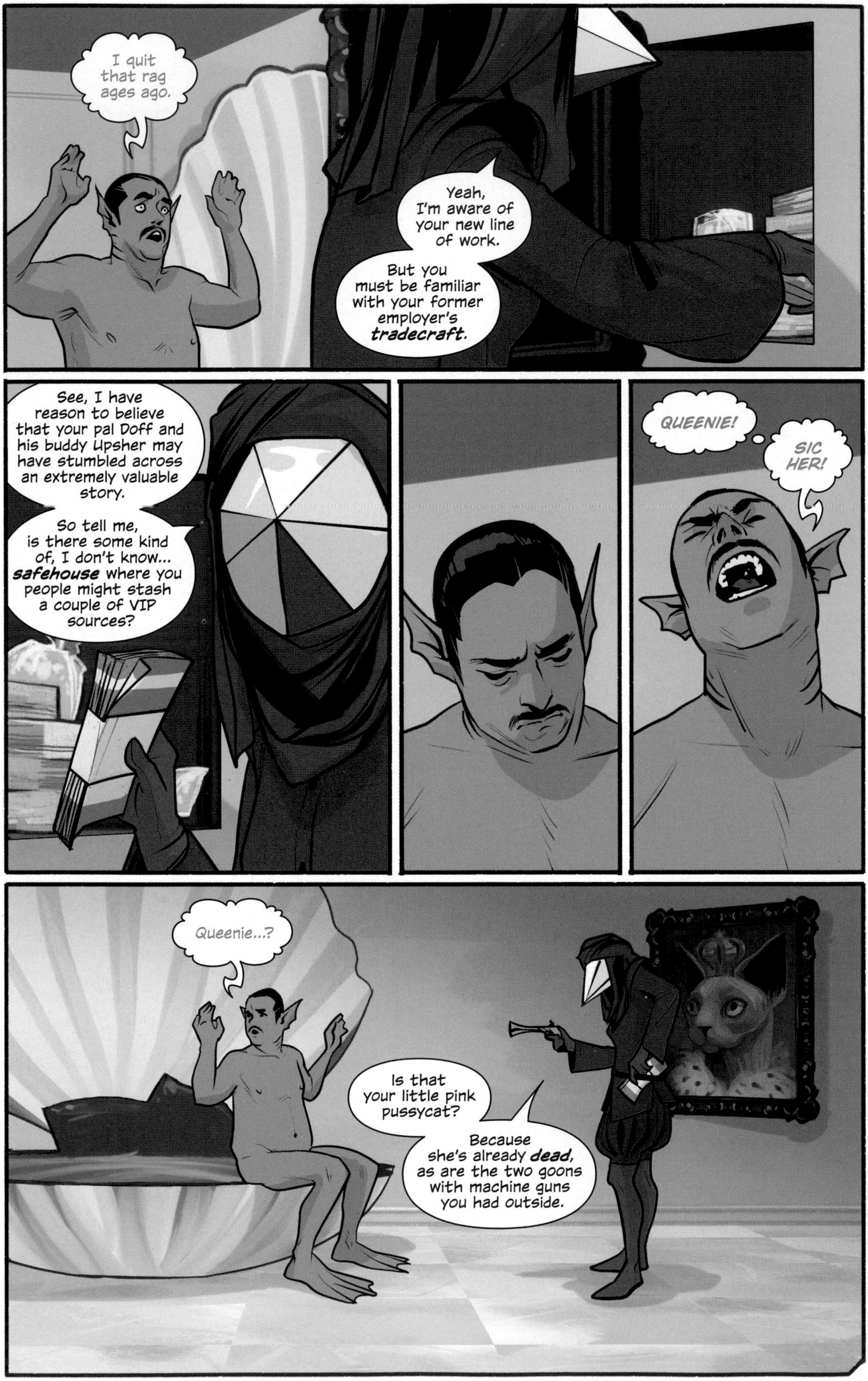
I quit that rag ages ago.
Yeah, I'm aware of your new line of work.
But you must be familiar with your former employer's *tradecraft*.
See, I have reason to believe that your pal Doff and his buddy Upsher may have stumbled across an extremely valuable story.
So tell me, is there some kind of, I don't know... *safehouse* where you people might stash a couple of VIP sources?
QUEENIE!
SIC HER!
Queenie...?
Is that your little pink pussycat?
Because she's already *dead*, as are the two goons with machine guns you had outside.

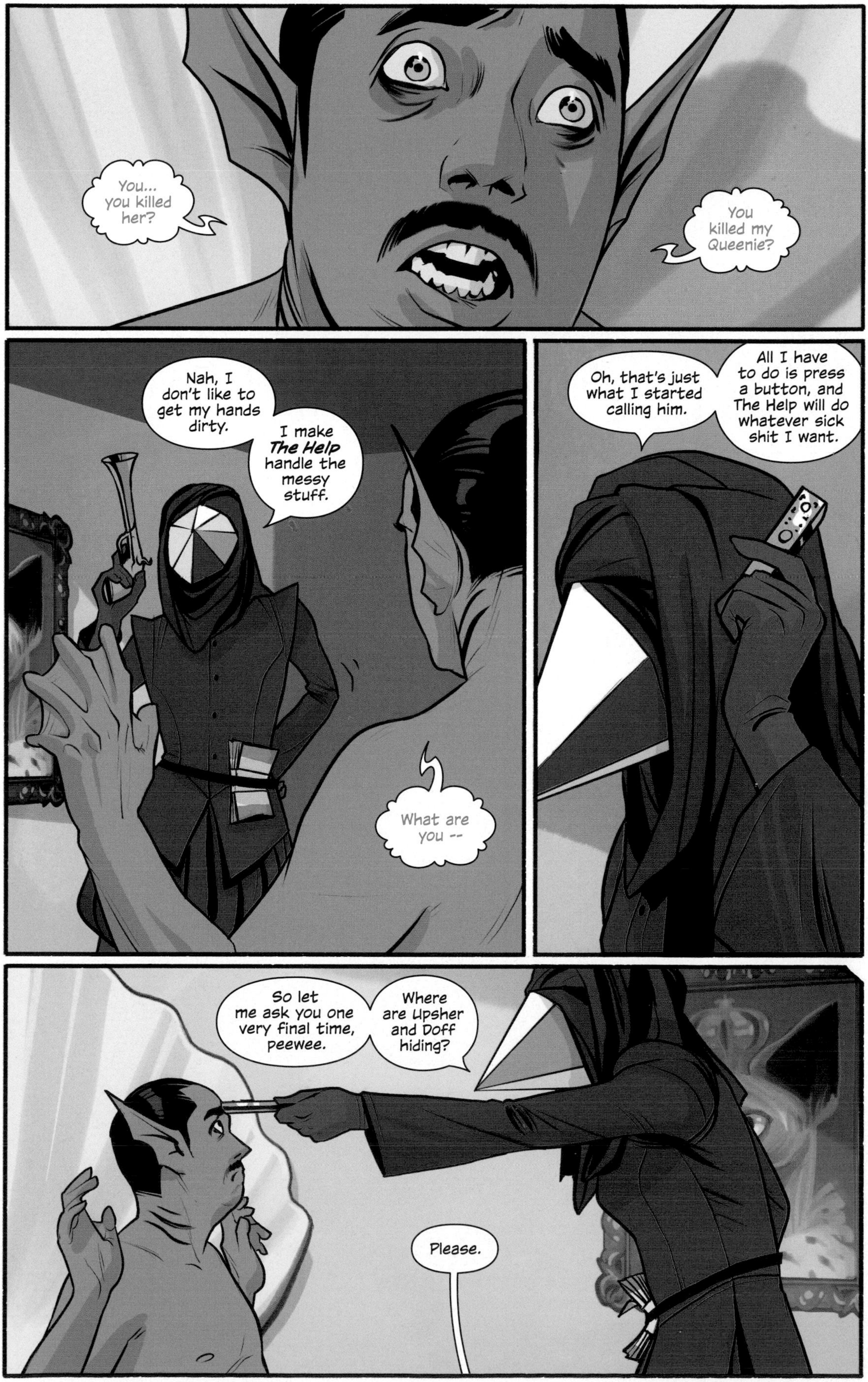

You... you killed her?
You killed my Queenie?
Nah, I don't like to get my hands dirty.
I make ***The Help*** handle the messy stuff.
What are you --
Oh, that's just what I started calling him.
All I have to do is press a button, and The Help will do whatever sick shit I want.
So let me ask you one very final time, peewee.
Where are Upsher and Doff hiding?
Please.

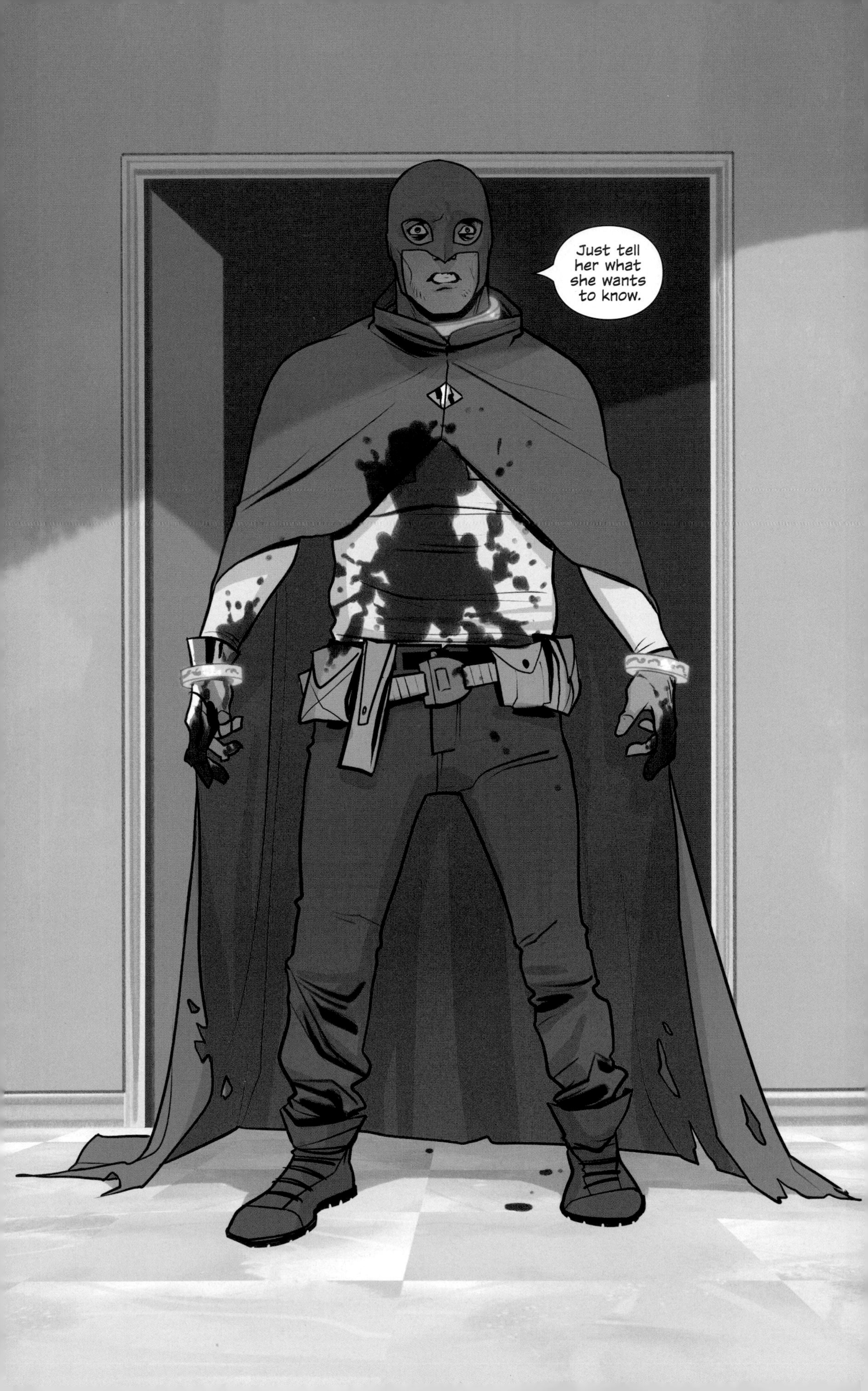
Just tell her what she wants to know.

end chapter fifty

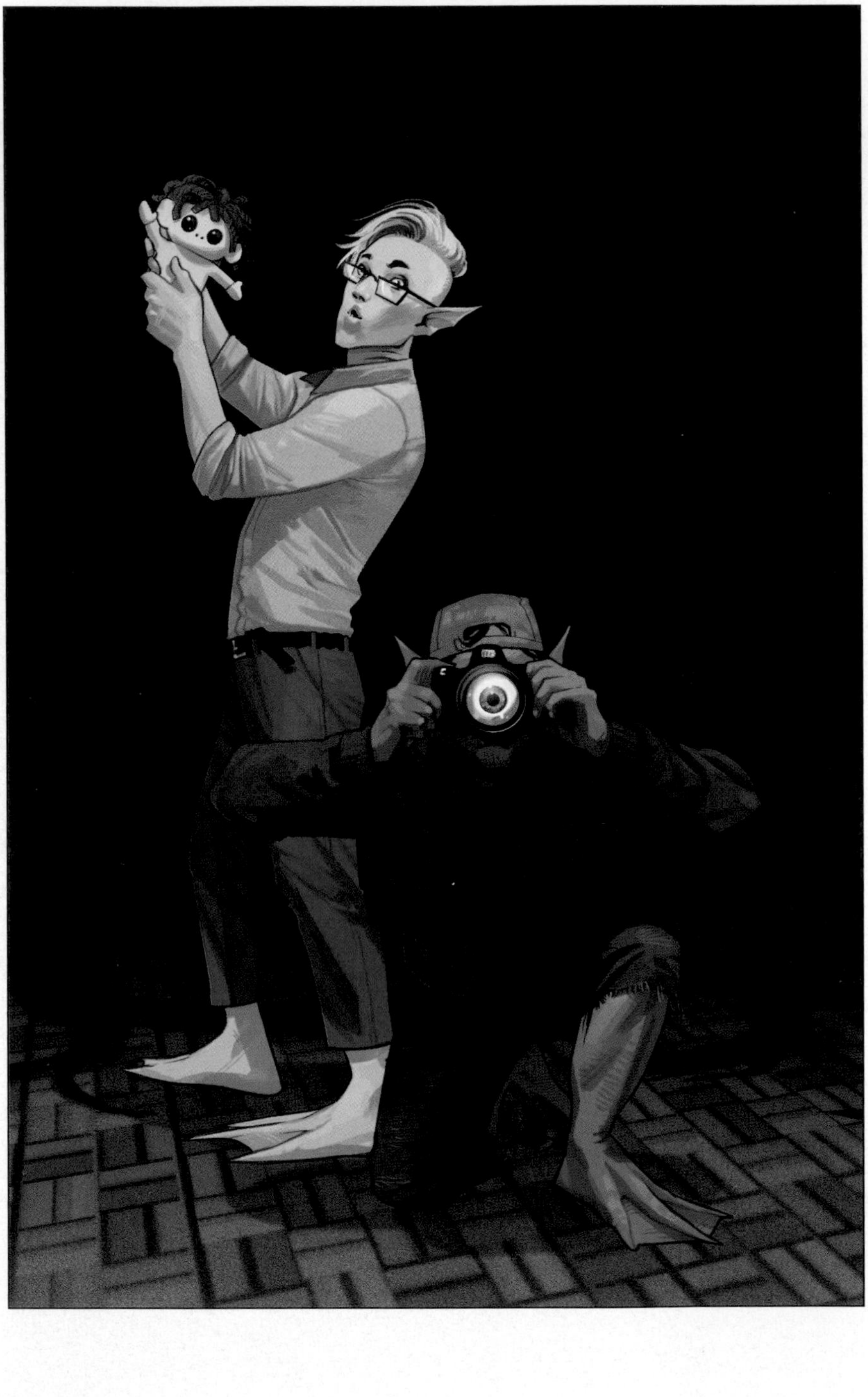

CHAPTER
FIFTY-ONE

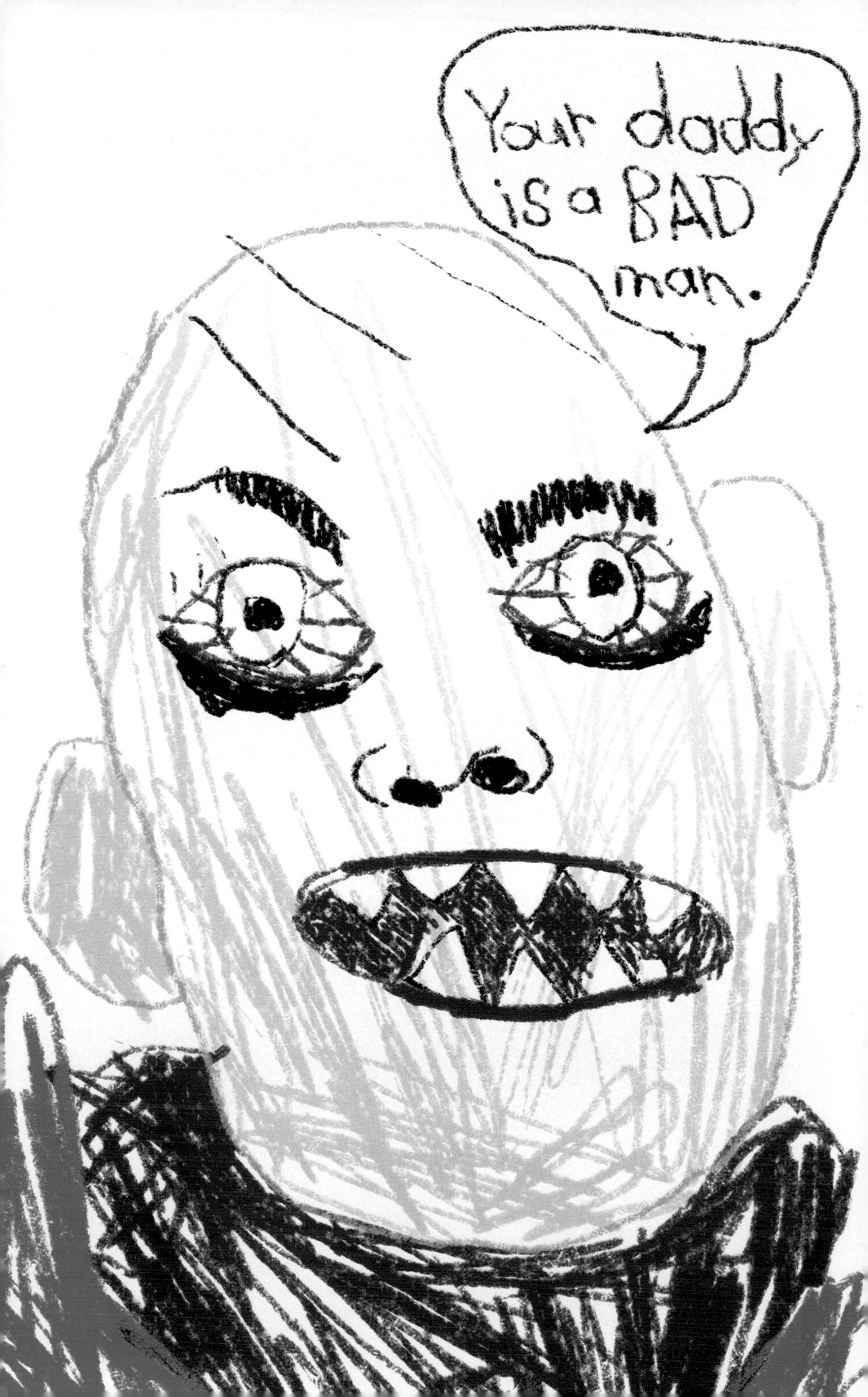
Your daddy is a BAD man.

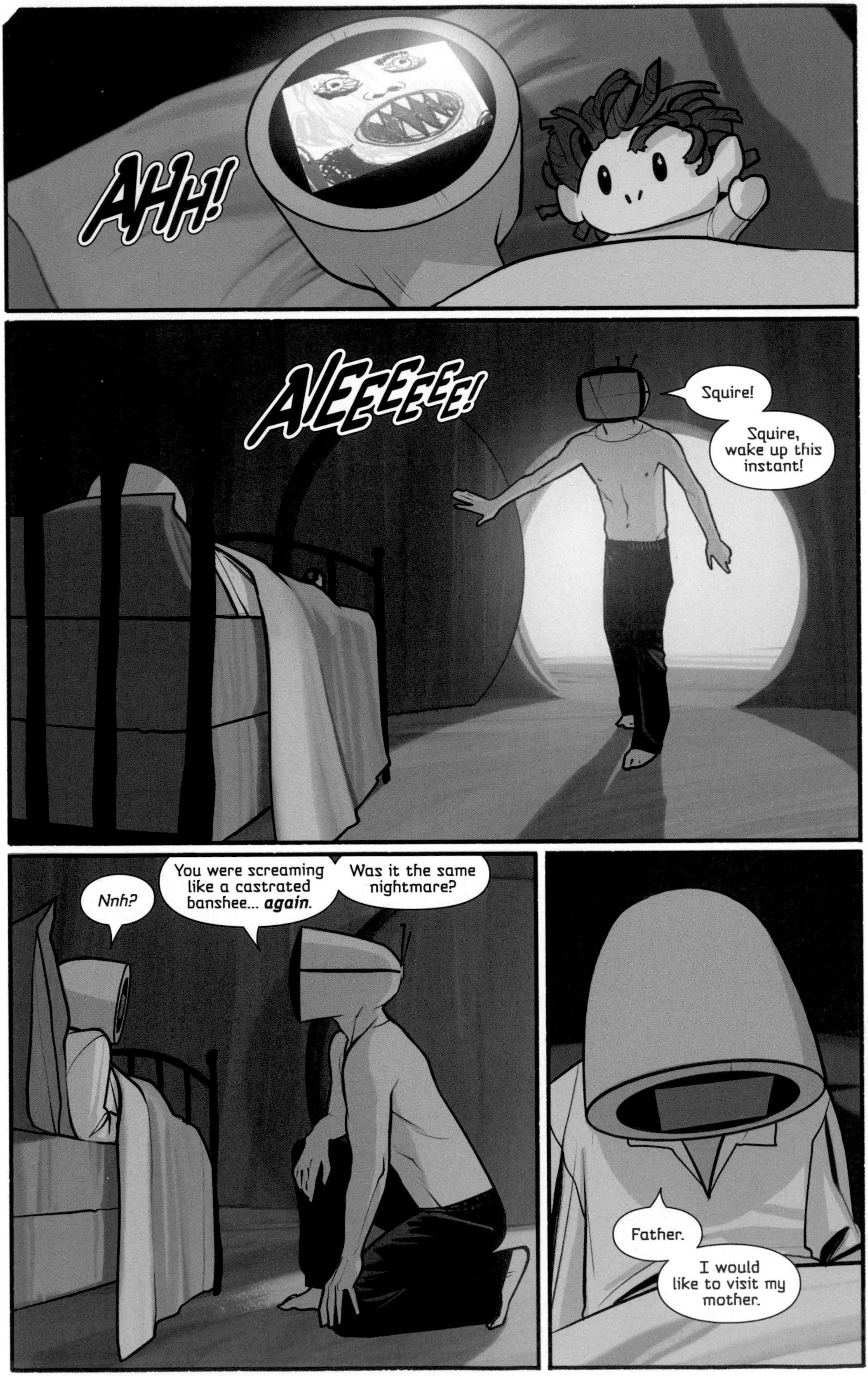
AHH!
AIEEEEEE!
Squire!
Squire, wake up this instant!
Nnh?
You were screaming like a castrated banshee... *again*.
Was it the same nightmare?
Father.
I would like to visit my mother.

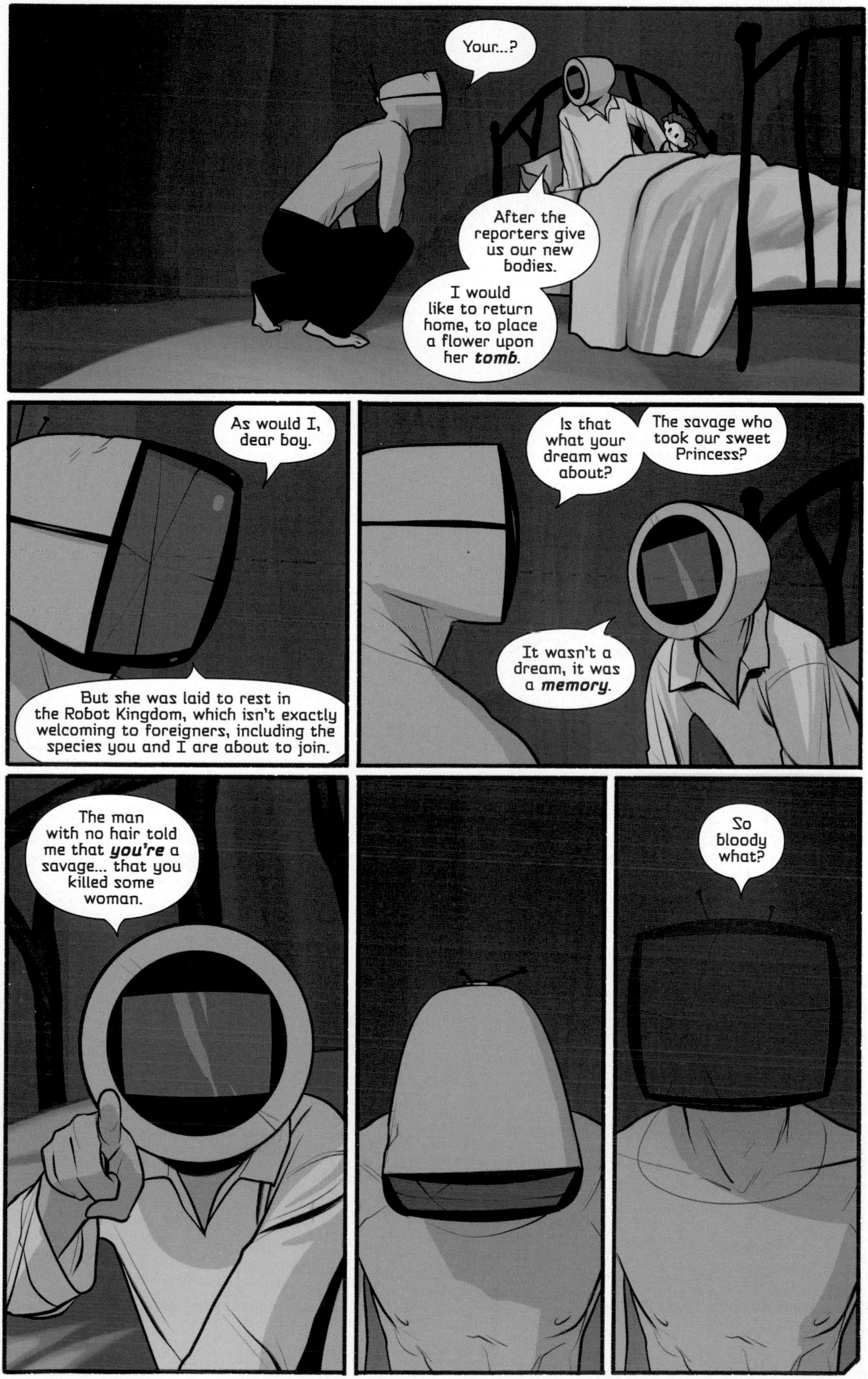
Your...?
After the reporters give us our new bodies.
I would like to return home, to place a flower upon her ***tomb***.
As would I, dear boy.
But she was laid to rest in the Robot Kingdom, which isn't exactly welcoming to foreigners, including the species you and I are about to join.
Is that what your dream was about?
The savage who took our sweet Princess?
It wasn't a dream, it was a ***memory***.
The man with no hair told me that ***you're*** a savage... that you killed some woman.
So bloody what?

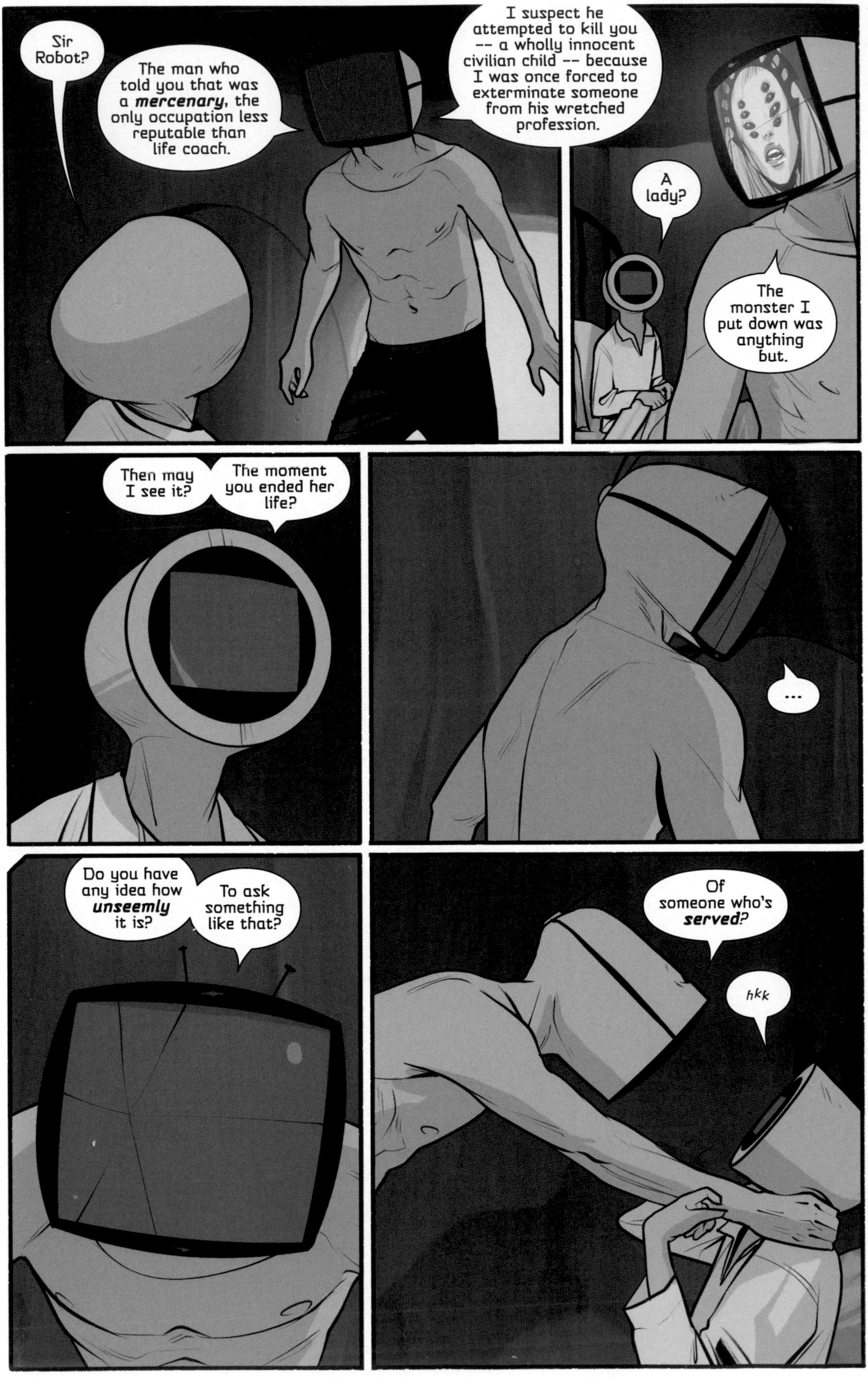
Sir Robot?
The man who told you that was a ***mercenary***, the only occupation less reputable than life coach.
I suspect he attempted to kill you -- a wholly innocent civilian child -- because I was once forced to exterminate someone from his wretched profession.
A lady?
The monster I put down was anything but.
Then may I see it?
The moment you ended her life?
...
Do you have any idea how ***unseemly*** it is?
To ask something like that?
Of someone who's ***served***?
hkk

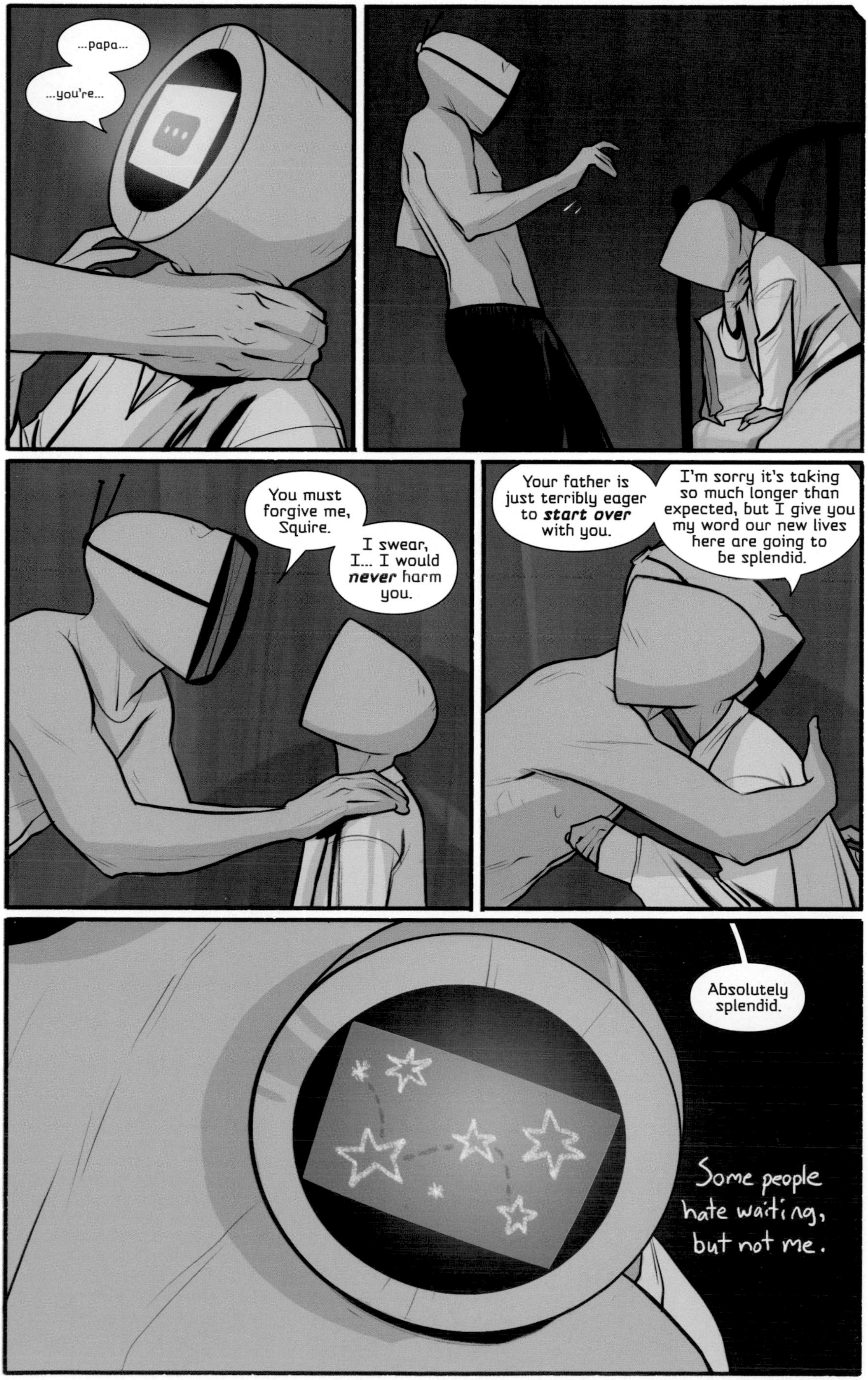
...papa...
...you're...
You must forgive me, Squire.
I swear, I... I would **never** harm you.
Your father is just terribly eager to ***start over*** with you.
I'm sorry it's taking so much longer than expected, but I give you my word our new lives here are going to be splendid.
Absolutely splendid.
Some people hate waiting, but not me.

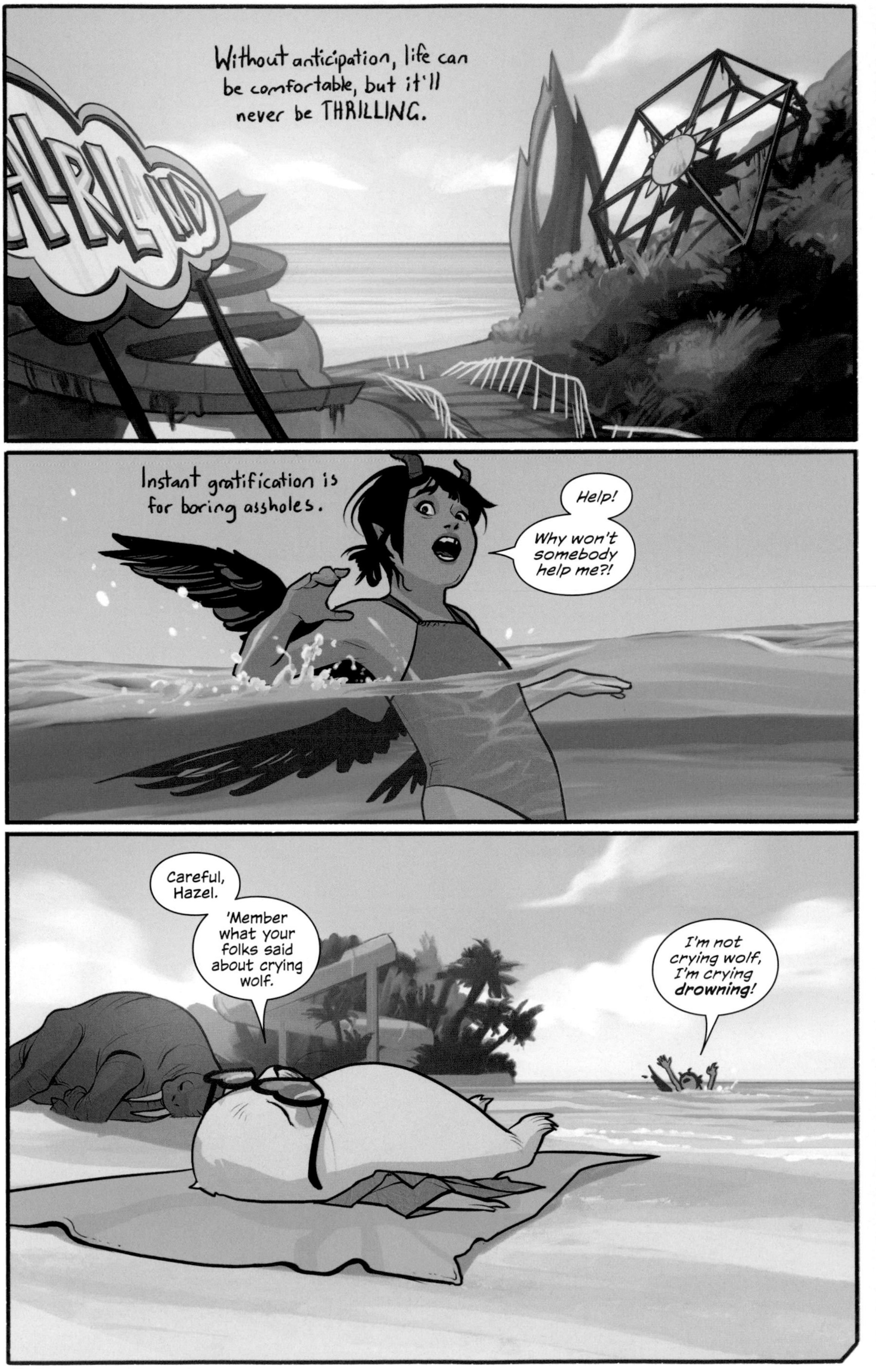

Without anticipation, life can be comfortable, but it'll never be THRILLING.
Instant gratification is for boring assholes.
Help!
Why won't somebody help me?!
Careful, Hazel.
'Member what your folks said about crying wolf.
I'm not crying wolf, I'm crying **drowning**!

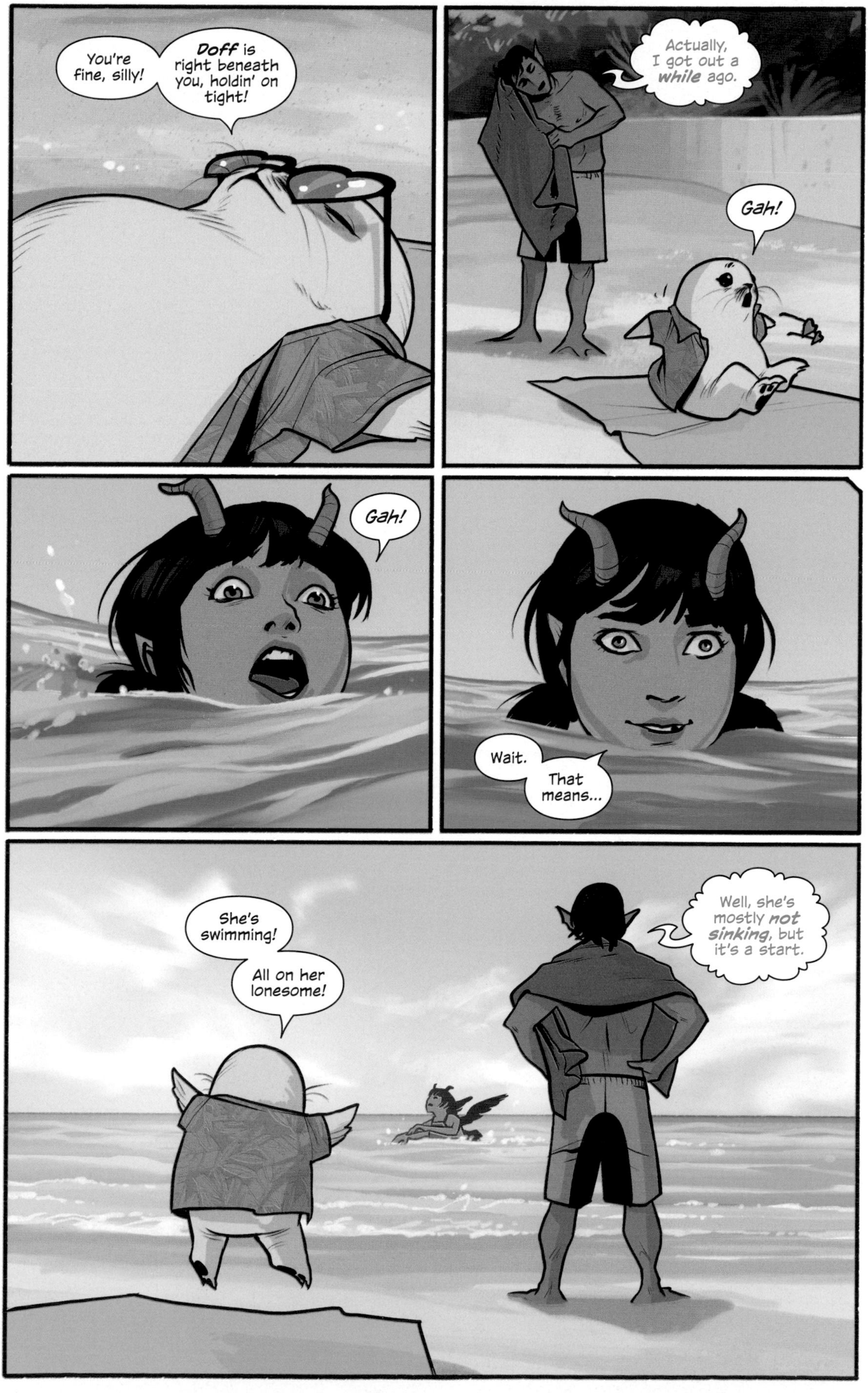

You're fine, silly!
Doff is right beneath you, holdin' on tight!
Actually, I got out a while ago.
Gah!
Gah!
Wait.
That means...
She's swimming!
All on her lonesome!
Well, she's mostly not sinking, but it's a start.

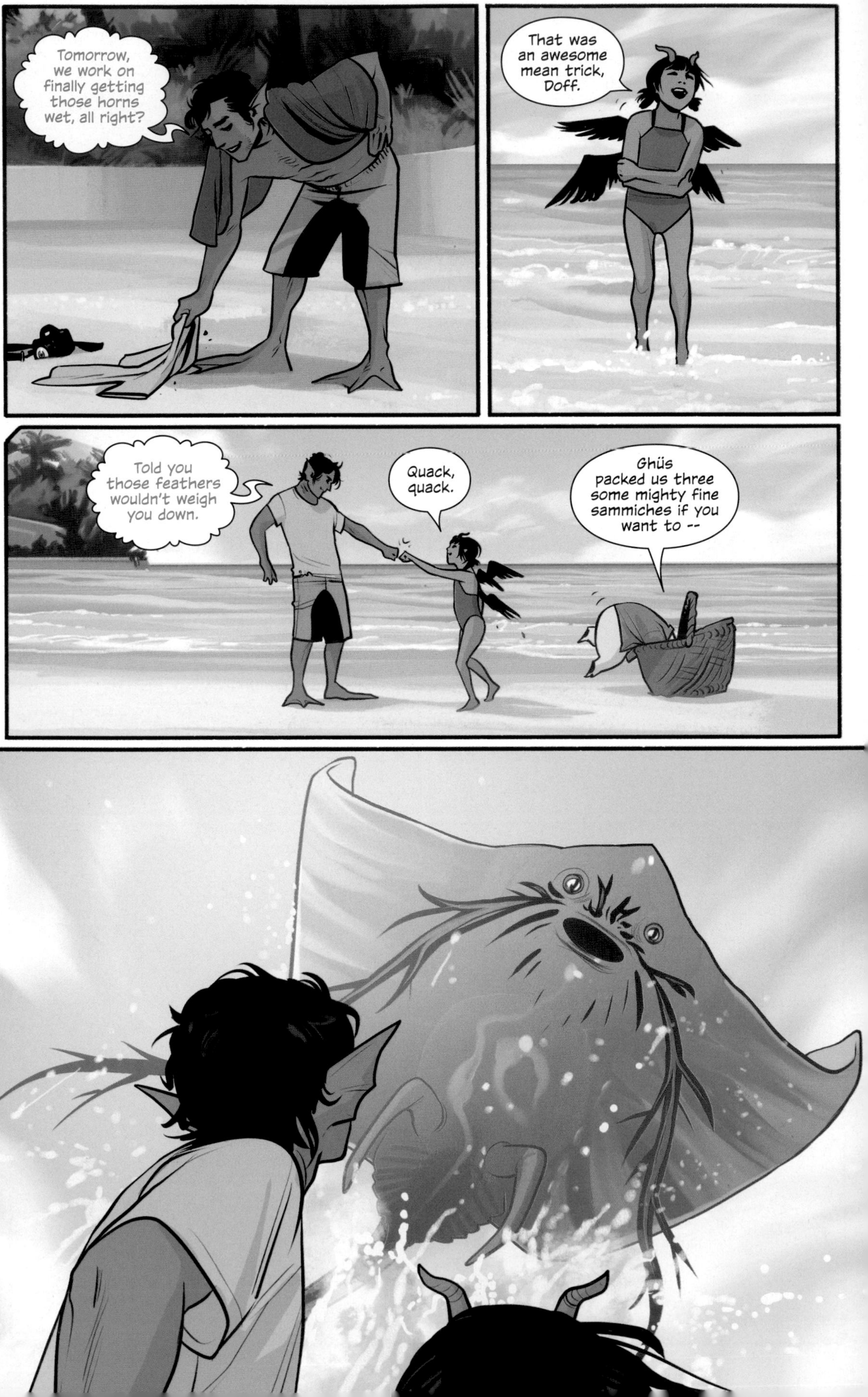

Tomorrow, we work on finally getting those horns wet, all right?
That was an awesome mean trick, Doff.
Told you those feathers wouldn't weigh you down.
Quack, quack.
Ghüs packed us three some mighty fine sammiches if you want to --

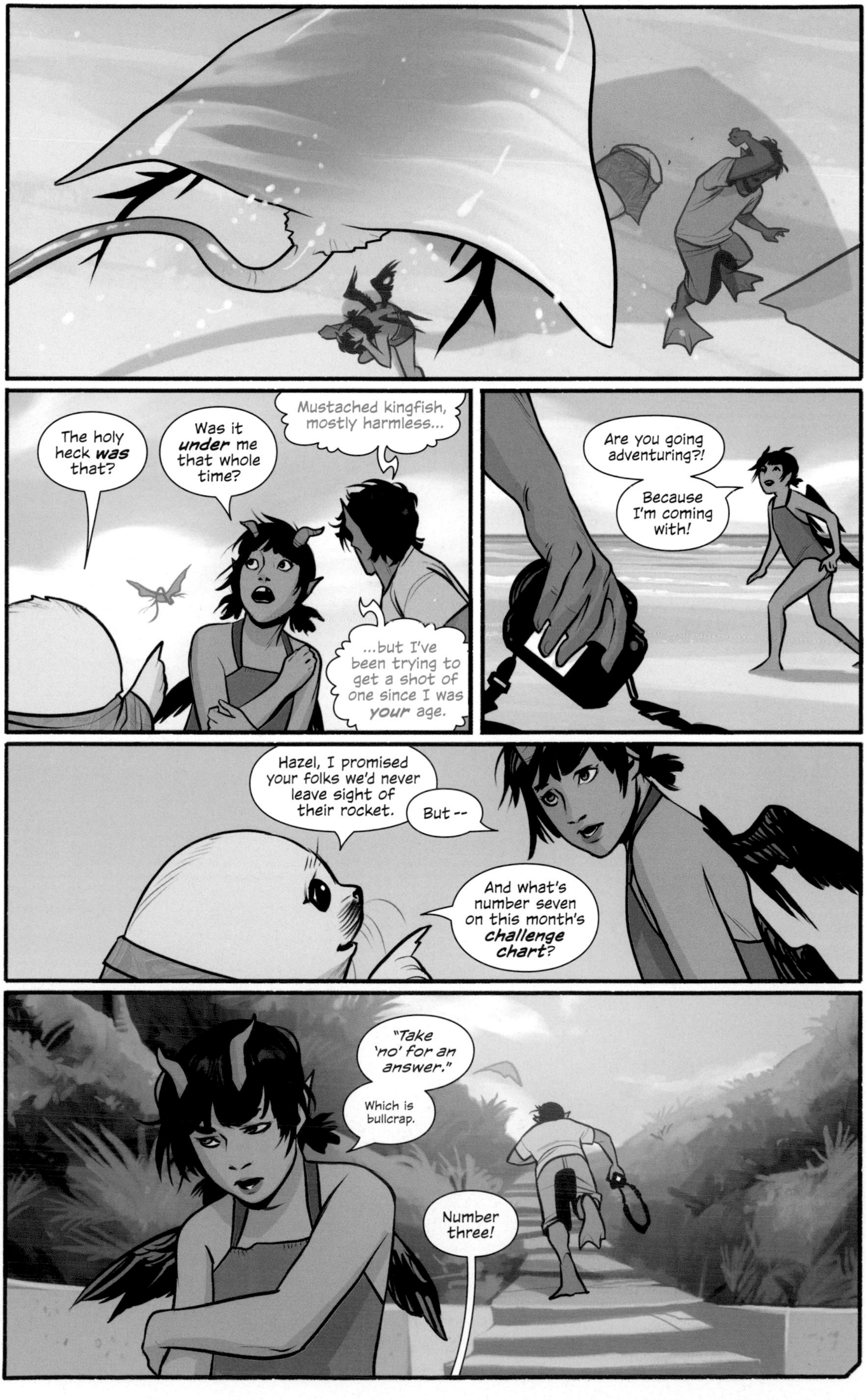

The holy heck *was* that?
Was it *under* me that whole time?
Mustached kingfish, mostly harmless...
...but I've been trying to get a shot of one since I was *your* age.
Are you going adventuring?!
Because I'm coming with!
Hazel, I promised your folks we'd never leave sight of their rocket.
But --
And what's number seven on this month's *challenge chart*?
"Take 'no' for an answer."
Which is bullcrap.
Number three!

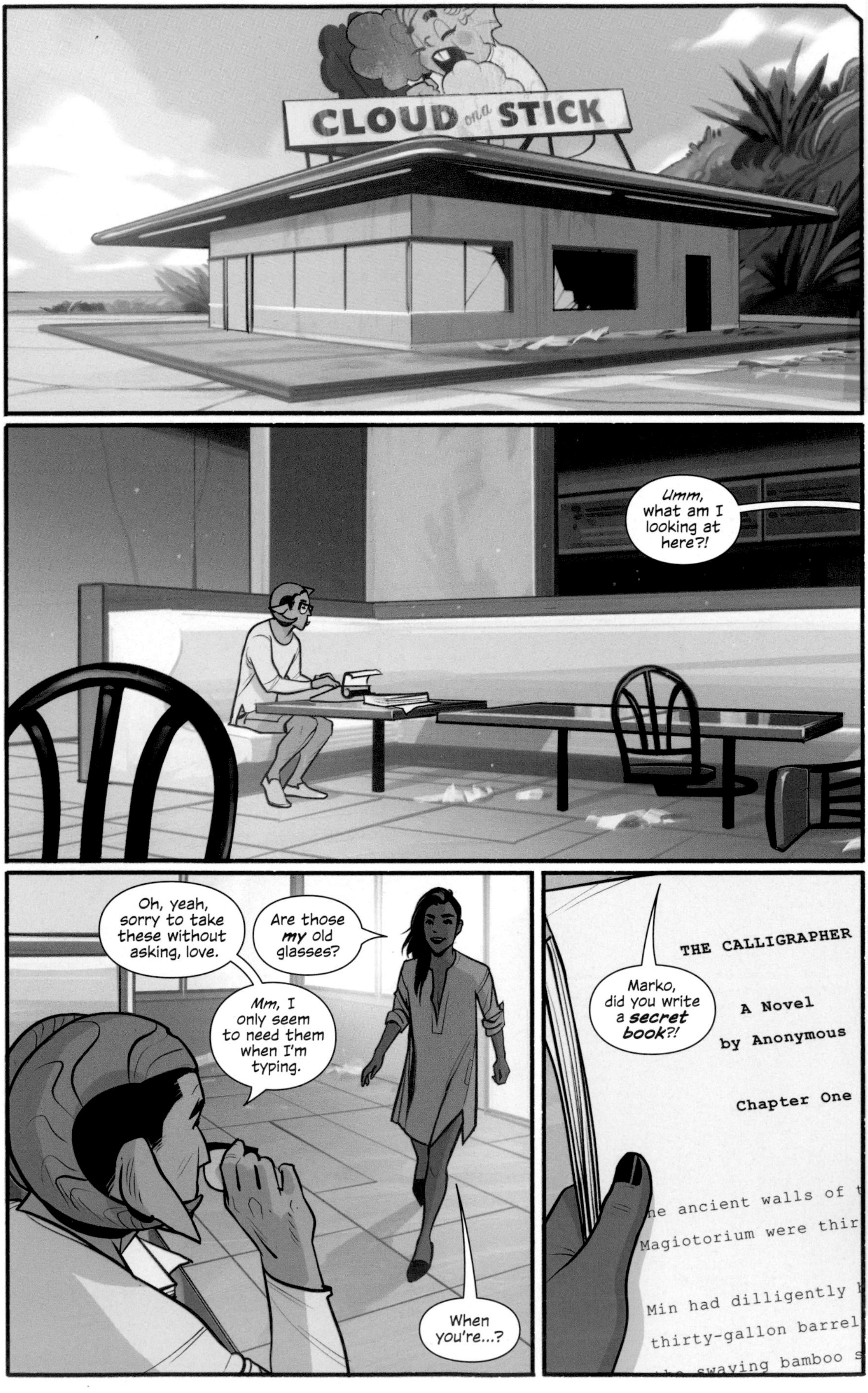
CLOUD on a STICK
Umm, what am I looking at here?!
Are those ***my*** old glasses?
Oh, yeah, sorry to take these without asking, love.
Mm, I only seem to need them when I'm typing.
When you're...?
Marko, did you write a ***secret book***?!
THE CALLIGRAPHER
A Novel
by Anonymous
Chapter One
he ancient walls of t
Magiotorium were thir
Min had dilligently
thirty-gallon barrel

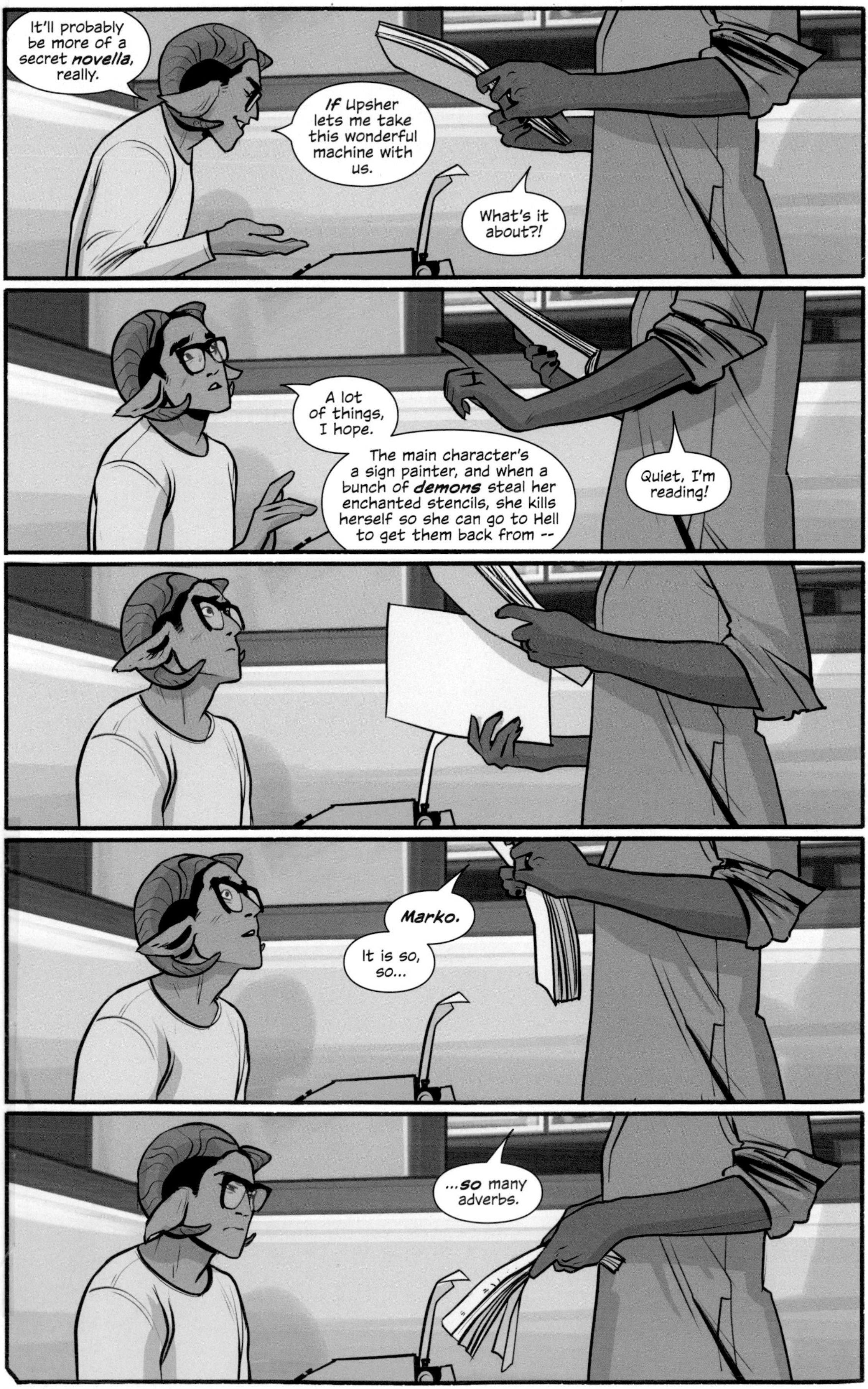

It'll probably be more of a secret *novella*, really.
If Upsher lets me take this wonderful machine with us.
What's it about?!
A lot of things, I hope.
The main character's a sign painter, and when a bunch of *demons* steal her enchanted stencils, she kills herself so she can go to Hell to get them back from --
Quiet, I'm reading!
Marko.
It is so, so...
...*so* many adverbs.

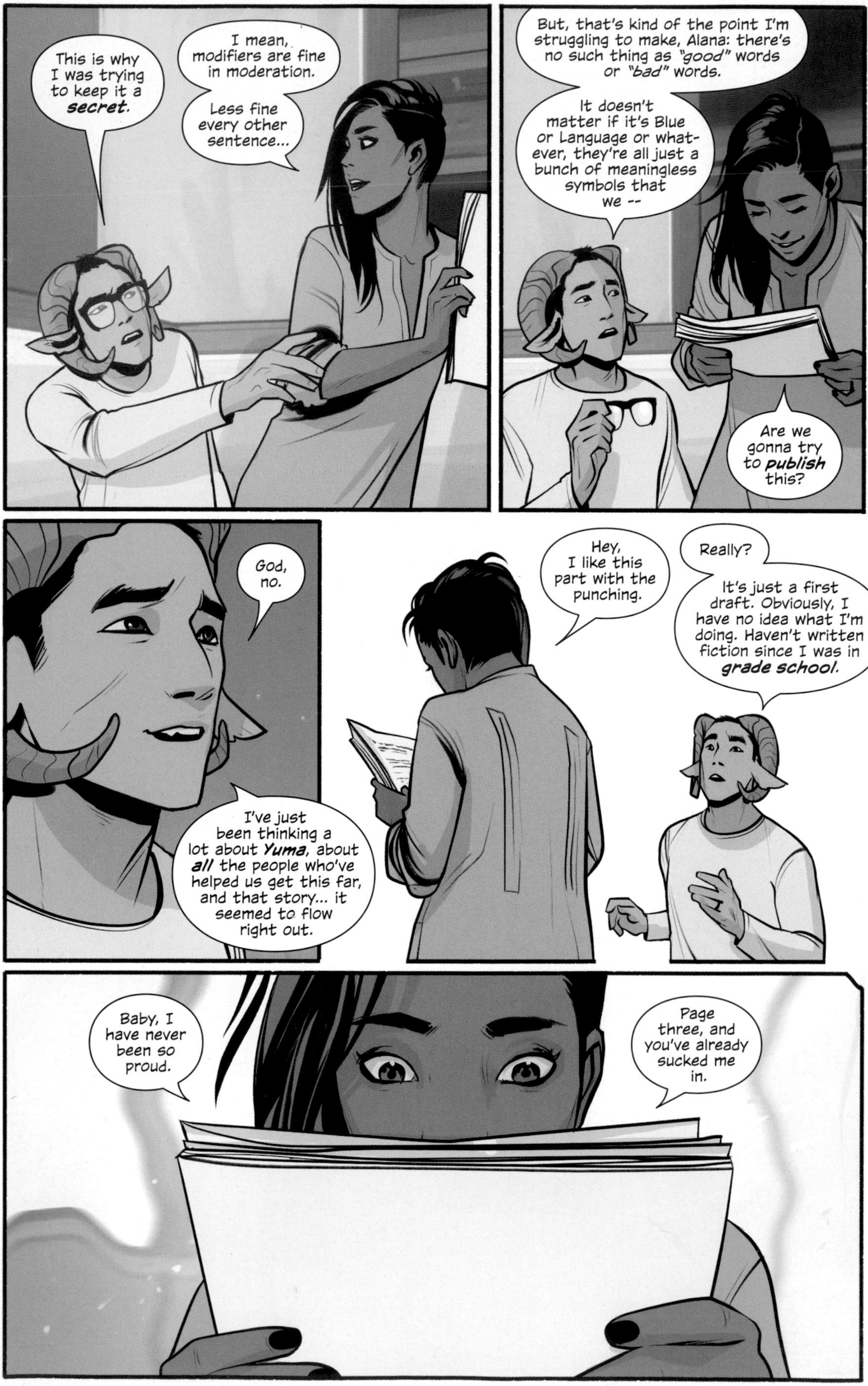

This is why I was trying to keep it a *secret*.
I mean, modifiers are fine in moderation.
Less fine every other sentence...
But, that's kind of the point I'm struggling to make, Alana: there's no such thing as "*good*" words or "*bad*" words.
It doesn't matter if it's Blue or Language or whatever, they're all just a bunch of meaningless symbols that we --
Are we gonna try to ***publish*** this?
God, no.
I've just been thinking a lot about *Yuma*, about ***all*** the people who've helped us get this far, and that story... it seemed to flow right out.
Hey, I like this part with the punching.
Really?
It's just a first draft. Obviously, I have no idea what I'm doing. Haven't written fiction since I was in ***grade school***.
Baby, I have never been so proud.
Page three, and you've already sucked me in.

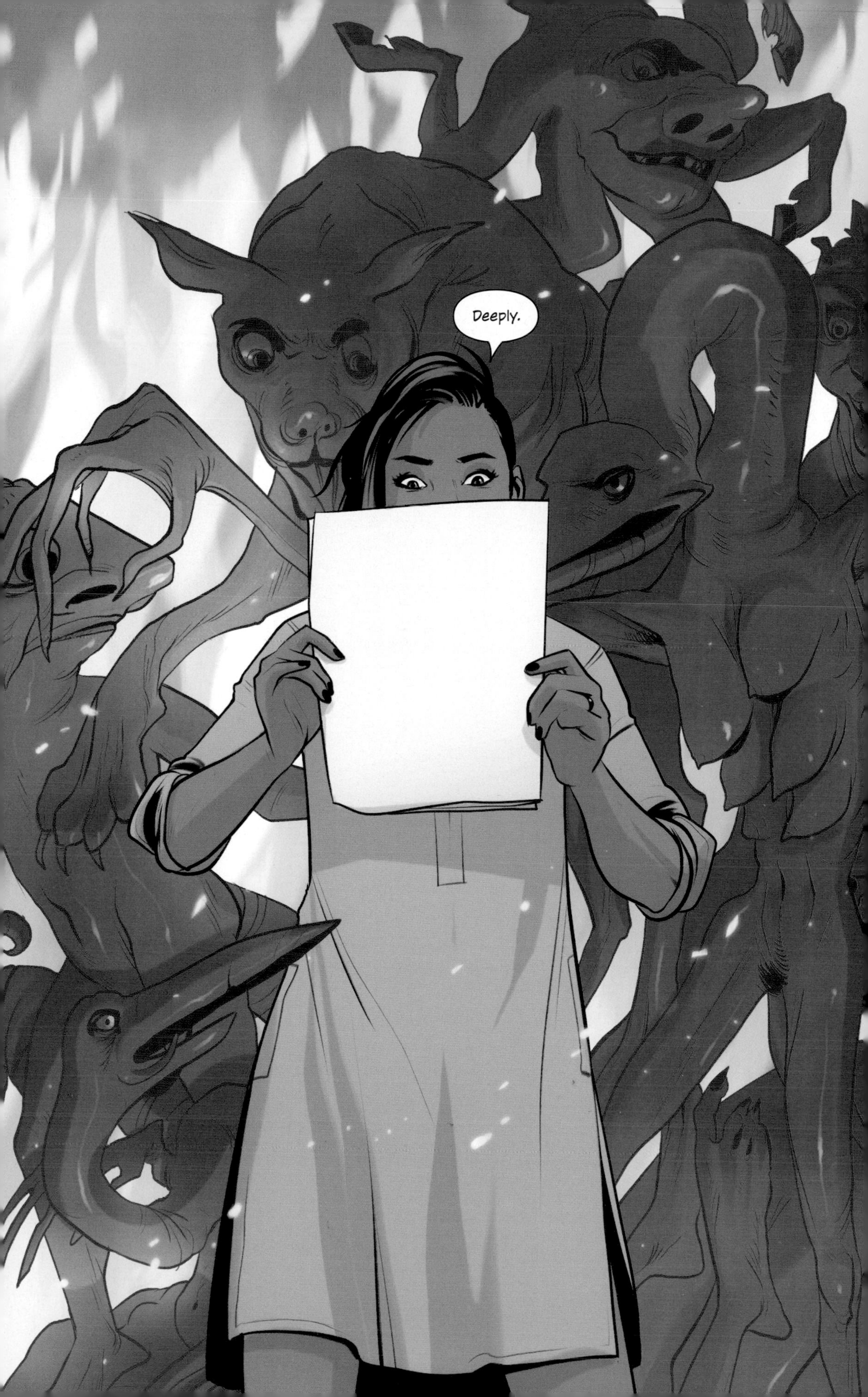
Deeply.

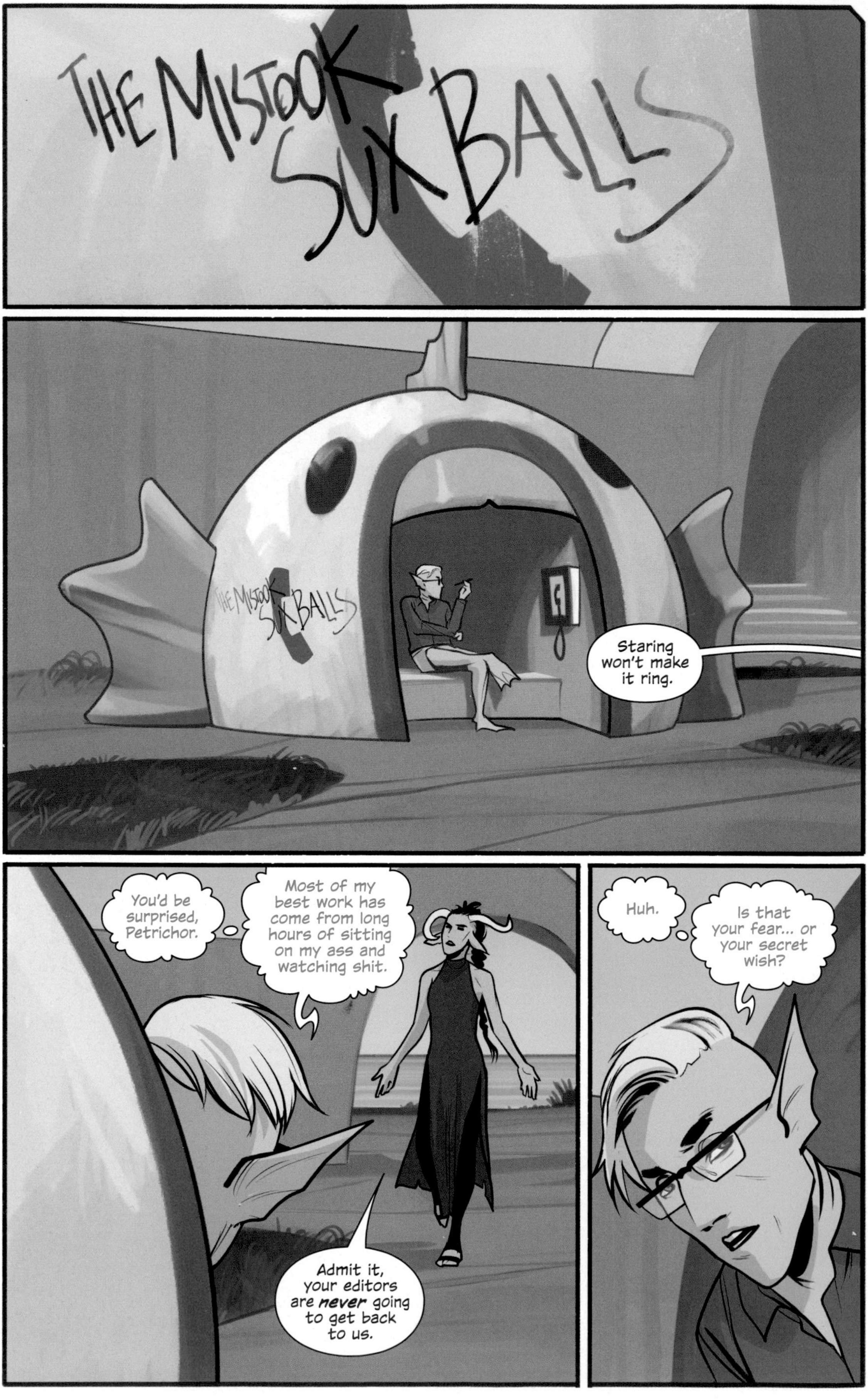
THE MISTOOK SUX BALLS
THE MISTOOK SUX BALLS
Staring won't make it ring.
You'd be surprised, Petrichor.
Most of my best work has come from long hours of sitting on my ass and watching shit.
Admit it, your editors are ***never*** going to get back to us.
Huh.
Is that your fear... or your secret wish?

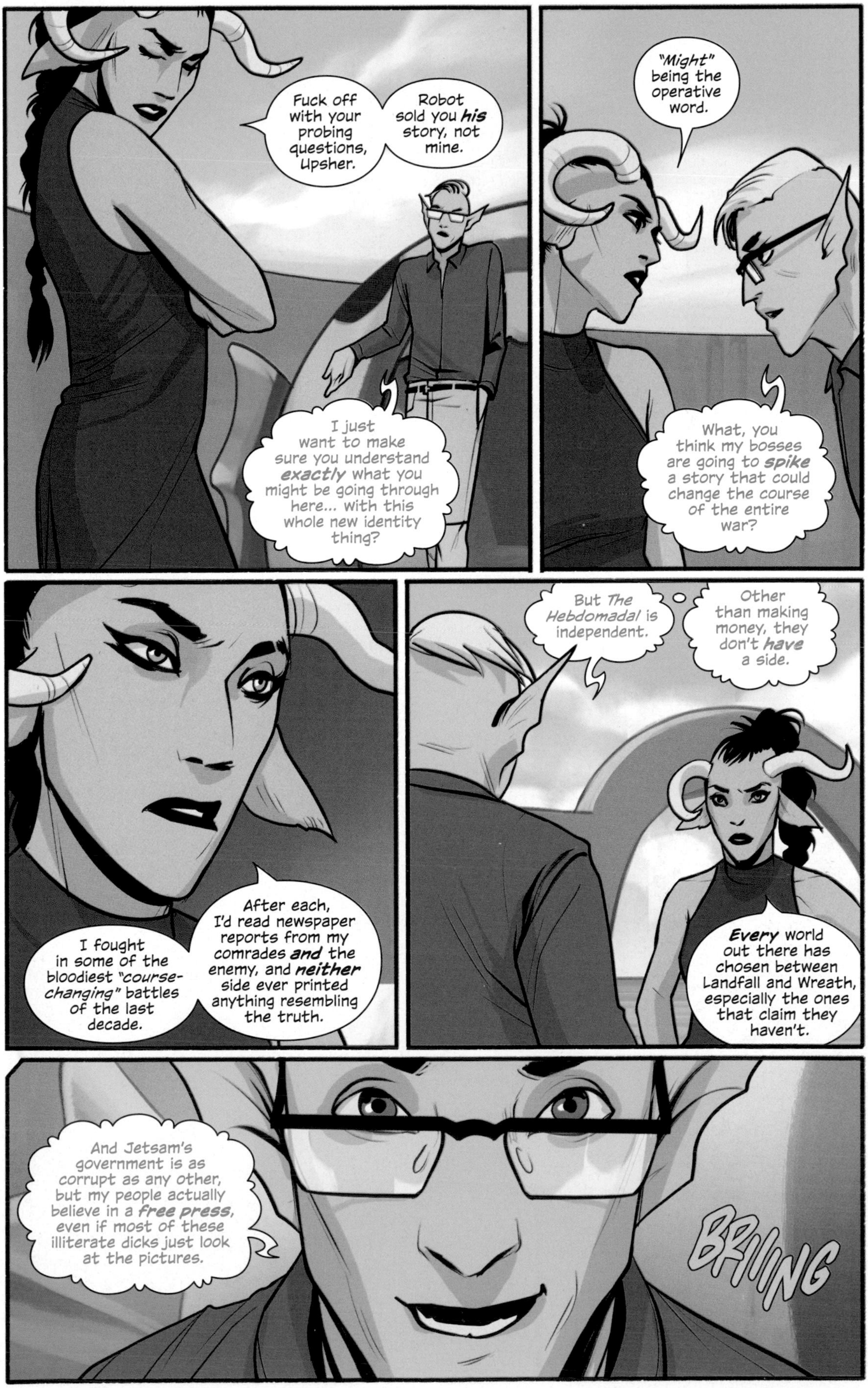
Fuck off with your probing questions, Upsher.
Robot sold you *his* story, not mine.
I just want to make sure you understand *exactly* what you might be going through here... with this whole new identity thing?
"*Might*" being the operative word.
What, you think my bosses are going to *spike* a story that could change the course of the entire war?
I fought in some of the bloodiest "*course-changing*" battles of the last decade.
After each, I'd read newspaper reports from my comrades *and* the enemy, and *neither* side ever printed anything resembling the truth.
But *The Hebdomadal* is independent.
Other than making money, they don't *have* a side.
Every world out there has chosen between Landfall and Wreath, especially the ones that claim they haven't.
And Jetsam's government is as corrupt as any other, but my people actually believe in a *free press*, even if most of these illiterate dicks just look at the pictures.
BRIIING

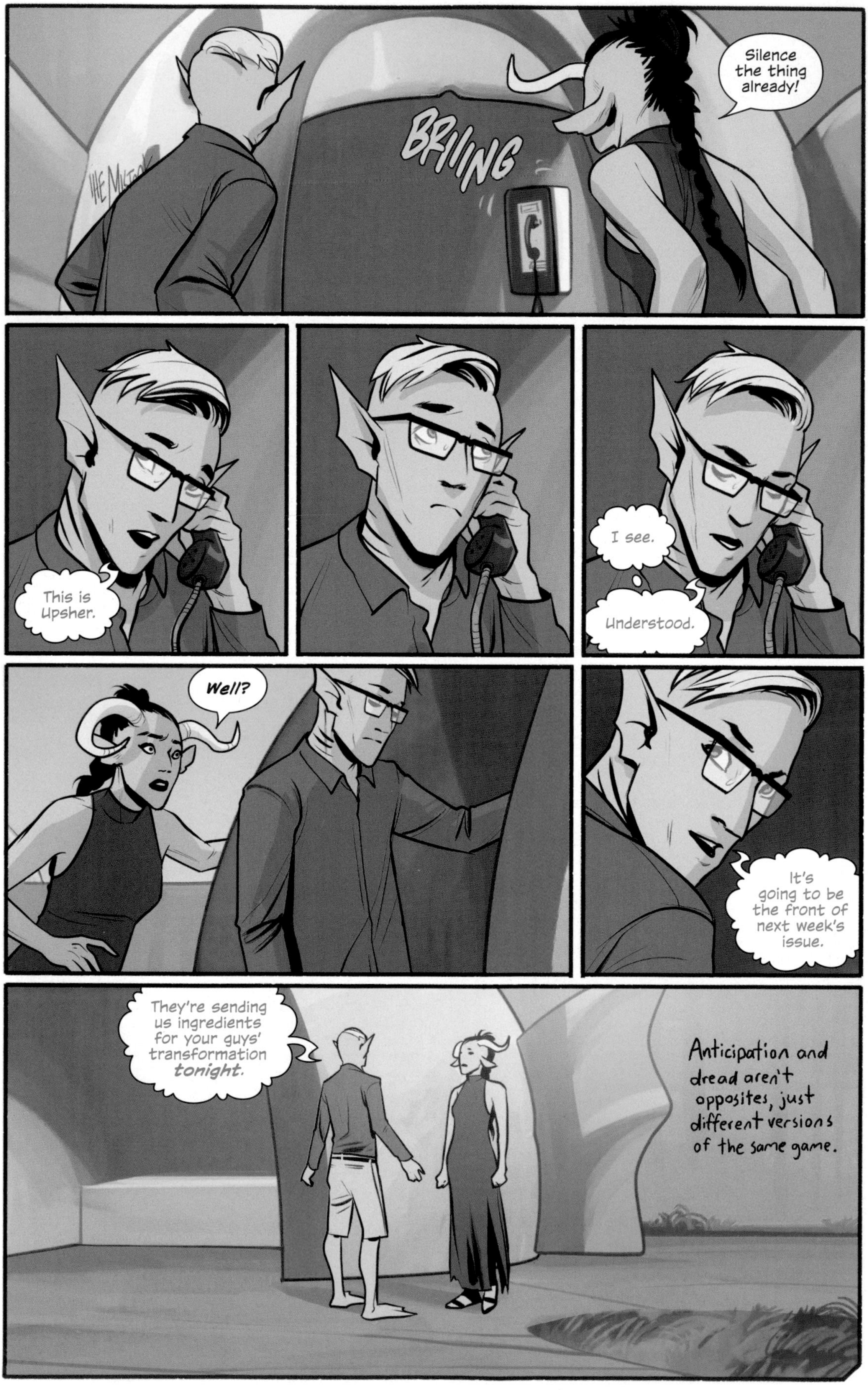
Silence the thing already!
BRIIING
This is Upsher.
I see.
Understood.
Well?
It's going to be the front of next week's issue.
They're sending us ingredients for your guys' transformation *tonight*.
Anticipation and dread aren't opposites, just different versions of the same game.

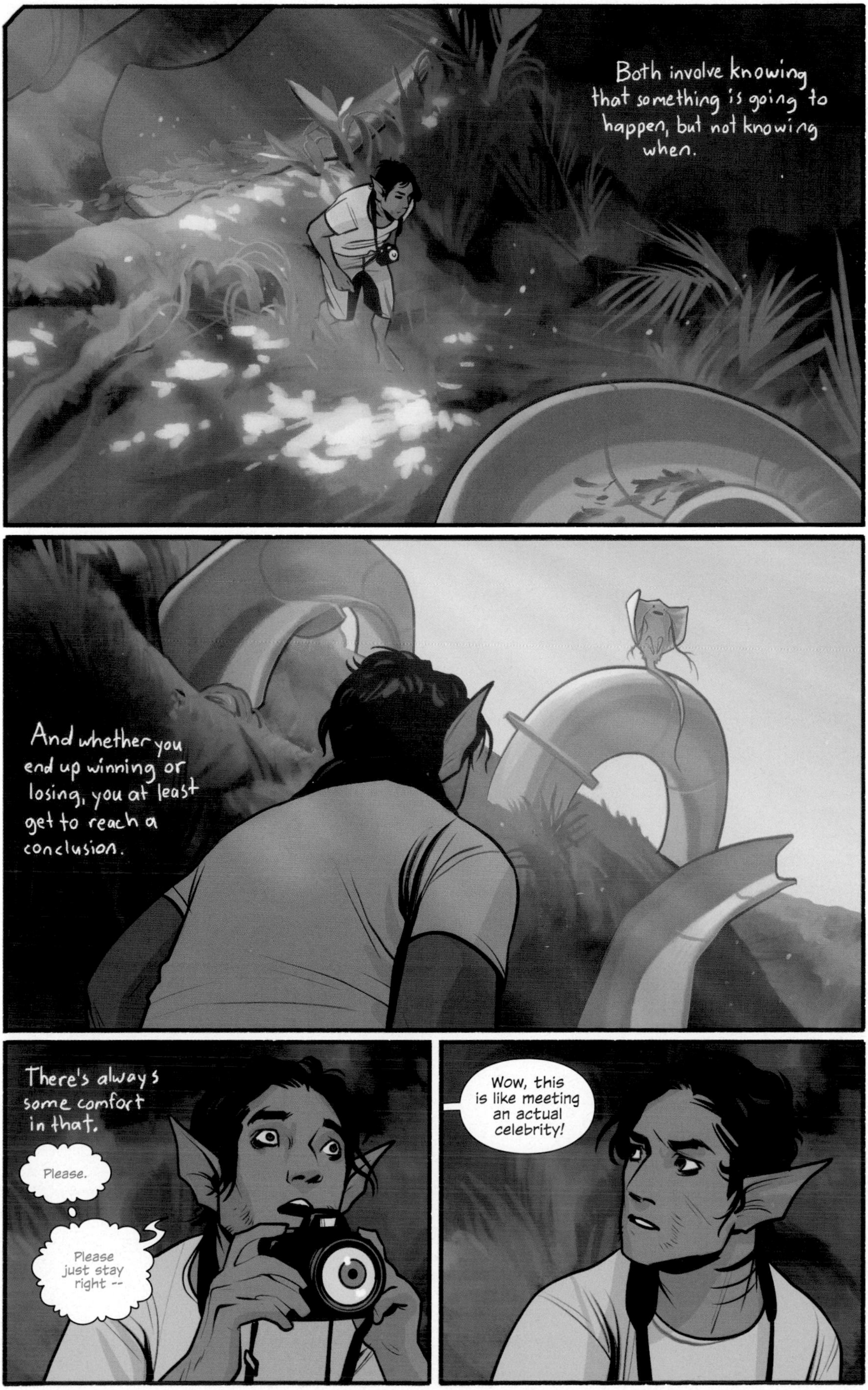
Both involve knowing that something is going to happen, but not knowing when.
And whether you end up winning or losing, you at least get to reach a conclusion.
There's always some comfort in that.
Please.
Please just stay right --
Wow, this is like meeting an actual celebrity!

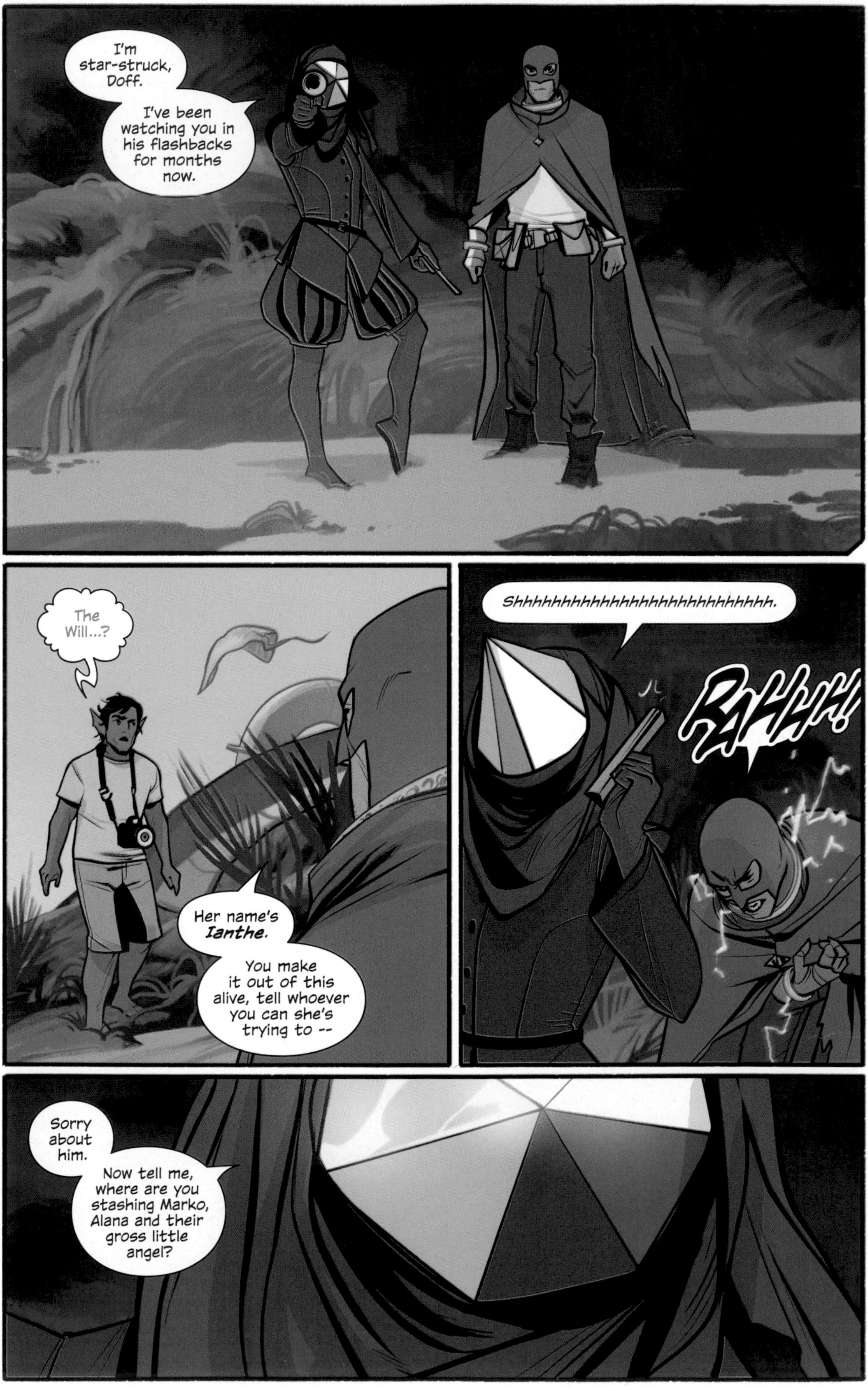
I'm star-struck, Doff.
I've been watching you in his flashbacks for months now.
The Will...?
Her name's *Ianthe*.
You make it out of this alive, tell whoever you can she's trying to --
Shhhhhhhhhhhhhhhhhhhhhhhhhhhhh.
RAHHH!
Sorry about him.
Now tell me, where are you stashing Marko, Alana and their gross little angel?

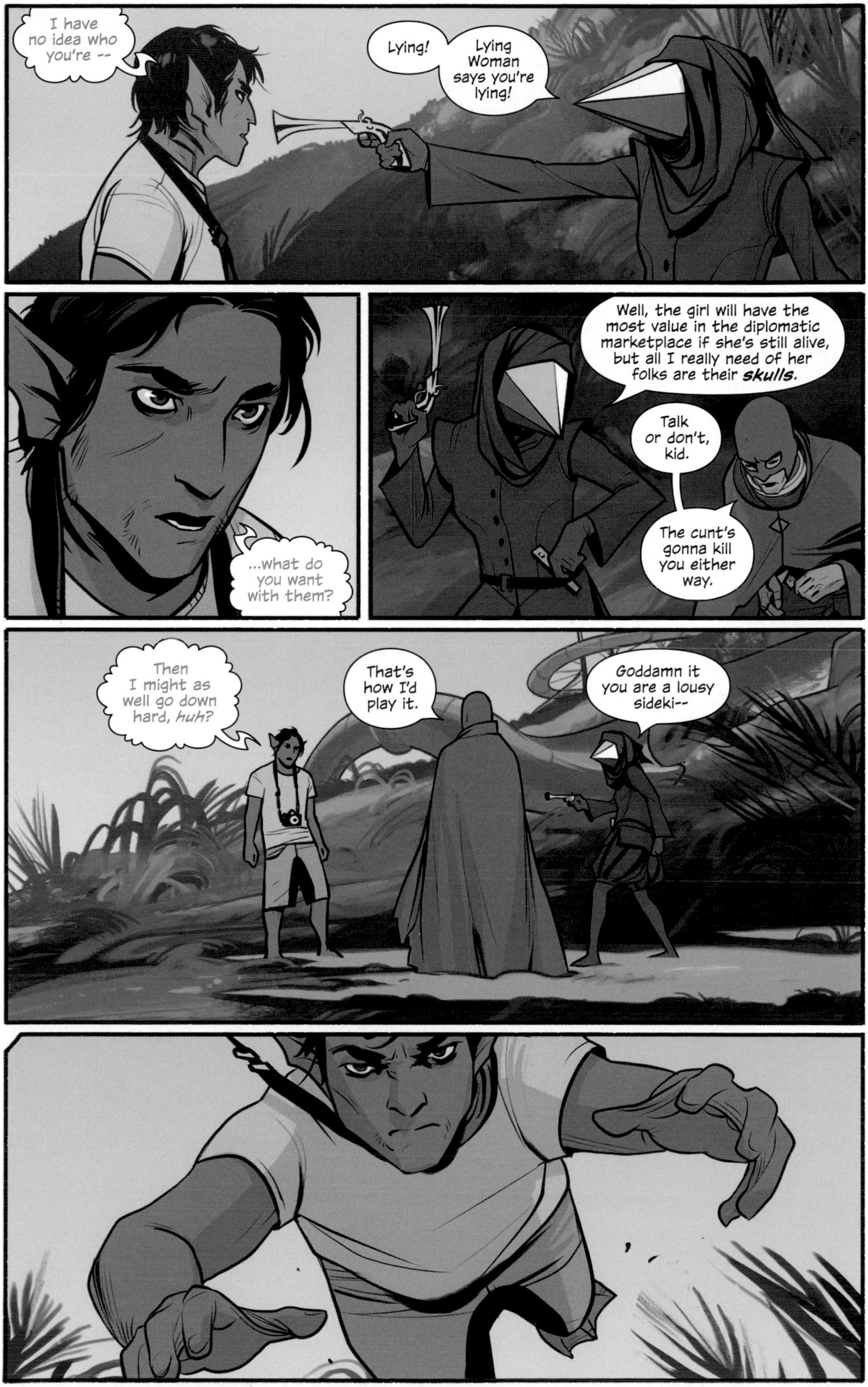

I have no idea who you're --
Lying!
Lying Woman says you're lying!
...what do you want with them?
Well, the girl will have the most value in the diplomatic marketplace if she's still alive, but all I really need of her folks are their *skulls*.
Talk or don't, kid.
The cunt's gonna kill you either way.
Then I might as well go down hard, *huh*?
That's how I'd play it.
Goddamn it you are a lousy sideki--

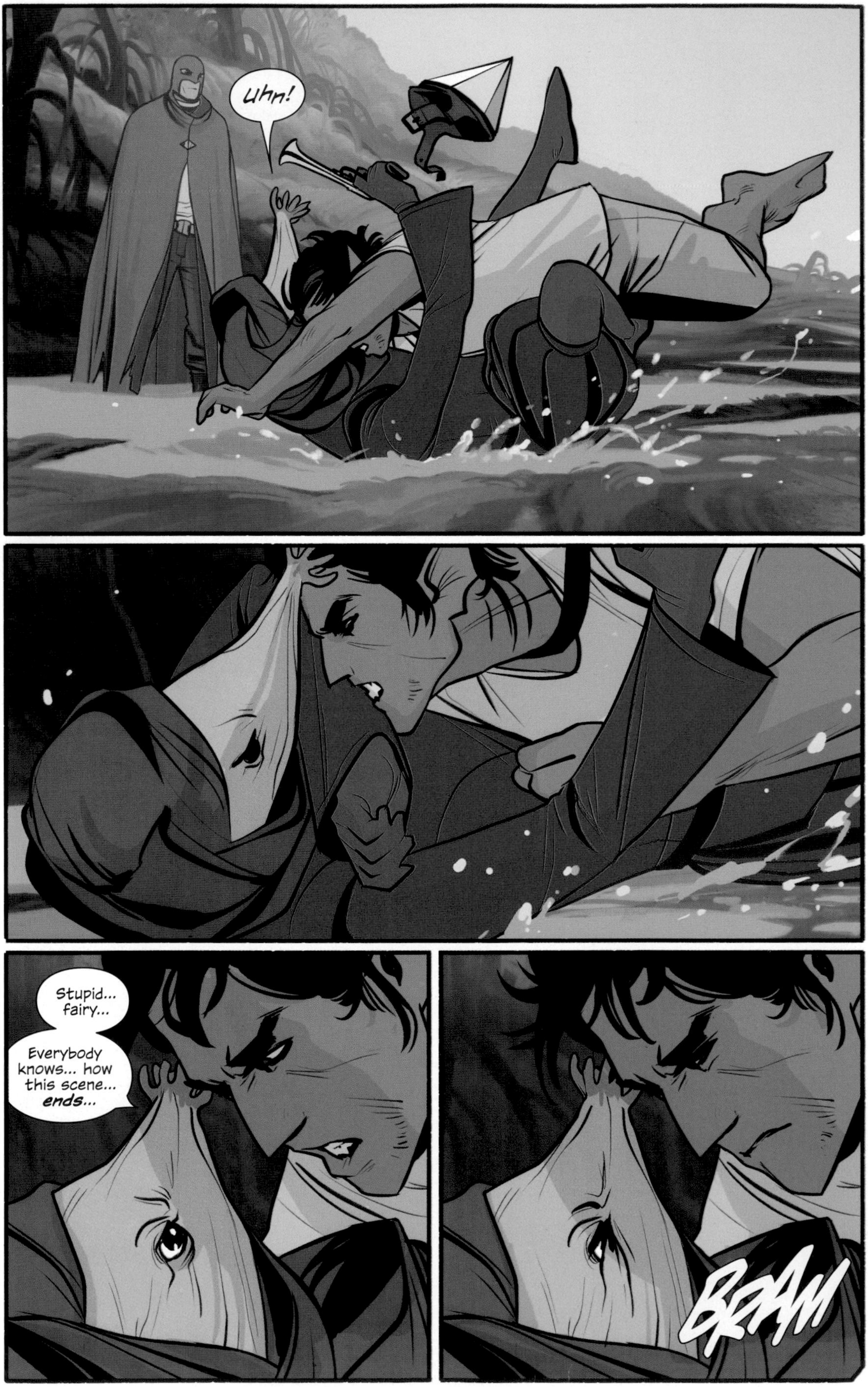
Uhn!
Stupid... fairy...
Everybody knows... how this scene... *ends*...
BRAM

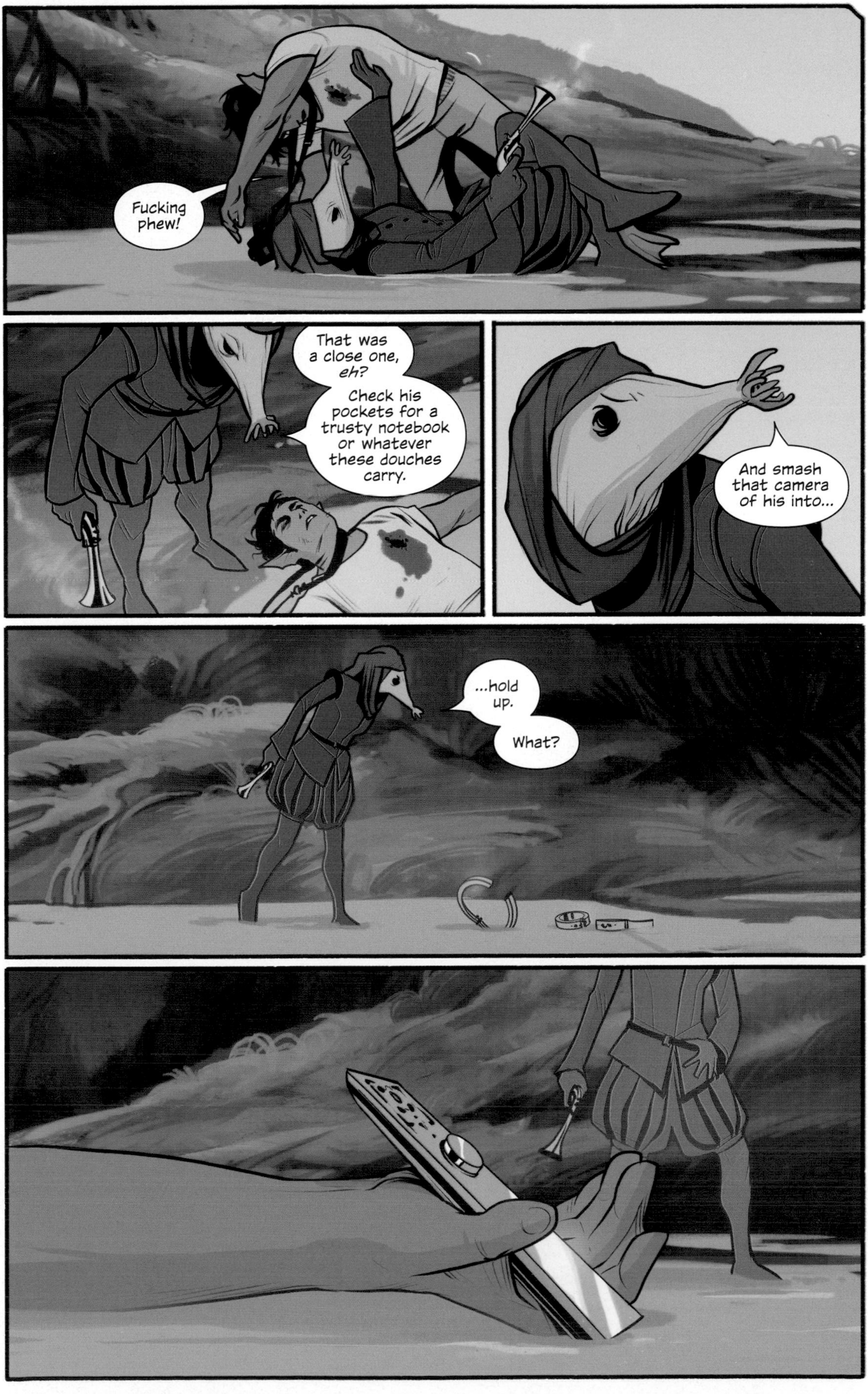
Fucking phew!
That was a close one, eh?
Check his pockets for a trusty notebook or whatever these douches carry.
And smash that camera of his into...
...hold up.
What?

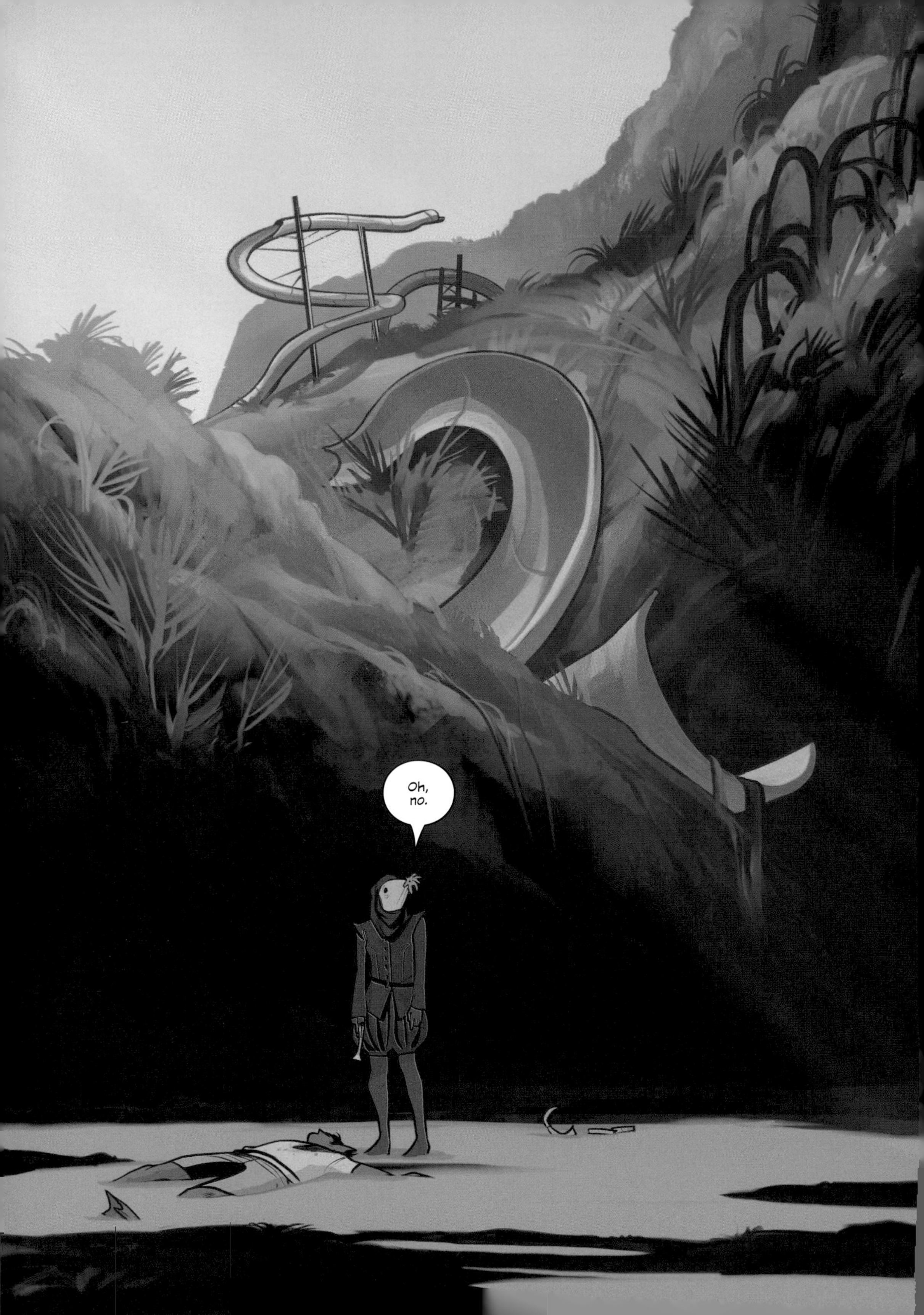
Oh, no.

end chapter fifty-one

CHAPTER

FIFTY-TWO

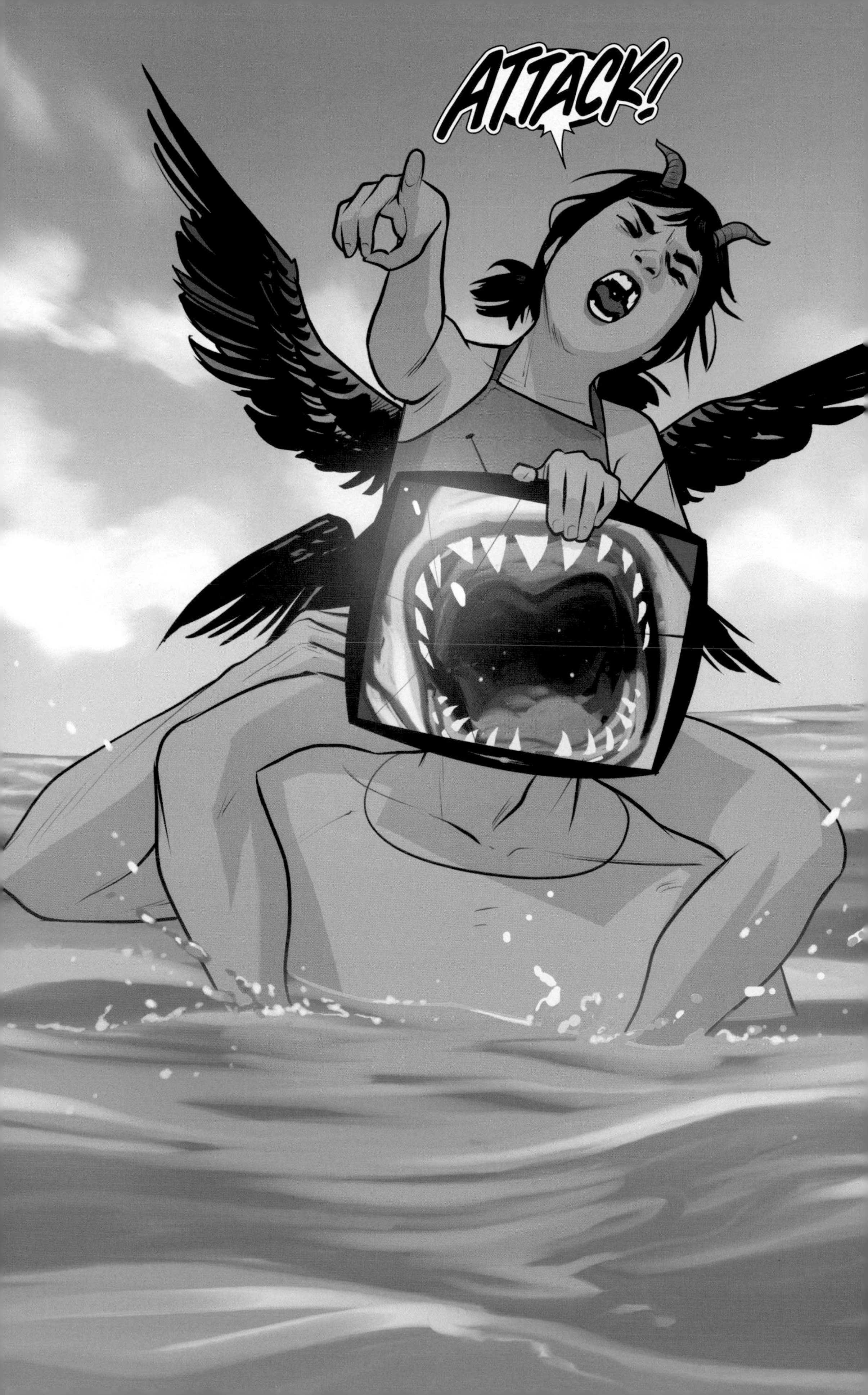
ATTACK!

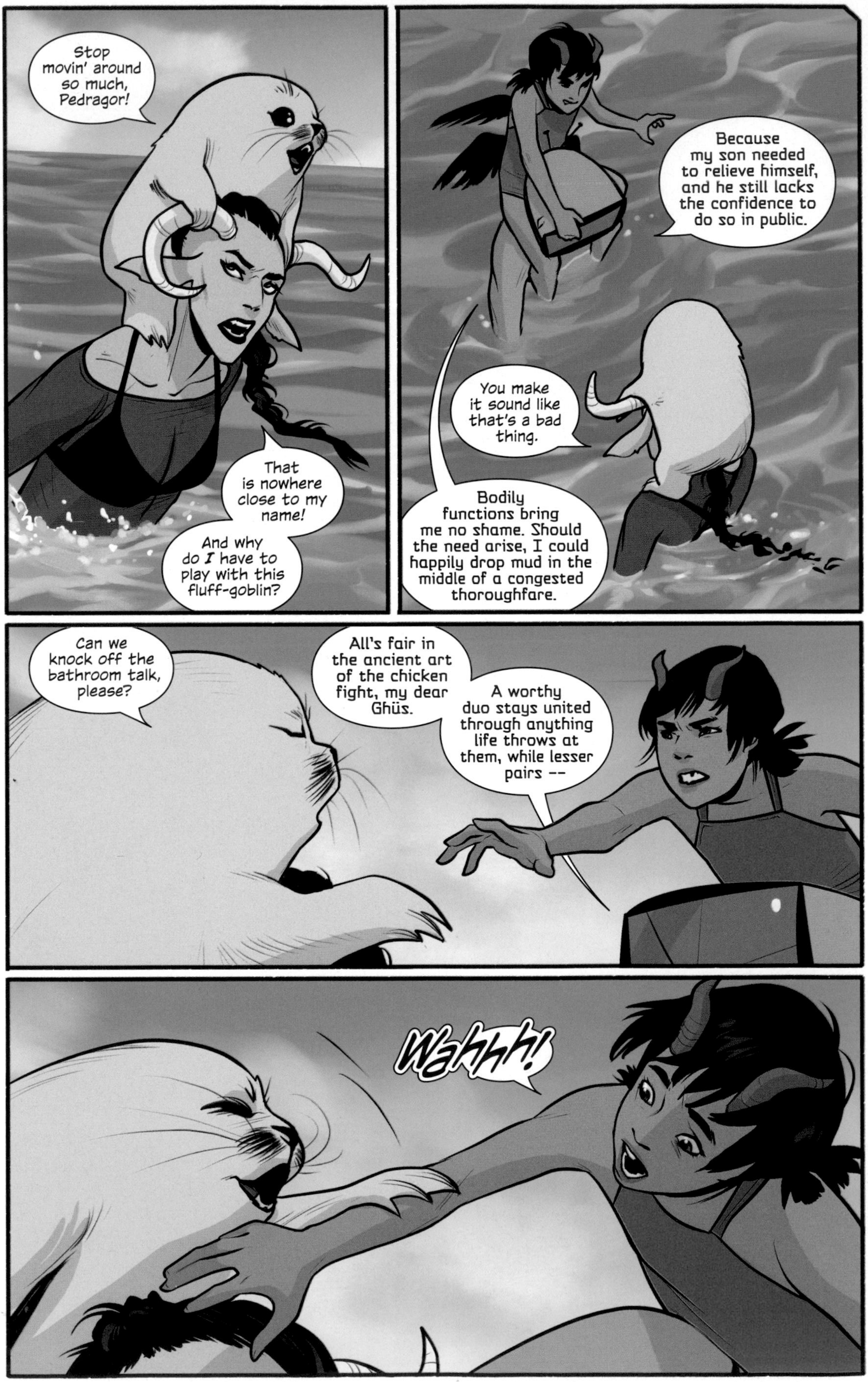
Stop movin' around so much, Pedragor!
That is nowhere close to my name!
And why do I have to play with this fluff-goblin?
Because my son needed to relieve himself, and he still lacks the confidence to do so in public.
You make it sound like that's a bad thing.
Bodily functions bring me no shame. Should the need arise, I could happily drop mud in the middle of a congested thoroughfare.
Can we knock off the bathroom talk, please?
All's fair in the ancient art of the chicken fight, my dear Ghüs.
A worthy duo stays united through anything life throws at them, while lesser pairs --
Wahhh!

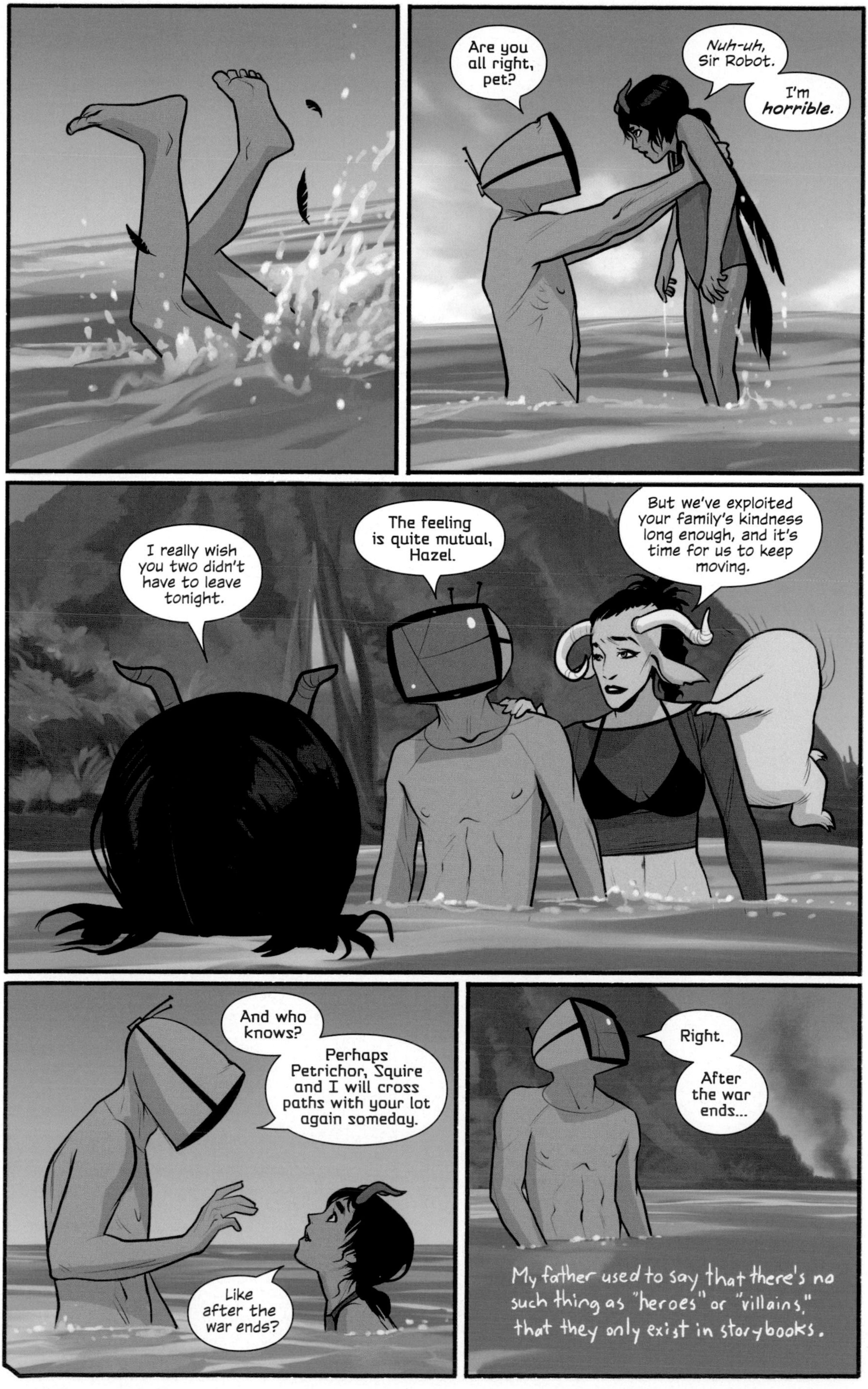
Are you all right, pet?
Nuh-uh, Sir Robot.
I'm horrible.
I really wish you two didn't have to leave tonight.
The feeling is quite mutual, Hazel.
But we've exploited your family's kindness long enough, and it's time for us to keep moving.
And who knows?
Perhaps Petrichor, Squire and I will cross paths with your lot again someday.
Like after the war ends?
Right.
After the war ends...
My father used to say that there's no such thing as "heroes" or "villains," that they only exist in storybooks.

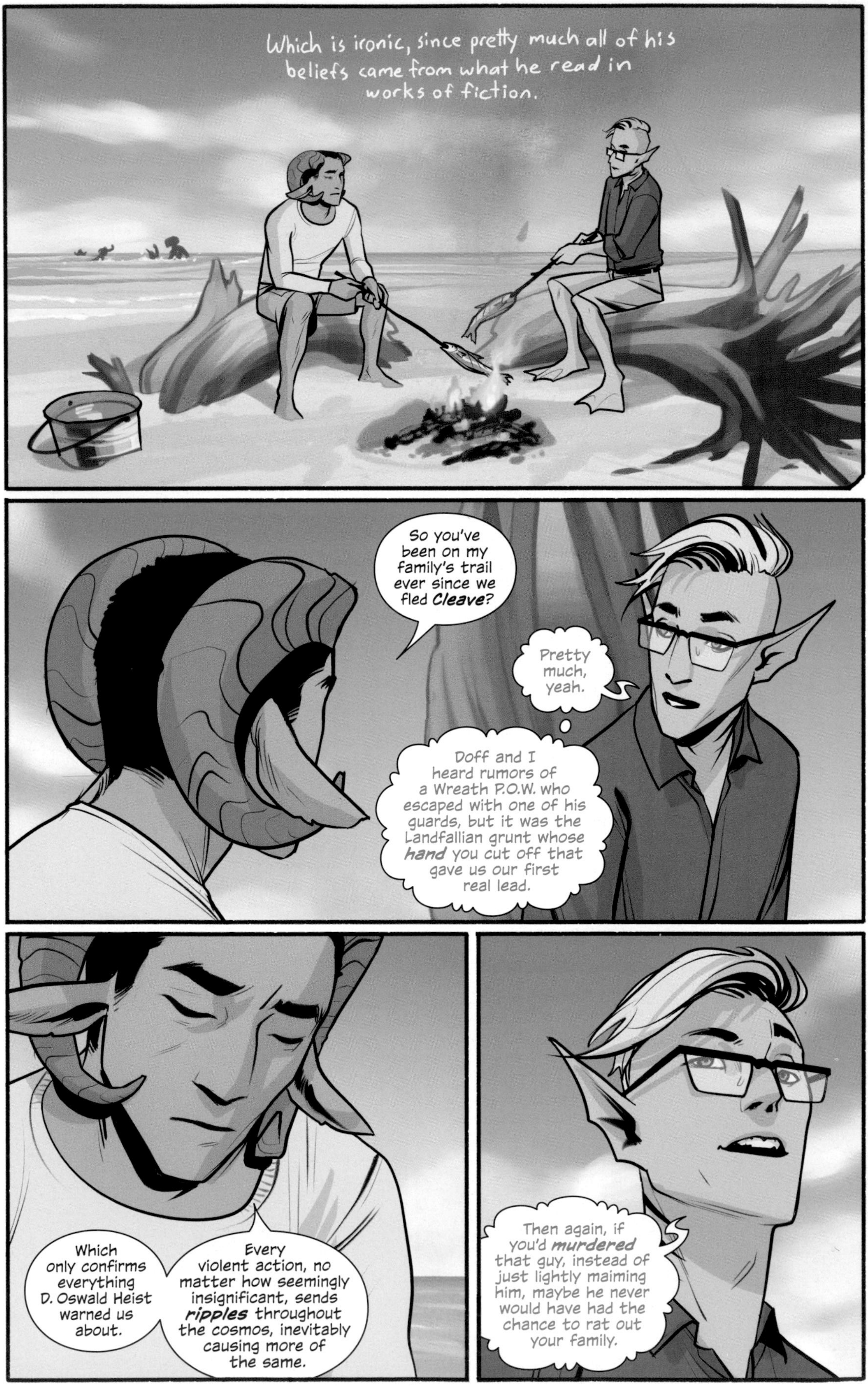

Which is ironic, since pretty much all of his beliefs came from what he read in works of fiction.
So you've been on my family's trail ever since we fled Cleave?
Pretty much, yeah.
Doff and I heard rumors of a Wreath P.O.W. who escaped with one of his guards, but it was the Landfallian grunt whose hand you cut off that gave us our first real lead.
Which only confirms everything D. Oswald Heist warned us about.
Every violent action, no matter how seemingly insignificant, sends ripples throughout the cosmos, inevitably causing more of the same.
Then again, if you'd murdered that guy, instead of just lightly maiming him, maybe he never would have had the chance to rat out your family.

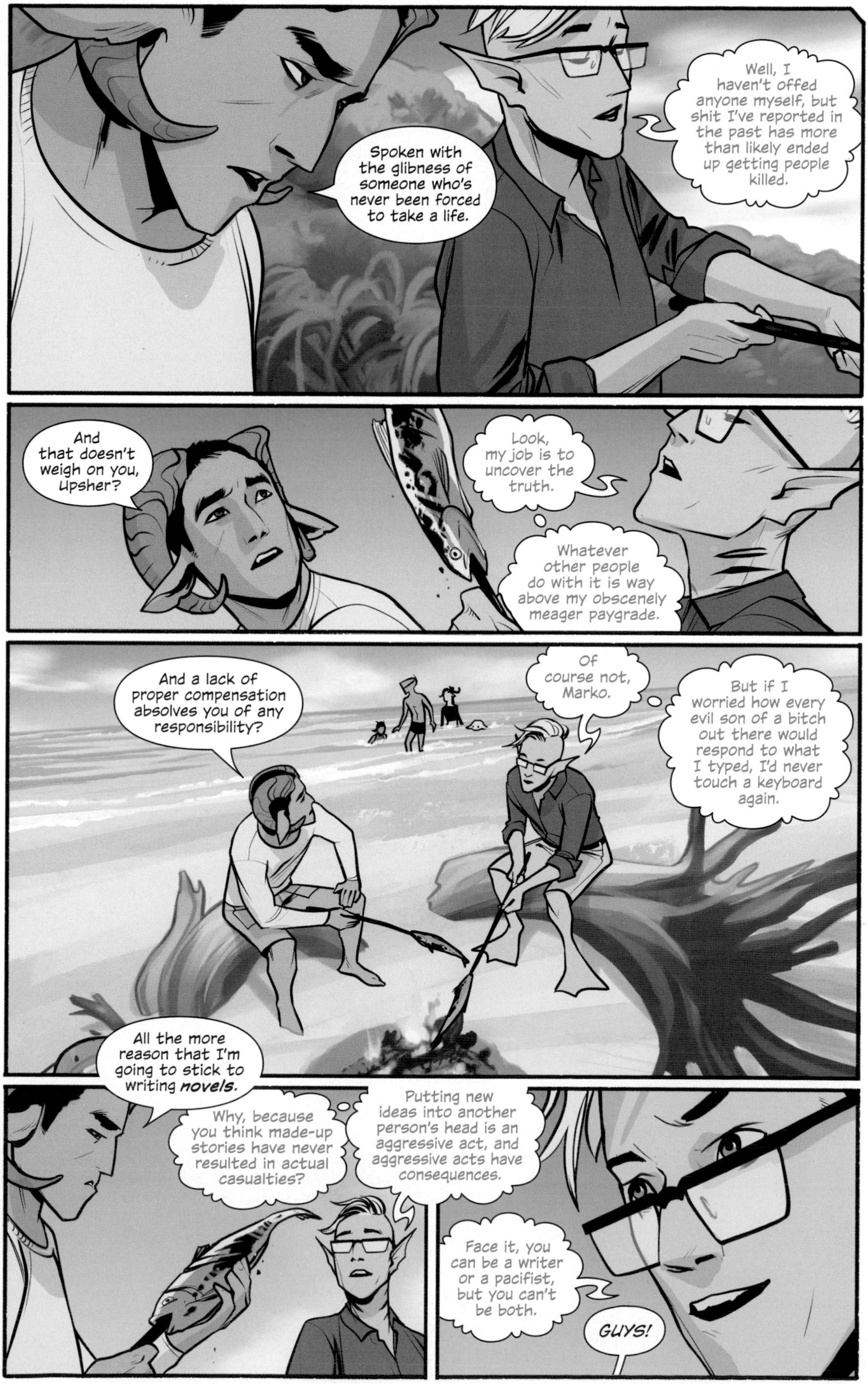
Well, I haven't offed anyone myself, but shit I've reported in the past has more than likely ended up getting people killed.
Spoken with the glibness of someone who's never been forced to take a life.
And that doesn't weigh on you, Upsher?
Look, my job is to uncover the truth.
Whatever other people do with it is way above my obscenely meager paygrade.
And a lack of proper compensation absolves you of any responsibility?
Of course not, Marko.
But if I worried how every evil son of a bitch out there would respond to what I typed, I'd never touch a keyboard again.
All the more reason that I'm going to stick to writing *novels*.
Why, because you think made-up stories have never resulted in actual casualties?
Putting new ideas into another person's head is an aggressive act, and aggressive acts have consequences.
Face it, you can be a writer or a pacifist, but you can't be both.
GUYS!

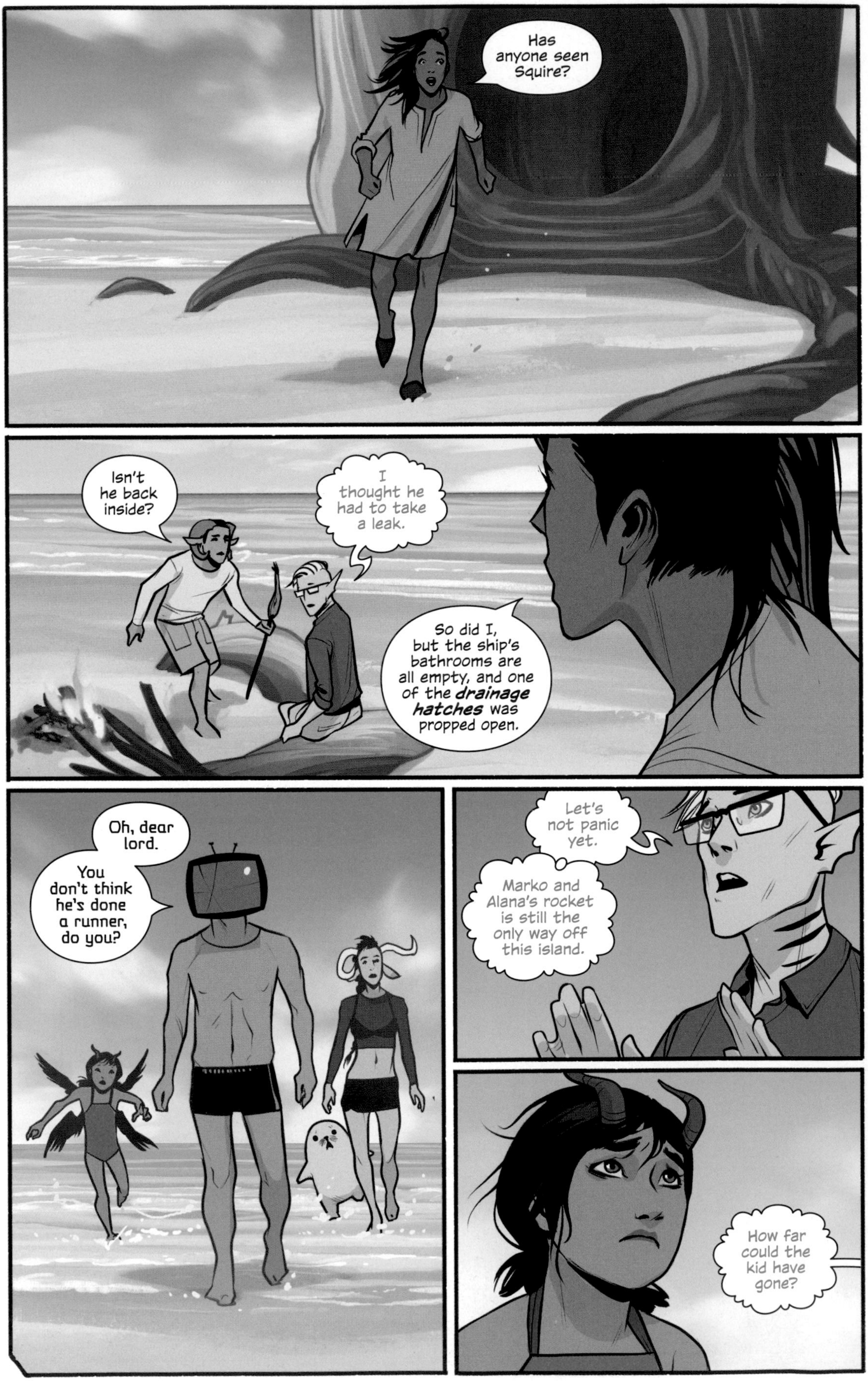
Has anyone seen Squire?
Isn't he back inside?
I thought he had to take a leak.
So did I, but the ship's bathrooms are all empty, and one of the **drainage hatches** was propped open.
Oh, dear lord.
You don't think he's done a runner, do you?
Let's not panic yet.
Marko and Alana's rocket is still the only way off this island.
How far could the kid have gone?

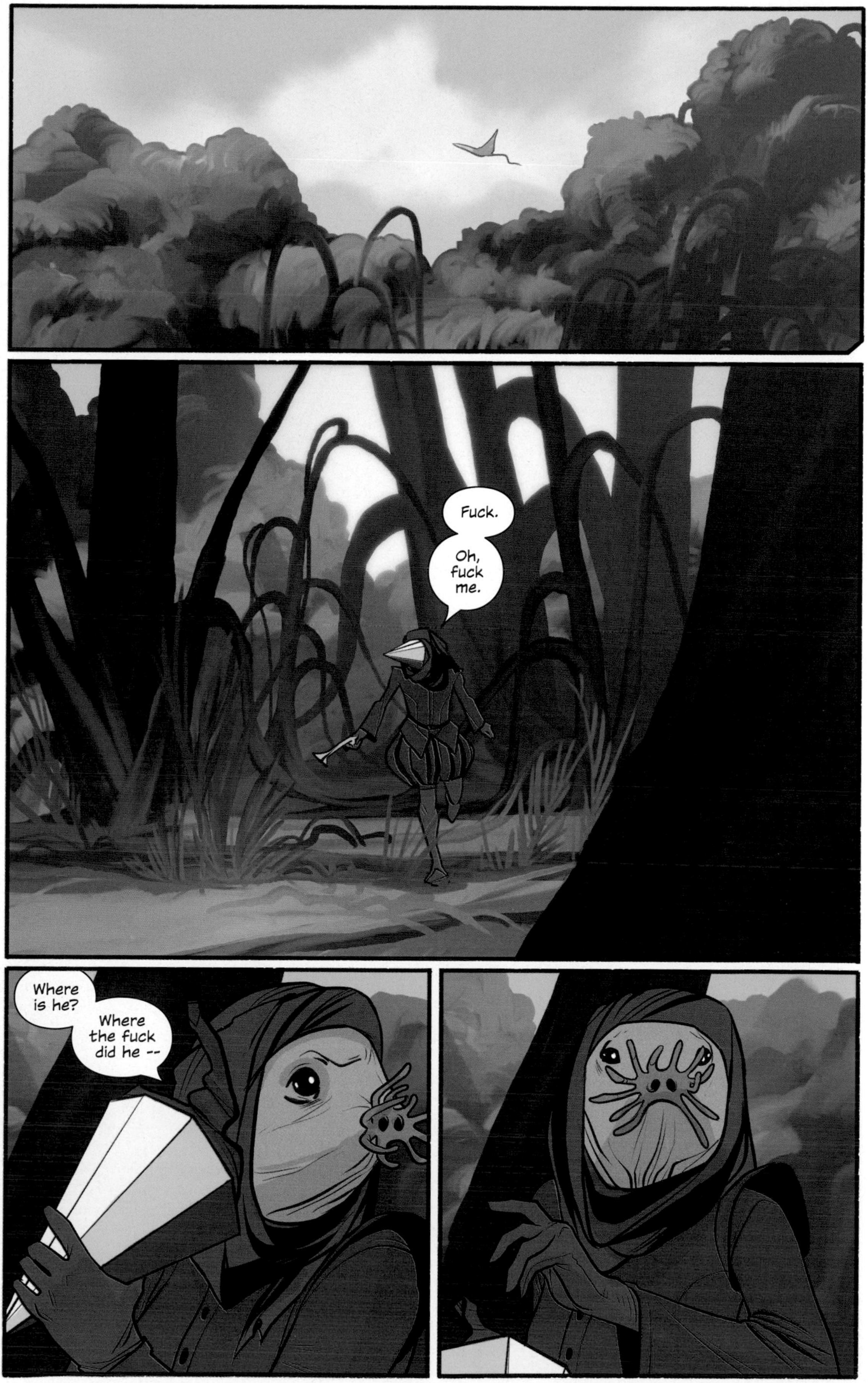
Fuck.
Oh, fuck me.
Where is he?
Where the fuck did he --

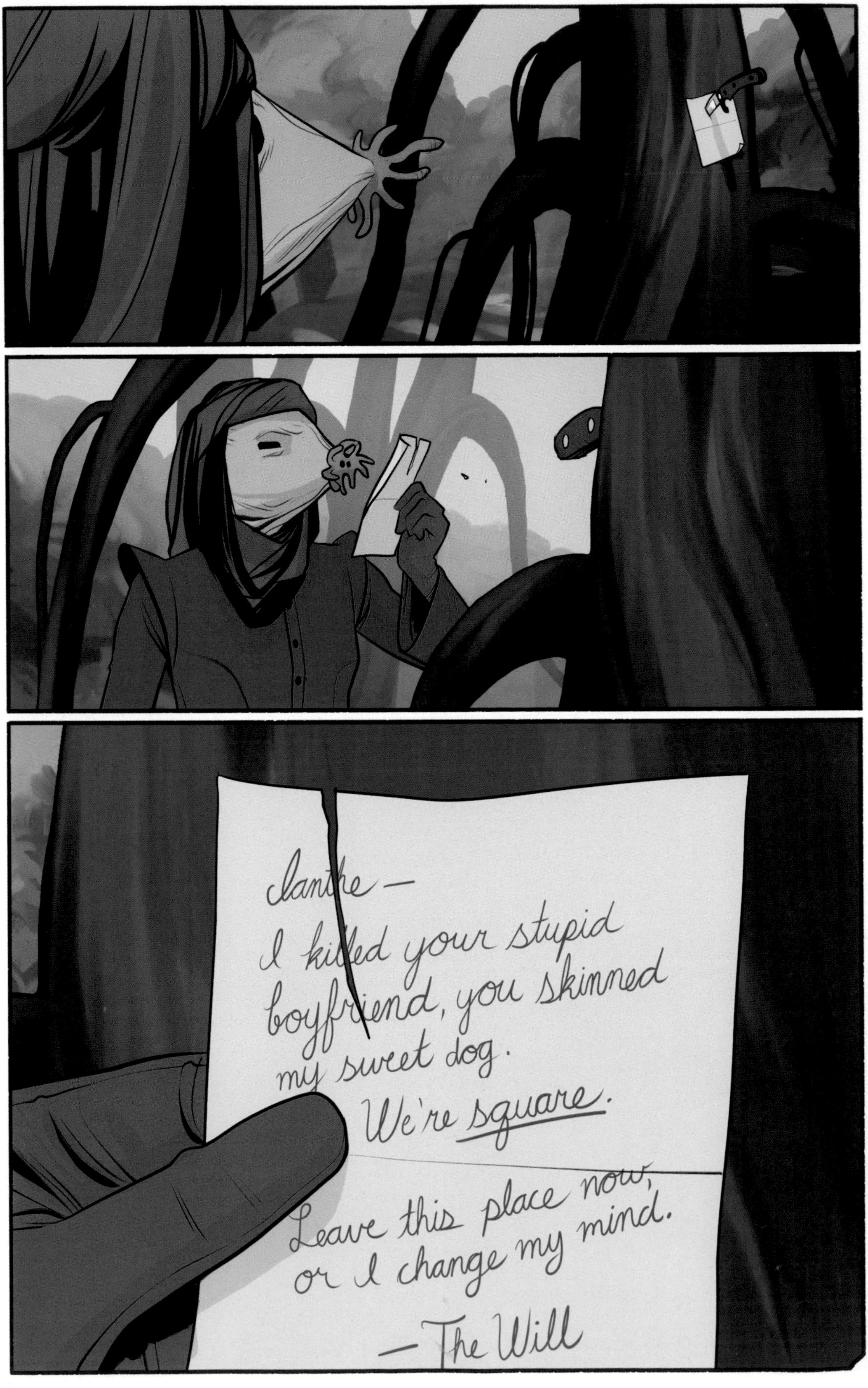

Ianthe —
I killed your stupid boyfriend, you skinned my sweet dog.
We're square.
Leave this place now, or I change my mind.
— The Will

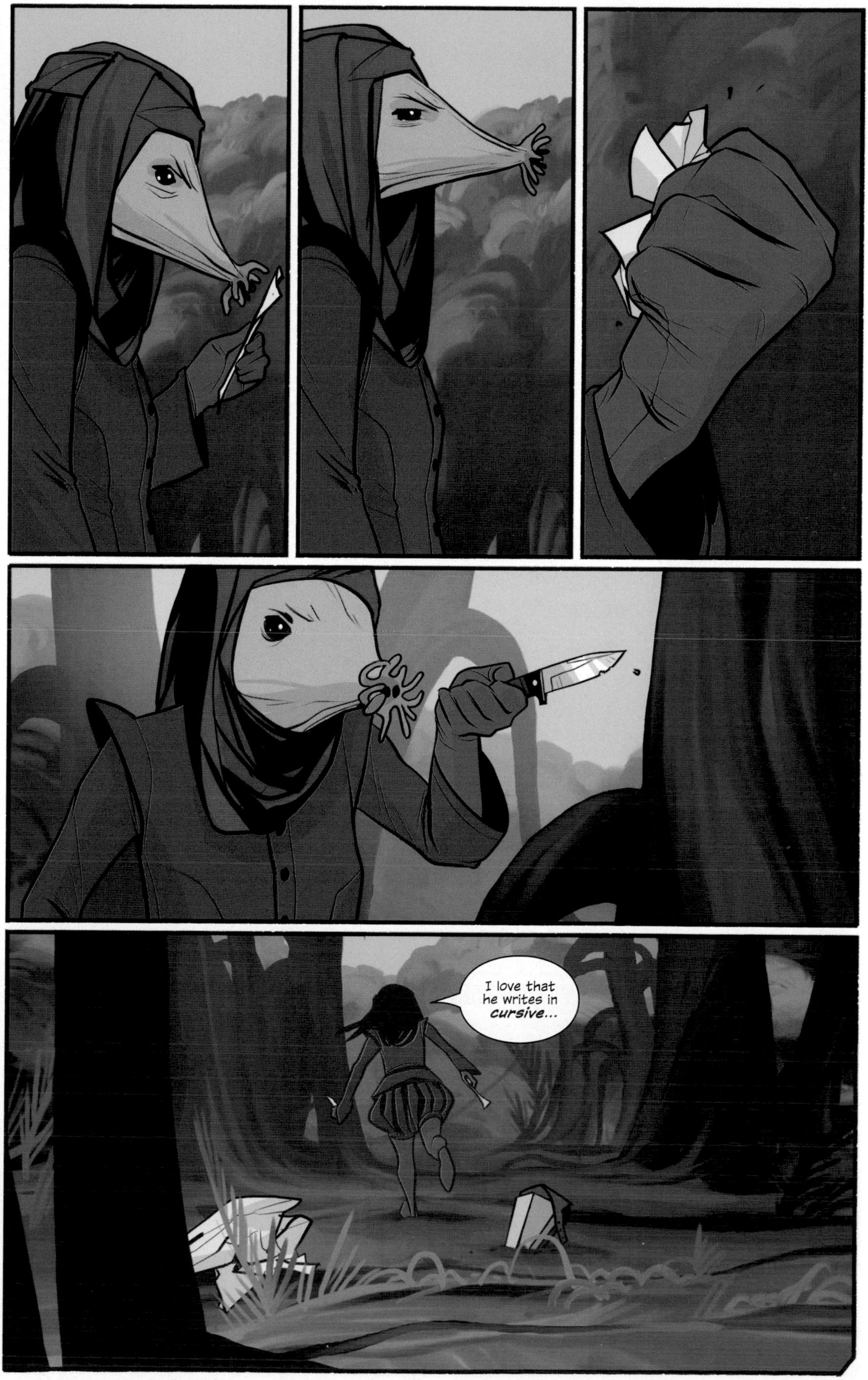
I love that he writes in *cursive*...

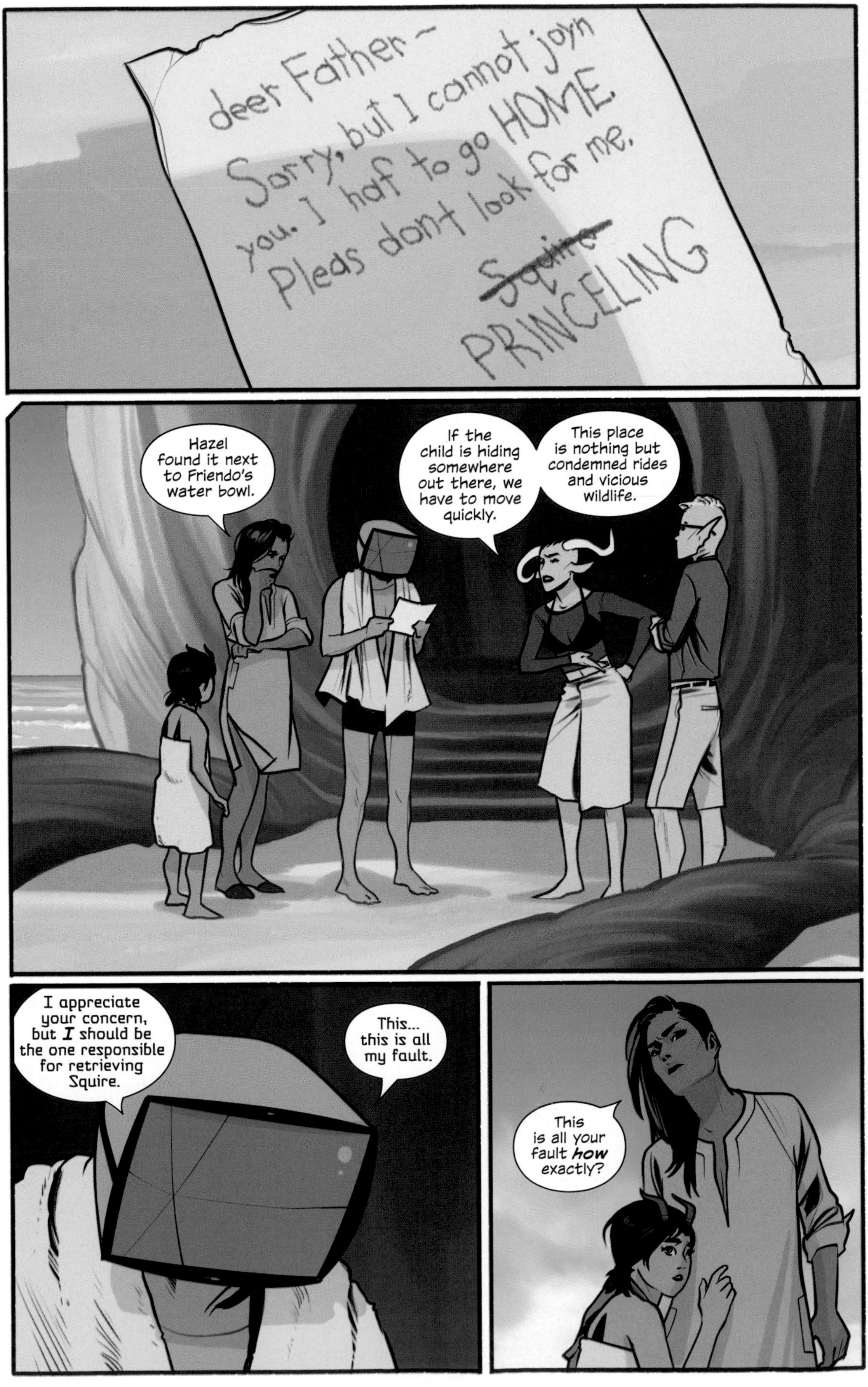
deer Father -
Sorry, but I cannot joyn you. I haf to go HOME. Pleas dont look for me.
~~Squire~~ PRINCELING
Hazel found it next to Friendo's water bowl.
If the child is hiding somewhere out there, we have to move quickly.
This place is nothing but condemned rides and vicious wildlife.
I appreciate your concern, but *I* should be the one responsible for retrieving Squire.
This... this is all my fault.
This is all your fault ***how*** exactly?

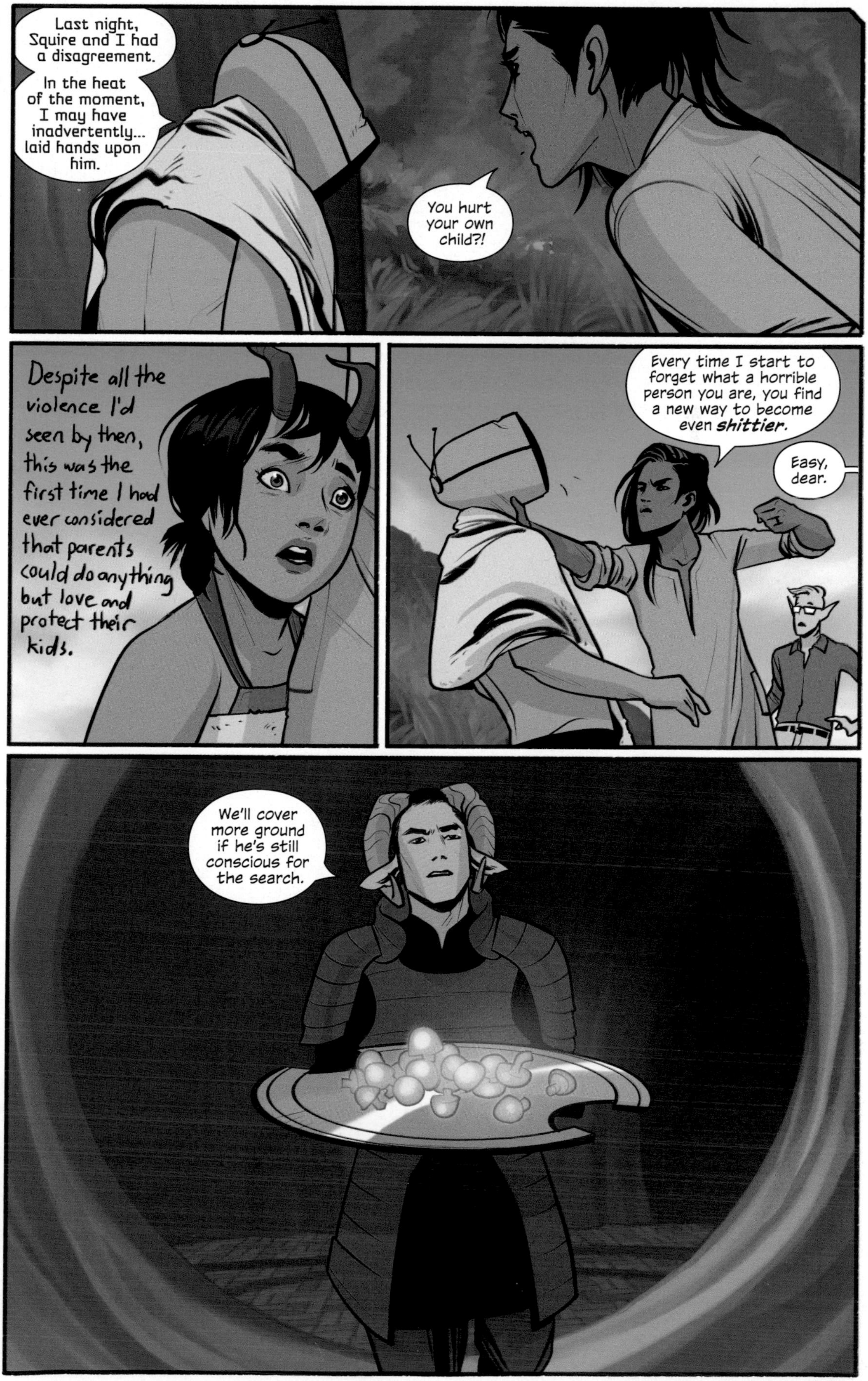
Last night, Squire and I had a disagreement.
In the heat of the moment, I may have inadvertently... laid hands upon him.
You hurt your own child?!
Despite all the violence I'd seen by then, this was the first time I had ever considered that parents could do anything but love and protect their kids.
Every time I start to forget what a horrible person you are, you find a new way to become even **shittier**.
Easy, dear.
We'll cover more ground if he's still conscious for the search.

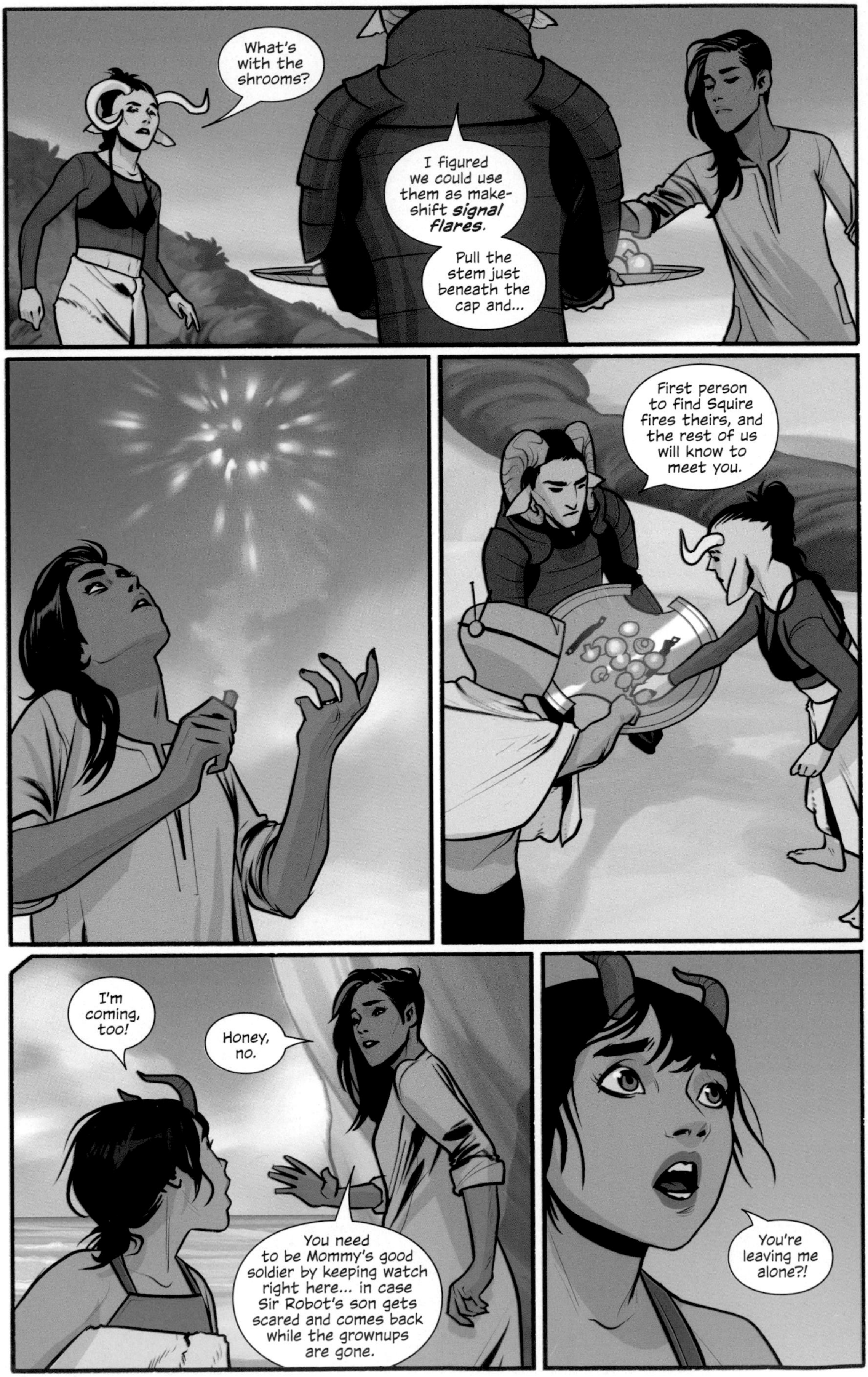
What's with the shrooms?
I figured we could use them as make-shift ***signal flares***.
Pull the stem just beneath the cap and...
First person to find Squire fires theirs, and the rest of us will know to meet you.
I'm coming, too!
Honey, no.
You need to be Mommy's good soldier by keeping watch right here... in case Sir Robot's son gets scared and comes back while the grownups are gone.
You're leaving me alone?!

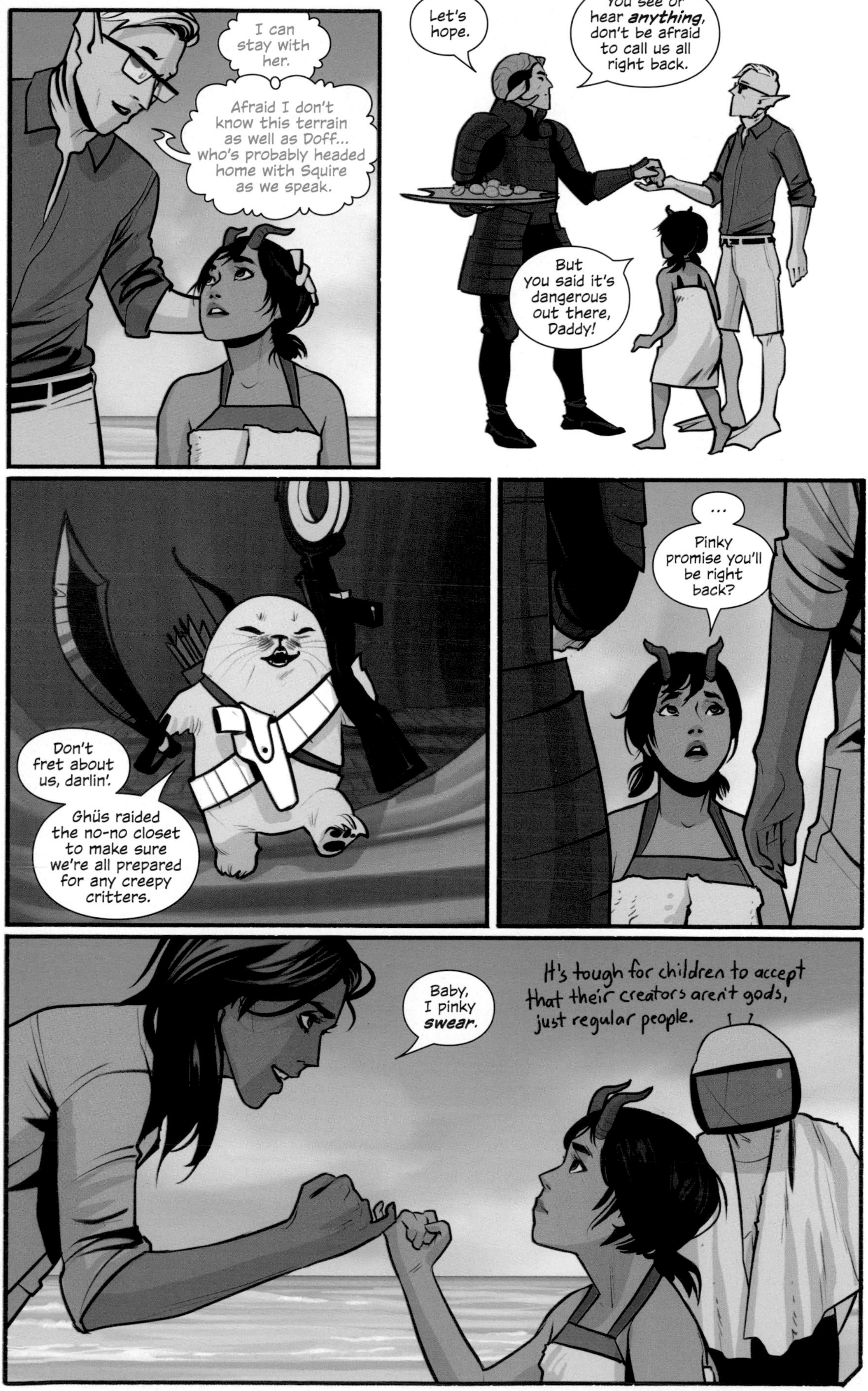

I can stay with her.
Afraid I don't know this terrain as well as Doff... who's probably headed home with Squire as we speak.
Let's hope.
You see or hear ***anything***, don't be afraid to call us all right back.
But you said it's dangerous out there, Daddy!
Don't fret about us, darlin'.
Ghüs raided the no-no closet to make sure we're all prepared for any creepy critters.
...
Pinky promise you'll be right back?
Baby, I pinky ***swear***.
It's tough for children to accept that their creators aren't gods, just regular people.

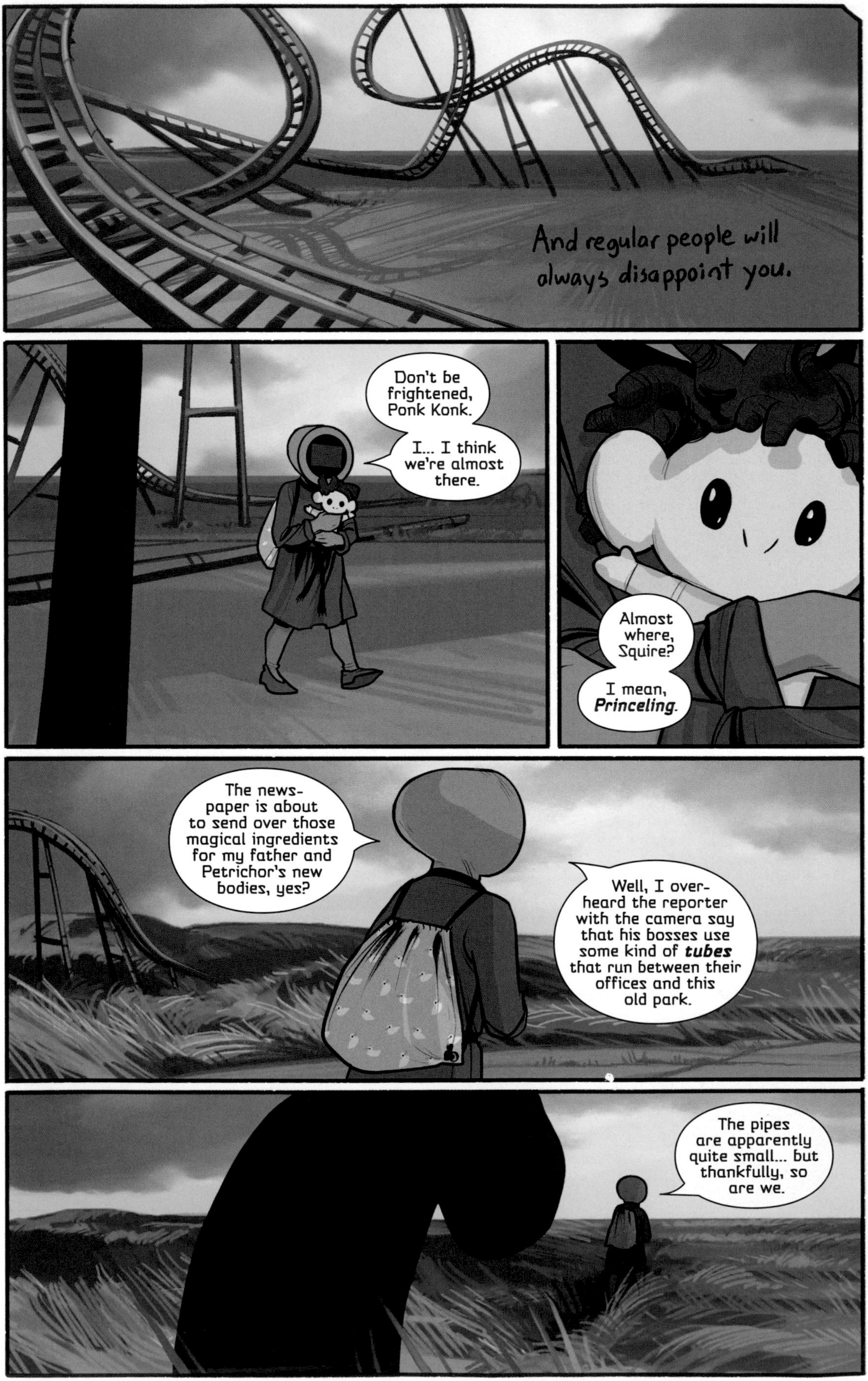
And regular people will always disappoint you.
Don't be frightened, Ponk Konk.
I... I think we're almost there.
Almost where, Squire?
I mean, ***Princeling***.
The news-paper is about to send over those magical ingredients for my father and Petrichor's new bodies, yes?
Well, I over-heard the reporter with the camera say that his bosses use some kind of ***tubes*** that run between their offices and this old park.
The pipes are apparently quite small... but thankfully, so are we.

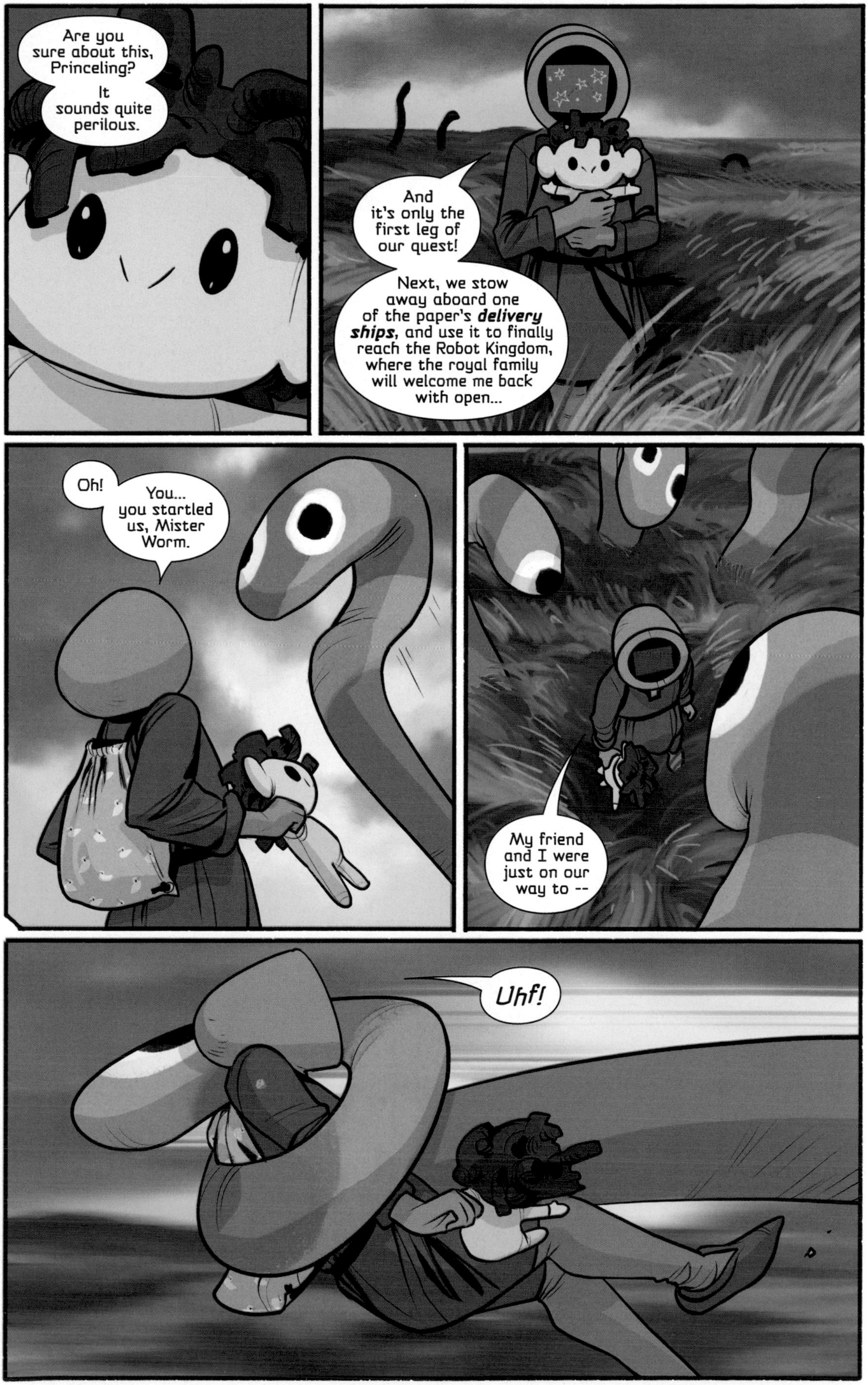
Are you sure about this, Princeling?
It sounds quite perilous.
And it's only the first leg of our quest!
Next, we stow away aboard one of the paper's ***delivery ships***, and use it to finally reach the Robot Kingdom, where the royal family will welcome me back with open...
Oh!
You... you startled us, Mister Worm.
My friend and I were just on our way to --
Uhf!

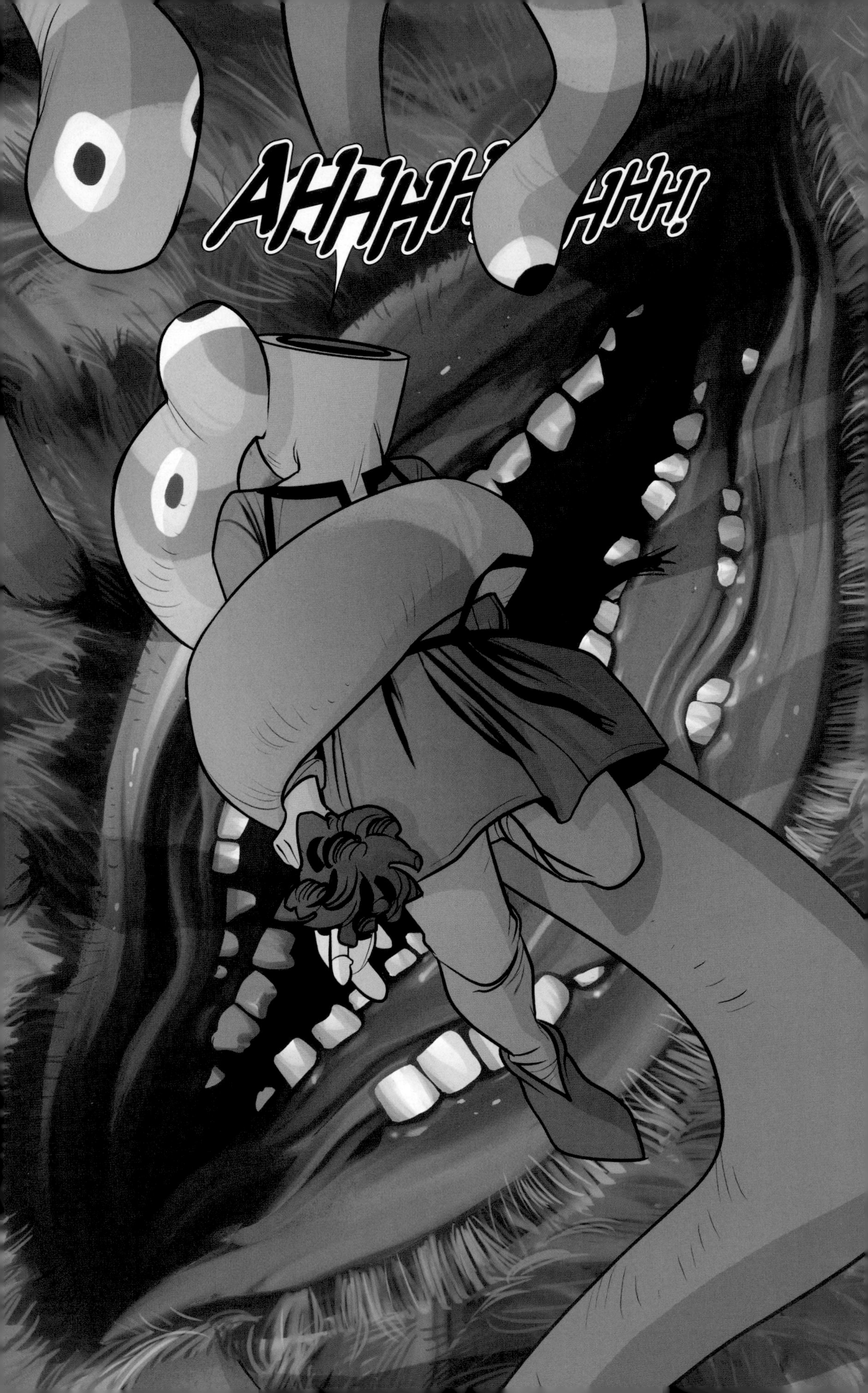
AHHHH HHH!

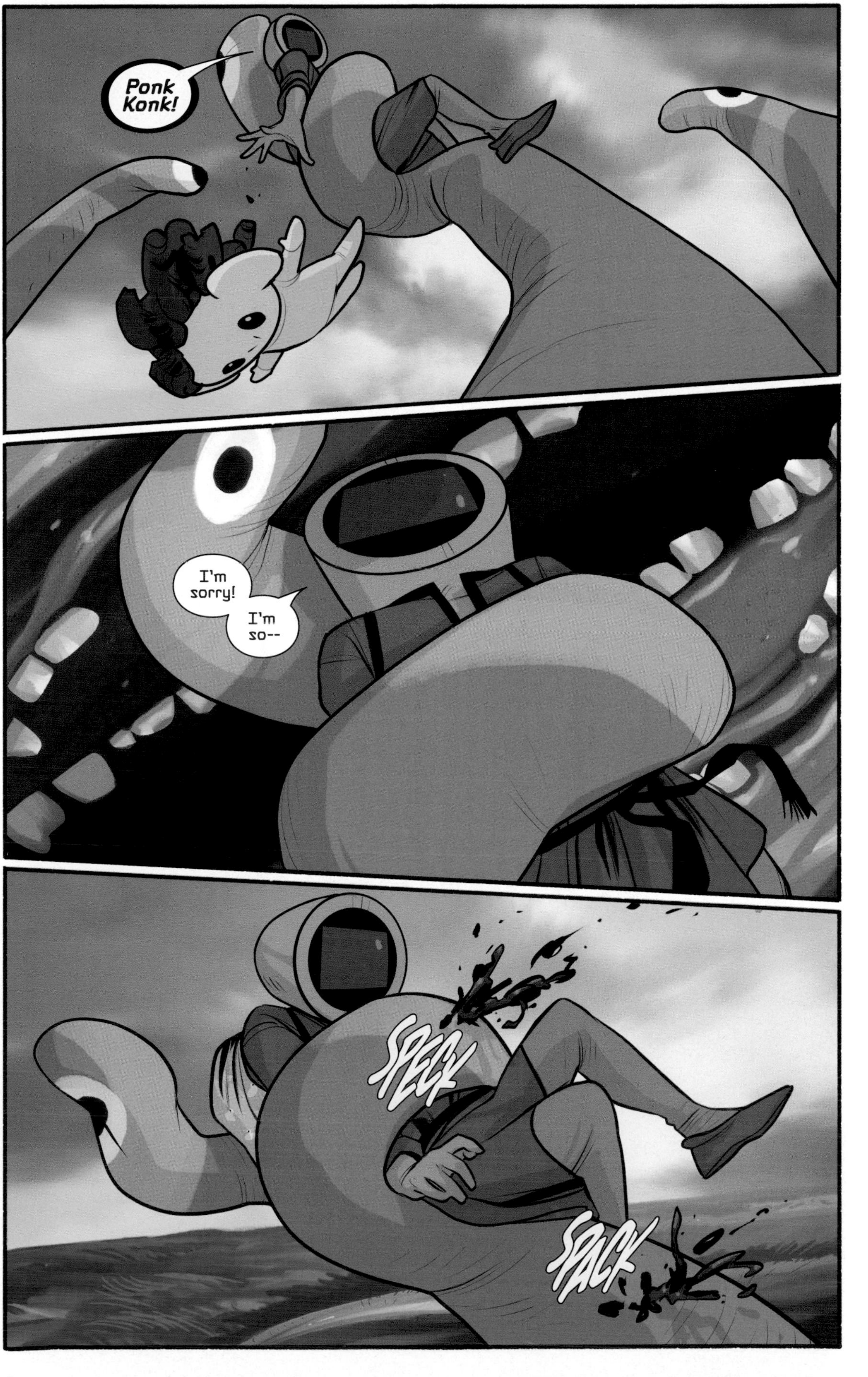
Ponk Konk!
I'm sorry!
I'm so--
SPECK
SPACK

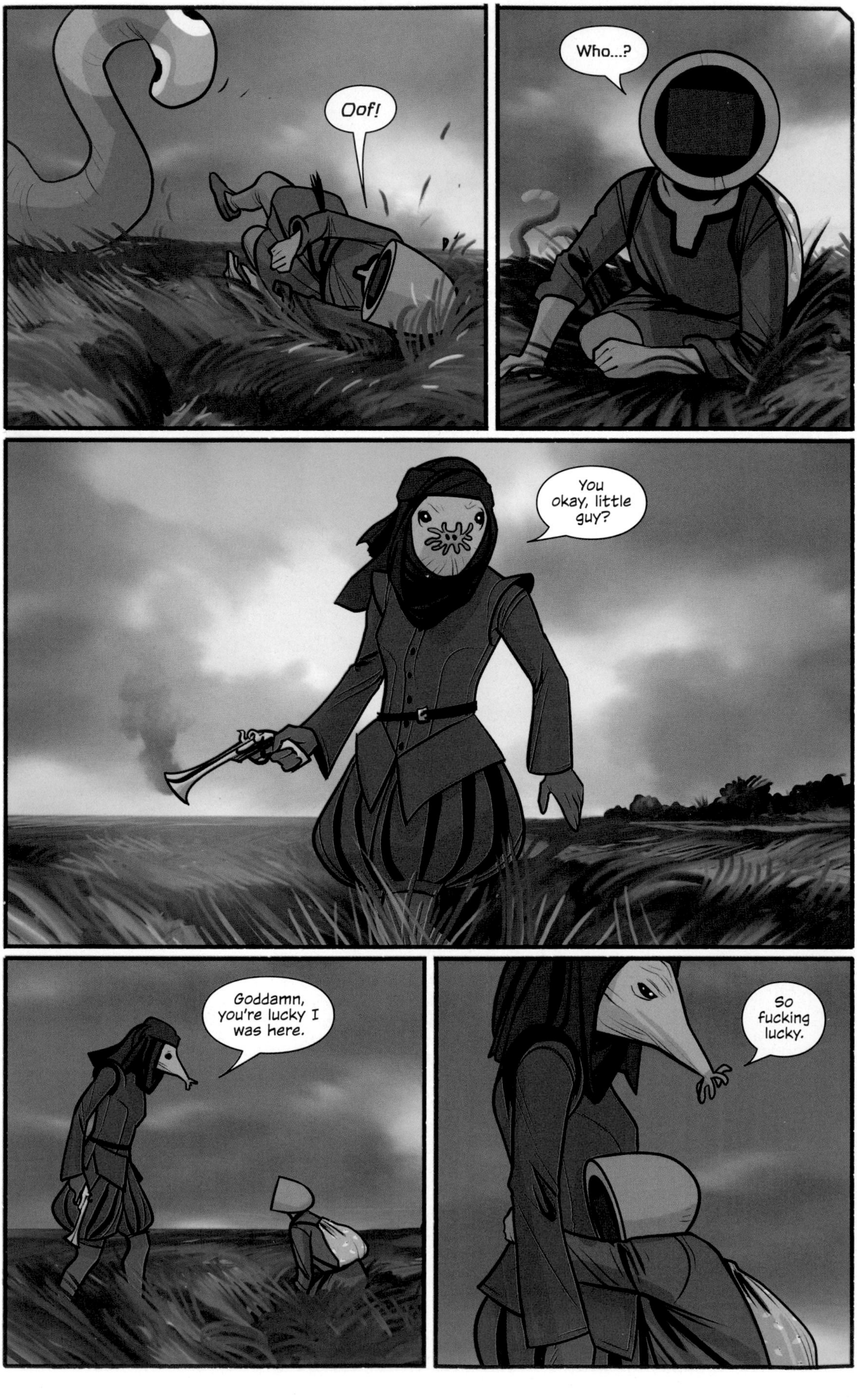
Oof!
Who...?
You okay, little guy?
Goddamn, you're lucky I was here.
So fucking lucky.

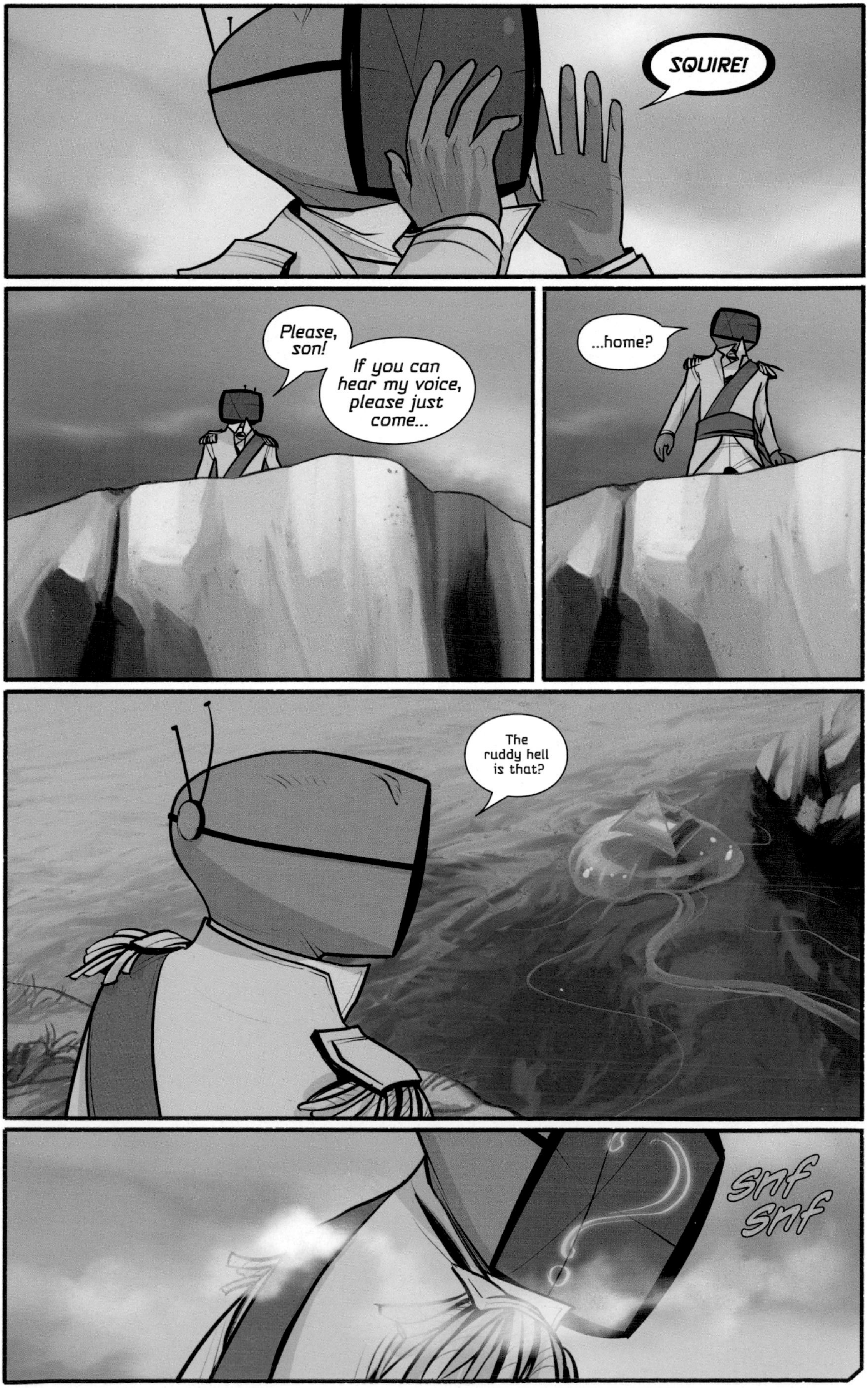
SQUIRE!
Please, son!
If you can hear my voice, please just come...
...home?
The ruddy hell is that?
snf snf

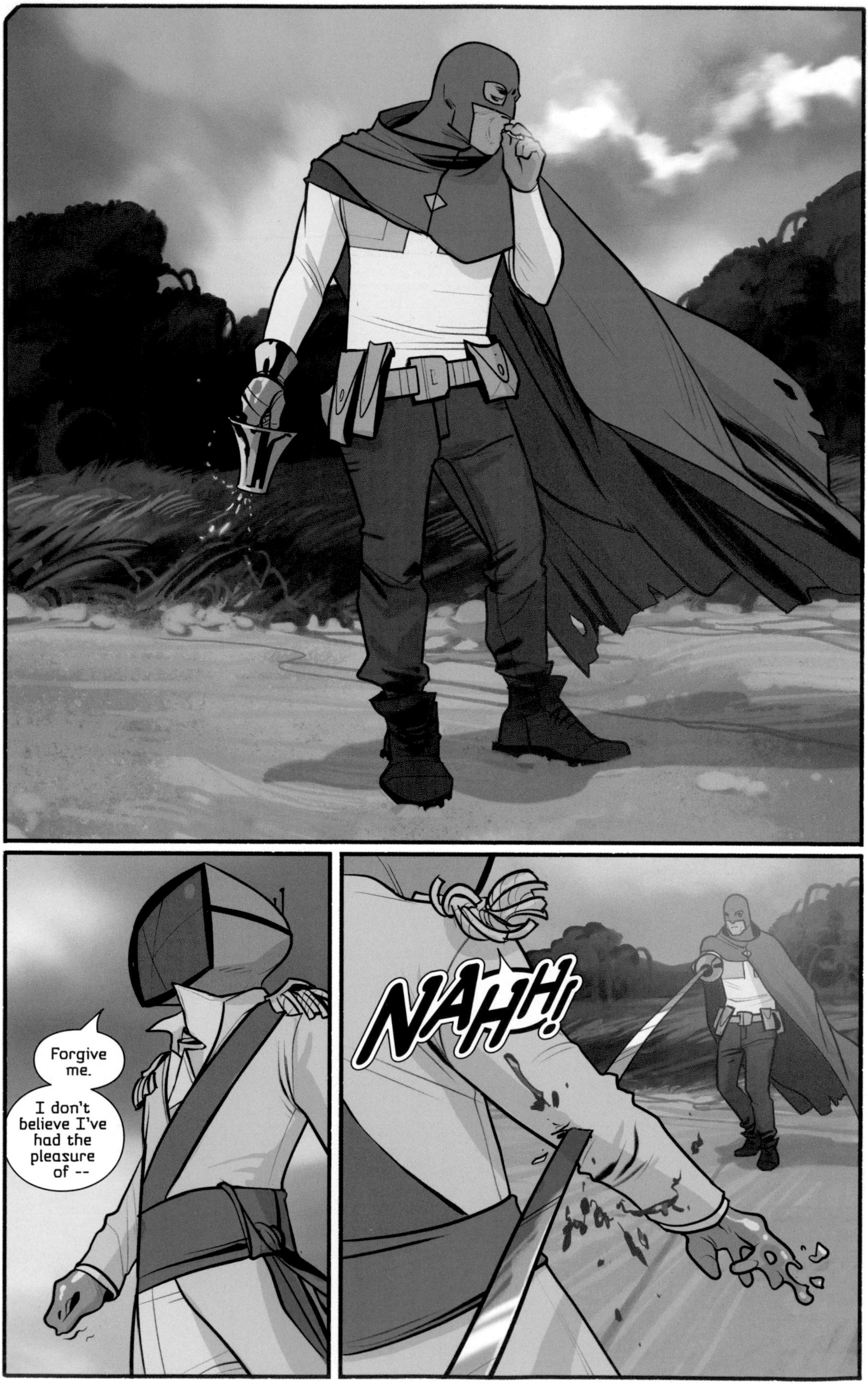
Forgive me.
I don't believe I've had the pleasure of --
NAHH!

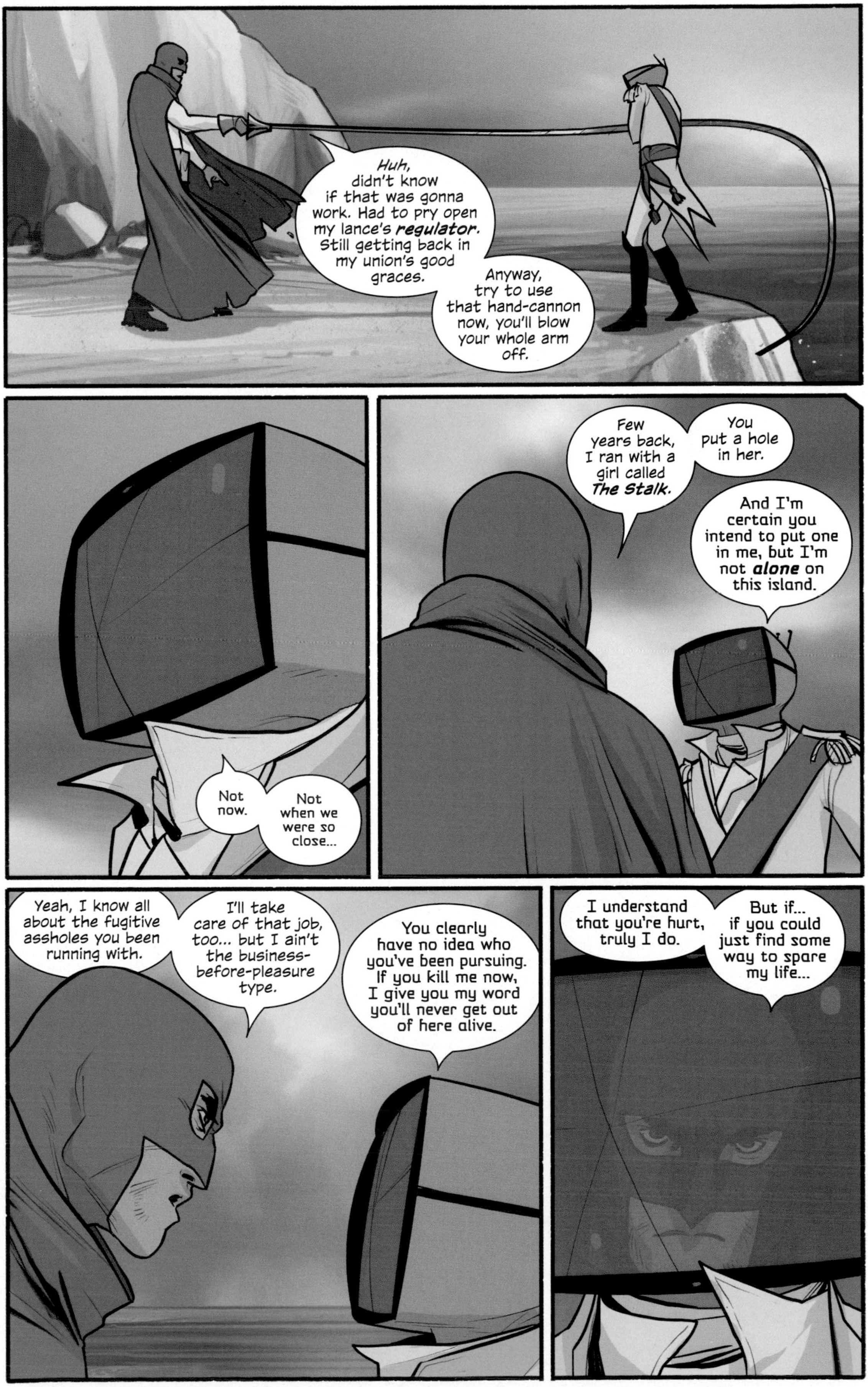
Huh, didn't know if that was gonna work. Had to pry open my lance's ***regulator***. Still getting back in my union's good graces.
Anyway, try to use that hand-cannon now, you'll blow your whole arm off.
Not now.
Not when we were so close...
Few years back, I ran with a girl called ***The Stalk***.
You put a hole in her.
And I'm certain you intend to put one in me, but I'm not ***alone*** on this island.
Yeah, I know all about the fugitive assholes you been running with.
I'll take care of that job, too... but I ain't the business-before-pleasure type.
You clearly have no idea who you've been pursuing. If you kill me now, I give you my word you'll never get out of here alive.
I understand that you're hurt, truly I do.
But if... if you could just find some way to spare my life...

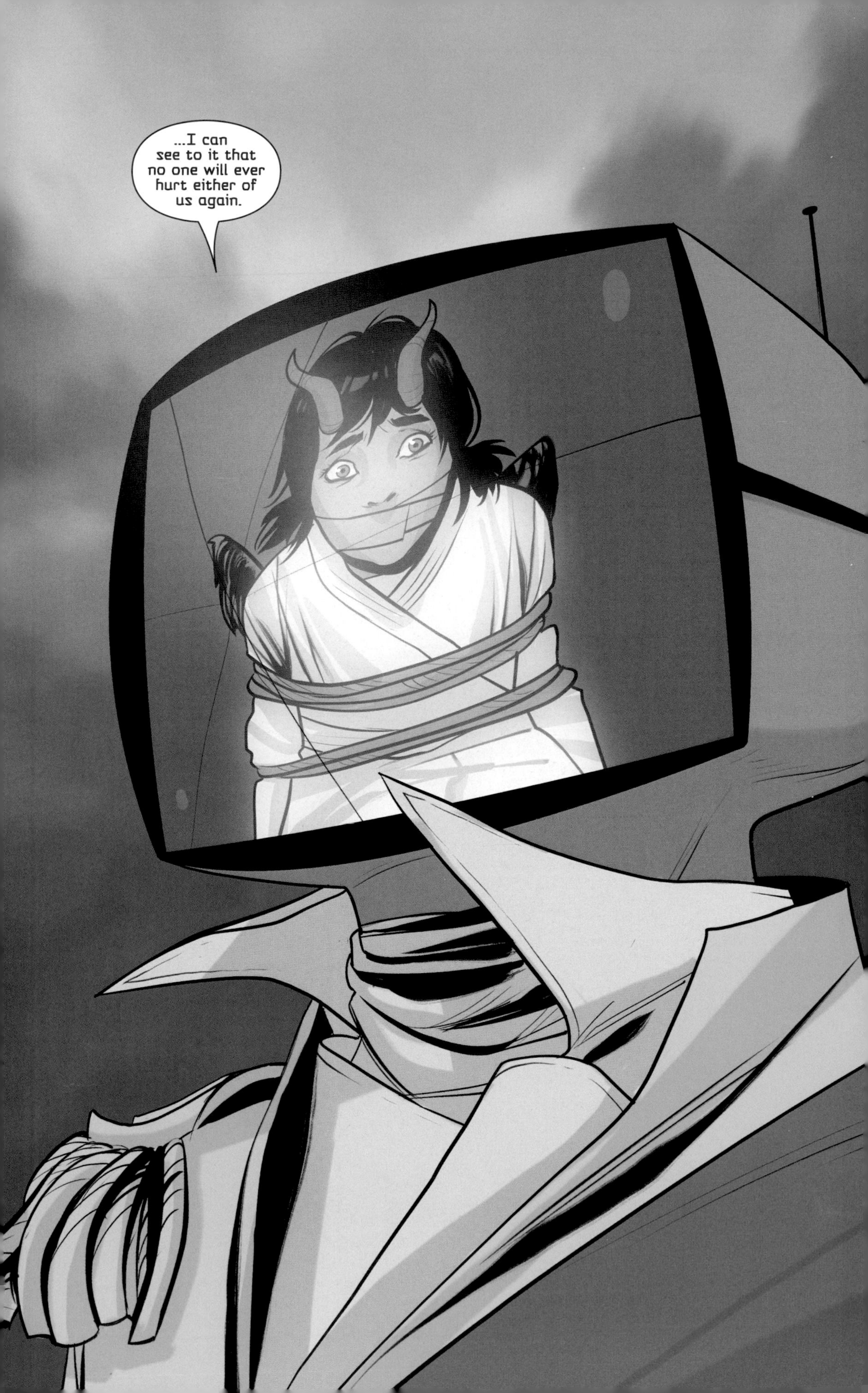
...I can see to it that no one will ever hurt either of us again.

end chapter fifty-two

CHAPTER
FIFTY-THREE

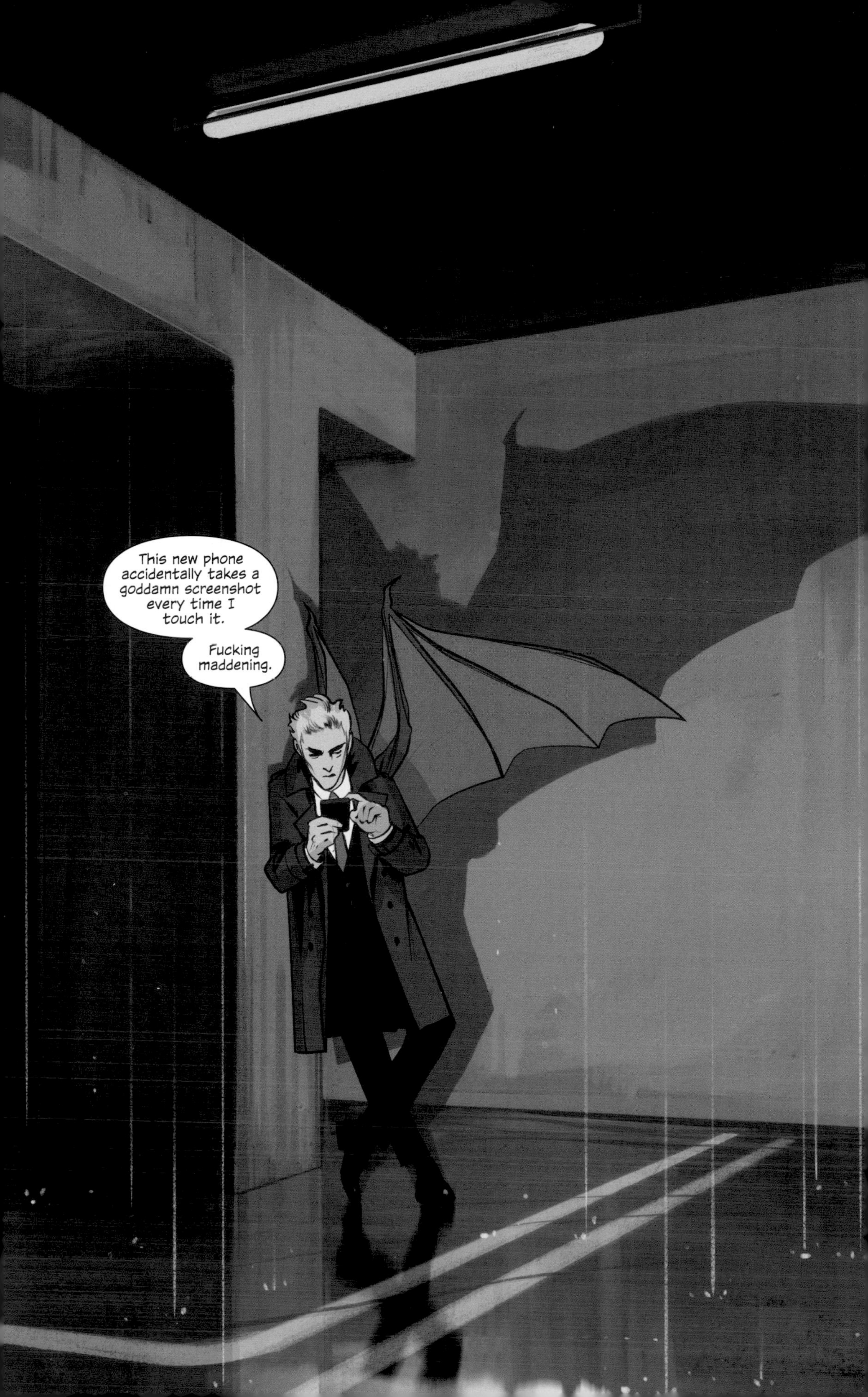
This new phone accidentally takes a goddamn screenshot every time I touch it.
Fucking maddening.

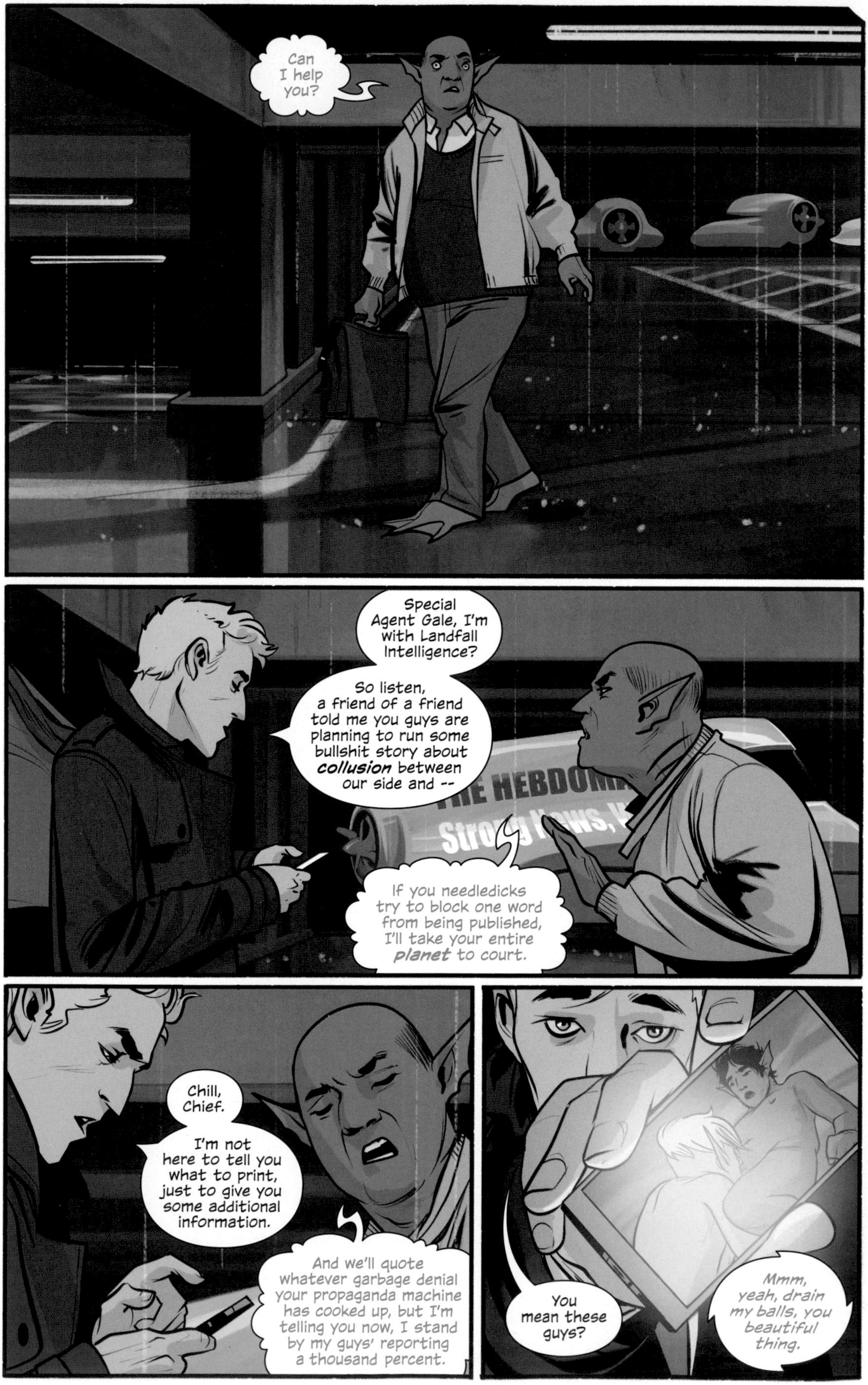

Can I help you?
Special Agent Gale, I'm with Landfall Intelligence?
So listen, a friend of a friend told me you guys are planning to run some bullshit story about *collusion* between our side and --
If you needledicks try to block one word from being published, I'll take your entire *planet* to court.
Chill, Chief.
I'm not here to tell you what to print, just to give you some additional information.
And we'll quote whatever garbage denial your propaganda machine has cooked up, but I'm telling you now, I stand by my guys' reporting a thousand percent.
You mean these guys?
Mmm, yeah, drain my balls, you beautiful thing.

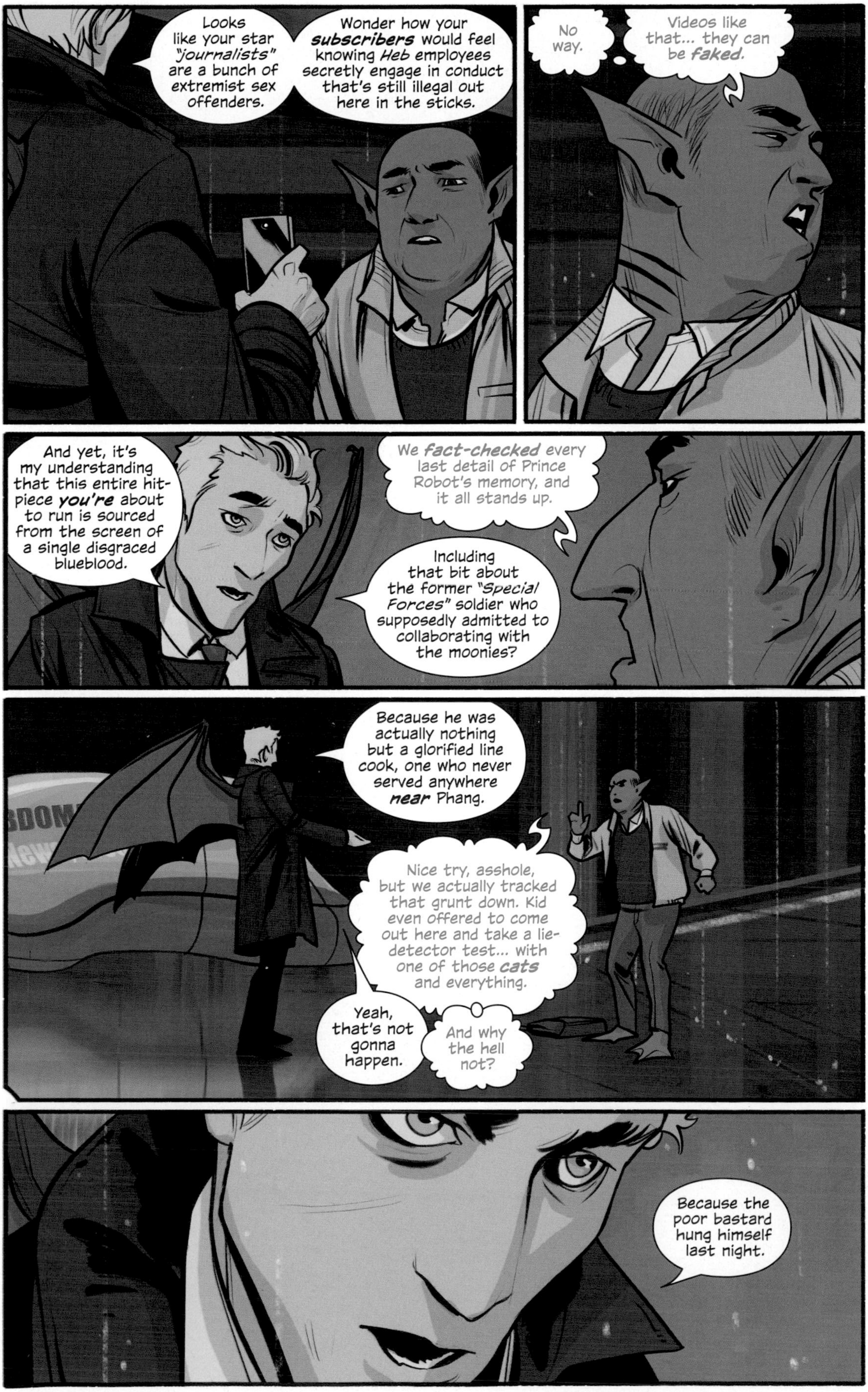
Looks like your star "journalists" are a bunch of extremist sex offenders.
Wonder how your subscribers would feel knowing Heb employees secretly engage in conduct that's still illegal out here in the sticks.
No way.
Videos like that... they can be faked.
And yet, it's my understanding that this entire hit-piece you're about to run is sourced from the screen of a single disgraced blueblood.
We fact-checked every last detail of Prince Robot's memory, and it all stands up.
Including that bit about the former "Special Forces" soldier who supposedly admitted to collaborating with the moonies?
Because he was actually nothing but a glorified line cook, one who never served anywhere near Phang.
Nice try, asshole, but we actually tracked that grunt down. Kid even offered to come out here and take a lie-detector test... with one of those cats and everything.
Yeah, that's not gonna happen.
And why the hell not?
Because the poor bastard hung himself last night.

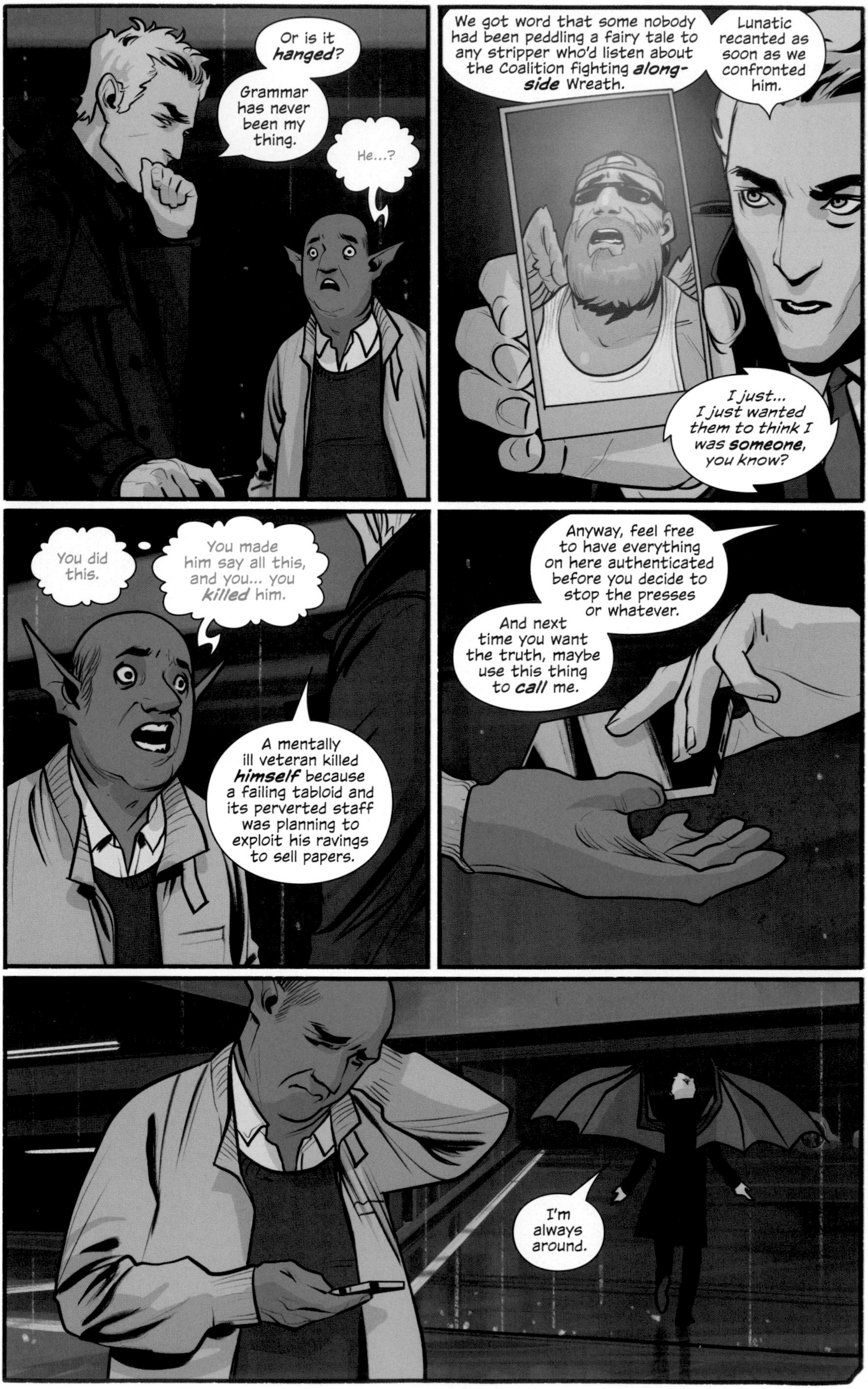
Or is it *hanged*?
Grammar has never been my thing.
He...?
We got word that some nobody had been peddling a fairy tale to any stripper who'd listen about the Coalition fighting *along-side* Wreath.
Lunatic recanted as soon as we confronted him.
I just... I just wanted them to think I was ***someone****, you know?*
You did this.
You made him say all this, and you... you *killed* him.
A mentally ill veteran killed *himself* because a failing tabloid and its perverted staff was planning to exploit his ravings to sell papers.
Anyway, feel free to have everything on here authenticated before you decide to stop the presses or whatever.
And next time you want the truth, maybe use this thing to *call* me.
I'm always around.

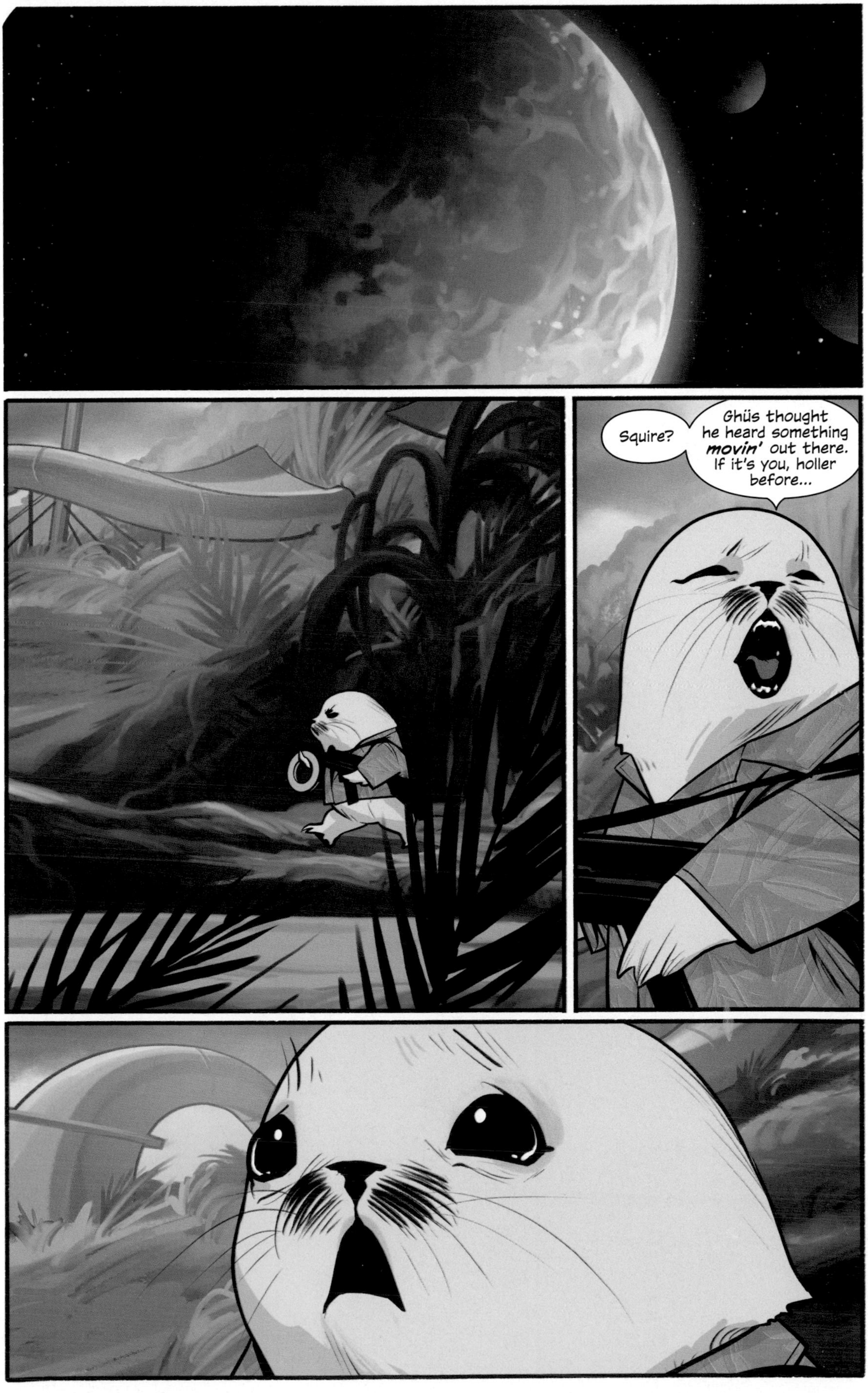
Squire?
Ghüs thought he heard something *movin'* out there. If it's you, holler before...

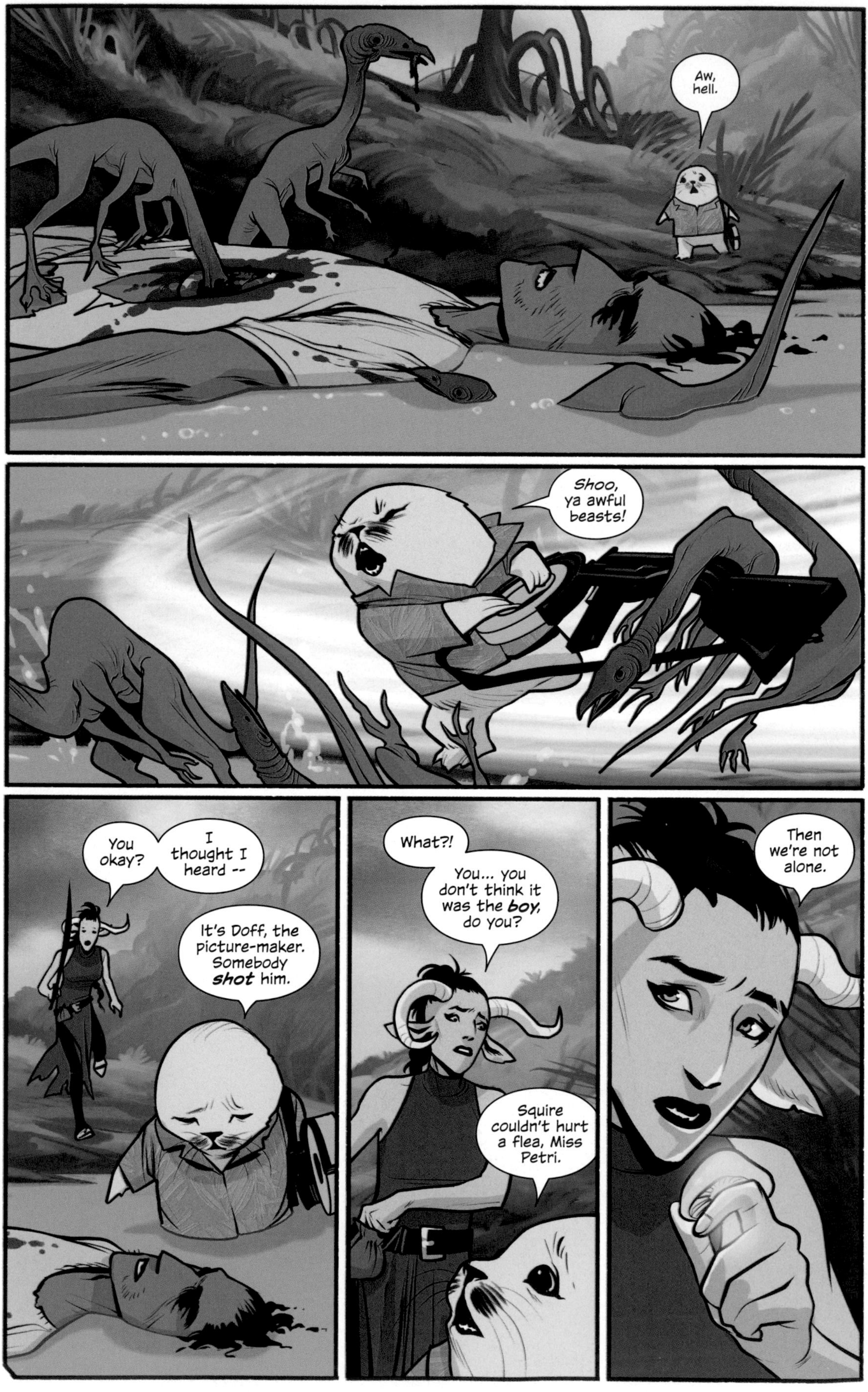
Aw, hell.
Shoo, ya awful beasts!
You okay?
I thought I heard --
It's Doff, the picture-maker. Somebody **shot** him.
What?!
You... you don't think it was the **boy**, do you?
Squire couldn't hurt a flea, Miss Petri.
Then we're not alone.

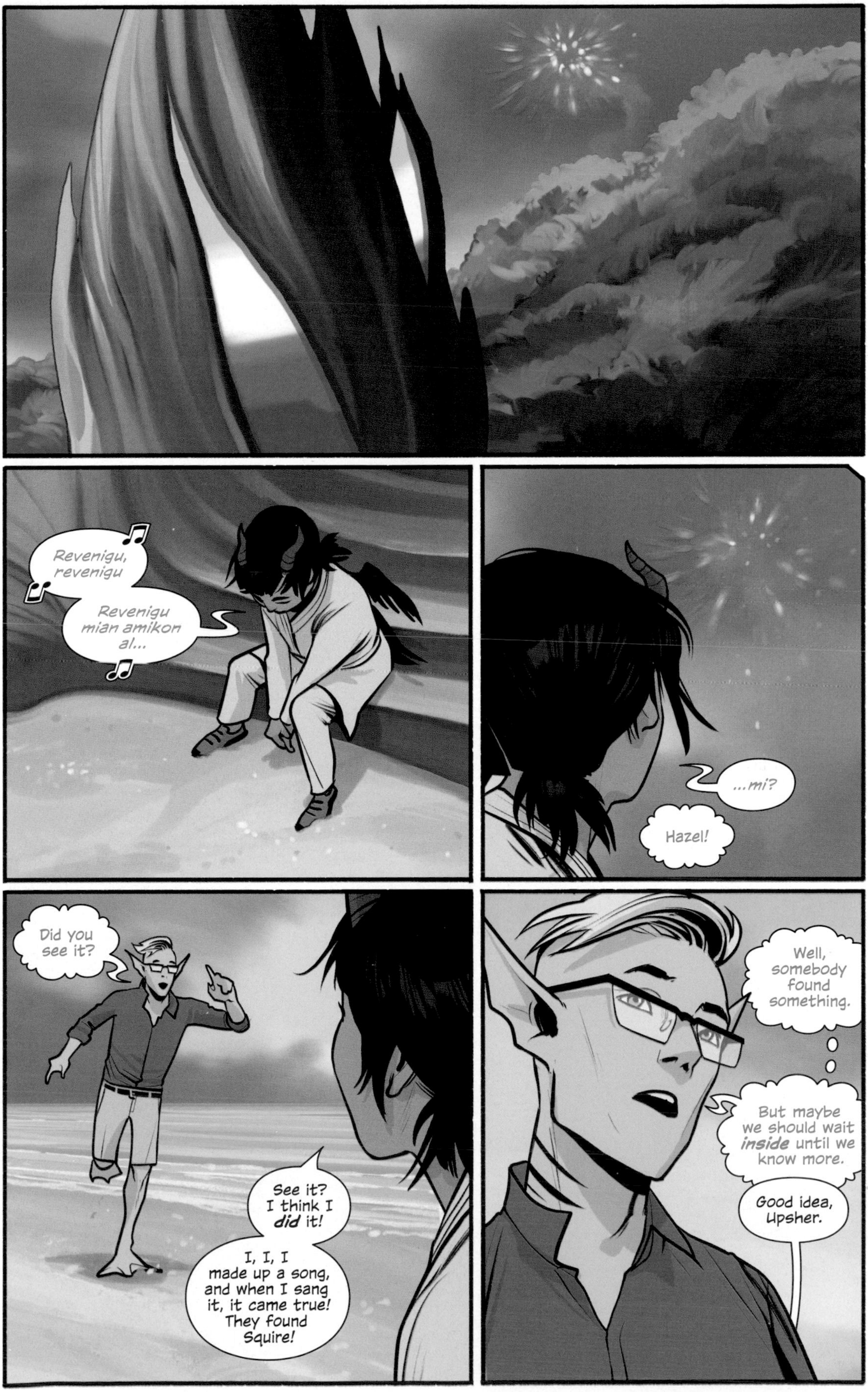
Revenigu, revenigu
Revenigu mian amikon al...
...mi?
Hazel!
Did you see it?
See it? I think I *did* it!
I, I, I made up a song, and when I sang it, it came true! They found Squire!
Well, somebody found something.
But maybe we should wait *inside* until we know more.
Good idea, Upsher.

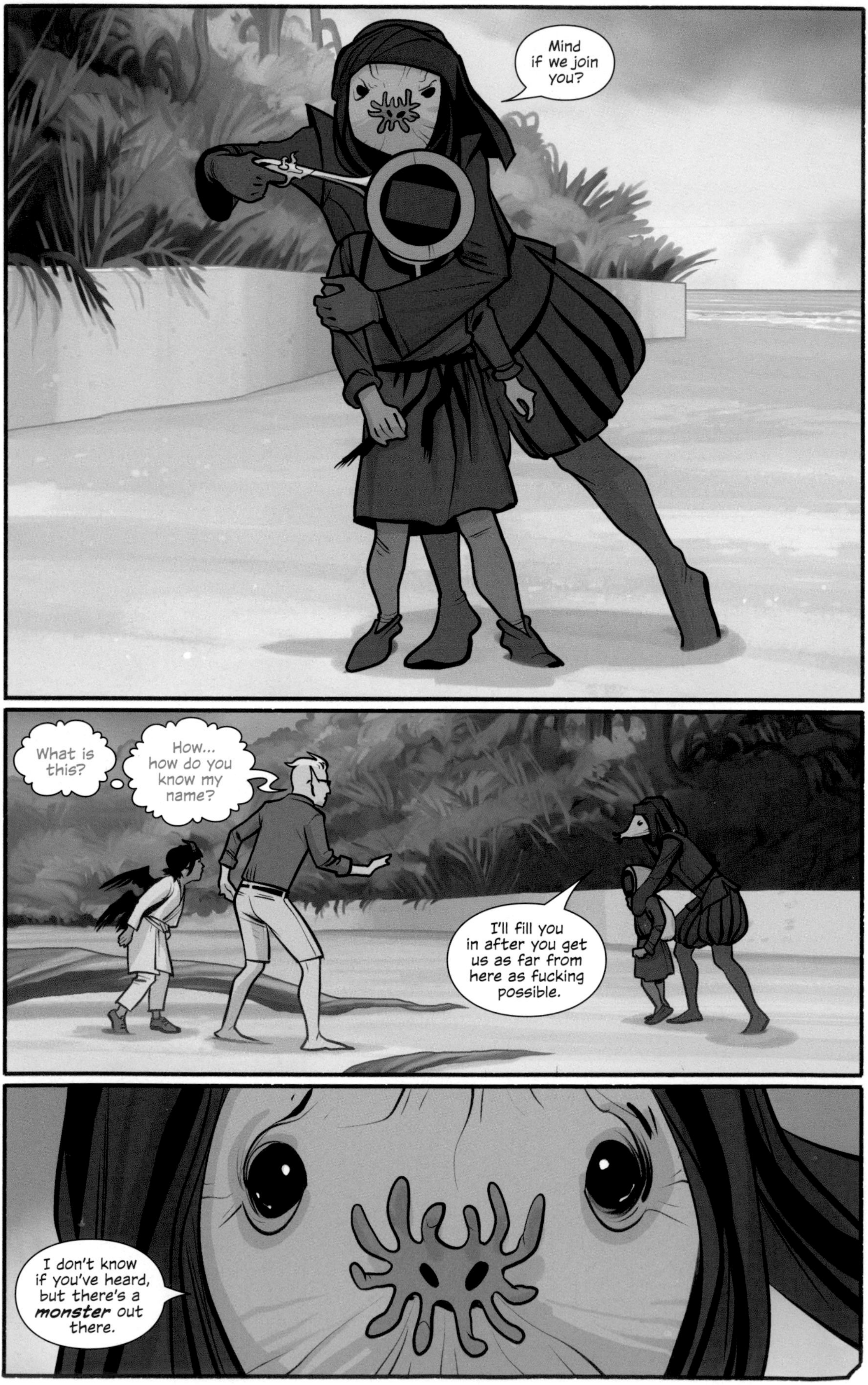
Mind if we join you?
What is this?
How... how do you know my name?
I'll fill you in after you get us as far from here as fucking possible.
I don't know if you've heard, but there's a *monster* out there.

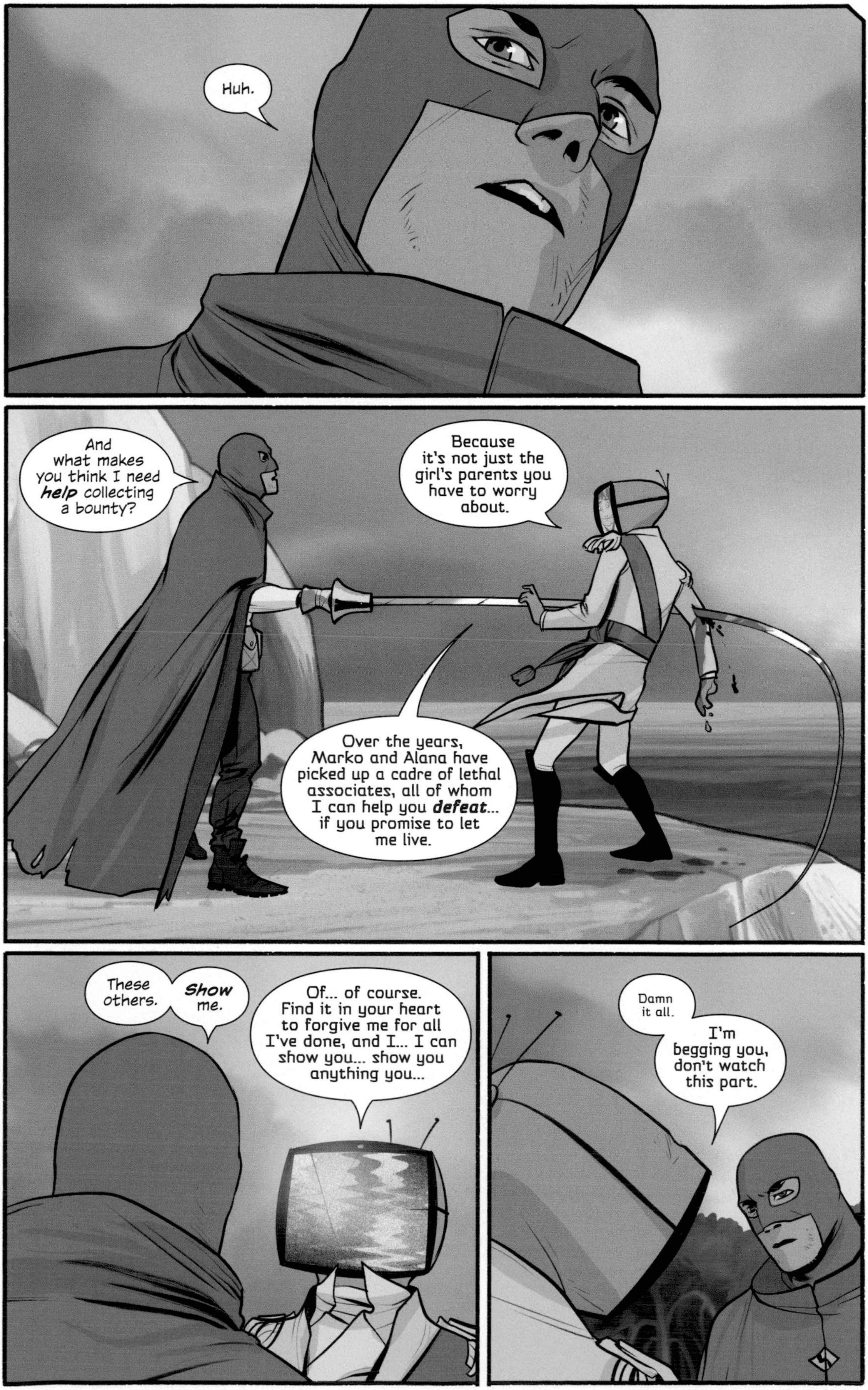
Huh.
And what makes you think I need ***help*** collecting a bounty?
Because it's not just the girl's parents you have to worry about.
Over the years, Marko and Alana have picked up a cadre of lethal associates, all of whom I can help you ***defeat***... if you promise to let me live.
These others.
Show me.
Of... of course. Find it in your heart to forgive me for all I've done, and I... I can show you... show you anything you...
Damn it all.
I'm begging you, don't watch this part.

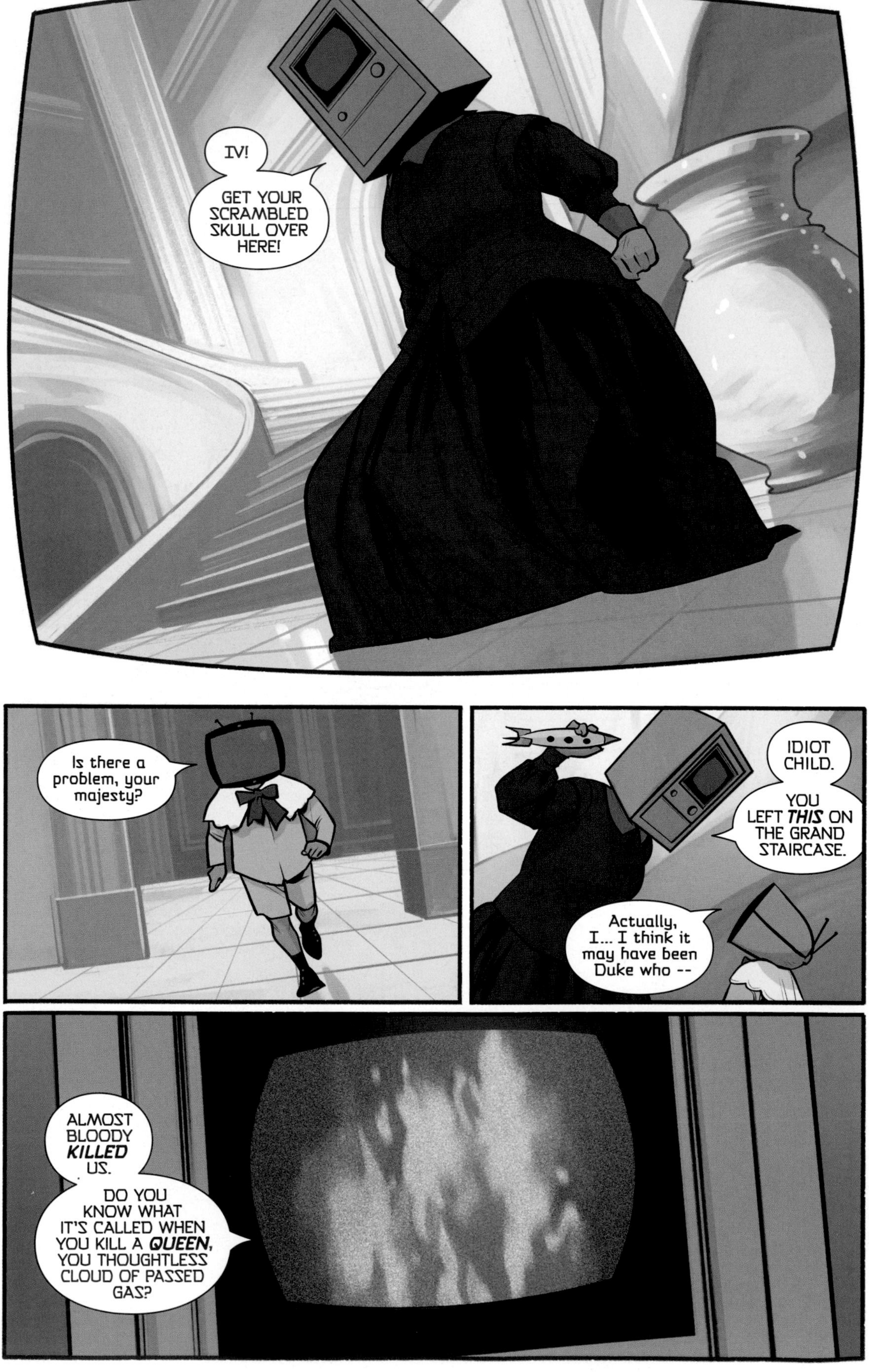
IV!
GET YOUR SCRAMBLED SKULL OVER HERE!
Is there a problem, your majesty?
IDIOT CHILD.
YOU LEFT THIS ON THE GRAND STAIRCASE.
Actually, I... I think it may have been Duke who --
ALMOST BLOODY KILLED US.
DO YOU KNOW WHAT IT'S CALLED WHEN YOU KILL A QUEEN, YOU THOUGHTLESS CLOUD OF PASSED GAS?

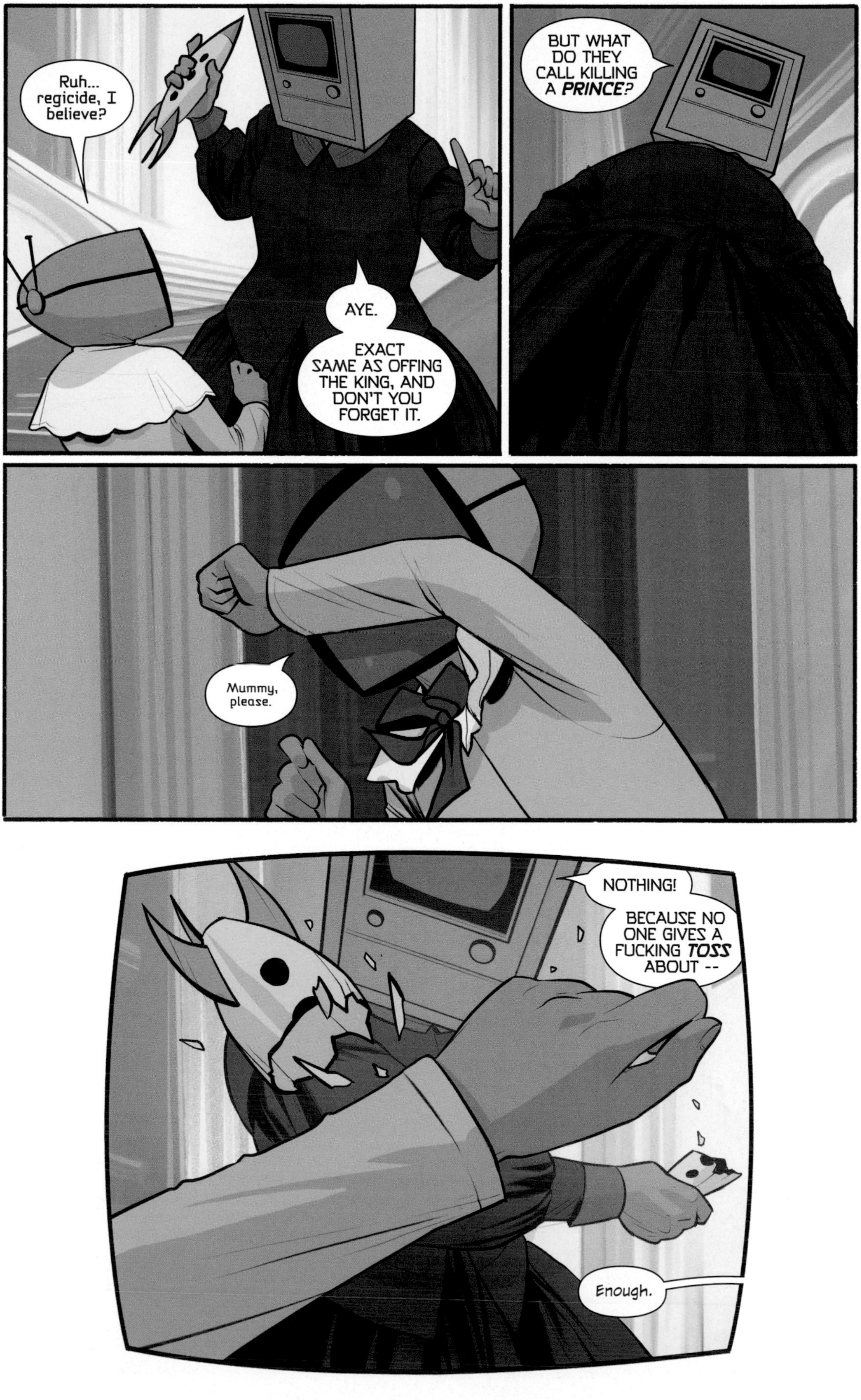
Ruh... regicide, I believe?
AYE.
EXACT SAME AS OFFING THE KING, AND DON'T YOU FORGET IT.
BUT WHAT DO THEY CALL KILLING A PRINCE?
Mummy, please.
NOTHING!
BECAUSE NO ONE GIVES A FUCKING TOSS ABOUT --
Enough.

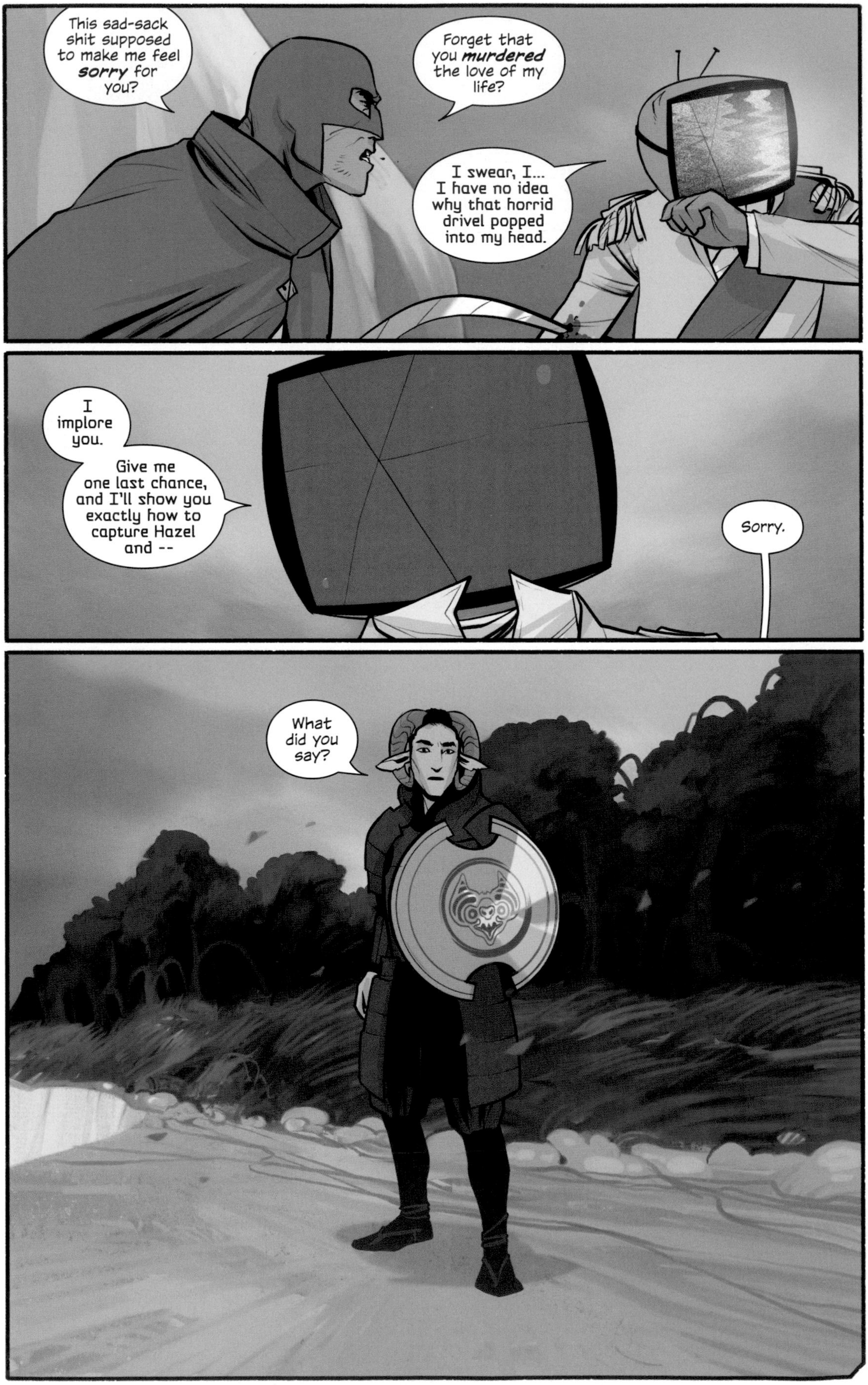
This sad-sack shit supposed to make me feel *sorry* for you?
Forget that you *murdered* the love of my life?
I swear, I... I have no idea why that horrid drivel popped into my head.
I implore you.
Give me one last chance, and I'll show you exactly how to capture Hazel and --
Sorry.
What did you say?

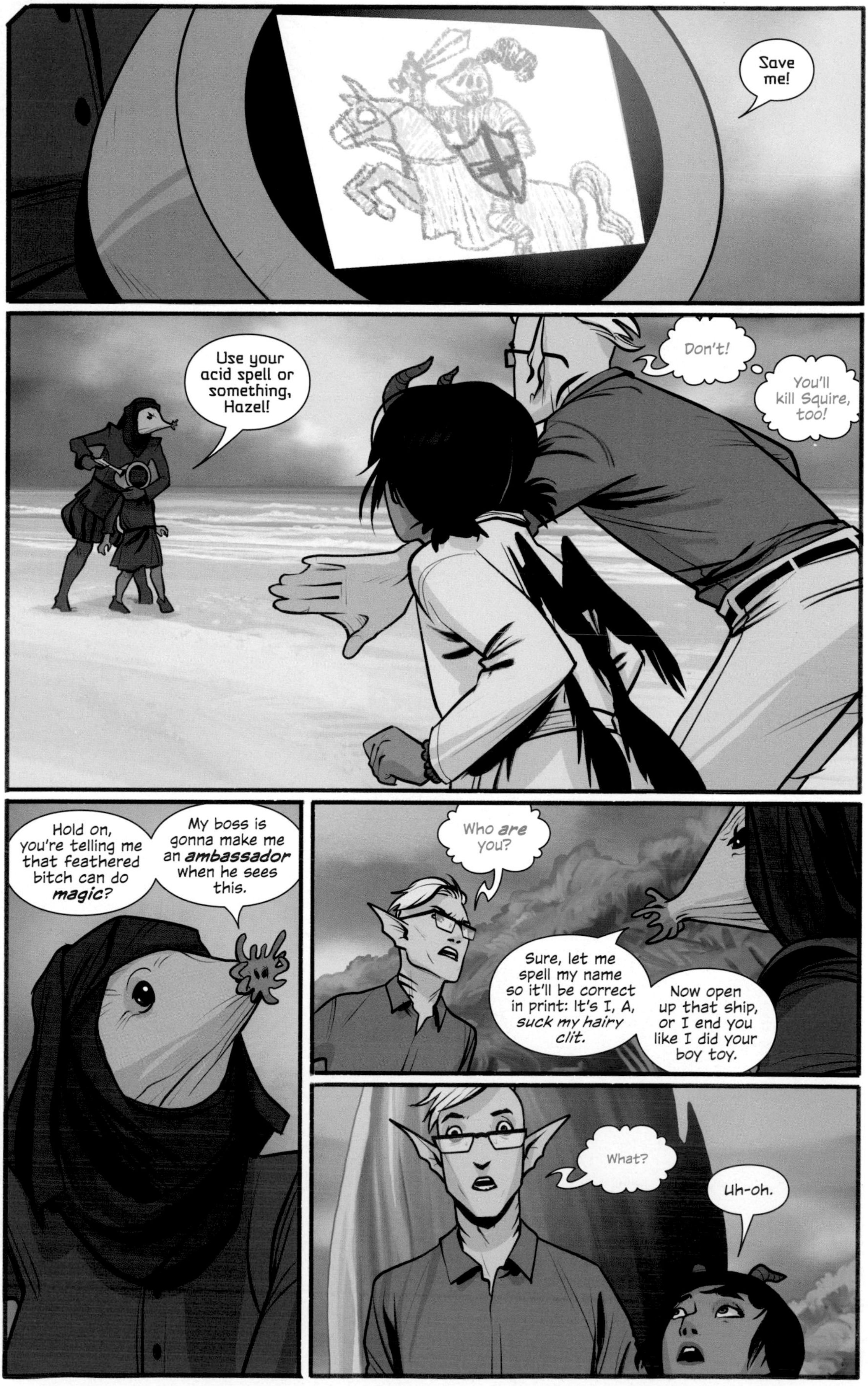
Save me!
Use your acid spell or something, Hazel!
Don't!
You'll kill Squire, too!
Hold on, you're telling me that feathered bitch can do *magic*?
My boss is gonna make me an *ambassador* when he sees this.
Who *are* you?
Sure, let me spell my name so it'll be correct in print: It's I, A, *suck my hairy clit.*
Now open up that ship, or I end you like I did your boy toy.
What?
Uh-oh.

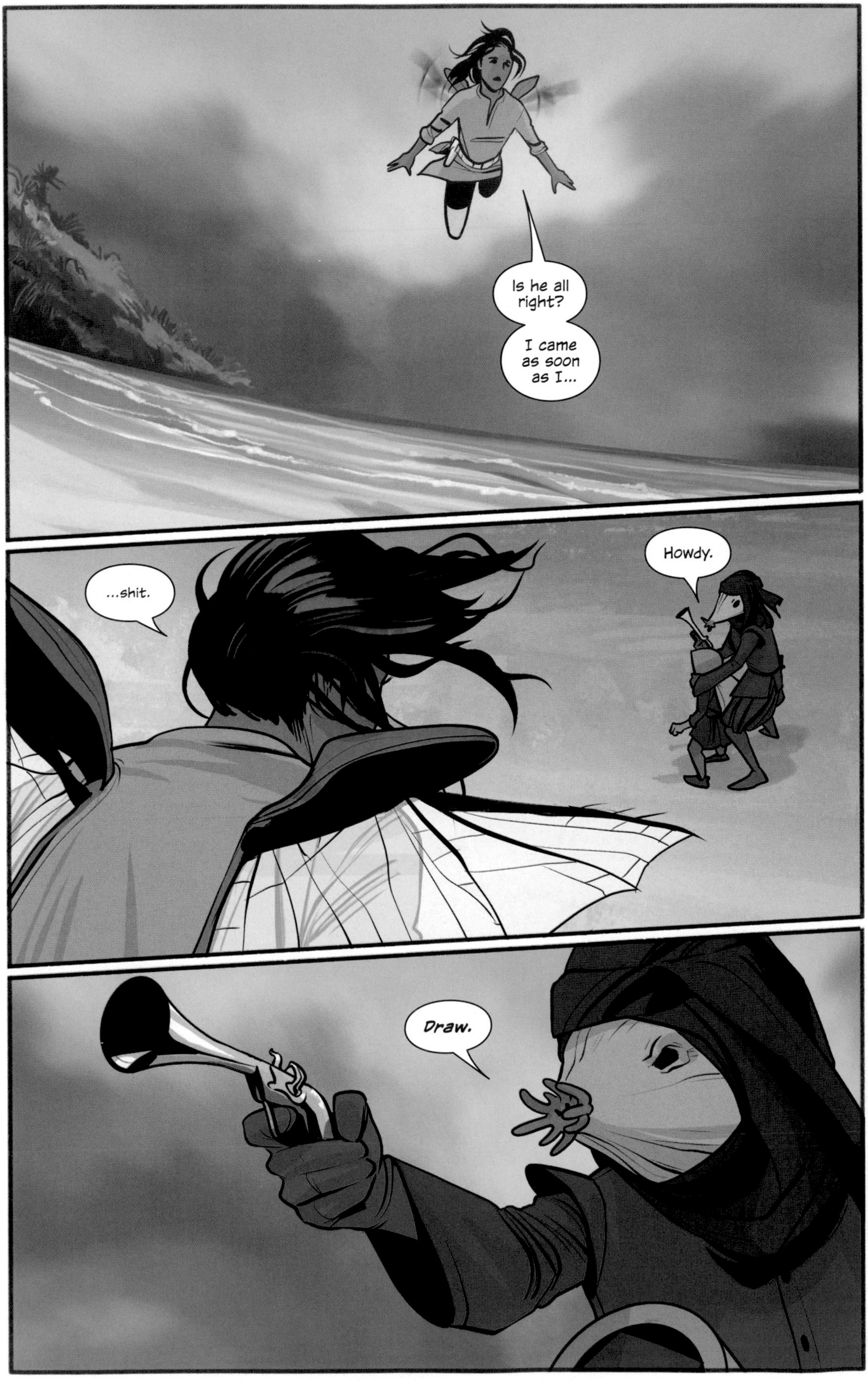
Is he all right?
I came as soon as I...
...shit.
Howdy.
Draw.

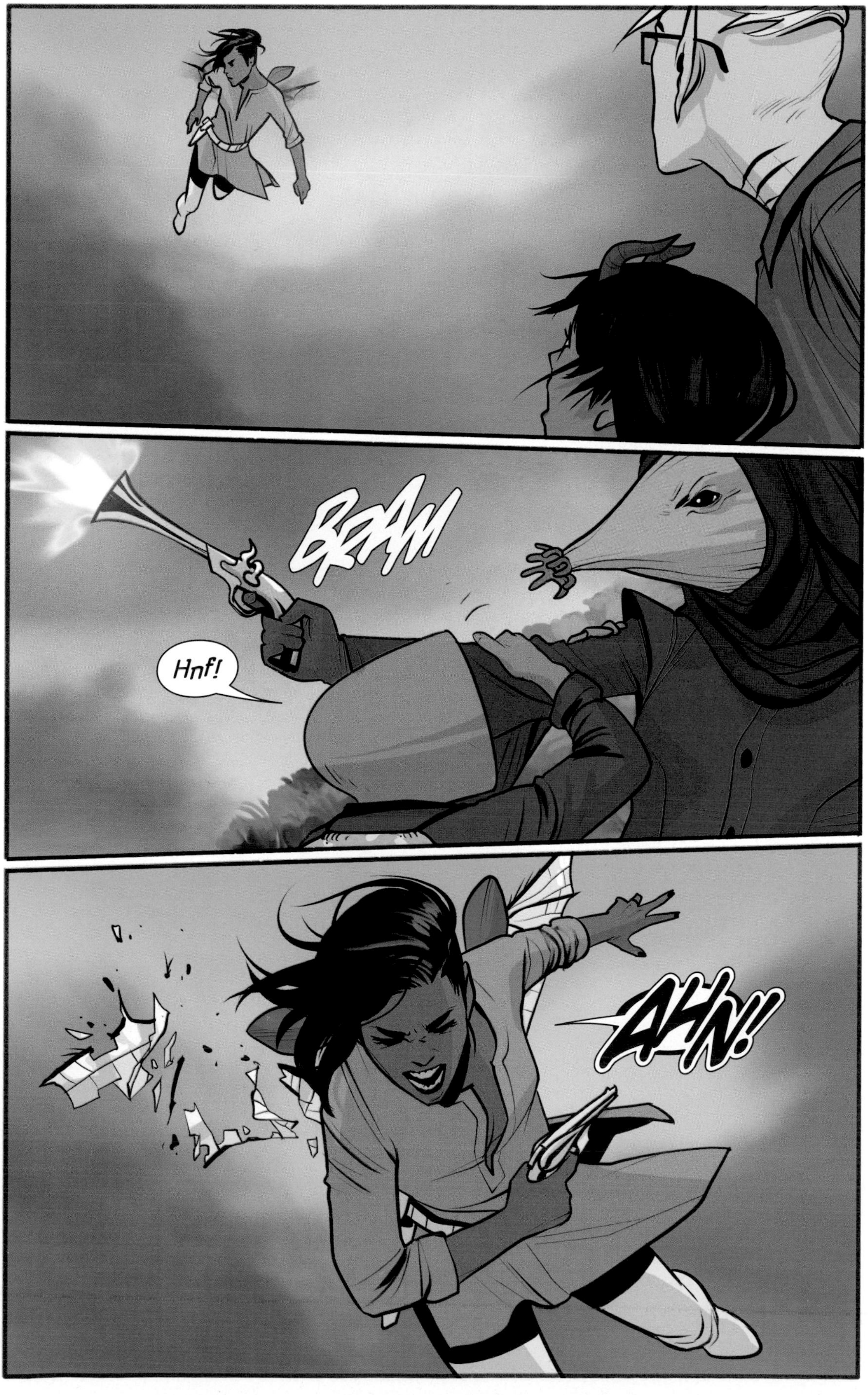
BRAM
Hnf!
AHN!

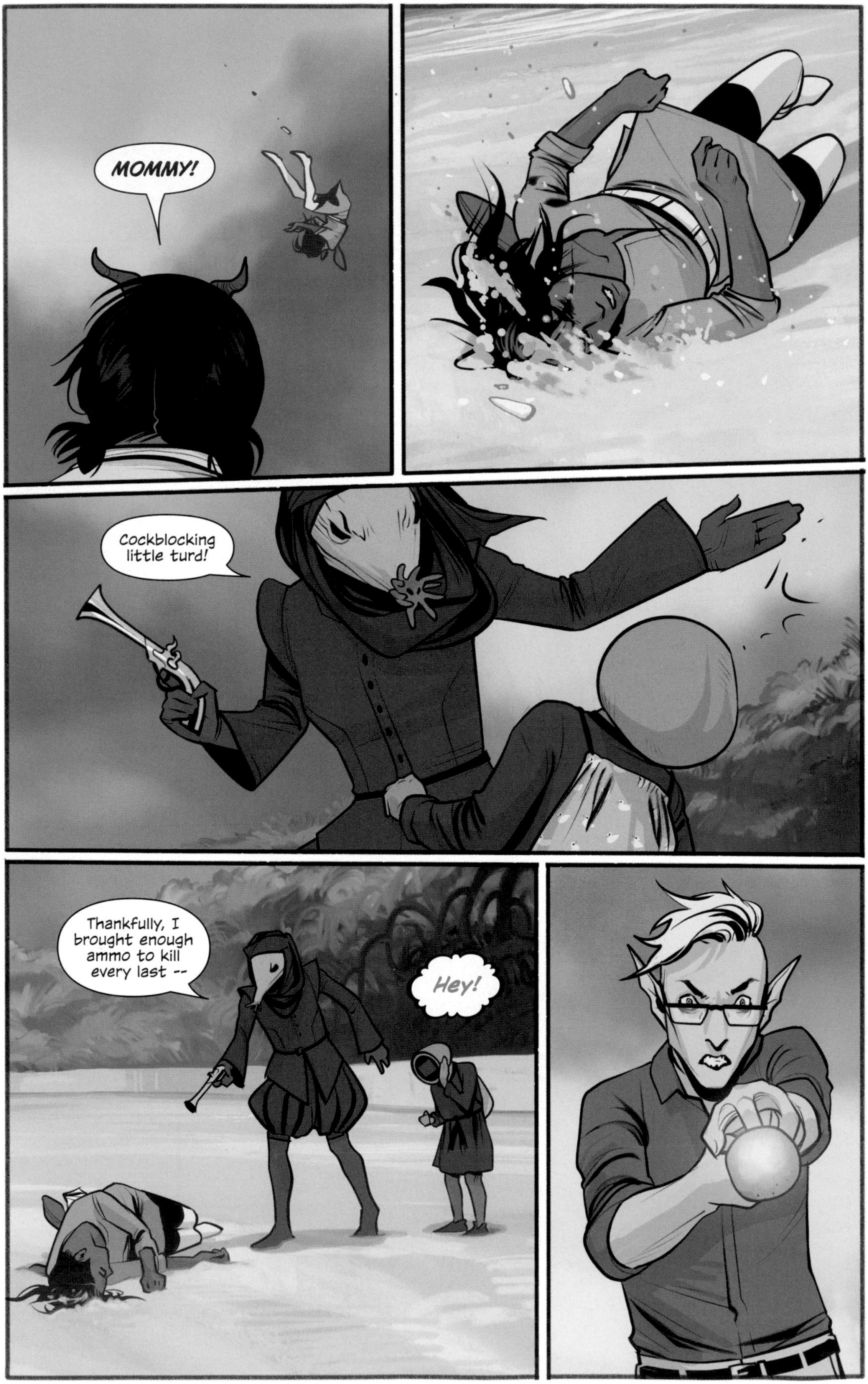
MOMMY!
Cockblocking little turd!
Thankfully, I brought enough ammo to kill every last --
Hey!

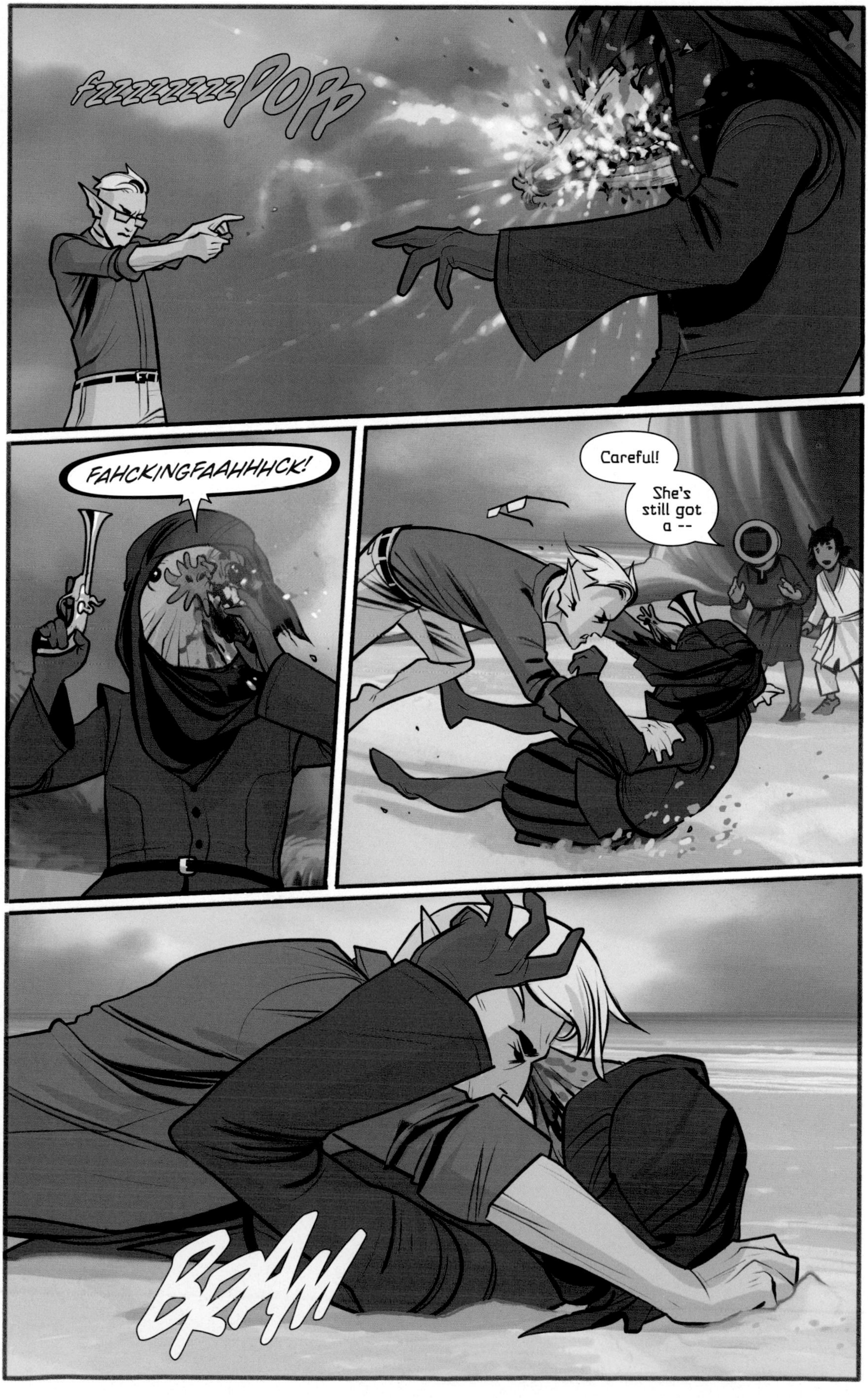
fzzzzzzzzzPOPP
FAHCKINGFAAHHHCK!
Careful!
She's still got a --
BRAM

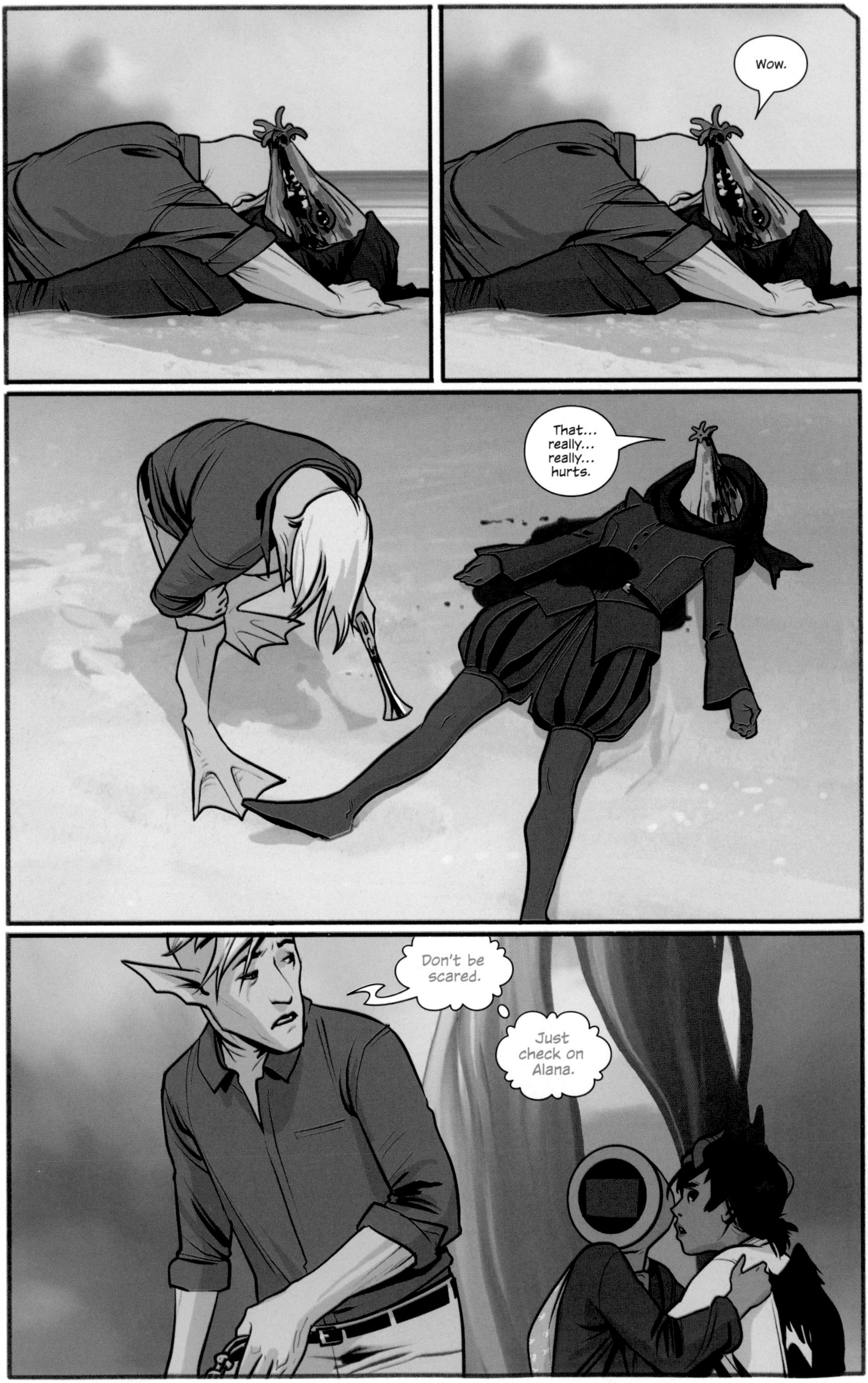
Wow.
That... really... really... hurts.
Don't be scared.
Just check on Alana.

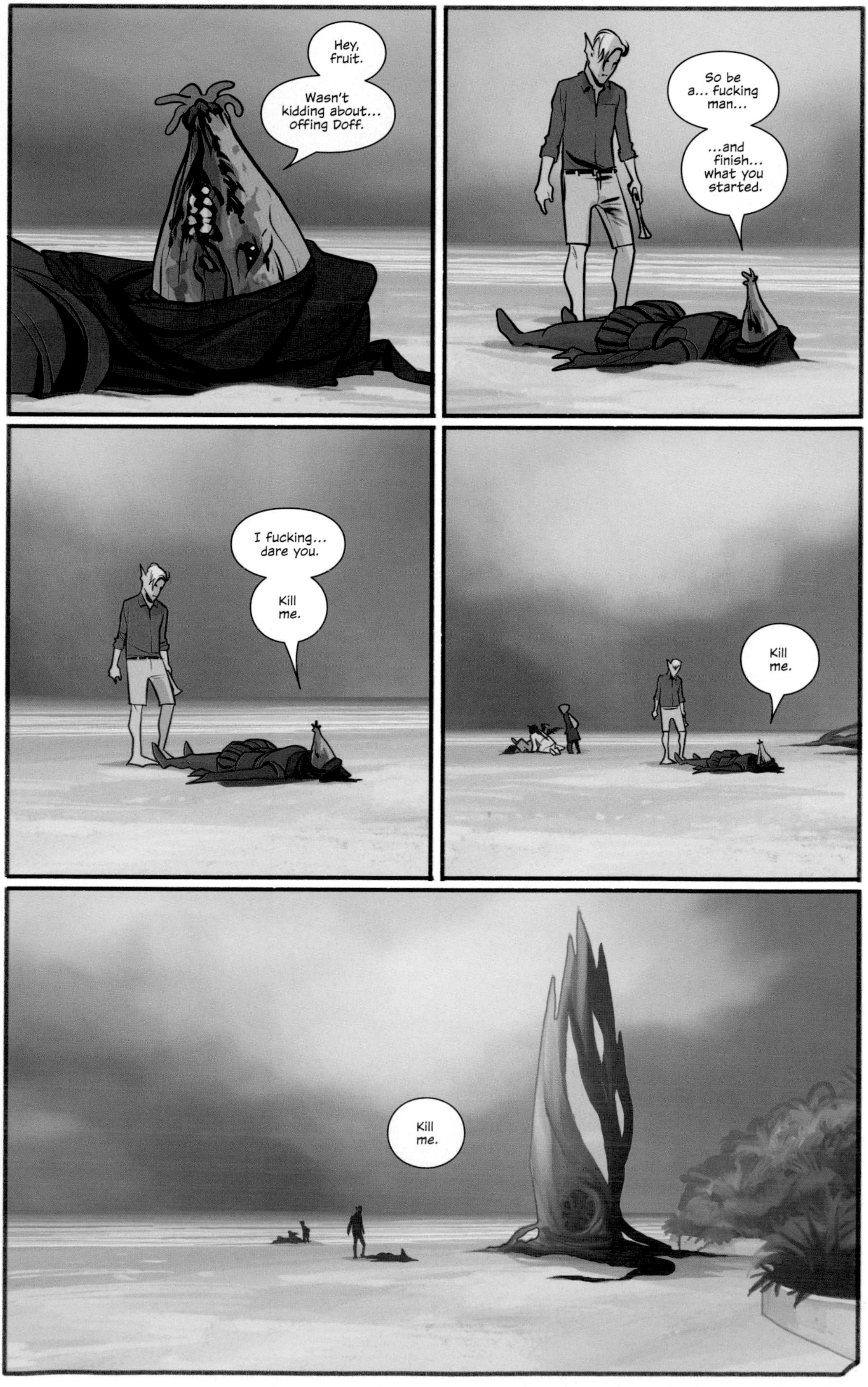
Hey, fruit.
Wasn't kidding about... offing Doff.
So be a... fucking man...
...and finish... what you started.
I fucking... dare you.
Kill me.
Kill me.
Kill me.

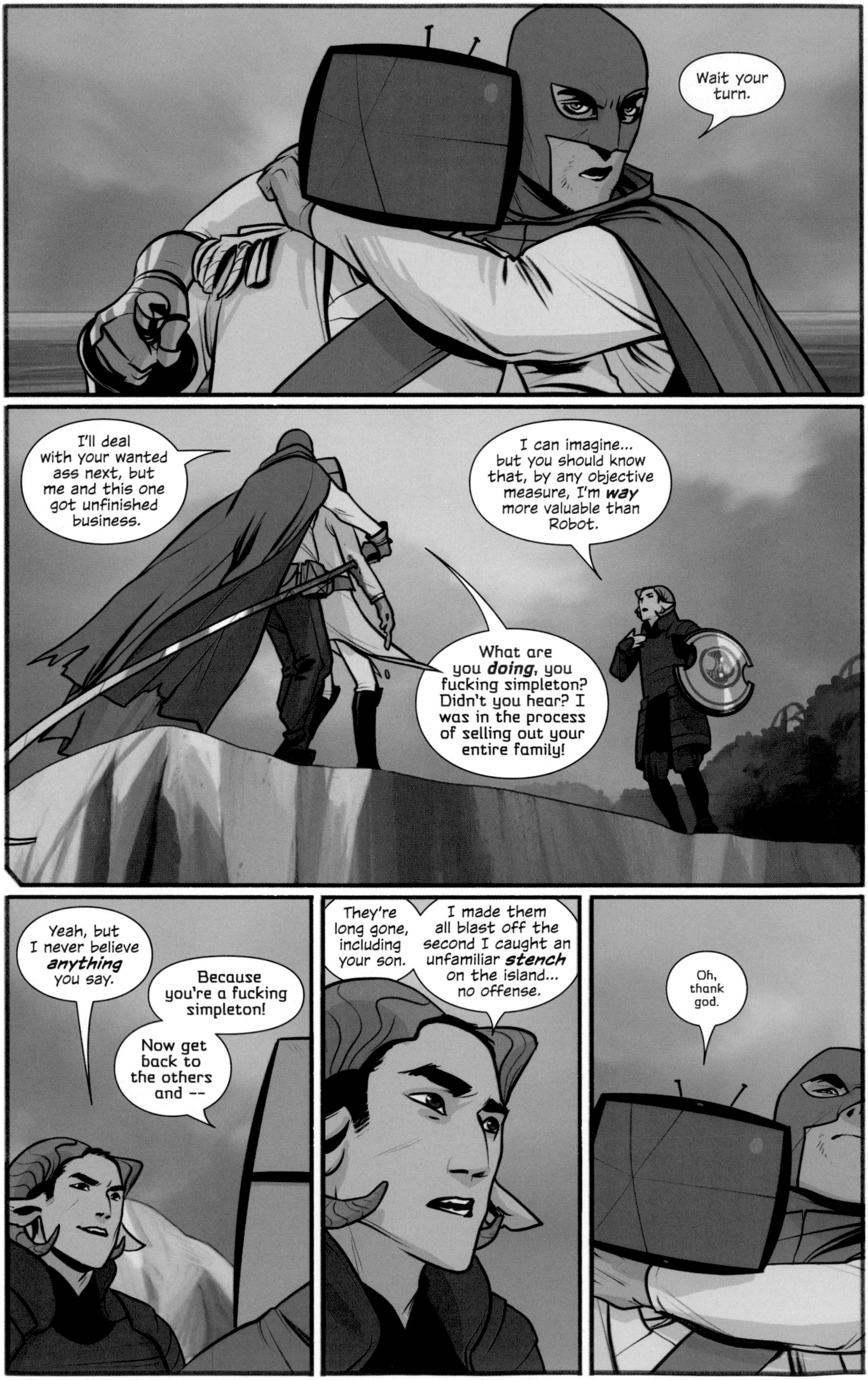

Wait your turn.
I'll deal with your wanted ass next, but me and this one got unfinished business.
I can imagine... but you should know that, by any objective measure, I'm **way** more valuable than Robot.
What are you **doing**, you fucking simpleton? Didn't you hear? I was in the process of selling out your entire family!
Yeah, but I never believe **anything** you say.
Because you're a fucking simpleton!
Now get back to the others and --
They're long gone, including your son.
I made them all blast off the second I caught an unfamiliar **stench** on the island... no offense.
Oh, thank god.

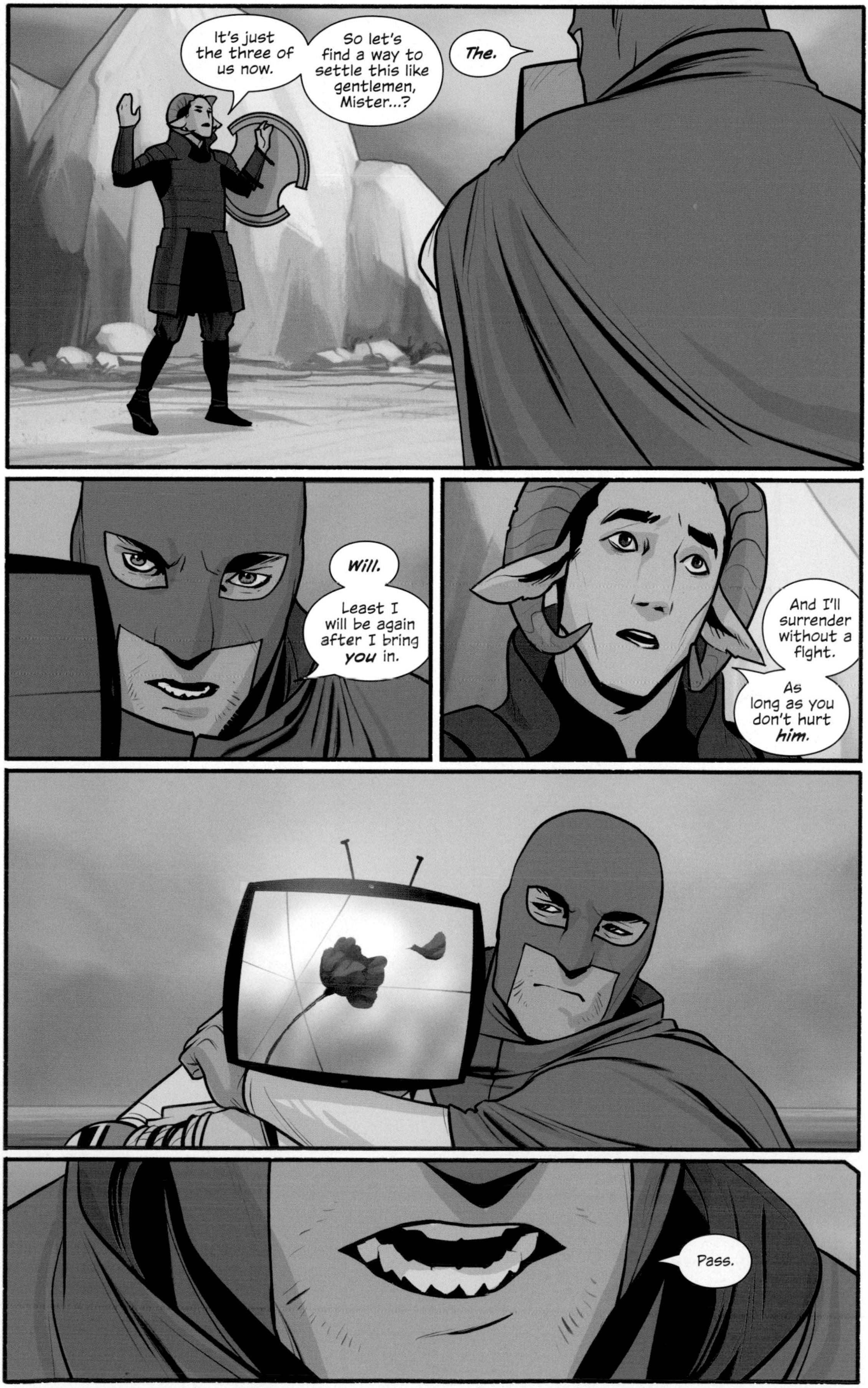
It's just the three of us now.
So let's find a way to settle this like gentlemen, Mister...?
The.
Will.
Least I will be again after I bring *you* in.
And I'll surrender without a fight.
As long as you don't hurt *him.*
Pass.

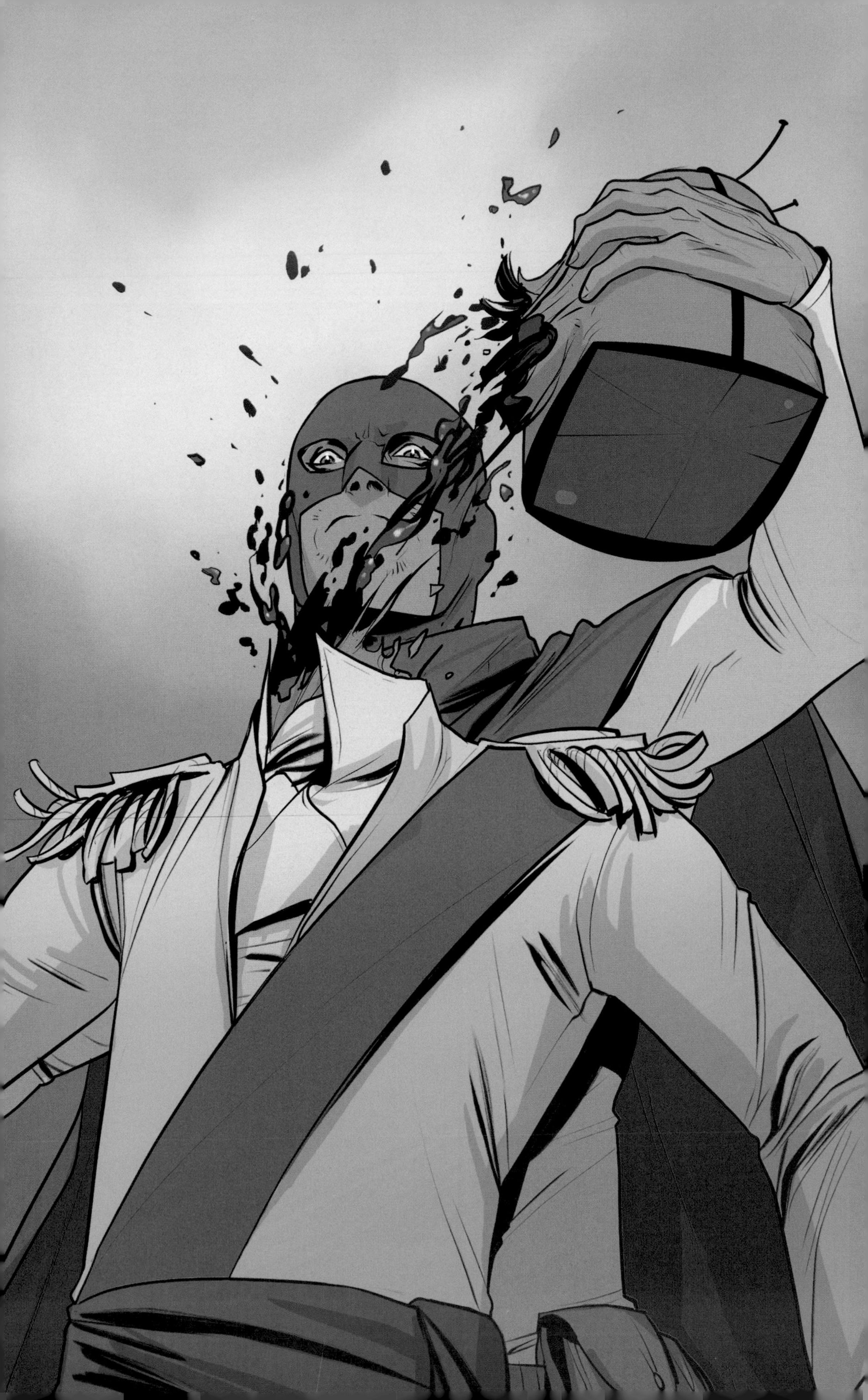

end chapter fifty-three

CHAPTER
FIFTY-FOUR

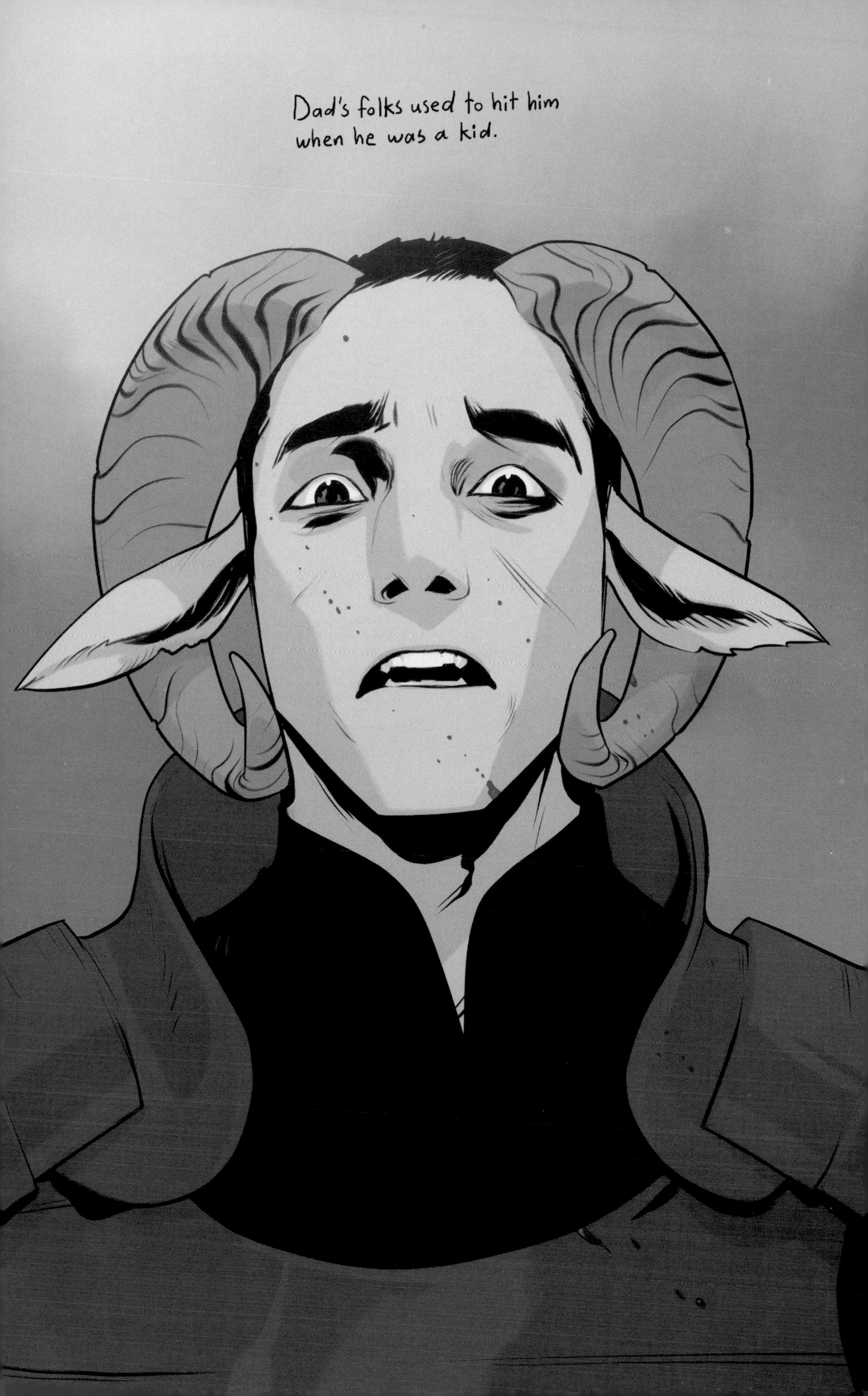
Dad's folks used to hit him when he was a kid.

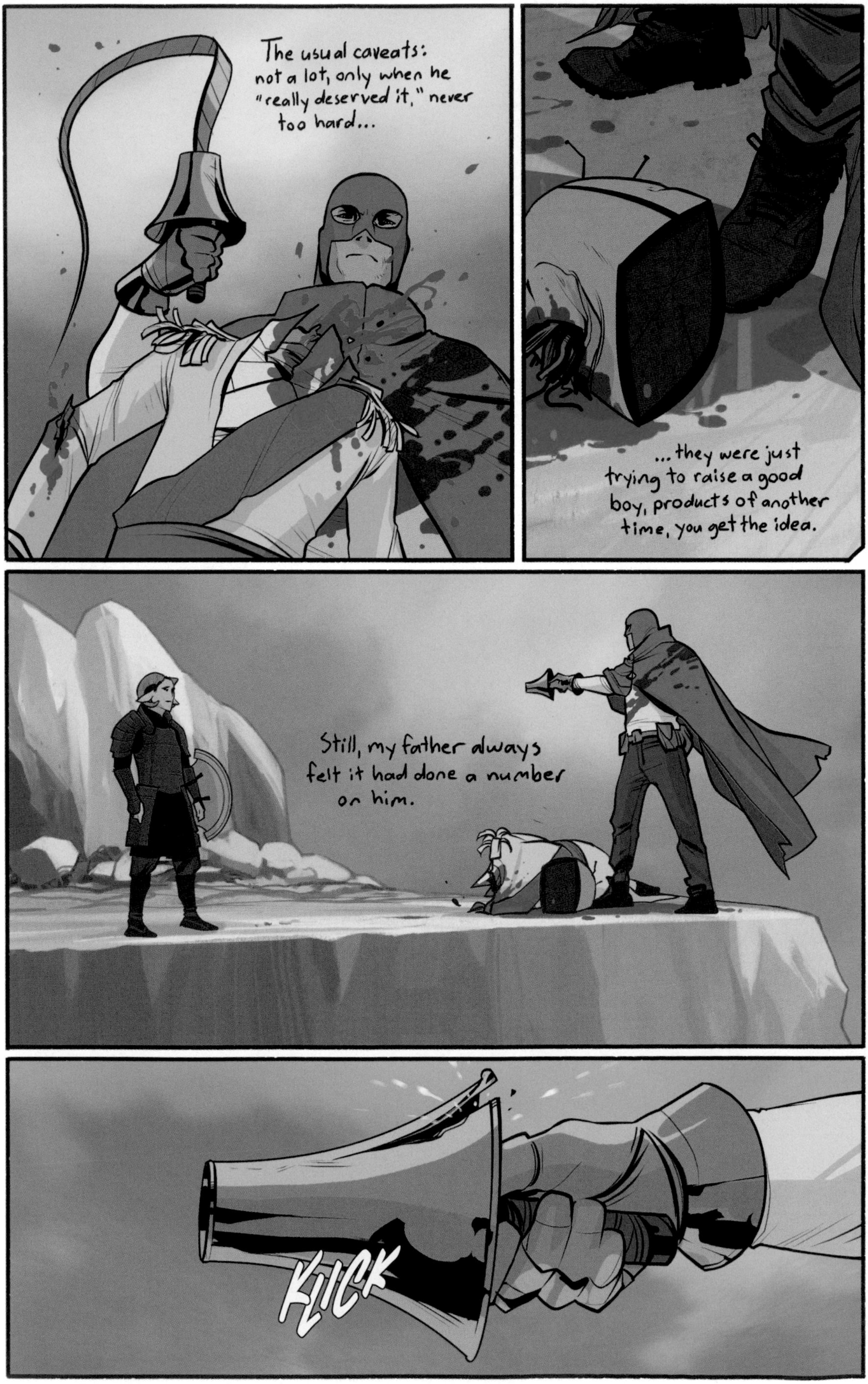
The usual caveats: not a lot, only when he "really deserved it," never too hard...
...they were just trying to raise a good boy, products of another time, you get the idea.
Still, my father always felt it had done a number on him.
KLICK

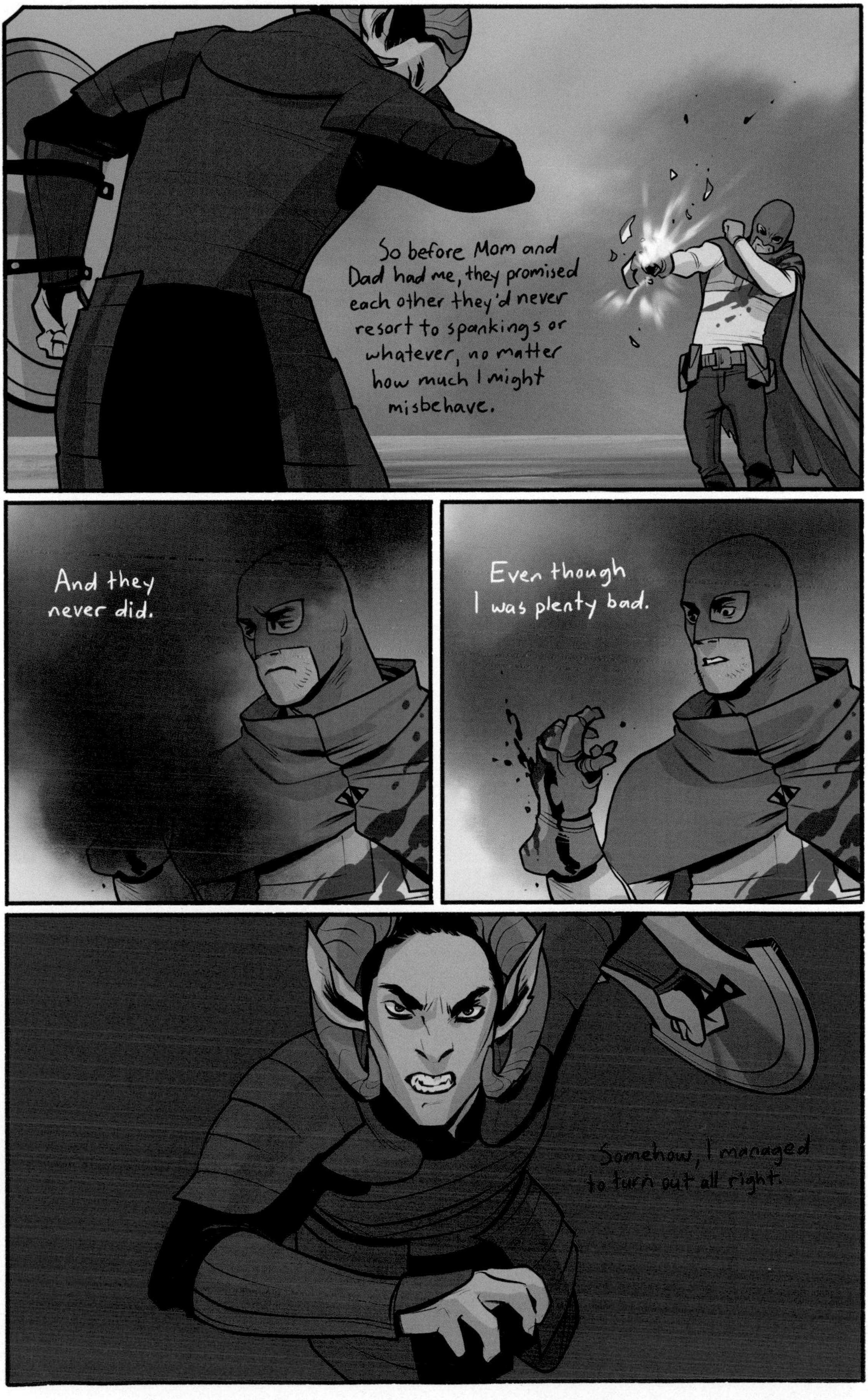
So before Mom and Dad had me, they promised each other they'd never resort to spankings or whatever, no matter how much I might misbehave.
And they never did.
Even though I was plenty bad.
Somehow, I managed to turn out all right.

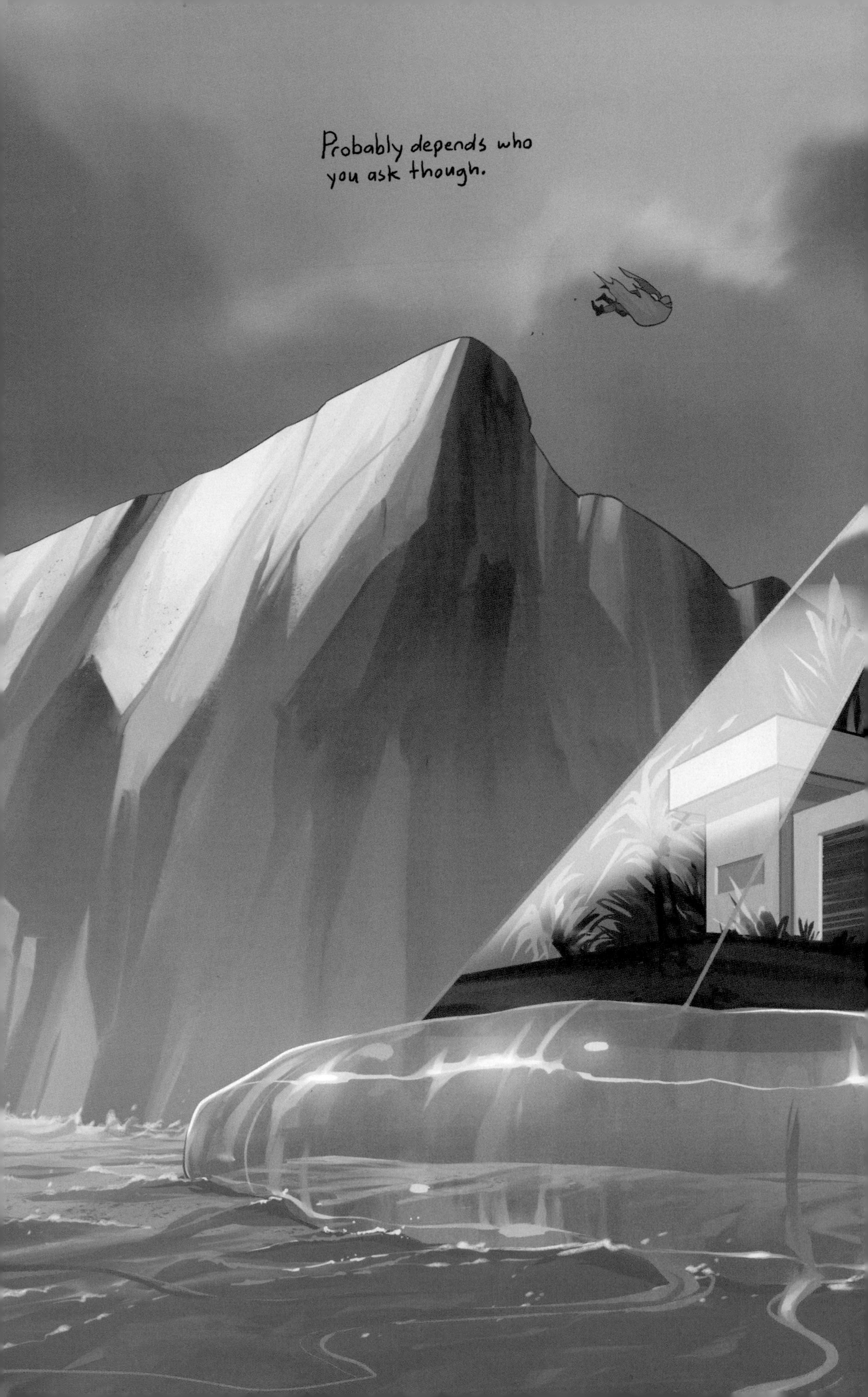
Probably depends who you ask though.

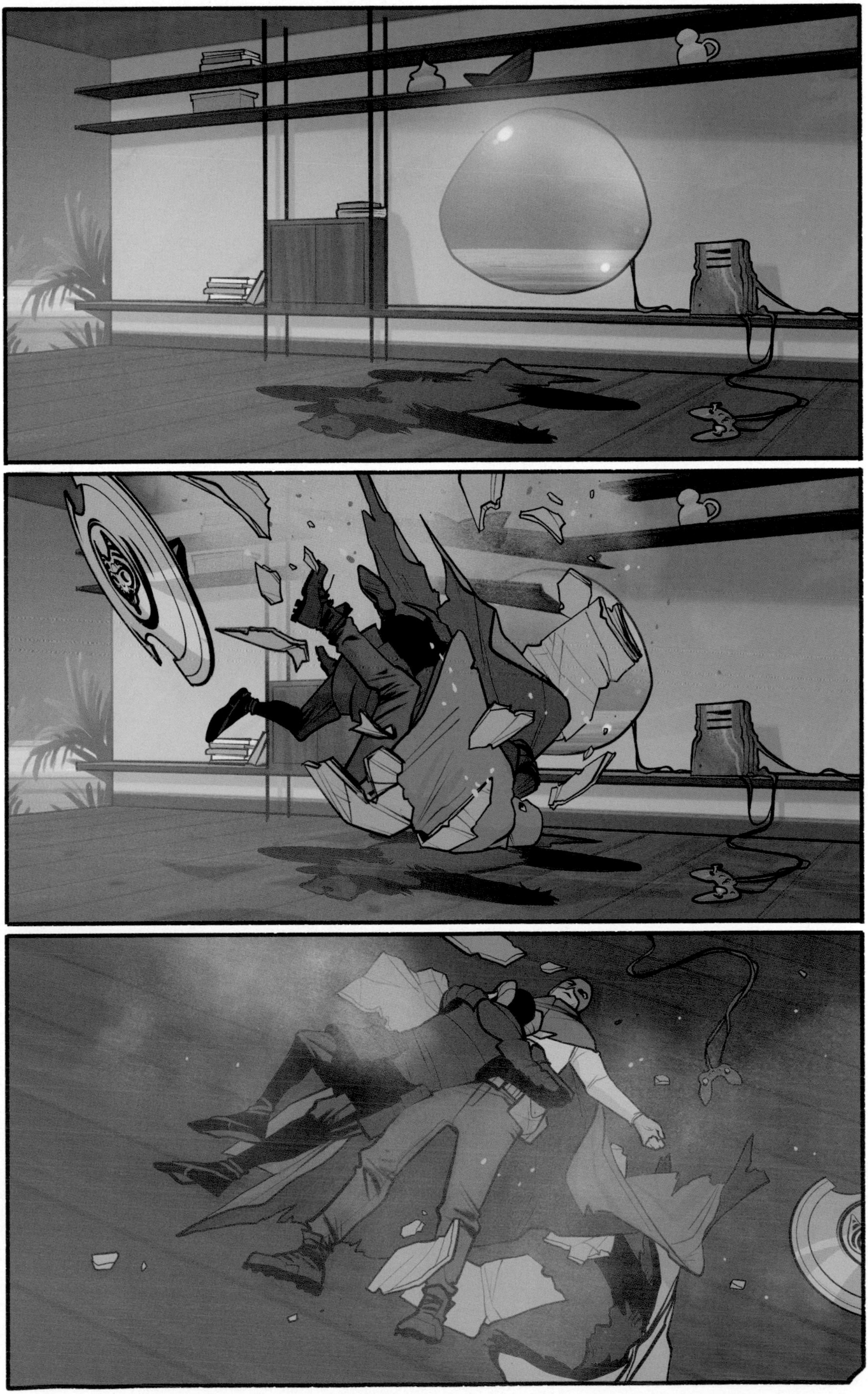

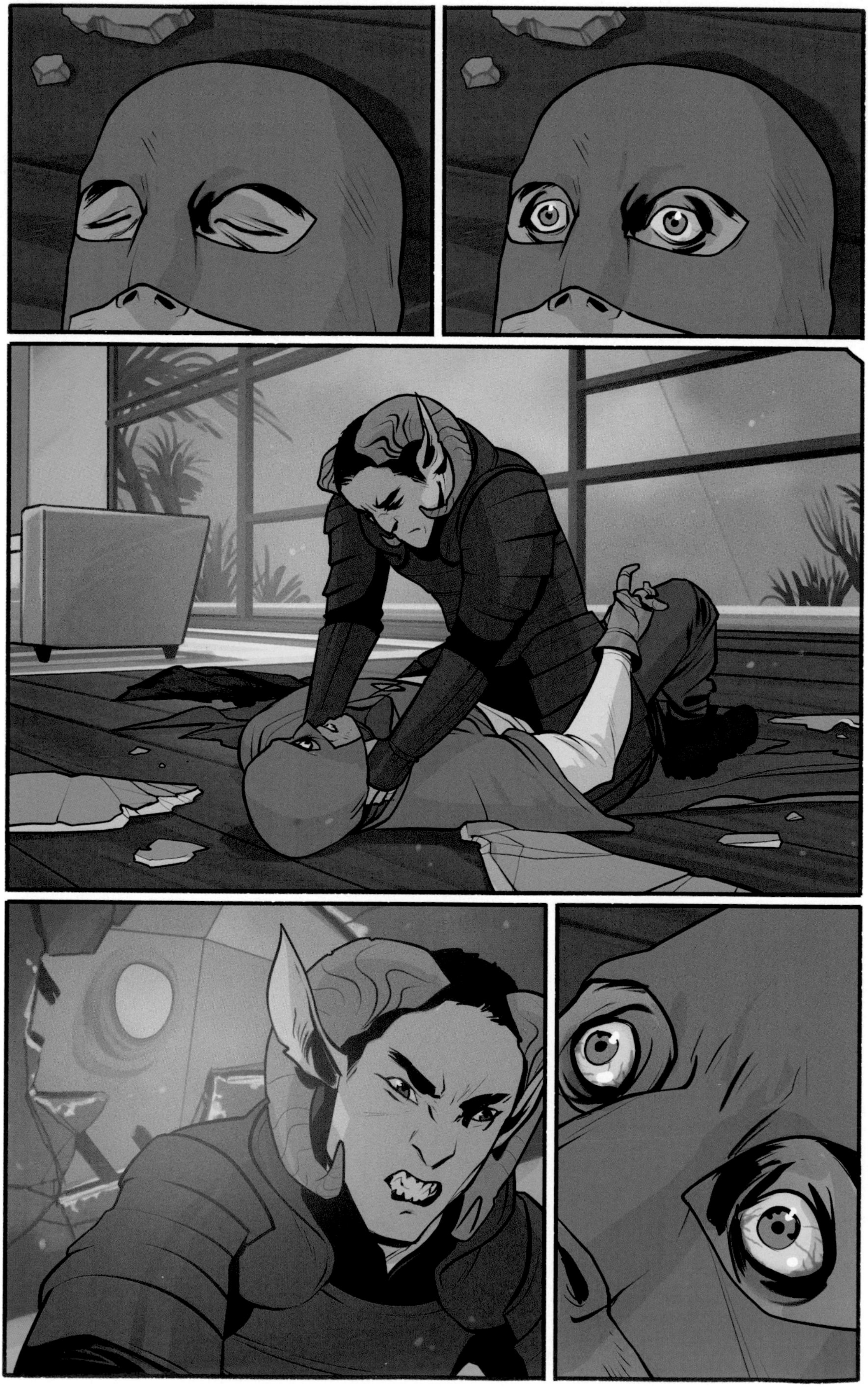

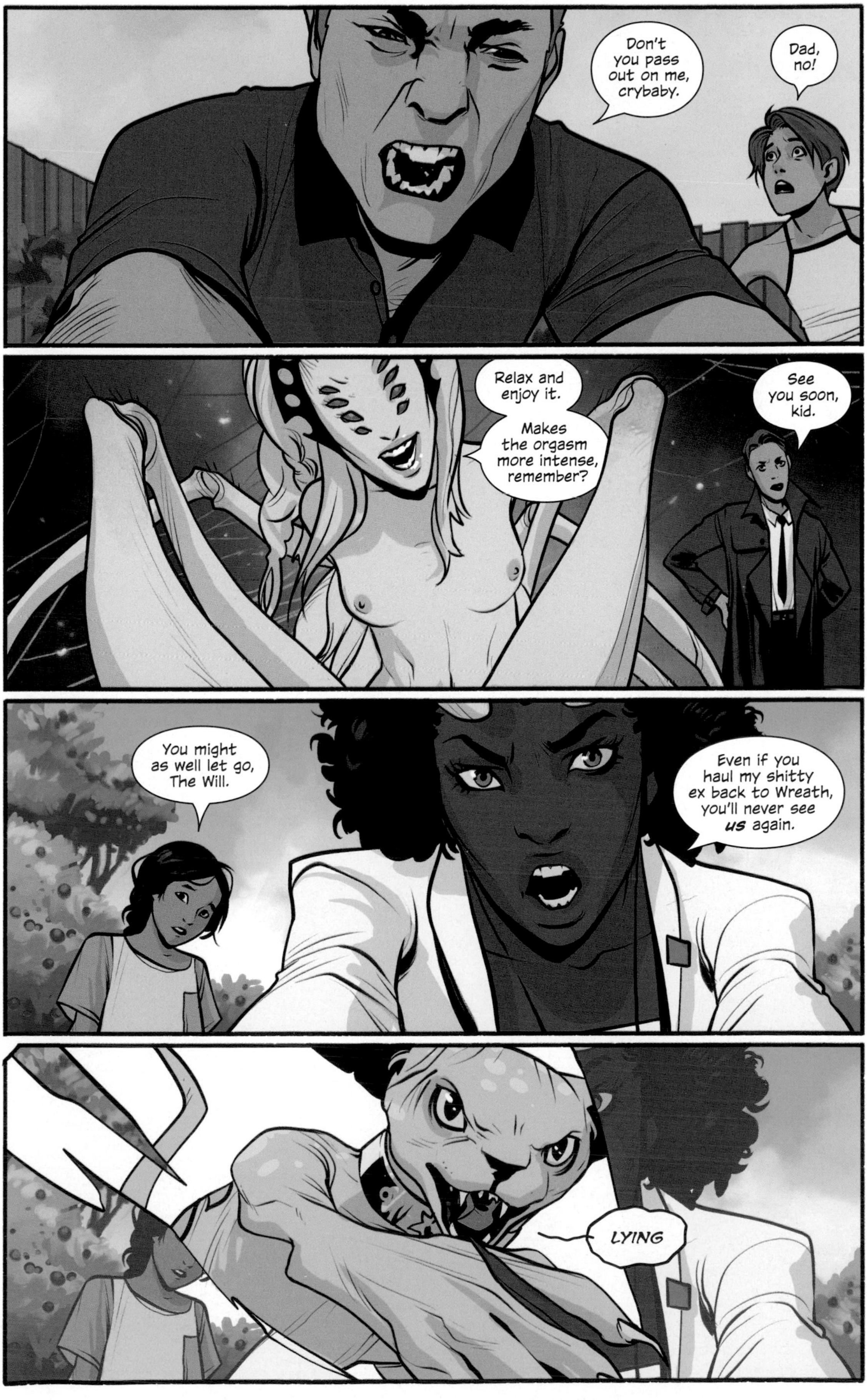
Don't you pass out on me, crybaby.
Dad, no!
Relax and enjoy it.
Makes the orgasm more intense, remember?
See you soon, kid.
You might as well let go, The Will.
Even if you haul my shitty ex back to Wreath, you'll never see *us* again.
LYING

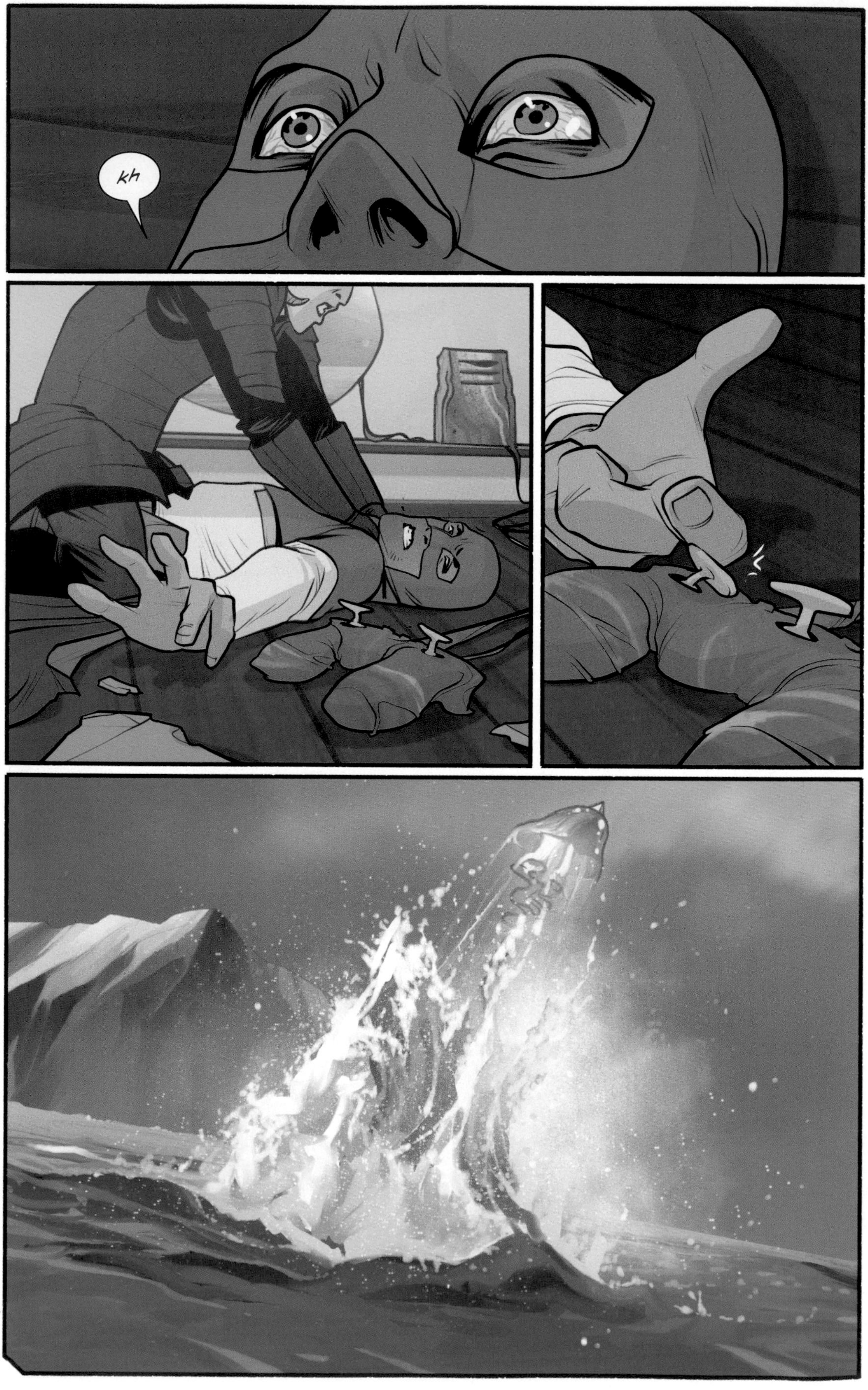
kh

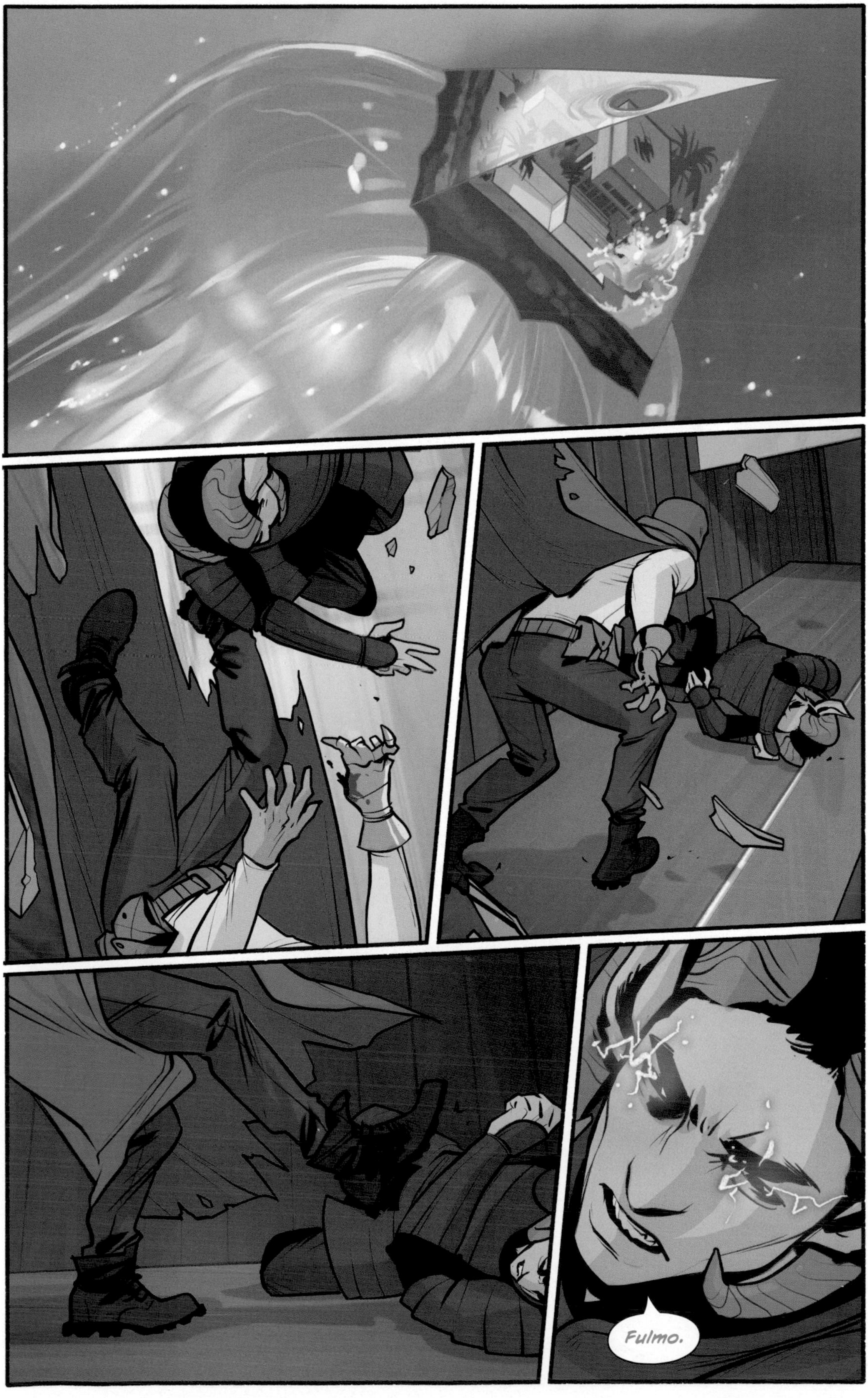
Fulmo.

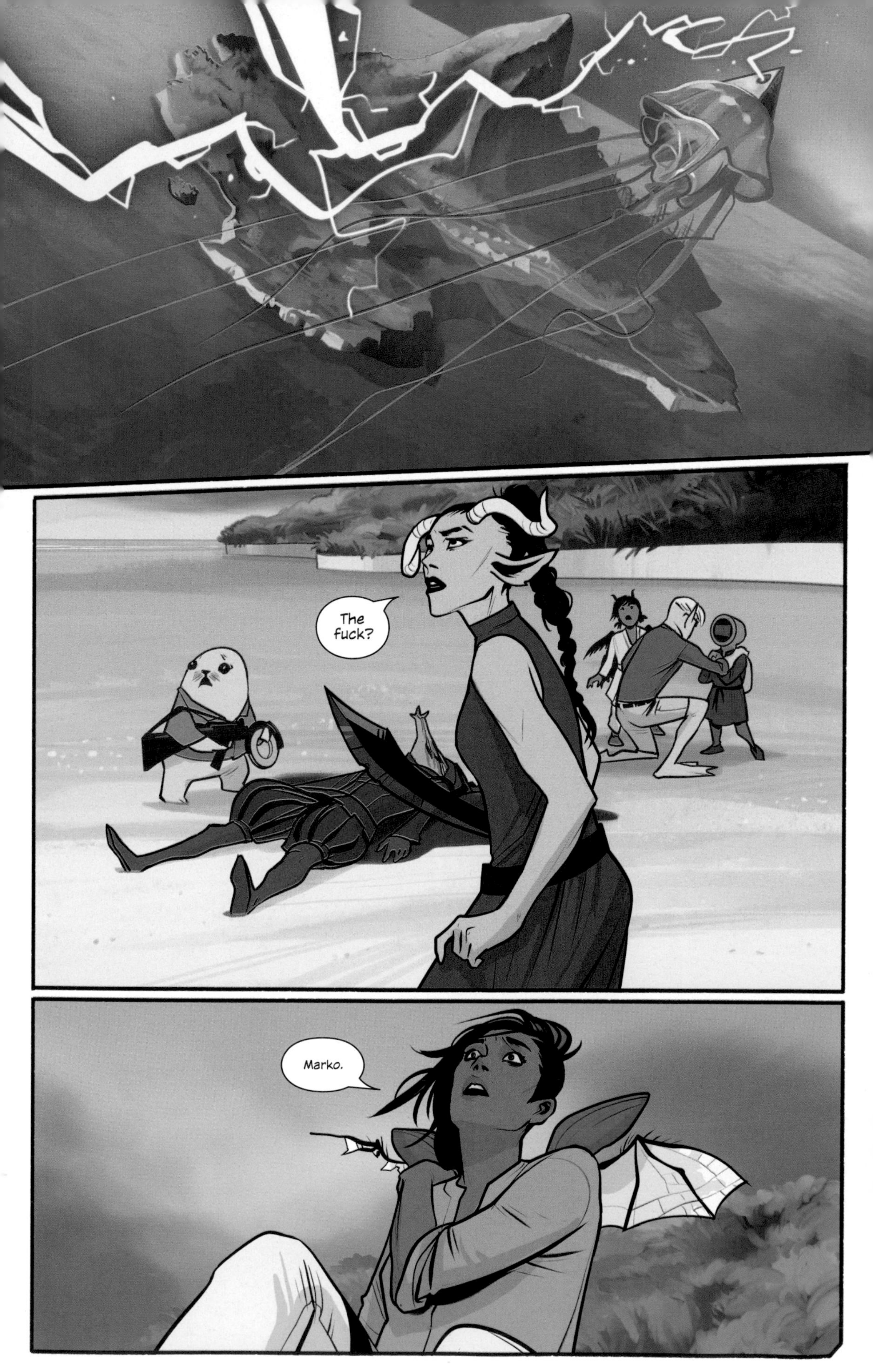
The fuck?
Marko.

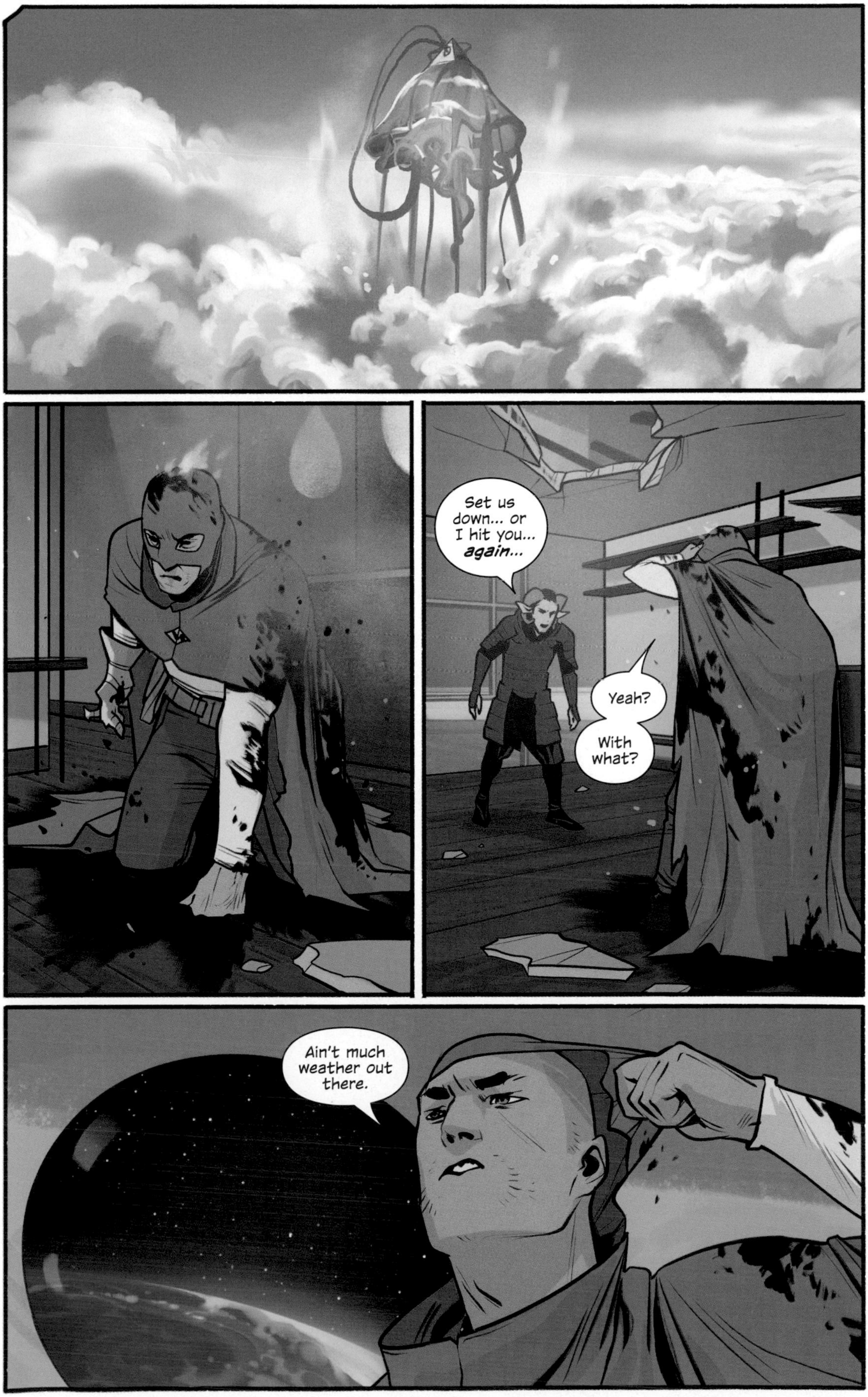

Set us down... or I hit you... *again*...
Yeah?
With what?
Ain't much weather out there.

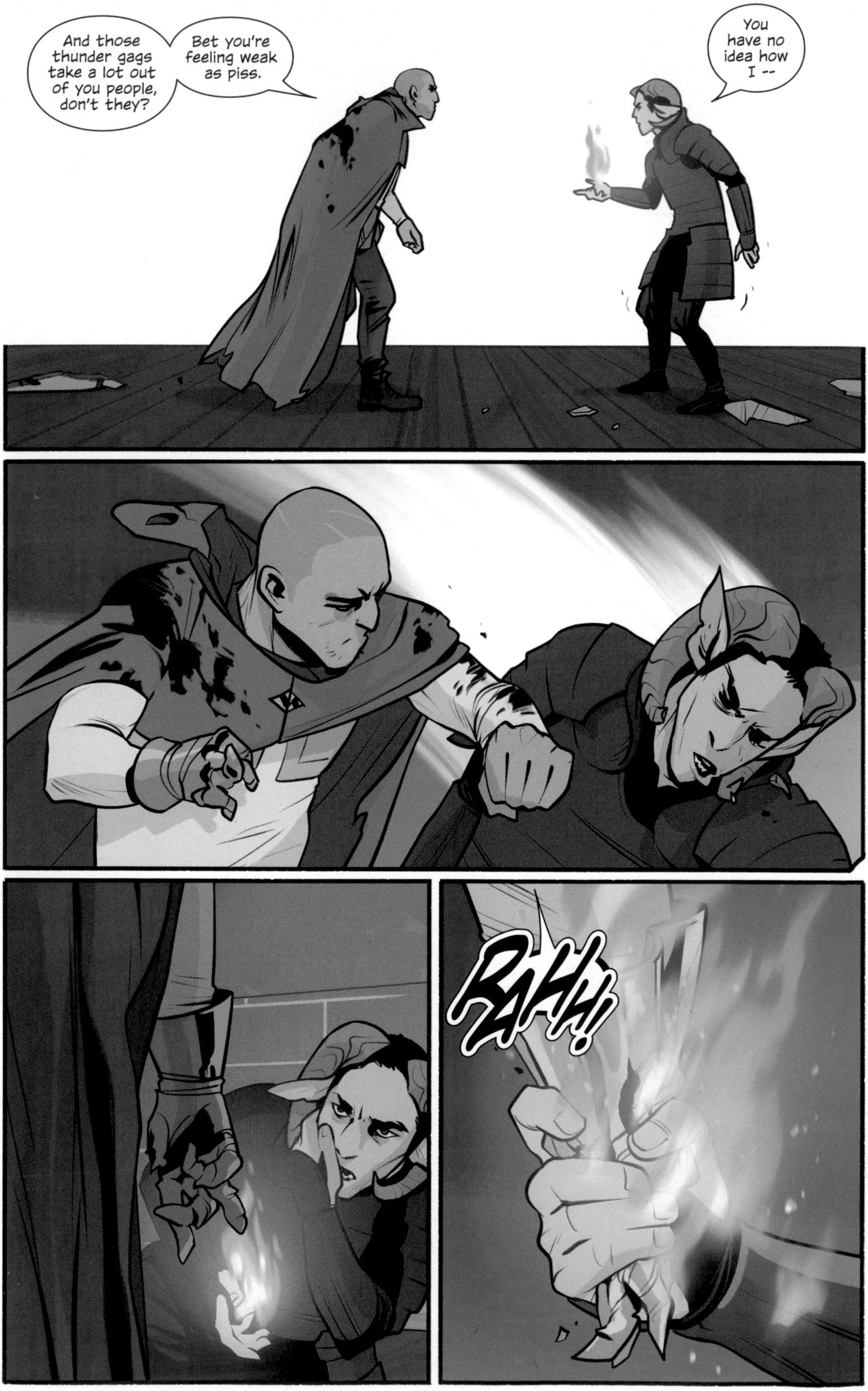
And those thunder gags take a lot out of you people, don't they?
Bet you're feeling weak as piss.
You have no idea how I --
RAHH!

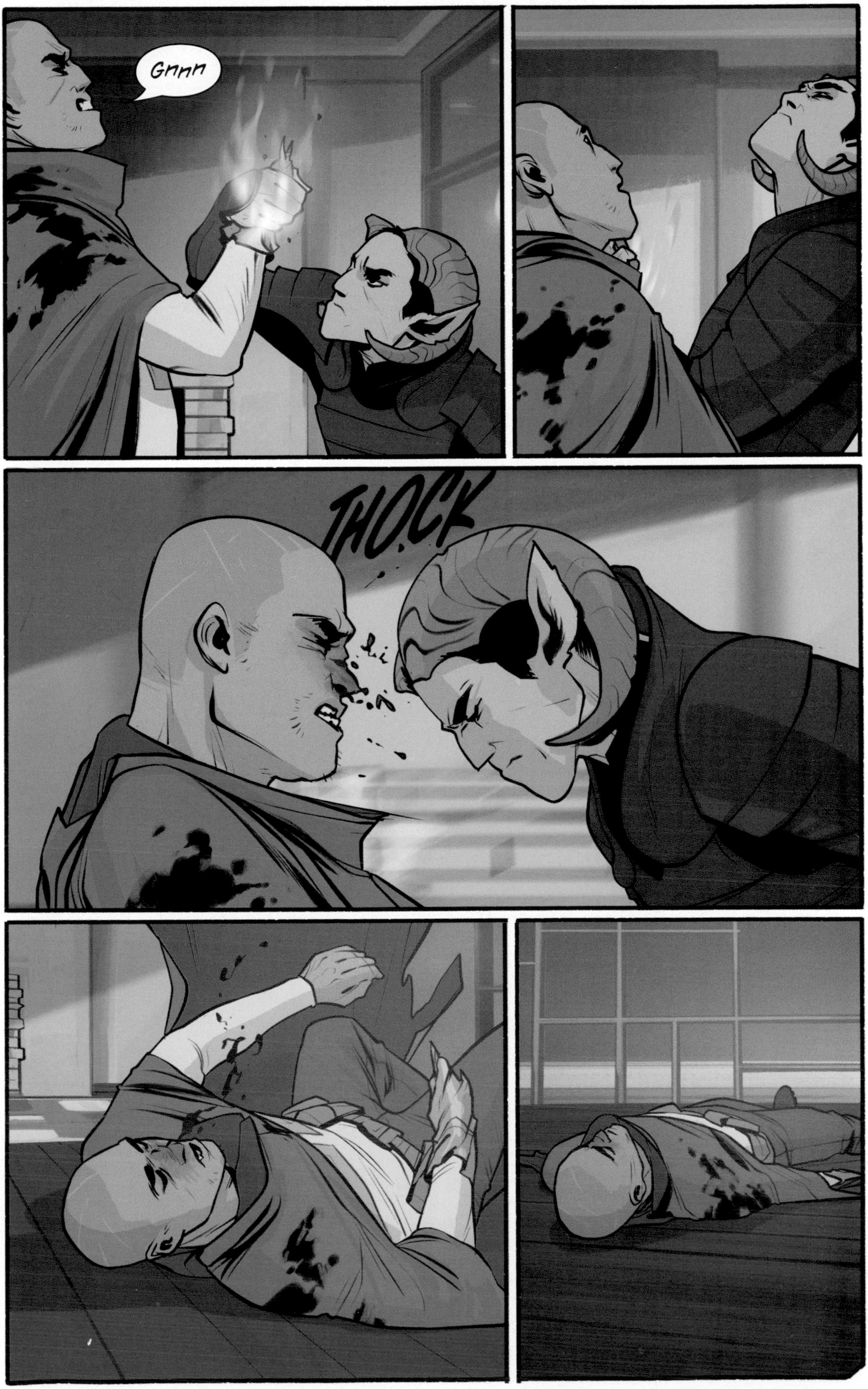
Gnnn
THOCK

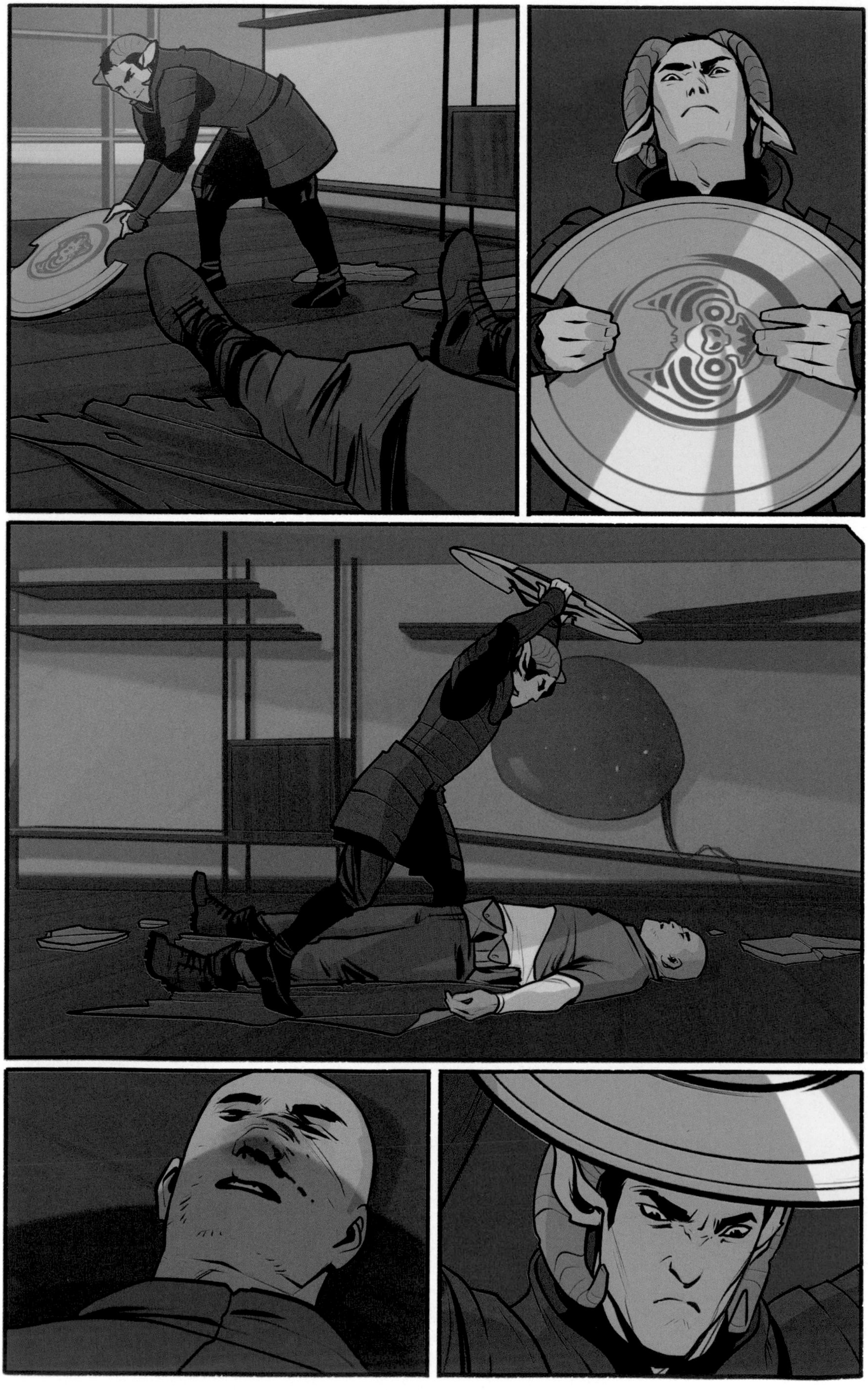

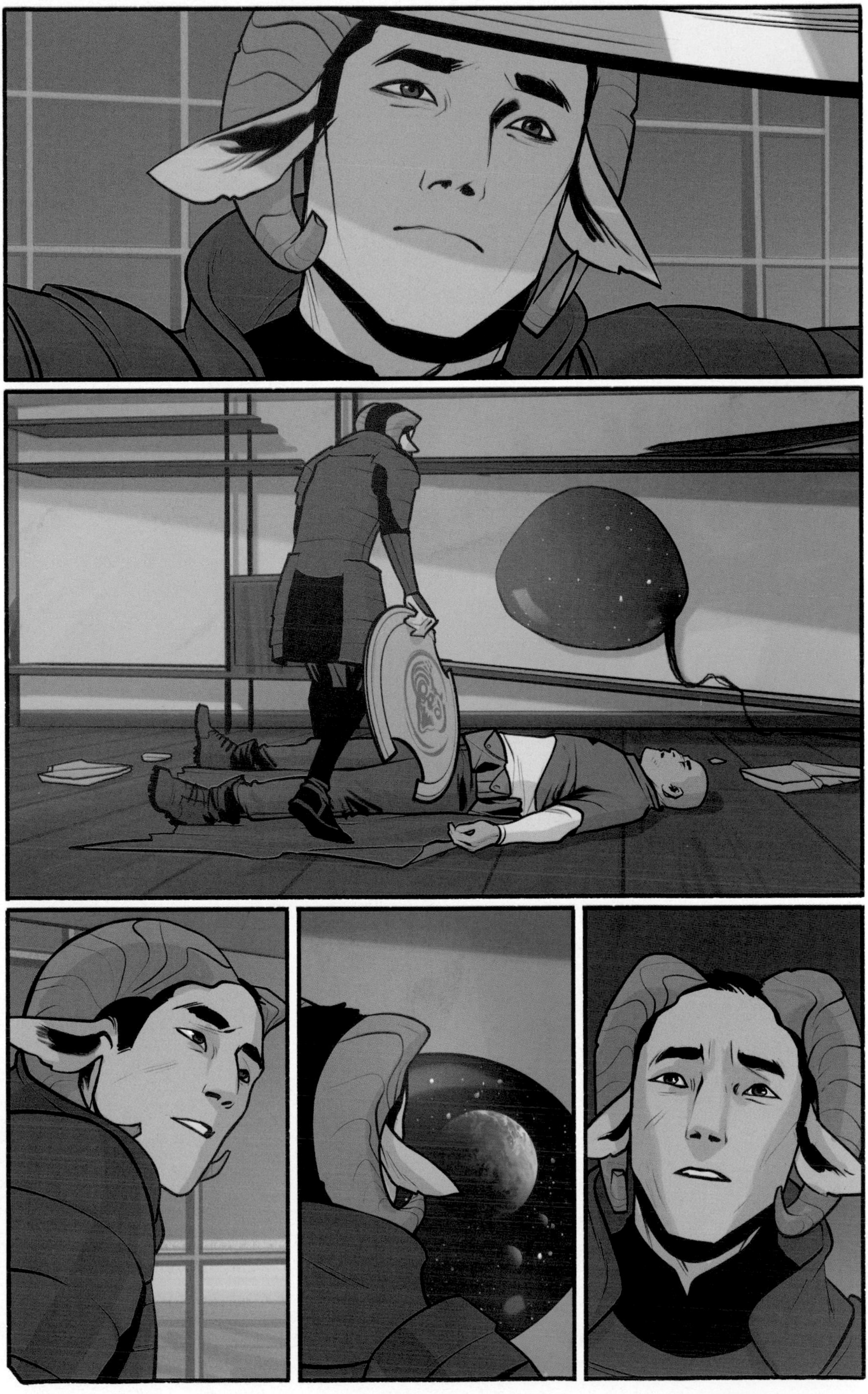

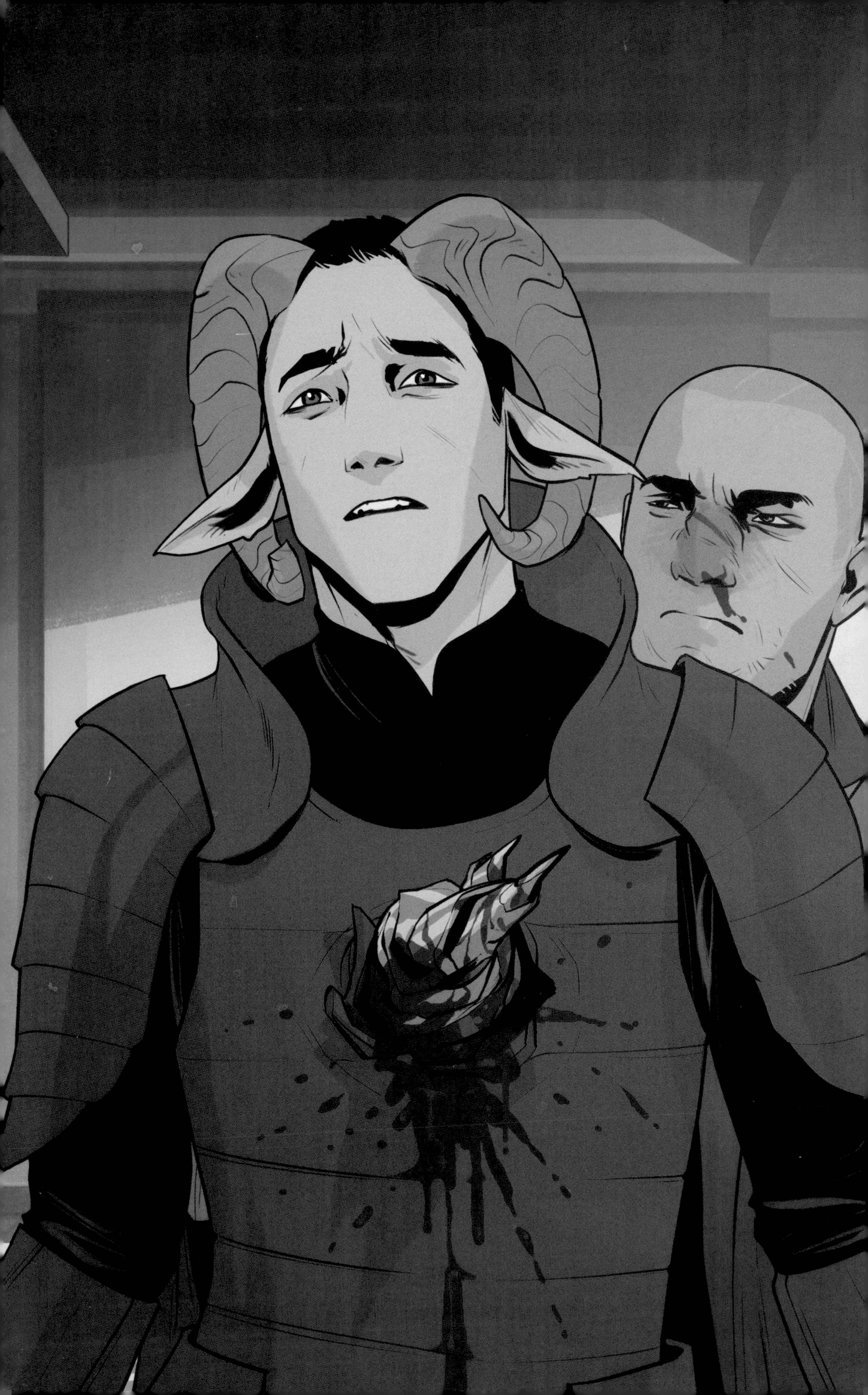

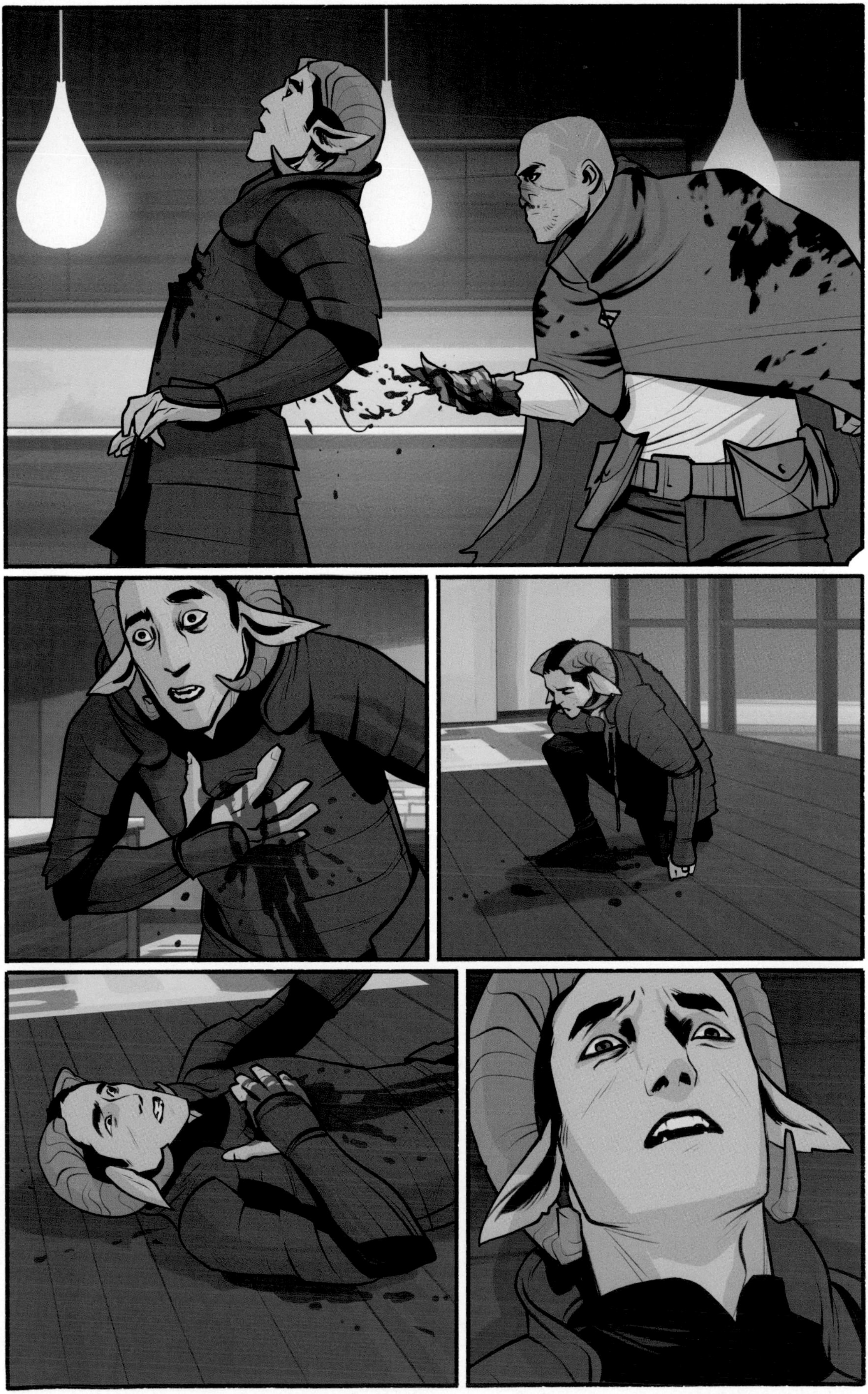

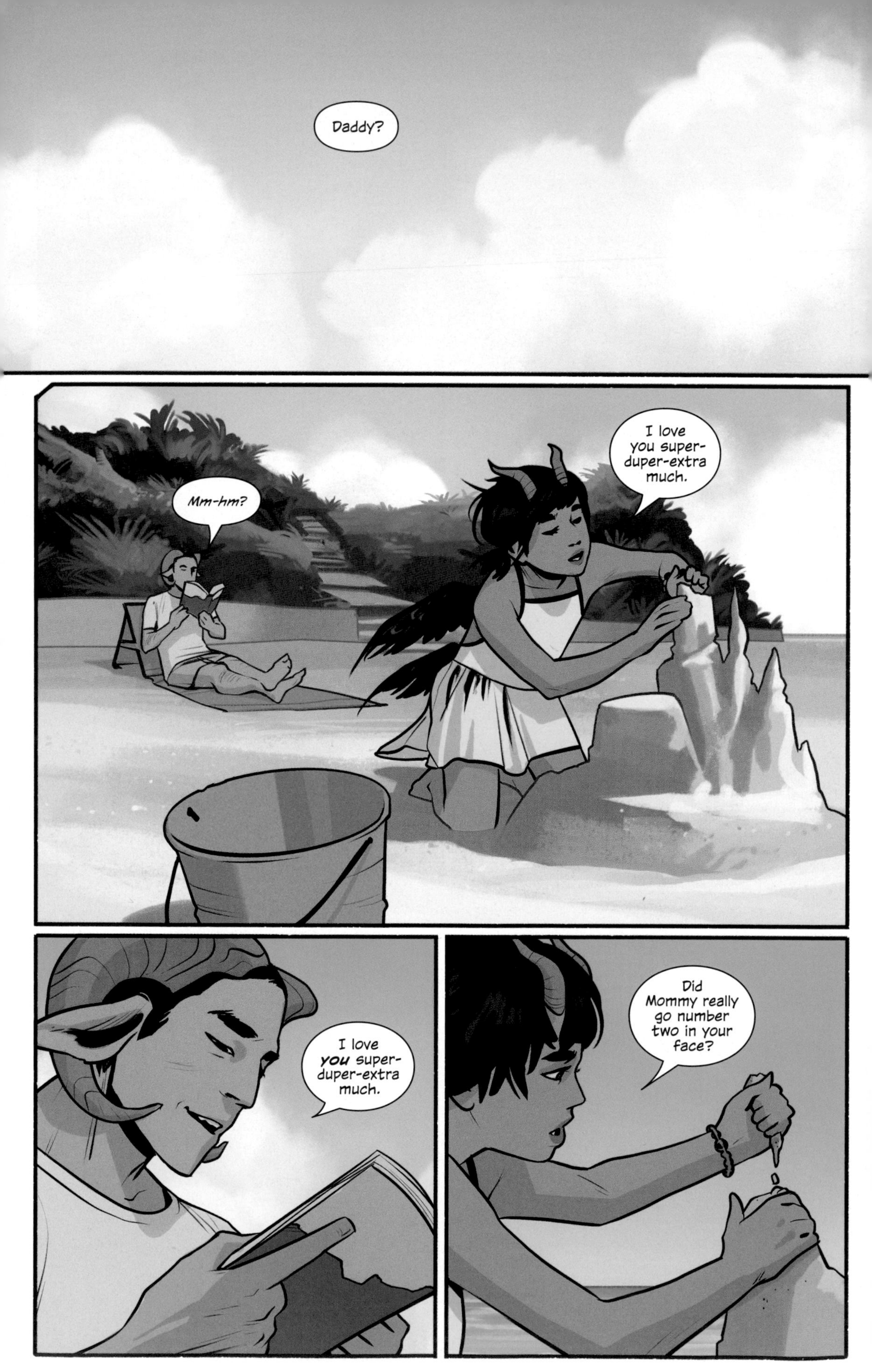
Daddy?
Mm-hm?
I love you super-duper-extra much.
I love *you* super-duper-extra much.
Did Mommy really go number two in your face?

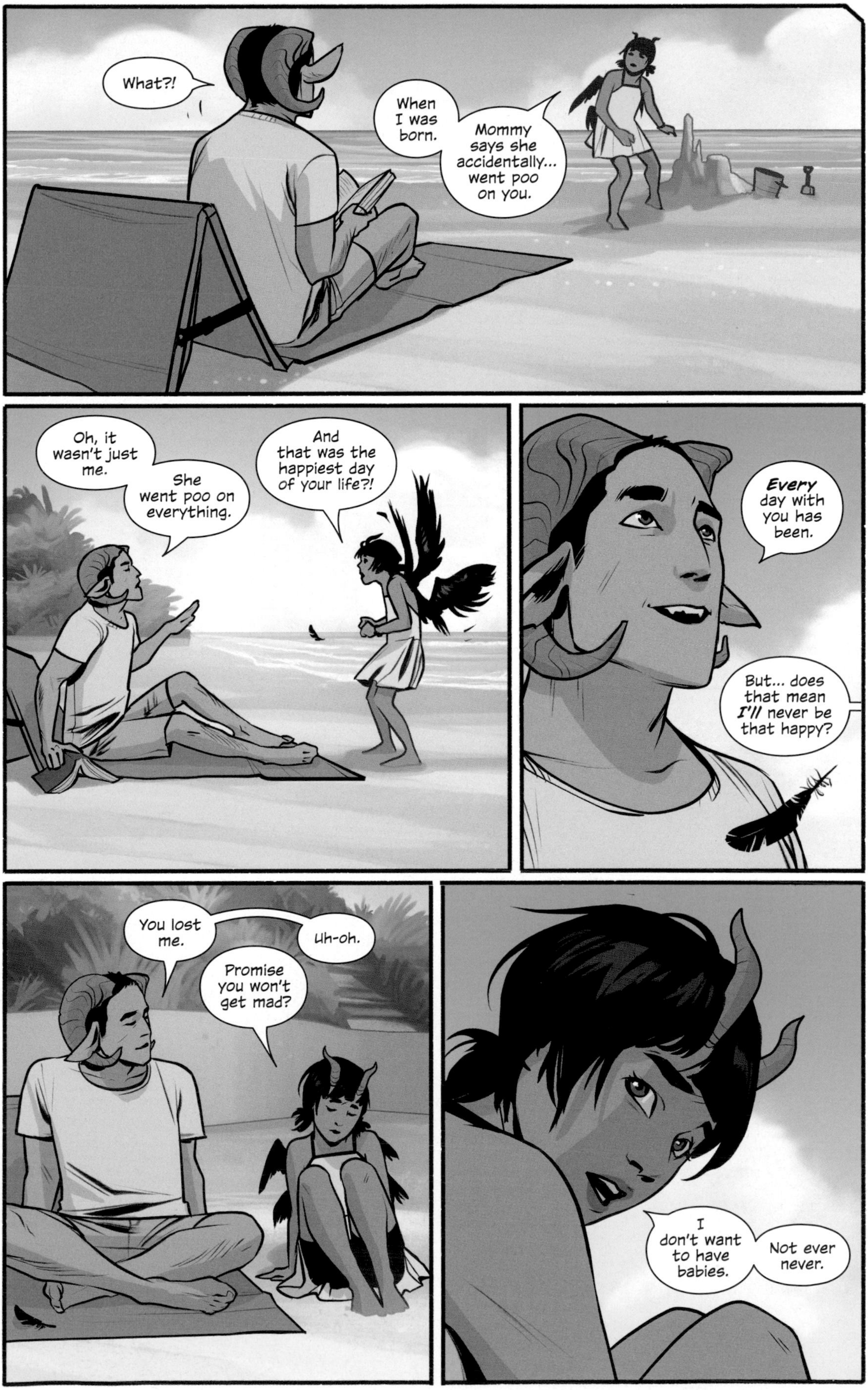
What?!
When I was born.
Mommy says she accidentally... went poo on you.
Oh, it wasn't just me.
She went poo on everything.
And that was the happiest day of your life?!
Every day with you has been.
But... does that mean I'll never be that happy?
You lost me.
Uh-oh.
Promise you won't get mad?
I don't want to have babies.
Not ever never.

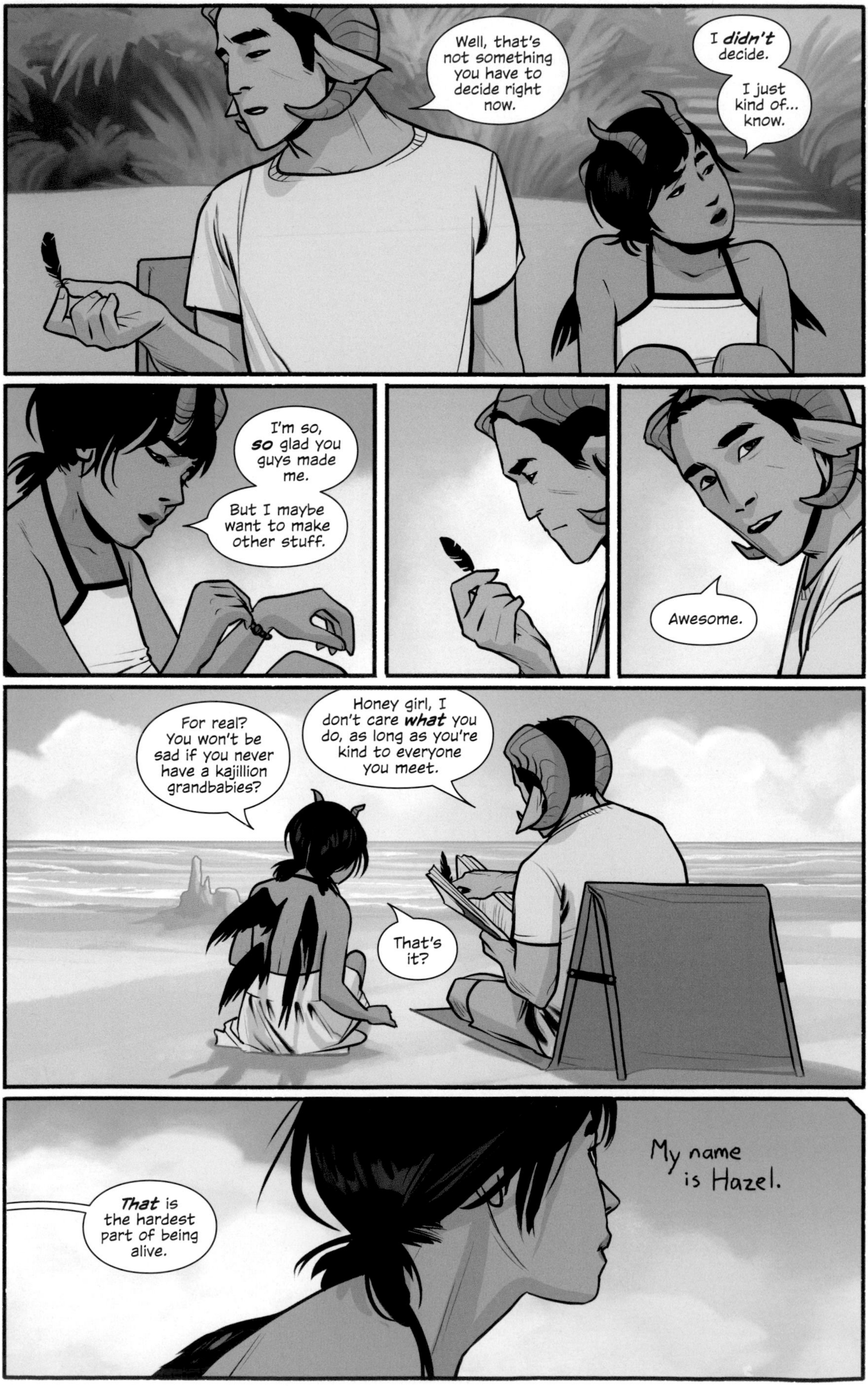
Well, that's not something you have to decide right now.
I *didn't* decide.
I just kind of... know.
I'm so, *so* glad you guys made me.
But I maybe want to make other stuff.
Awesome.
For real? You won't be sad if you never have a kajillion grandbabies?
Honey girl, I don't care *what* you do, as long as you're kind to everyone you meet.
That's it?
My name is Hazel.
That is the hardest part of being alive.

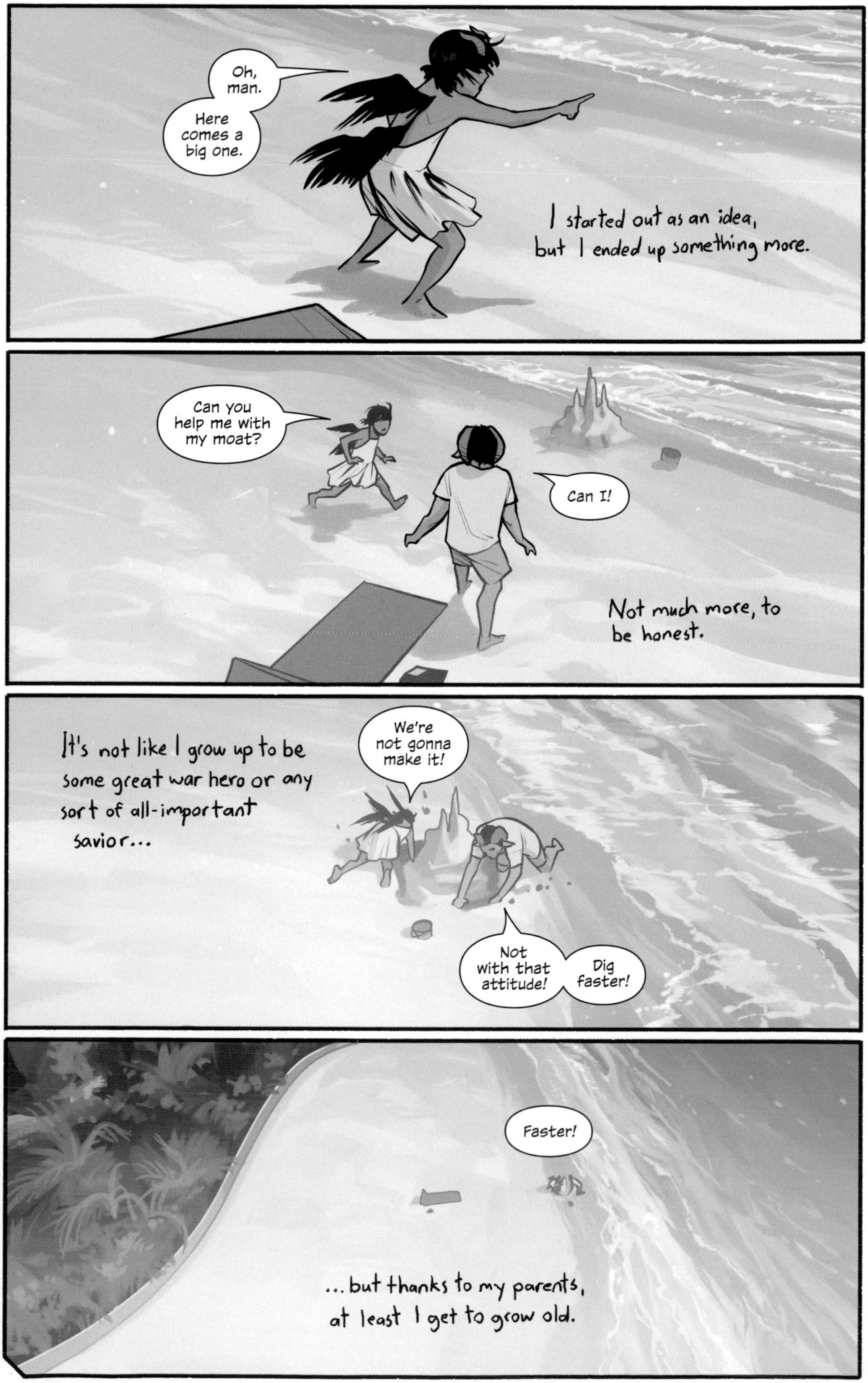
Oh, man.
Here comes a big one.
I started out as an idea, but I ended up something more.
Can you help me with my moat?
Can I!
Not much more, to be honest.
It's not like I grow up to be some great war hero or any sort of all-important savior...
We're not gonna make it!
Not with that attitude!
Dig faster!
Faster!
...but thanks to my parents, at least I get to grow old.

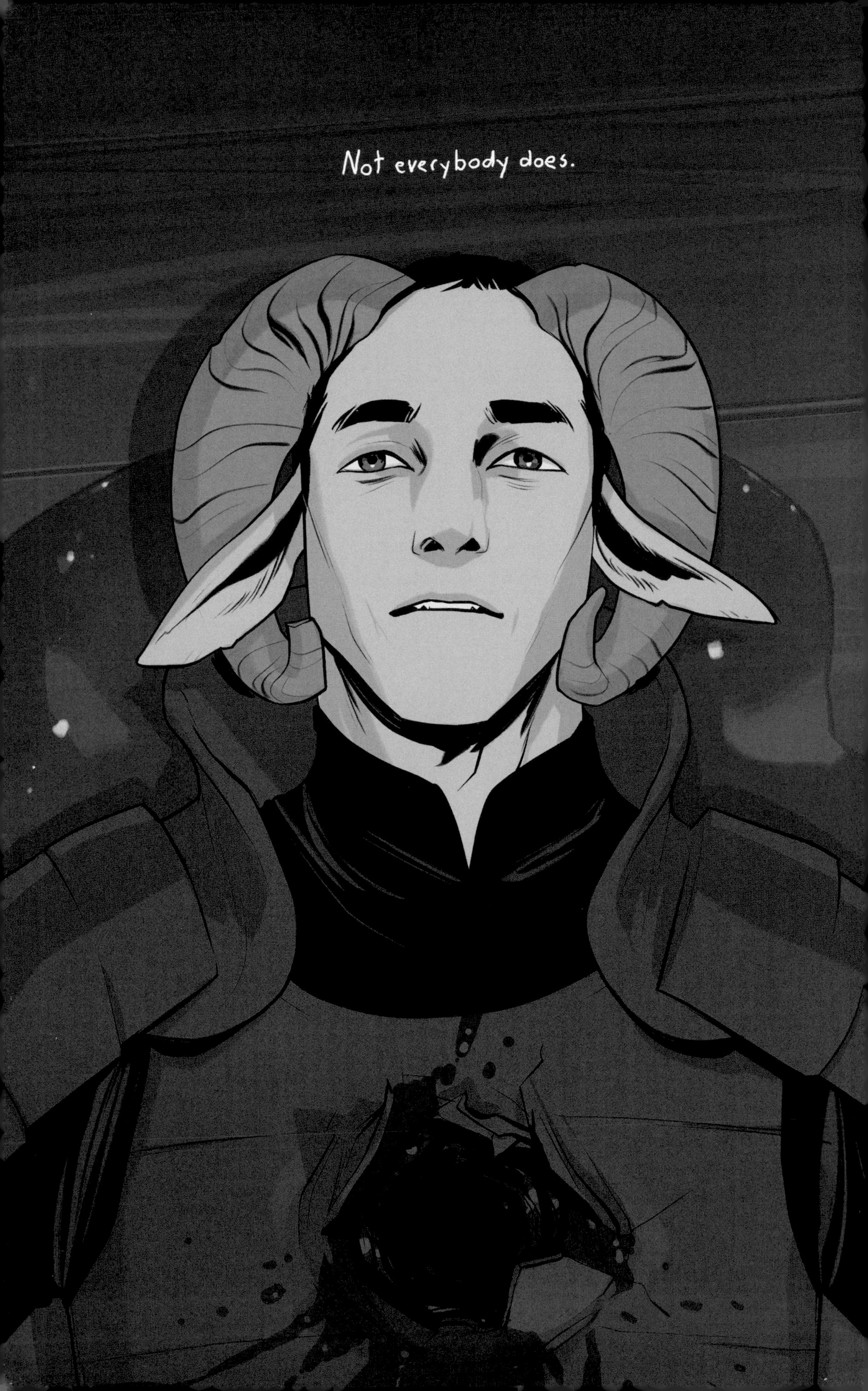
Not everybody does.

to be continued

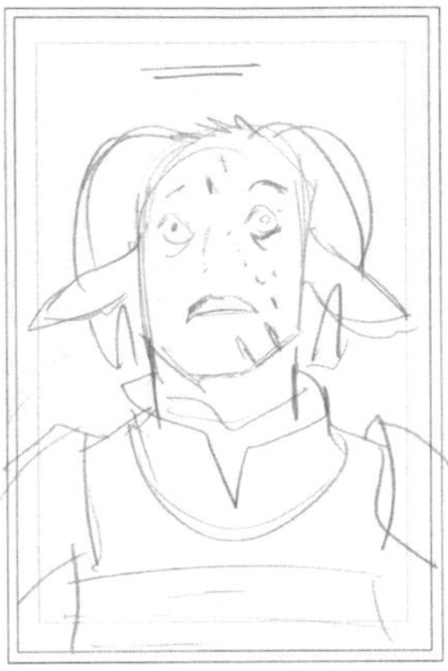

1

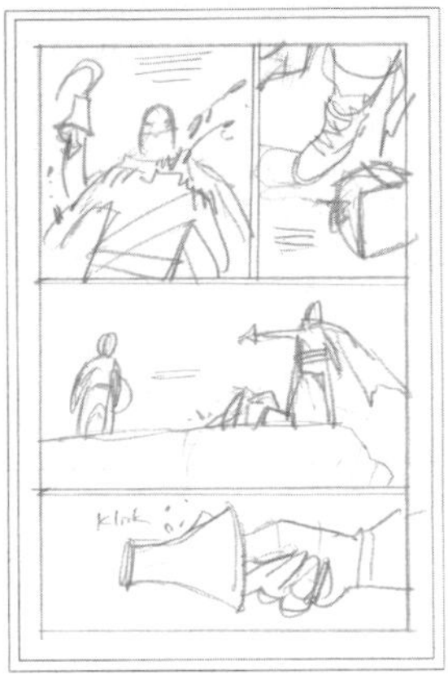

2

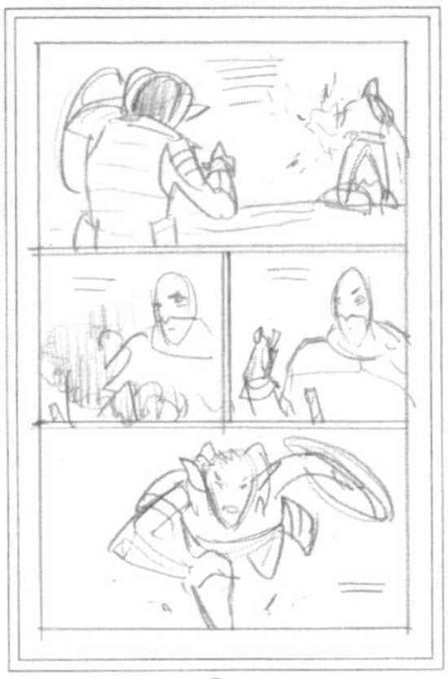

3

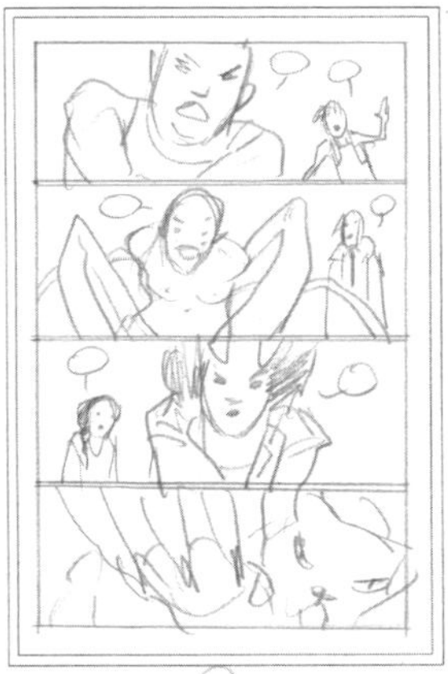

7

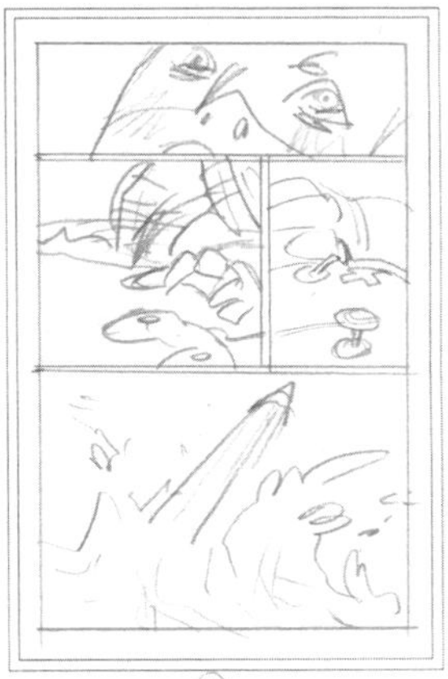

8

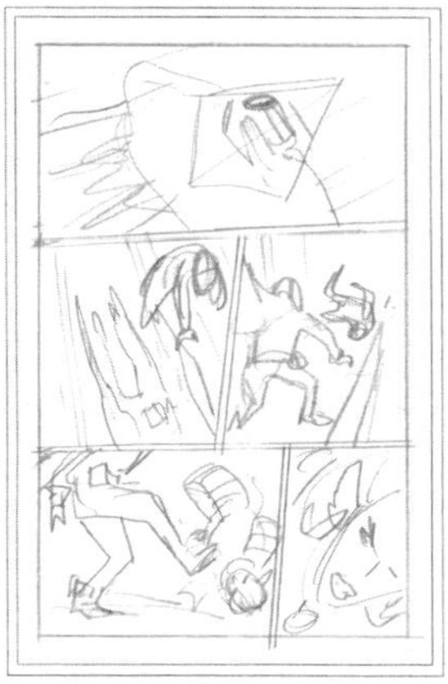

9

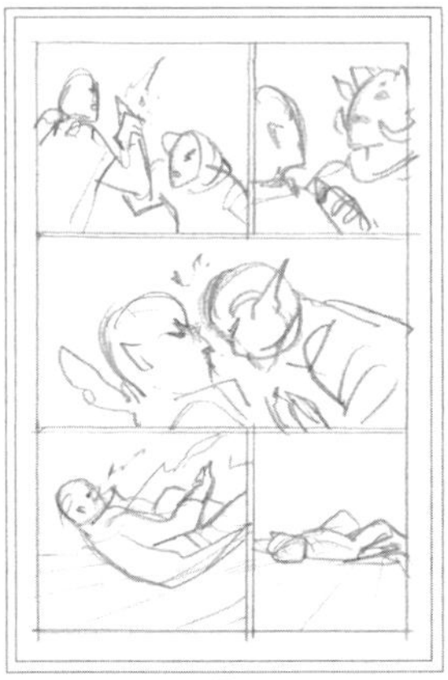

13

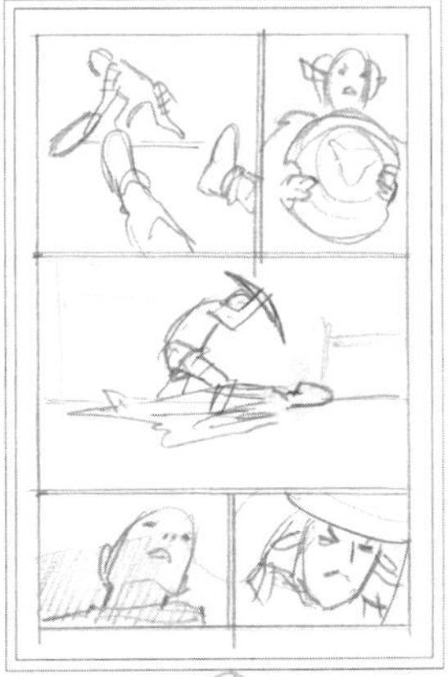

14

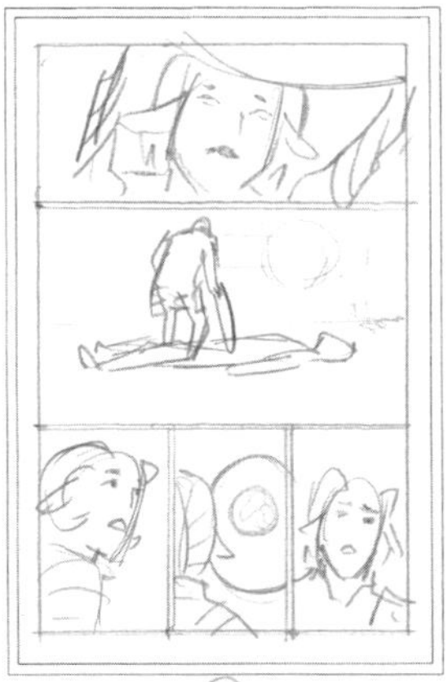

15

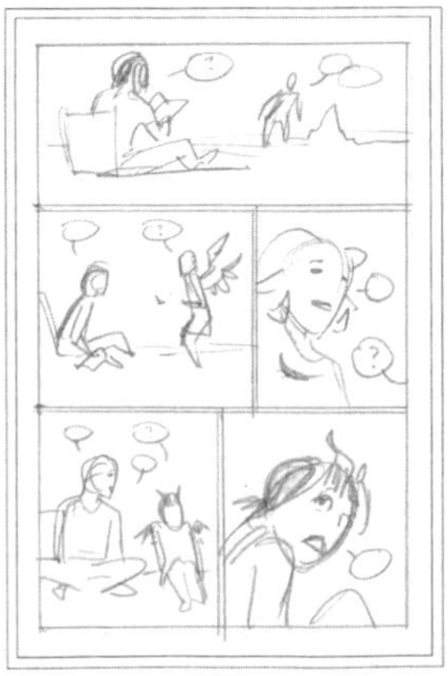

19

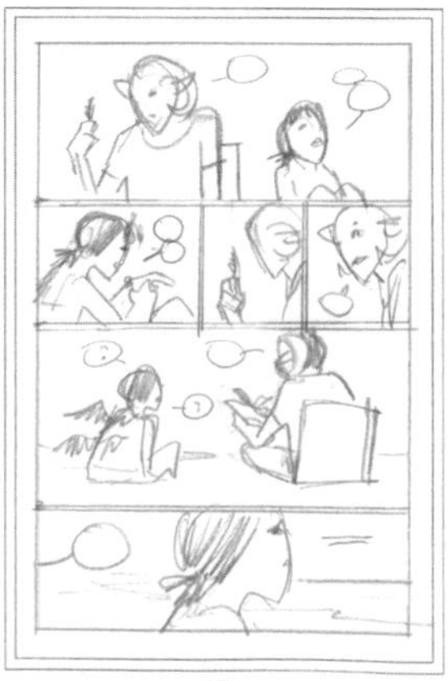

20

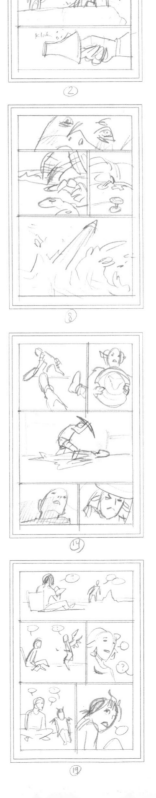

Fiona's thumbnail sketches…

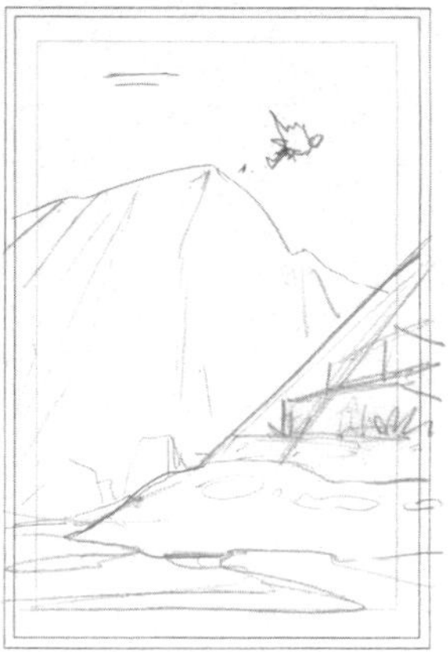

4

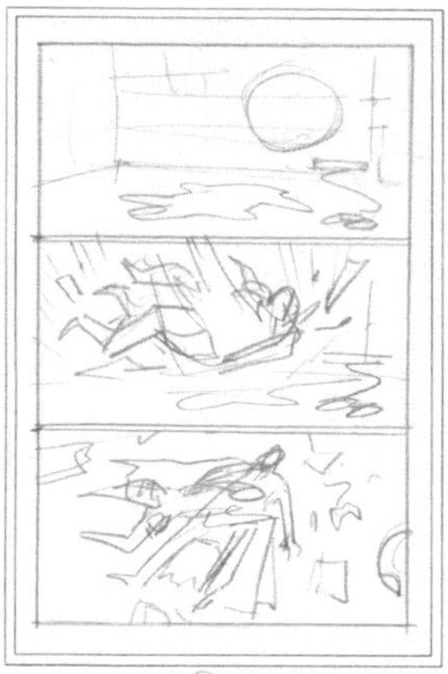

5

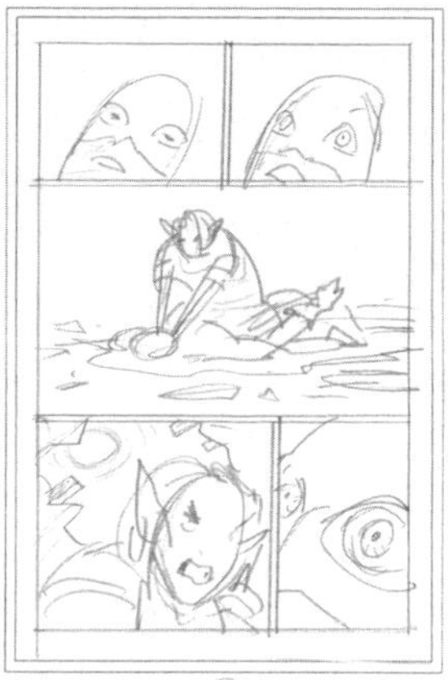

6

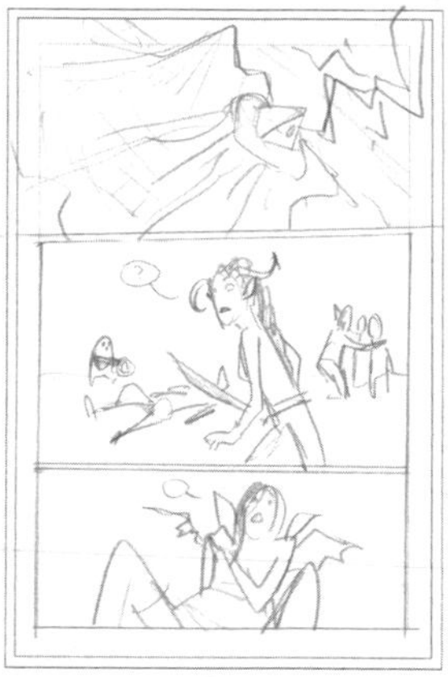

10

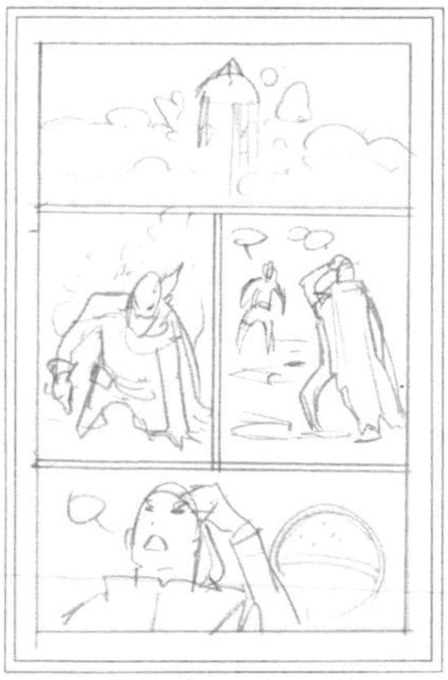

11

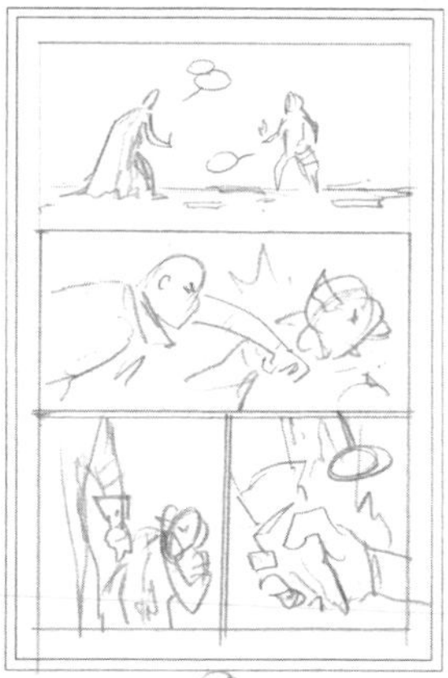

12

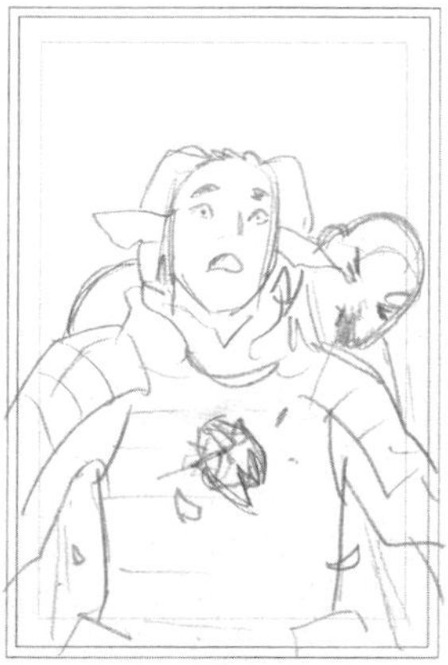

14

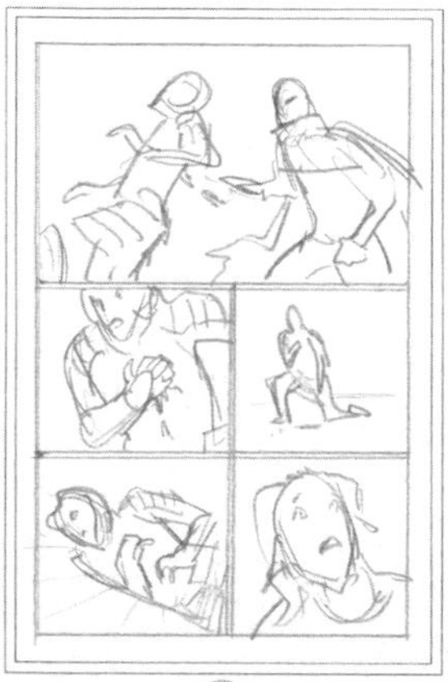

17

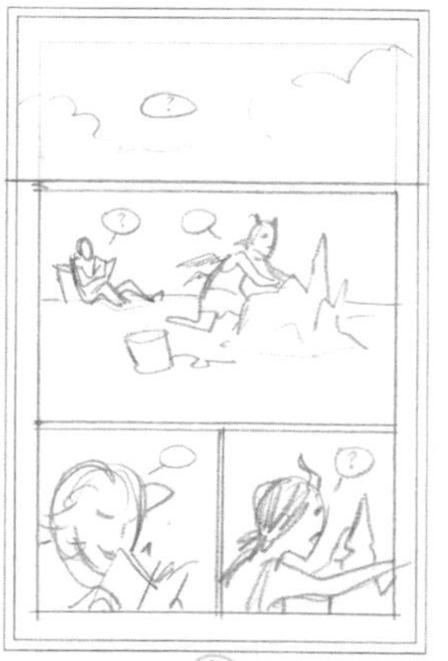

18

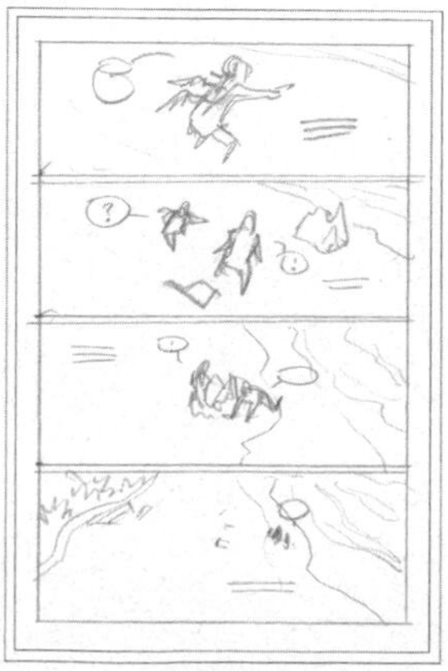

21

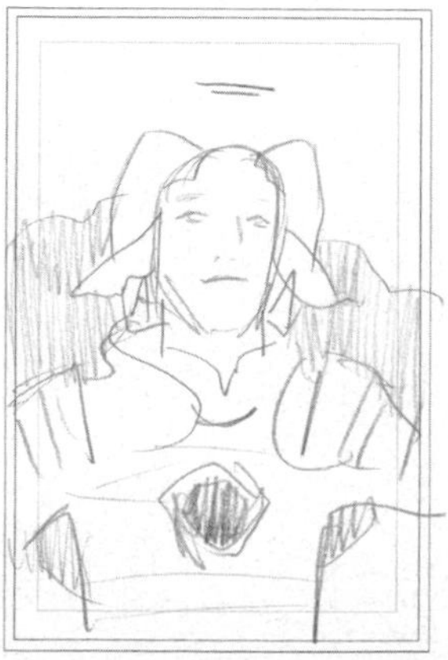

22

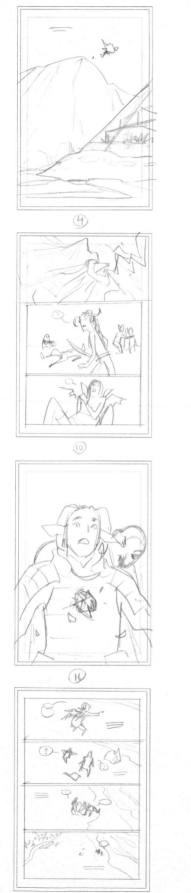

…for Chapter Fifty-four.

Paper Girls

VOLUME FOUR

COLLECTING ISSUES 16-20
AVAILABLE NOW

BRIAN K. VAUGHAN
CLIFF CHIANG
MATT WILSON
JARED K. FLETCHER

image